FILTHY JEALOUS HEIR

DUET ONE

HEIRS OF ALL HALLOWS'

CAITLYN DARE

Copyright © 2024 by Caitlyn Dare

All rights reserved.

No part of this book may be reproduced in any form or by any electronic or mechanical means, including information storage and retrieval systems, without written permission from the author, except for the use of brief quotations in a book review.

Editing by Pinpoint Editing

Proofread by Sisters Get Lit(erary) Author Services.

Cover and Interior by Sammi Bee Designs

WICKED HEINOUS HEIRS

HEIRS OF ALL HALLOWS' PREQUEL

1

REESE

"What did they do to your brother the night he initiated?" Oakley asks Elliot a second before he tips his bottle to his lips, downing what's left of his beer.

Elliot shrugs. "Fuck knows. We all know they're a bunch of bullshitters. They make out that it's all dark and twisted tasks to prove our worth, but really, what are they going to make us do that we haven't already done? Drink their piss or something?" He laughs, reaching for his own beer.

"Don't joke, man," Theo says, taking a hit on his joint. "I've heard some wild fucking stories about initiation night."

I sit back in my chair, swiping the blunt from Theo's fingers the second he's done, and purse my lips, toking on it until my lungs burn.

It's exactly what I fucking need. Weed, alcohol, and my boys. The perfect distraction for whatever tonight is going to throw at us.

Theo is right, we've already endured plenty of fucked-up things that Scott and his crew have forced on us during our first year of sixth form. Since our journey toward becoming

Heirs started. But I can't deny the adrenaline already pumping through my veins for what might be to come.

My fists curl on my lap as I allow my mind to wander over the things we've been subjected to so far.

What I need tonight is pain.

Lots and lots of fucking pain.

"Like what?" I ask, needing to lose myself in Theo's stories, even if they're likely to be complete bullshit as Elliot suggested.

"The guys before Scott," he says, leaning forward and resting his elbows on his knees. "I heard they were made to kill and gut a sheep."

"That's not so bad," Oakley says, rolling another joint after noticing I maxed out on the last one.

"And then they made them eat the heart."

Elliot's face pales.

"And the intestines."

"Bullshit. They did not," I bark.

"And the Heirs before them had buckets of shit tipped over them."

Elliot looks on the verge of gagging at the thought of that alone. "Nah, it's all hearsay. We know full well it's never as bad as they claim."

"I dunno, man," I say. "That fight ring they set up at the beginning of the year was pretty brutal."

"I've still got the scars to prove it," Oakley agrees, running a hand over his chest. "They told us to meet them at the Hideout at eight. They'll just ink us and make us down a fifth of vodka or something before throwing us to the wolves."

"Hell yes," I announce, uncapping another bottle of beer with my teeth and spitting it across Oakley's room, much to his irritation.

Motherfucker shouldn't be such a neat freak, if you ask me. Even his fucking sister lives a little more wildly—not that I've spent a whole lot of time inside her room. "I'm fucking desperate to find out who my girl is gonna be." I thrust my hips forward, mimicking how I hope to be spending most of my night.

"Fuck, yes," Oakley agrees.

"What if she's a minger?" Elliot asks.

"Then I'll take her from behind." I roll my eyes at him as if it's obvious.

"Just like you did with Daniella over Easter?" he teases.

"I thought we promised never to talk about that again," I hiss, still not over that little drunken mistake a few months ago. "I'm fucking ready for it, boys. We're finally gonna be fucking Heirs, and we're gonna have all the girls dropping to their motherfucking knees."

"Like they don't already," Theo says smugly.

"Things are only gonna get better from here on out, my friends," I promise, although not a single one of them knows what I really mean by that.

Our lives might be about to change forever after this stupid initiation ceremony tonight, but they have no idea that mine is going to be significantly different by the time the new school year rolls around.

Thank fucking God.

Conversation turns to plans for the summer before the sound of pounding feet outside Oakley's room hits my ears.

"What that—"

"GET ON YOUR FUCKING KNEES," three masked guys bellow as they storm the room, making my heart jump into my throat.

None of us move, too startled by Scott, Evan, and Liam's arrival.

"I said, get on your MOTHERFUCKING KNEES," Scott booms.

One by one, starting with Elliot, we all follow orders. My

knees hit the hard, wooden floor a second before Evan and Liam drag sacks over Elliot and Theo's heads.

"Oh no, I don't fucking think so," I bark, but it's too late. Scott has already moved behind me, dragging my arms back and binding them while I was distracted by watching my boys have their vision removed.

"You don't get a fucking say tonight, Whitfield." He pulls the cable ties tighter, ensuring they cut into my skin before the sack covers my eyes.

My heart rate picks up, the anger I've been battling to keep contained for the past week threatening to overspill.

"Motherfuckers," Oakley barks beside me.

"You told us to fucking meet you there," Elliot hisses.

"Yeah, and you're forgetting who's still in charge, little brother," Scott snarls, dragging me to my feet. His fingers wrap around one of my forearms before I'm shoved forward.

Someone, I'm assuming Oakley, crashes into my shoulder.

"Careful, arsehole," I bark.

"Pussy," Evan jokes.

We're frog-marched out of Oakley's room and turned toward the stairs. My irritation at being manhandled gets the better of me as I'm forcefully shoved forward once more.

A roar that I barely even recognise as my own rips from my throat as I spin around on Scott. If I'm right and he's got his other hand on Oakley, then he's half distracted right now.

"Dickhead," I bellow, lunging for him, slamming his body back into the wall.

"Motherfucker," he grunts, his breath leaving his lungs in a rush as I bend lower, shaking the sack from my head.

The sound of a door opening somehow manages to force its way through the blood rushing through my ears, and the second I look up, I find her standing there.

She's wearing an oversized All Hallows' hoodie, her bare legs sticking out the bottom with her hair piled on top of her head and not a scrap of makeup on her face.

There might have been a time I'd have checked Olivia Beckworth out, looking like that. Sure, as one of my best friend's sisters—twin no less—she's more than off limits, but fuck, I'm still a guy.

But now, everything has changed. And the only thing I feel as I look at her is disgust and betrayal.

Olivia rolls her eyes as she takes us in, placing her hands on her hips and making the hem of her hoodie lift, exposing more of her thighs.

My top lip peels back as I glare pure hate at her.

"Enjoy drinking cat piss. Idiots," she mutters as Scott recovers from my attack and my vision is cut off once more.

"You better fucking be there tonight, Liv," Oakley calls, having heard his sister's voice.

"I think I might be busy tidying up my ribbon collection."

"Olivia," Oakley growls.

"Come on, Olive," I snarl, aware of just how much she hates that little nickname. "If you're lucky, maybe your name will be pulled out of the jar and you'll get to spend your night with a real man."

"Shut your fucking mouth, Reese," Oakley barks as we're shoved forward once more. "You gotta be there, Liv. Promise me."

"Stupid little shits," she mutters under her breath before her bedroom door swings closed.

"Let's fucking go, boys. We don't have all night," Scott snarls, damn near throwing me down the stairs when we get there.

Only a few minutes later, we're thrown inside what I assume is a van and driven out of the Beckworth driveway. The floor rumbles beneath my body as the engine comes to life.

"Is this really fucking necessary?" Theo booms, making me jump—not that I'd admit to it.

There's no response from any of the dickheads who threw us in here.

Feet pound on the floor, making it vibrate beneath my arse as my boys protest.

"Scott, you motherfucker," both Oakley and Theo bellow.

I don't bother joining in.

It's pointless.

Plus, I want to save my energy for the party later. I have every intention of getting as fucked up as I possibly can.

We drive for so long, I start to wonder if we're actually heading to the Hideout or not.

My senses are sharp as the van finally pulls to a stop and whoever's driving kills the engine.

"Time to get this party started, motherfuckers," Scott booms excitedly the second the door is slid open.

"You're not fucking funny," Elliot snarls.

"Ah, little brother, enjoy it while you can. This is child's play compared to what we're about to go through," he explains, referring to the fact he and his friends are due to start university. "And you've only got a year before you get that joy, too."

"Great," Elliot mutters as hands grab my upper arms and I'm hauled out of the van.

I don't get a chance to find my footing as two of the existing Heirs drag me across rough gravel before dumping me on the floor. "Un-fucking-tie us," I growl, thrashing about the best I can with my wrists still bound.

"Reese," Elliot hisses in his attempt to get me to follow the rules.

I know why. Doing this initiation, finally getting to take over All Hallows' is something the four of us have been dreaming about for years, and we're right on the cusp of it. But the reality is nothing like I was expecting. Well, it might seem like everything the guys have ever wanted, but while my world implodes around me, it feels nothing but pointless, entitled bullshit.

Learning what I have, discovering the secrets that everyone seems to have around me, has put all this shit into perspective, and now it seems nowhere near as important as I thought it once was.

Suddenly, the sack is ripped from my head, and the light floods my eyes, making them burn and water instantly. It takes more than a good few blinks to clear my vision, and when I do, I find we're exactly where I expected to be. A circle of floodlights points right at us as the rest of Scott's inner circle and most of the rugby team staring at us with hunger in their eyes.

Scott stands before us, Evan and Liam flanking his sides. Their masks have now gone, along with their shirts, showing off their Heir tattoos. The ones we all expect to have finished tonight.

"Tonight," he booms, "marks a new beginning. It's time to hand the baton over to my little brother and his crew. But before I do that, they need to complete the final tasks and receive their marks."

The floor beneath me vibrates violently as multiple pairs of heavy feet stomp on the wooden floorboards in response to Scott's words.

"Heirs," he shouts over the excitement. "ARE YOU READY?"

"Fuck yeah, we're ready," Elliot, Oakley, and Theo shout back.

"Louder. I want to hear that you are fucking ready." His eyes find mine, clearly not missing that I said nothing that first time.

Aware that the only way to get to the party that's waiting

for us at the clearing in the woods behind the Beckworth house, I force down my hesitation and get involved.

"WE ARE READY," we shout in unison.

I always thought this night would be the best one of my life. The night we become men, fucking gods around All Hallows'. The night we embark on the first steps to the future that's been mapped out since before our mothers gave birth to us.

But right now, that future I always thought I was going to have to endure is far from my mind. A different one, one that I've craved for more than a few years now is in touching distance. And I can barely wait any fucking longer.

"Let the games begin," Scott shouts, the words quickly followed by another round of cabin-shaking excitement.

Two guys step up to Evan and Liam, handing them jugs of suspicious-looking liquid.

"You've all heard stories about what these initiations consist of. And let me tell you, none of it is bullshit. Every single story you've heard is true. Each task is thought up by the departing Heirs, getting more and more... inventive"—a roguish grin tugs at his mouth—"every single time control changes hands."

A ripple of anticipation rushes through the air as the four of them step closer.

"Tonight, we start with the Heirs' signature cocktail. Open wide, boys. We... concocted this especially for the four of you."

My stomach clenches in anticipation as wicked intent flashes in Scott's eyes. He's always been a bit of an evil motherfucker, but I've never seen it shining quite so bright as it is now.

"Heads back. It's time for your baptism."

"And don't you fucking dare shut your eyes," Liam adds.

I suck in a breath a beat before Evan starts pouring his jug of fuck knows what over my face. "Swallow, Whitfield. Or the next thing in your mouth will be a hell of a lot worse than this."

I do as I'm told, not willing to make this worse than it needs to be. The liquid is warm, too fucking warm, and it makes me want to retch.

They don't stop pouring the ominous yellow liquid all over us until each jug is empty. I fight to catch my breath as they step away, glancing over at my boys, finding them sucking in deep lungfuls of air, their clothes sopping wet with... My stomach convulses at the thought of what we just consumed.

"Release their arms," Scott commands.

His four little bitches follow orders and step behind us, thankfully cutting us free.

My muscles ache like a motherfucker as I lift my hands in front of me, inspecting the lacerations on my wrists from the tight cable ties.

My eyes catch on Scott's and narrow in warning. *I will fucking hurt you for this*, I silently promise.

I don't give a shit if his position as a soon-to-be Scion means he's above us, or that he's Elliot's big brother.

I want to take him to the fucking ground for his unnecessary bullshit.

"Strip down to your underwear. I really fucking hope you're wearing some," he taunts.

Reluctantly, I do as I'm told, ripping my shirt over my head and kicking my trousers off my legs and onto the little makeshift stage they have us on.

"Get on your fronts," Scott shouts as a familiar buzzing erupts from behind us.

We got the first part of our Heir tattoos the summer before we started sixth form. But tonight, we get our addition to prove our worth, our position at All Hallows' School, and this whole motherfucking town.

And even though I no longer want it, I can't help the rush of power that surges through my body, filling my veins and making my muscles bunch at the thought of being one of only a few men who bear this mark, even if I'm not going to get a chance to see out my time as an Heir.

Hands grip my arms, making a show of holding me down as if I'd fucking run away from the barely-there pain of a tattoo gun. They're going to need to do better than this if they have any intention of breaking me.

2

OLIVIA

"Liv, sweetheart," Dad says, looking up as I enter the kitchen. "You're not dressed."

"I'm not going."

"Olivia." He drops his papers on the breakfast counter and lets out a heavy sigh. "Your brother—"

"I love Oakley, Dad. He's a part of me." We are twins, after all. "But this initiation stuff is so dumb."

"It's an age-old rite of passage." His lip quirks with amusement. "One that you can't possibly understand because—"

"Because I'm a girl. Really, Dad?" I huff.

"No, not because you're a girl. But because you're too damn smart for your own good. Let the boys have their fun. Being an Heir is—"

"Yeah, yeah, save me the speech, Dad." I know all about the hardship of being an Heir.

The parties and god-like worship at school. The ridiculous pranks and initiations.

For Oakley and the other sons of the founding families of Saints Cross, being an Heir is a rite of passage. One that will see them transform into more unbearable, arrogant, and cocky arseholes than they already are.

"You should be there tonight, Liv." He pins me with a stern look.

"Yeah," I concede. Because he's right.

I should be there.

This is Oakley's life—his future. Even if I think it's a bunch of archaic, juvenile, chauvinistic bullshit, he's still my brother.

And family is everything to me.

"I'll head over there in a little bit."

From the way Scott Eaton and his friends burst in here earlier, I have a feeling they'll be putting my brother and the rest of the guys through their paces for a while.

"But don't blame me if Oakley ends up in A&E tonight."

Dad chuckles. "The older boys know not to push too hard. It's a bit of harmless fun."

My brow lifts. "We'll see." I go to leave, but his voice gives me pause.

"And sweetheart?"

"Yeah, Dad?" I glance back.

"I'm proud of you. Both of you. I know it isn't always easy to live with me and your brother, but it won't be like this forever."

My brows furrow at his strange choice of words. It's been the three of us since Mum died when Oak and I were just kids. But he's never made us feel anything less than loved, even if we do live a life slightly outside of the norm.

I guess that's to be expected when your dad is one of the best defence lawyers in the country.

"Have you met someone?" I ask, hopeful.

"Oh, sweetheart, don't you think I'm too old for all that?"

I go to him and wrap my arms around his neck. "You deserve to be happy, Dad."

"I am happy, sweetheart. I've got you and your brother and a good life. What more could a man want?"

But there's a note of sadness in his voice from the hole in his heart that I'm not sure will ever be filled.

The walk down to the location of tonight's end of year party doesn't take me long. Set in a vast clearing in the dense woods behind our house, it's a popular haunt for the kids of Saints Cross. My brother and his friends often come down here on a weekend to drink and get high and generally get up to no good.

Laughter echoes around me, rising over the din of the music in the distance. I can just make out the flames licking the dusky sky through the trees.

I didn't bother dressing up, sticking to a denim skirt and a plain black crop top with an All Hallows' grey hoodie tied around my waist for later, when the temperature drops.

The trees begin to thin, revealing the chaos before me. The party is already in full swing, but there's no sign of my brother and his friends.

"Liv," a saccharine voice says, and I turn to find Darcie Porter smiling at me.

"Darcie." I fight the urge to scowl.

Darcie is... well, she's *that* girl. The one who will walk over your corpse so long as it gives her a leg up the social ladder. And she's been after my brother for years.

Thankfully, Oakley sees her for what she is. A fake, money-grabbing bitch.

"I didn't think you'd come."

"Of course I came. Oakley wants me here."

My words land their intended mark, and she blanches. "Yeah, but it's got to suck that they'll be Heirs next year and you'll be left behind."

"Go suck a dick, Darcie, since you're so good at it."

Her cheeks burn, but in true Darcie fashion, she stands her ground. I'm aware that we've begun to draw a small crowd, but I really couldn't care. I'm not here to gain popularity or friends. I'm a Beckworth. Christian Beckworth's daughter. That affords me some measure of respect from my classmates. Maybe even a line of girls wanting to be my friend and boys wanting to get in my knickers.

But I don't make a habit of surrounding myself with fake bitches and entitled dickheads. My brother and his friends notwithstanding.

"At least I'm getting some dick, Olivia." She smirks, glancing at her little huddle of friends.

"Good for you. But make sure you keep a list, so you know who the baby daddy is when you get knocked up."

Darcie's gasp barely hits my ears as I spin on my heel and stalk away from her, irritation trickling down my spine.

A couple of guys flash me a knowing grin, obviously having overheard the conversation. If you could call it that. I ignore them trudging deeper into the party. The guys must still be at the Hideout, if that's where Scott has taken them. But I know better than to venture out there uninvited. Especially tonight.

Shaking my head, I snag a beer from one of the coolers and find a quiet spot to wait. Because they'll be here soon. That's what everyone's waiting for, after all—to see the old Heirs pass the new Heirs the keys to the kingdom.

Or as I like to think of it, the baton of stupidity.

I just hope they're in one piece.

Because everyone knows the rugby players can be brutal.

And no one is more twisted than Scott Eaton.

The crackle of anticipation in the air is the first sign that something is happening. A rumble of chatter goes up around me, and I follow the crowd as they move excitedly toward the path leading to the Hideout. It's a strange thing to behold, a group of trashed teenagers lining the dirt track, all waiting to pay homage to their beloved Saints.

I choose a shadowy spot in the back. The couple of beers I've had warm my body, but I still had to slip on my hoodie earlier to fend off the cool night air. I look nothing like the other girls here, in their floaty summer dresses and little shorts and cute blouses. But I've never been that girl.

I don't try too hard or seek attention. I'm more comfortable in jeans, t-shirts, and trainers than dresses, skirts, and sandals.

Oakley likes to tease me and call me Oliver, but it doesn't bother me. Growing up surrounded by boys has rubbed off on me.

The noise of the crowd grows louder, and I'm not surprised when I see Elliot Eaton appear with my brother, Theo Ashworth, and Reese Whitfield trailing behind.

But I am surprised by the state of them.

"What the—" I clap a hand over my mouth, trapping the bark of laughter.

They look utterly ridiculous.

It isn't the smears of mud and blood crusted on their faces or even the ripening bruises, it's the bright red royal capes hanging off their shoulders and cheap and tacky crowns perched atop their heads.

Jesus, I knew tonight would be full of over-the-top displays of manly bullshit, but the capes and crowns are a whole new level.

Elliot is stone-faced, ignoring every single person cheering his name as he leads his friends down the long path toward the Heirs' thrones—four ugly-as-hell, hand-carved chairs that have withstood the test of time. My father's initials are etched on one of those chairs, just as Elliot and Theo's dads are. And their fathers before them, and so on. The only person not to have one of his parents' names there is Reese, and that's because it isn't his father who comes from the Heir line—it's his mum.

I can barely restrain my eye-rolling as I watch them each take their seats, only to throw my arm over my eyes when I realise they're butt naked underneath, save for some tight white boxer shorts.

Really freaking tight.

Jesus. I need more beer. Or vodka.

Yeah, vodka sounds like a good plan.

Oakley scans the crowd, catching my eye. His big, goofy smile softens something inside of me, but then my gaze snags on Reese and he glowers.

Arsehole.

Of all the Heirs-to-be, Reese is the one who gets under my skin the most. Probably because he's the one who constantly pushes my buttons. Theo and Elliot have always accepted my presence without question. Because although I'm not truly one of them, I am a part of Oakley. But Reese has only ever tolerated me. Something that seems to have only gotten worse this year.

"All Hallows'," Scott's voice rings out through the woods, and everyone goes wild. "Tonight, we gather to officially see in the new Heirs. And, of course, celebrate in style."

"Fuck yeah," somebody yells, and I shake my head.

Sheep.

That's what they remind me of. How easily they follow the stupid rules and expectations. How eager they are to fall into line and kiss arse.

Heir arse, to be precise.

"Elliot." Scott beckons for his brother to stand, moving closer to him. "You know what this is?" Elliot glances down at the ornate key in Scott's hand and nods. "It's yours now. Yours to use as you see fit. But let it be known that the Heir in possession of this key is the Heir who has the final say."

Scott offers Elliot the key and an eerie silence falls over the clearing.

I almost want to yell something to interrupt their little ceremony. But I don't. Because this is how it's always been, and some traditions will never die.

The two of them share a long, silent look, and then Elliot retreats to his wooden throne, his expression as cold and aloof as ever.

"Now to the fun part. Evan, if you will."

One of Scott's friends steps up to him and presents a small glass jar filled with slips of paper.

"Your Saints chosen for the night." Scott smirks before shoving his hand inside and plucking a slip out. "Oakley, rise." He does with a knowing grin. "Your chosen... Sophie Lister."

A girl shrieks with delight, and a small blonde bursts from the crowd, practically throwing herself at my brother. Ever the gentleman, he catches her and wraps his arm around her waist.

Please.

This whole thing is a joke.

I don't want to stick around and watch this, but maybe I'm not that much better than everyone else, because curiosity gets the better of me and I move closer to the fray.

"Okay, next up. Reese, step forward."

I hadn't noticed it earlier, but there's something different about him tonight. He's always been a cocky, arrogant arsehole, but he doesn't usually look so... so angry.

Huh.

I'm so fixed on the tension in his face, the storm swirling in his eyes, that I don't hear my name called.

Not until Scott repeats it with an amused look on his face. "Olivia Beckworth, come on down."

"What the hell, Eaton?" Oakley snarls. "Her name shouldn't be in there."

Someone pushes me and I stumble forward, right into their

path. "This is low, Scott," I accuse, anger and embarrassment warring inside me. "Even for you."

"Don't look at me, little Beckworth." He chuckles darkly. "I had nothing to do with this."

"Doesn't matter, because it's not fucking happening."

"Oakley," I snap. "I can handle my own—"

"Over my dead body."

My head whips around to Reese and I narrow my eyes, my pulse thundering in my ears. "What did you say?"

"I said, *Olive*"—he takes a step forward, and the air vanishes between us—"Over. My. Dead. Body."

"Like I'd ever let you anywhere near me. You and your stupid game can go fuck itself." Tears prick my eyes as every single person stares at me. At us.

"Liv." Oakley reaches for me. "No one is gonna make you do anything. This is just some sick joke. Right, Eaton?" He pins Scott with a desperate look.

"Like I said, this isn't on me. But rules are rules, and tradition states that the girl picked from the jar is the girl each Heir has to—"

"I swear to fucking God, Eaton, if you don't shut the fuck up—"

"Oakley!" I hiss.

This cannot be happening, it cannot—

"Let him pick again," Elliot says coolly. "The sooner we're done with this, the sooner we can get fucked up."

My gaze flicks to Reese, but I immediately wish it hadn't. He looks murderous, and it's all aimed at me.

What the hell is his problem?

"Nah, little brother, that's not how it works." Scott taunts, clearly enjoying this. "Her name was in there, therefore she has to—"

"I'd rather fuck a corpse. Motherfucker—" Reese roars as Oakley punches him square on the jaw and the two of them start going at it.

"Oh my God," I breathe, a crushing weight on my chest.

Theo calls, "My money is on Beckworth."

"Seriously, Theo? Do something," I implore, but cheers and catcalls go up around us, drowning out the violent beat of my heart.

"Fucking idiots," Elliot mutters, standing up and storming over to them. He rips my brother off Reese and shoves him toward his girl.

"Fucking pussy," Oakley spits.

"You almost sound like you want me to fuck your sister, Beckworth." Reese smears a hand across his bloody mouth, giving him a feral appearance.

"Whitfield," Elliot barks. "Stop baiting him. No one expects you and Liv to..." He offers me an apologetic glance. But I'm done.

I'm so done.

"I'm leaving," I grit out, failing to hide the quiver in my voice.

"No, don't go, Liv," Oakley says. "This is just a misunderstanding. Right, Eaton?" He looks at Scott, who seems more than a little amused by the dramatic turn of events.

"You're the Heirs now. You figure it out." He shrugs.

They all turn to Reese, who casts me a scathing look before striding toward the crowd. He grabs Darcie—of all the girls here—and twists his fingers into the front of her dress, smashing his mouth down on hers and kissing her hard.

"There." Elliot says with complete indifference. "Problem solved."

"Liv," Oakley says, concern etched into his face.

"I need a drink," I murmur, hugging myself tight.

He runs a hand down his face, blowing out a strained breath. "Just don't run off. Once this is all done, we'll get a drink." He winks, and I manage a small smile.

One drink?

Something tells me I'm going to need the whole damn bottle.

3

REESE

"She's not meant to be a part of this," Oakley roars, getting in Scott's face about this Olivia bullshit for the second time in thirty minutes.

"Too late now, man. Her name was pulled." He shrugs, giving less than zero fucks about Oakley's opinion on this.

But he's right. Sisters are off limits. Even to Heirs.

Her name shouldn't have been in that jar. But it was, and it was pulled for me.

I couldn't have planned it better myself. And I'm kinda pissed I didn't think it up, to be honest. Having her in my possession to do with as I please for the night seems like the perfect opportunity for us to have a little... chat, shall we say.

I've been watching her for the last few weeks. Trying to figure out what angle she's playing, what she's trying to get out of the secrets she's hiding. But as far as I can see, she's just playing with people's lives, covering up indiscretions that aren't hers to hide and ultimately betraying those who don't deserve it.

Oakley's muscles are pulled tight even though Sophie is all over him like a fucking rash. She's about ten seconds from shoving her hand down the front of his boxers with the way she's going, but even that isn't enough to distract him from my ownership of his sister.

"Don't you trust me, Oak?" I ask, throwing back a shot of vodka, quickly followed by the others.

The rest of the party is stuck with shitty beer and cheap spirits. As Heirs, though, we get as much of the good shit as we can handle, thanks to Mr. Eaton. As the father of the old and new lead Heir, he's the one responsible for this ceremony. And seeing as he's about as fucked up as his oldest son, I didn't really expect anything but the kind of night most college kids can only dream of.

"Smoke this and let it go, Oak," Theo says, passing over a joint and pushing it between Oakley's lips the second they part.

"She's my fucking sister," he complains, sounding like nothing more than a broken record.

"Yeah, and Reese will take good care of her tonight. Right, Whitfield?" Elliot teases, looking more than just a little drunk after Scott challenged him to an entire row of shots when we finally made it offstage not so long ago.

Tonight has been brutal. And I'm more than ready to get a good buzz going, then find my way to some dark corner of the woods with my chosen one for the night.

The party is meant to be about celebrating new beginnings. But I have every intention of laying a few ghosts to rest and finding out the truth, no matter how dirty I need to get in order to drag out the information I really need.

"Oh yeah," I quip, aware that it's probably going to earn me another punch from my best friend, but who gives a fuck. All's fair in love and war, right? "You all know I'm more than capable of showing her what she's been missing out on all this time."

Predictably, Oakley lunges for me, but Theo and Elliot manage to get the upper hand this time, holding him back from me as he snarls. "If you so much as fucking touch my sister,

Whitfield, I'll cut that useless little cock of yours off in your sleep."

I smile at him. A dark and twisted kind of smile that feeds the beast that's only been growing inside me since the night I learned the truth.

I focus on tomorrow. On the peace that's heading my way, the relief of losing the shackles that have been weighing me down for as long as I can remember, and I smile back at Oak. An almost-genuine smile.

"Trust me, man." I'm only going to give her exactly what she deserves.

My eyes find hers through the crowd. If I were a weaker guy, then the hate spilling from them might affect me. But as it is, those daggers she's throwing barely scratch the surface.

"Olive," I purr when she's close enough to hear. "Missing me already, sweet cheeks?"

"Fuck you," she snarls, turning her back on me in favour of focusing on her brother.

I have no idea what she says, but only seconds later Sophie slinks off into the crowd and the two of them move away from us slightly, leaning close in a hushed yet heated conversation.

Curiosity burns through me like a wildfire as I watch the two of them. Oak and I have been close for as long as I can remember. He's my ride or die, always has been. But she's always fucking there too, only two steps behind him wherever we go.

I thought it was cute when we were kids. But the older we've got, and especially recently, I've noticed just how fucking annoying it is. He's meant to be one of us. But he's always got one foot with us and one foot with his sister.

She's like a little devil—or angel, I guess seeing as some of the things she has an opinion on are less than upstanding. But she's always there, whispering in his ear, trying to control him, and I'm fucking sick of it.

"What the fuck crawled up your arse tonight, Reese?"

Elliot asks, following my line of sight toward the Beckworth twins.

"Nothing," I grunt, reaching for the half-empty bottle of vodka sitting only a foot away with my fucking name on it.

I forgo the shot glass this time and chug it straight from the bottle. It burns like a motherfucker, but I don't give a shit and keep going.

"Bullshit," he snaps. "You're planning something, I can see it in your eyes."

"Hell, yeah. I'm planning on getting as wasted as fucking possible and then getting my dick wet in as many willing girls as I can find," I announce, lifting my bottle and saluting Oak and Olivia when they look over. Both of them are still wearing scowls, but as the alcohol starts to take effect, Oak's irritation with me is already beginning to weaken.

"What do you say, Olive? Wanna be my first and kick the celebrations off with your chosen Heir?" I offer with a smirk.

"He's going to fucking kill you if you keep this shit up," Elliot warns.

"He knows I'm only teasing," I breathe.

"Fuck you," the little spitfire herself hisses. "I'd rather stuff a cactus up my vag sideways than let your limp dick anywhere near it."

Oak throws his arm around his sister's shoulder protectively. "Whoops," he says with an insincere grin. "I don't think I was meant to tell you that story."

Fury surges through me. I knew that little shit couldn't keep anything from her.

"Fuck you, Oak. I was off my fucking face that night and she... she sucked cock like a fucking dead fish."

Olivia's eyes shoot up in amusement. "Funny," she smiles, but it's full of bite, "because I thought all the girls you hung out with sucked dick like that. Thought you'd be used to it by now."

Her dark and angry eyes break from mine for a beat. I

quickly realise why when Darcie's overpowering perfume hits my nose a second before her hand slips inside my cape as if she fucking owns me. I swear to fuck, my cock literally tries to shrivel up inside my body.

I don't want Darcie Porter. I never have. I just dragged her out of the crowd earlier knowing it would torment Olivia. The two of them hate each other with a fiery passion, so it seemed like fate that she was one of the closest girls to me as I duelled with her.

She drags her fake, pointed nails up my abs, and the vodka filling my stomach threatens to make a reappearance.

"Case in point," Olivia mutters, reaching for her own drink and turning away from us. Although, not enough that she can't see when I pull Darcie in front of me and lean down to whisper in her ear.

"You need to play nice," I warn. "You piss off one of us, you piss off all of us. And that's not how you want your night to go, is it?"

A shudder rips through her body, and anyone watching would probably think it's desire. I mean, it might be. Darcie is pretty fucked up like that, but I'm sure there's a good heap of fear thrown in there for good measure.

Olivia bristles, but she refuses to react other than that.

"Come dance with me, Reese," Darcie purrs, ignoring my threat in favour of what else I can offer her tonight.

"I'd love to," I say, taking her hips in my hands and walking her backward toward the dancing crowd on the edge of the woods behind us.

"Careful, the last guy she got too close to ended up with one hell of a case of crabs," a familiar voice calls from behind me.

"You sound awful jealous, Olive," I shoot over my shoulder.

"Nah, you can keep the crabs."

A growl of irritation rips from Darcie's lips, but I move

before she can respond to Olivia and the crowd swallows us up.

It's not exactly where I want to be right now, but I can't deny that while Darcie's personality might leave a little—or a lot—to be desired, the girl can fucking dance.

Turning her back on me, she thrusts her arse into my junk and starts moving, her arms reaching back so her fingers can twist in my hair. "Alone at last," she breathes in my ear.

I mean, no, not really. We're surrounded by half the fucking sixth form at All Hallows', but I guess she doesn't mean them.

It means she can't feel the death stare from behind that's searing through my skin.

"Whitfield," someone booms over the pounding music.

With the help of the alcohol filling my veins and Olivia's hatred warming my skin, I've been able to let go for a bit.

The anger that's been consuming me for the past few weeks ebbed away slightly, and I lost myself in Darcie. It was easy to forget who she was as my head started to spin.

She's nothing but a body, a more than willing one that I can bend to my wishes, knowing that she's going to be along for the ride.

"Whitfield, get your arse over here." It's Scott this time, and I immediately stop what I'm doing, dropping Darcie.

"Reese," she whines, setting my teeth on edge.

"Go find another dick to grind on for a bit. I'm being summoned," I growl, forcing the words out between gritted teeth.

I walk over to where the crowd is watching the guys get set up with beer bongs as a smirk curls my lips.

"About fucking time," Evan hisses.

"I was busy, arsehole."

"Not busy enough, evidently," Liam comments. "Most guys would have had Darcie on her knees in the woods by now. Did you know she doesn't have a gag reflex?"

I push past him, shoulder checking him as I go. They might always hold power over us, but we're officially Heirs now, so all three of them can go fuck themselves. Or Darcie, if they so wish.

"You seem to be playing with the wrong girl, Whitfield," Scott snaps, his eyes shooting to Olivia, who's still watching us from by the coolers with a beer in her hand. "You know the rules, Reese. One girl, one night, no holds barred."

A growl rumbles in Oakley's chest, but when I glance over at him, I find that both Evan and Liam are holding him in the chair they've already tipped back for this game.

"Is that how it worked for you, Scott?" I quip, meeting his girl's eyes over his shoulder. "Wasn't Zoey's name pulled the night of your final initiation? Pretty sure there's been more than one night there."

He bristles at my comment. He might be a sadistic cunt, but he's also severely jealous and possessive over his girl. One wrong look in her direction has sent more than a few guys to A&E over the two years of his reign.

"Zoey is none of your fucking business."

"Just like Olivia should be none of mine. Seems like the rules only stick when they suit you, huh?"

The muscle in his temple tics with irritation. "Sit your arse down and follow my rules, Whitfield," he snarls, taking a threatening step toward me.

But I don't back down. Not like most would.

"You're not in charge anymore, Eaton. You've handed the key to Elliot. So maybe we should see what he thinks about this."

Tension ripples around us. I don't need to rip my eyes from Scott's to know we've got the attention of the entire sixth form on us right now.

"Fine," he concedes surprisingly. "Elliot, what are you saying?"

"Sit down, Reese, and just fucking try to enjoy yourself."

"Pussy," I hiss under my breath, making Elliot's eyes narrow on me as *she* steps up beside her brother. "Fine. But only because I want good stuff." My eyes flick momentarily to the bottles of top shelf scotch and vodka the appointed bartender is pouring into the assembled cups.

An identical smirk pulls at the left-hand side of their lips as I stumble back into my seat.

"You motherfuckers are going down," I bark at my boys as Elliot and I take our seats.

"You're all fucking mouth, Whitfield," Theo bites back.

"Say that again while you're barfing up the contents of your stomach in a few minutes."

He flips me off as Scott announces for his guys to get ready to start.

I've never lost a game of fucking beer bong, and I'm not intending on starting now.

My head spins as I sit up, beer running down my chest and soaking into the stupid tighty whities Scott insisted we wear for this fucking show.

As predicted, Theo is already puking, and Elliot looks like he might be about ready to blow.

"You're all a bunch of lightweight pussies," I tell them, pushing from the chair and stumbling a little as I try to find my footing.

"You were saying?" Oak asks with amusement, watching me with glassy eyes.

Movement over his shoulder catches my eyes, and when I manage to focus, I spot Olivia heading for the darkness of the trees in the distance. My heart thrashes in my chest that she's about to escape and I'm going to lose my opportunity to get close to her.

"I need a piss," I announce, stumbling in the direction she's just disappeared in.

Look out, little Olive. The big bad wolf is coming to play.

4

OLIVIA

Stupid boys and their stupid, juvenile games. I still can't believe my name was ever in that jar. Or that Scott allowed Reese to humiliate me so quite spectacularly.

Red-hot anger trickles down my spine. God, I hate him.

I've always known Reese can be an arsehole, but I didn't think he'd ever be so brash about it. And in front of Oakley, no less.

Stupid boy.

A bitter, strangled laugh spills from my lips. Because Reese Whitfield isn't a boy. None of him and the other Heirs are. They're man-boys with their ridiculous good looks and chiselled bodies. All that muscle and tanned skin. And did I mention muscle?

I throw out a hand and steady myself against a tree. Maybe I drank more than I realised. But I needed the distraction while sitting with my brother and the rest of them. He owes me big time for this. For coming here and subjecting myself to him.

Ugh.

Reese Baron Whitfield-Brown.

The bane of my existence.

There's always been a strange rivalry between us. He's one of Oakley's best friends, and I'm literally part of Oakley. It was bound to happen. The jealousy, the silly rivalry as we both vie for Oak's attention.

But tonight has been different. Every time I've felt his eyes on me—

A shiver runs through my body.

He can go to hell, as far as I'm concerned. They all can.

I stomp deeper into the woods. Eventually, I'll find the path back to the house. But it's really dark out here, and the vodka haze isn't helping. My fingers clutch my cell phone in my pocket, ready to call Oakley to come and rescue me. I won't, though. I'm stubborn to boot. Even if I know the right thing to do is call him to make sure I don't end up lost out here.

Growing up with Oakley and the other Heirs has hardened something inside me. It's had to. Being the only female in their generation affords me certain protections, but it's all bullshit. Guys would use me without hesitation if it meant they could get to my brother and his friends, and girls would cut me down if I tried to stand in their way. Not that I ever would. I don't give two shits who they hook up with.

Except Darcie.

Damn Reese. He just had to pick her out of the crowd.

Of course, he did it to get a rise out of me. To bait me into playing his stupid little game. Well, she's welcome to him. She's sucked almost every other dick on the rugby team. She might as well add an Heir to her list of stellar achievements.

"Stupid fucking boys," I mutter, kicking a stone with my Converse. It zips across the ground, landing with a soft *plunk*.

Humming quietly to myself, the noise from the party fades into the distance as I keep walking toward where I hope will be the well-trodden path.

But a rustle behind me catches my attention and I freeze, icy cold fear fisting my heart.

"Hello?" I call out with fake bravado.

But only silence answers.

My pulse picks up speed a little. These woods are familiar territory. I know if I scream, someone will hear me and come looking. Or maybe I should call—

"Boo." A dark figure steps out of the shadows, and my heart catapults into my throat.

"Reese?" I spit, irritation coursing through me. "Creeper, much."

"Oak sent me to keep an eye on you, make sure you get home okay."

I narrow my eyes, considering his words. My gaze snags on the impressive bruise on his jaw. "No he didn't. There's no way he'd send you."

A slow, wicked smirk tugs at his mouth. "See something you like, Olive?"

"Don't call me that," I snarl, confused at the lick of heat in my stomach.

Reese is good looking, sure, in an arrogant, knows-it-and-flaunts-it kind of way. He's infuriating. The way his dark eyes bore into mine, daring me to take the bait, to play his stupid game.

"You can leave now," I snap, unwilling to engage.

"Leave?" He takes a step forward and I inch back. "I'm not going anywhere, Olive."

"I said stop—" Fists clenched at my sides, I inhale a sharp breath, forcing myself to calm down. To rise above it—above him—and be the bigger person. The better person.

"Fine. If you won't leave, I will." I go to move around him since he's blocking my path, but Reese's hand shoots out and grabs my arm.

"Not so fast." He backs me up against a tree, pinning me there. My mouth falls open as I gawk at him. The audacity. "Cat got your tongue, Olive?" he teases, smirking, and I swear I'm about one second away from kneeing him in the balls.

"You are such a—"

His grip on my arm tightens and I wince, silently fuming at him.

"Go on, Olive..." He leans in, his breath mingling with mine.

Too close.

He's too close, and the air feels too thick.

"Why don't you tell me exactly what you think of me, since you're such a self-righteous bitch."

A beat passes.

And another.

But I can't think straight, the alcohol in my veins saturating any sense of rationality I had left.

Reese's lip curls into a snarl. "Didn't think so."

"I hate you." The words fall from my lips, shattering whatever is growing between us. But he simply laughs. A deep, dark chuckle that does strange things to me. Unwanted things.

What is happening?

Maybe someone slipped something in my beer. Because I don't find Reese attractive. I don't. Not in any of the ways that matter to me, at least.

He's filthy rich and entitled and vulgar. And he might be one of my brother's best friends, but he's never been mine.

"Your body says otherwise," he drawls, letting his finger trail down my cheek and over my jaw. He slides it down my throat and dips it inside my top.

"Don't," I breathe, aware of the rush of desire his touch evokes.

It's just a natural reaction. It doesn't mean anything. How could it, when Reese represents everything I despise?

"Scared I'm right?" he taunts, his eyes molten. "Scared you'll... like it?"

"Please." My eyes roll dramatically. "I doubt you would ever know what to do with a girl like me. You know, a girl with half a brain cell."

"Big words, Olive, considering I have you pinned to a tree with no means of escape."

"Why?" I ask. "Why bother with me at all? You were just as horrified when my name was pulled from the jar."

I'd seen the disgust in his eyes. The utter disdain.

Well, the feeling is entirely mutual.

"Why?" His brow lifts as he dips his head to my ear. "Because I can. And it's so much fun, proving a liar wrong."

"I'm not— Ah..." A breathy moan escapes my lips the second his teeth clamp down on the soft flesh of my earlobe. "Reese."

God, why does it sound like I'm moaning his name?

I'm not.

That's not what this is.

And yet...

The flames inside me rise higher as he drags his treacherous lips down my throat, licking and nipping the skin there.

"Reese, stop..." His hand finds my bare thigh, sliding north, leaving a burning path in its wake. "Stop." The demand catches in my throat, sounding more like a ragged plea.

But I don't want this...

Do I?

For the last two years, I've watched Reese, my brother and their friends fuck their way through the girls in our town, always wondering what the appeal was.

But I can't deny the hum of power in my veins as Reese runs his hand up my thigh. His eyes are hooded with lust, swirling with hunger.

And I realise in this moment, he might hate me—but he also wants me.

Even more terrifyingly, I realise that maybe a small part of me wants him, too. Not because I like him or am even attracted to him beyond his physical appearance, but because for once, just once, I want to know what it feels like to have an Heir's sole attention.

"Knew you didn't have it in you, Olive." He drops his face to my neck again, breathing me in. "Always walking around like you're better than us, better than me. But you're just like the rest of us. Wicked, little liar." His mouth latches onto my neck, sucking hard, a bolt of pure lust shooting through me.

"Oh God," I whimper. Because it's both too much and not nearly enough.

Reese lifts his head, eyes as black as the night and stares at me, the air crackling between us. "You're nothing—"

I fist his robe and crush him against me as I kiss him. I don't want to hear his cruel words. I don't want to play this strange game of cat and mouse we seem to be caught in. I just want to feel, more of his lips, his teeth, his tongue.

"Fuck, Olivia." He breathes the words onto my lips, collaring my throat with his big, calloused hand.

Reese holds me there, my chest heaving and heavy between us.

"What are you—"

He dives back in, plastering his body against mine and capturing my lips in a bruising kiss. I'm no longer in control here, but I don't care, because his kiss, the taste of him is—

Realisation slams into me and I shove him back. "What the hell are we doing?"

Oh God. My stomach roils and Reese smirks, running his thumb across his bottom lip as he watches me calculatingly.

"You need to leave."

I can't do this.

But Reese closes the space between us again and pins me with a dark look as his hand grips my thigh, sliding upward until he's cupping me.

"Reese," I choke out. Because no one has ever touched me so indecently before.

"You're wet for me, aren't you, little liar." He hooks the damp material aside and slides his fingers through my folds.

"Reese, please..." Blood roars in my ears as my body melts under his possessive, filthy touch. "We can't."

"Oh, but we can." He grins. "Hate sex will blow your mind."

A cold blast goes through me.

"So you're admitting it. You hate me?"

"I don't just hate you, Olive. I want to fucking ruin you."

"Wha— Ah."

He pushes two fingers deep inside me, curling them deep while his thumb circles my clit, sending my heart into a free fall. "Jesus, Liv, you're so fucking tight."

Liv.

He's never called me that before. Before I can stop her, my stupid, fickle heart latches on to it.

Liv.

I like the way it rolled off his tongue. A little too much.

But all thoughts fly out of my head when he picks me up and cages me against the tree.

"Reese, what are you—"

"Just once," he grits out, fumbling between us.

I feel it then. His thick, long, bare dick pressed up against me.

"We can't," I repeat, part of me fully aware what a bad, bad idea this is.

But when he slides his dick through my wetness, nudging my clit, I cry out, all doubts melting away.

"Hold on," he orders, lining himself up.

"Reese, wait—"

He pushes inside me, a low growl rumbling in his chest. "Just fucking once," he grits out, as if his restraint is on a razor's edge.

"Reese, what are—"

He kisses me, drowning out my words as he rocks into me,

right to the hilt. My body shudders, stretching to accommodate him.

I'm having sex with Reese Whitfield. I should be freaking out, thinking about all the consequences if my brother or dad ever find out. But all I can think is *more*... I need more. Because he feels so fucking good, and we fit together so right.

I loop my arms around his neck, anchoring us together. "You feel so good," I pant.

"What do you need, Olive?" His fingers flex around my throat. "Say it."

"I want you to move... I need you to move."

"Beg."

"Please... Reese... God, please, I'm so close..."

Something glints in his eyes, and then I'm falling. I don't even realise what's happening until my arse hits the ground hard next to the tree, my back smarting from the scrape of the bark.

"R-Reese, what are you—"

He cuts me with an icy cold expression that takes my breath away. "Did you honestly think I'd ever fuck a girl like you?"

"W-what?" I croak as I stare up at him, dumbfounded. "I don't understand. You were inside me, you were—"

"And you begged for it so well, little liar. *More, Reese,*" he mocks me. "*Please, Reese... God, please, I'm so close.*"

Realisation slams into me, my heart dropping. "No. You wanted it, you... you wanted me."

"No, Olive. I told you I wanted to ruin you." He pulls out his mobile phone and points it at me, the flash blinding me for a second as he takes photo after photo.

"Reese!" I bark, panic flooding me. "Delete those." I clamber to my feet, aware that I'm a dishevelled mess. "Delete them right now."

I lunge for him, but he swats me away with ease.

"I don't think so. Consider it insurance. Breathe a word of

this to Oak or anyone else and I'll make sure everyone at All Hallows' knows what a dirty little whore Olivia Beckworth really is."

Tears burn the backs of my eyes, but I blink them away. I will not cry. I will not give him the satisfaction.

"You bastard."

"Never claimed to be anything else." A smug smirk curls at his mouth. "This was fun and all, but I've promised Darcie I'll fuck her senseless tonight." He winks before walking off. But I stand there, frozen. Paralysed at the turn of events. At how foolish I've been.

At the last second, Reese glances back.

"What?" I snap, feeling myself unravel.

He throws his head back and laughs. Laughs. When his eyes settle on me again, something cracks inside me.

"How does it feel, knowing that every time you're with a guy from here on out, you'll always think of this moment? The moment I *almost* fucked you."

I press my trembling lips together, refusing to give him so much as another breath.

Reese Whitfield is dead to me.

And I hope he rots in hell.

FILTHY JEALOUS HEIR: PART ONE

HEIRS OF ALL HALLOWS' BOOK ONE

1

REESE

I bring my car to a stop outside the only house I've ever known and sigh.

It's been ten weeks since I threw a bag into the boot and hightailed it out of Saints Cross, leaving the vivid memories of the night before behind. Or at least, that was the plan.

I might not have got the answers I wanted that night, but I sure left town with a fuck load of new material for my wank bank. After turning off my phone, I'd headed into the sunset on the promise of a new life. A promise that has kept me going through the summer.

But that dream wasn't exactly all it was cracked up to be.

It could have been. It could have been everything I wanted. Everything I've craved since Mum signed my life away.

But the lying son of a bitch I get to call Dad fucked it all up.

All the promises he'd made me about starting over, about cutting ties with our old life... they were all bullshit.

My fingers tighten on the wheel as I stare up at the house, anger bubbling up inside me and threatening to overspill at the fact that I'm back here. That I have been given zero fucking choice but to come back here. For now, at least.

My phone buzzes in my pocket, but I ignore it.

I turned it on before I got in my car and instantly wished I hadn't.

I haven't spoken to anyone since the night of the initiation.

The second I left that party, I disconnected from my past and looked to the future.

It hurt. Fuck yeah, it did. Those boys—my best friends Oakley Beckworth, Elliot Eaton, and Theo Ashworth—have been my life. My brothers. My ride or fucking dies.

But they'd got what they wanted. They were Heirs. They had their tattoos; Elliot had the key to the Chapel, and they all had the power.

They'd rule All Hallows' Sixth Form with an iron fist—and I had no doubt that they'd be fucking good at it, too.

They probably barely even noticed that four had become three with the hordes of girls I'm sure they've been fighting off since that night. I bet they can hardly think fucking straight from the sheer number of free blow jobs and pussy offered to them in the past few weeks.

Reaching down, I tug at my sweats, the memories of that night affecting me as if I'm right back there.

I slam those thoughts down.

The only reason they're bubbling under the surface is because my dick's seen less than zero action besides my right hand since getting out of his hellhole and it's desperate. I'm desperate. Even Darcie fucking Porter, the Queen Bitch of All Hallows', could get it hard with one look right now.

That thought sends a violent shudder down my spine.

I shove my door open, frustration seeping through my veins as I trudge to the boot and pull out the one bag I packed to take with me all those weeks ago.

Hitching it up onto my shoulder, I head toward the door.

I was half expecting Mum to be here. For her to be waiting

for me. But that doesn't seem to be the case. The driveway is empty, and as far as I can tell, so is the house.

There's certainly no big welcome home party.

Hell, there's not even a greeting.

I'm halfway up the steps to the front door when a note taped to the glass catches my eye. A frown pulls at my brows as I consider her being aware of my arrival and still not making the fucking effort to be here.

I guess it should be exactly what I expected. She's a lying, cheating control freak after all, and it seems those traits might extend to her relationship with me now.

My bag hits the ground with a thud as I step up to the familiar handwriting on the note. The second the words register in my head, my heart drops to my feet and my blood turns to ice.

Reese,
Surprise! We have moved in with the Beckworths.
Mum x

Hooking my fingers under the small scrap of paper, I tear it from the door. My hand trembles with barely restrained aggression. "No," I spit. "Fuck no, this is not happening."

Ripping my bag open, I search the bottom for my keys. Keys which I haven't used in fucking forever, because there was always someone inside this house. Always someone to greet me when I did show my face, even if it was our housekeeper.

Finding them, I pick out the one I need and move it toward the lock. Only, when I get it there, it doesn't fucking fit.

A bitter laugh of disbelief falls from my lips, but despite knowing what she's done, I keep pushing, desperate to get inside, to walk into my room, curl up in my bed and fall asleep with the hope that I can wake up six months ago and that none of this is happening.

I can't move in with the Beckworths. I can't…

Dropping my hand, my keys fall to the floor as I stumble back until my legs hit the small wall of our porch and I flop down. My head lowers into my hands as I fight to stop it from spinning.

There was a time when we were like, eight or nine when Oakley and I came up with a plan for me to move in with them. It was stupid childish shit. But I'd wanted it. I wanted what they had. Oakley and Olivia Beckworth.

Oakley might have been my boy. My best fucking friend in the entire world. But we would never share the connection that he and Olivia had.

Even as a kid, jealousy used to ravage me when I'd catch them sharing a knowing look that they both fully understood but I had no fucking clue about. It was a twin thing. They could finish each other's sentences. Hell, at times, they even knew what the other was doing without being told.

It was weird. It was impressive. But mostly, it made me fucking lonely.

Mum and Dad were always busy and almost always out of the house, leaving me to be cared for by nannies. Oak and Olivia didn't have that either. Their mum was incredible. Kind, caring, loving. They had a family, a home. And it was everything I wanted.

Don't get me wrong, my parents were great. They were happy, they loved each other, and they made sure I had everything I could ever want. They had no idea that deep down, what I really needed was… them.

Looking back now, I wonder how blind I was to it all. They put on such a united front, showed the world that they were the perfect couple with the successful jobs, the happy family, the beautiful home. All the things people crave in life. But when it came down to it, it was all lies.

There was nothing but lies, secrets, and betrayal hiding beneath the perfect veneer they had painted on our lives.

My arms fall, my fingers wrapping around the edge of the wall until it hurts and I tip my face up to the sky.

It's the perfect summer's day. Not a cloud in the sky. One of those days as a kid that you never want to end, because you know that every one you have edges you closer to growing up, to facing the brutal reality of life and the things you have no choice but to become.

Or maybe that was just me.

I hated that I'd had my life mapped out for me, hated that every day I woke got me closer to the inevitable.

I have no idea how long I sit there, putting off doing what I need to do, but eventually my phone buzzes and I pull it free.

Anger licks at my insides, my hand trembling as I swipe the screen to open what he has to say.

> Dad: I'm sorry, Son. But we both know it's for the best. Saints Cross is where you really belong.

My eyes lift from the screen as my grip turns so tight I'm amazed I don't crack it. What I really want to do is get in my car and go straight back to where I came from to hide. But I can't.

My only choice is here, or...

My eyes find my car as the option of getting in it and driving plays out in my mind. I don't have access to the kind of money I need right now to start over. That's why I'm here. Although I'm sure I've got enough to at least get started.

But I need to be here.

I need to be here and show this entire town what lying, cowardly, manipulative arseholes my parents really are. And then, and only then, I might be able to leave with my head held high. I might be able to start over.

Nodding to myself, I find my feet, determination pulsing through my veins.

I can do that. I can endure stepping foot back inside that house, living with those liars so long as at the end of it, I show the town exactly who they are, exactly what they do to people's lives.

My hands tremble around the wheel as I make my way toward the house that I know almost as well as the one I just left. Hell, there's every chance that over the years, I've spent as much time under the Beckworths' roof as I have my own.

The sight of their mansion makes my stomach knot. I have no idea what kind of reception I can expect. Mum knows I'm coming, although she thinks I'm turning up tomorrow. But the others?

What has she told them? Where do the boys think I've gone?

Are they relieved that I'm no longer in their lives?

I bet Olivia is.

For the briefest moment, I allow myself to think back to our final meeting in the woods. Her scent, her addictive taste, the way her pussy gripped me so fucking tight, trying to draw me deeper.

"Fuck," I bark, slamming my hand down on the wheel.

I told myself as I walked away from her that night that I wasn't going to think about it again. That what happened under the cover of darkness, deep in the trees was nothing but a show.

A show of power over the girl who was just as bad as my parents.

I wanted to see her broken. Ruined. I wanted to see her fucking tarnished for what she was doing, what she was hiding, and as she curled up on the cold, dark ground at my feet, I almost got my wish.

But it wasn't enough.

I knew instantly that what we shared that night wasn't

enough. Not enough to break her, and certainly not enough to sate my twisted need, my darkest fantasy, my... obsession with the girl I could never have.

Unlike my house, there are cars parked in the driveway here. The windows are open with soft music pouring from inside.

My heart pounds harder as I consider the fact that they're all in there, playing happy families.

Is she being a better mum to them than she's been to me?

I sit there for the longest time, staring up at the house I once felt so at home in. But it's different now. It's tainted right along with my memories of everything that happened inside it.

Aware that I'm going to be caught if I sit out here like a creep for much longer, I push the door open and drag my bag out that I dumped on the passenger seat before leaving... home.

I shake my head. That house is apparently not my home anymore.

This is.

A house where my mum and my what... my new stepfamily are.

Please.

My eyes roll and my fists clench as I head toward the front door. The music gets louder, and it becomes more than obvious that it's Oakley's as I get closer.

A sense of longing pulls at my tight muscles, the need to kick back in my best friend's room with some beats pouring from his speakers as we forget about the world and all the bullshit in it.

But something tells me that after the stunt I pulled, I'm not going to be welcomed back with open arms.

I don't have a key this time, so I reach for the handle, hoping like hell that it's open and I'm not going to have to ring the bell and wait to be invited inside.

Thankfully, it twists, and only a second later, I've thrown the door wide open and stepped into their massive hallway.

Their house always did put our mini mansion to shame, but after living in a beach house in a small seaside town for the last few weeks, it seems even more fucking ridiculous than ever.

Voices float down to me from the kitchen at the back of the house. The scent of something cooking hits my nose and makes my stomach growl loudly.

Dumping my bag on the marble floor tiles, I take a step forward, but a shadow falls in a doorway beside me.

My heart jumps into my throat, but I don't get a chance to turn his way, to say anything before Oakley roars, "You motherfucker!" and flies at me.

His fist collides with my jaw and my head snaps back as pain explodes across my face and down my neck. My head spins and my vision blurs for a beat, his punch is a hell of a lot harder than I ever remember them being in the past. But after what I've done, I guess I deserve it.

A blurred figure races down the stairs as I fight to recover from the surprise attack, but the second my vision clears and I find her dark, angry eyes, everything comes crashing down around me. Literally.

2

OLIVIA

The hand-painted Moorcroft vase lays scattered at Reese's feet as he stares blankly at me.

"You threw a vase at my head."

I cock a brow and smirk. "Shame it missed."

"You're fucking crazy."

"And you're a piece of shit."

"Liv," Oakley warns, stepping in between us.

"Control your psycho bitch sister, Beckworth, or I'll—"

I grab the next item off the sideboard and haul it above my head. "Or you'll what?" I threaten, unsure how likely I am to follow through on my intentions.

Seeing Reese Whitfield-Brown standing at our door unleashed something in me. Something I thought I'd long let go of.

He's been gone all summer, ever since the end of year party.

A night I've tried my hardest to pretend never happened.

"Okay, okay, everyone just calm the fuck down," Oakley barks, holding out his hands as if he's physically trying to keep me and Reese apart. Which is rich, seeing he was the first one to land a punch.

"He started it," I snap, the anger I feel at seeing Reese again bubbling over.

"Liv, not helping."

"What are you doing here, Reese?"

His expression falters, and for a second, I see behind the icy cold veneer he's wearing.

"You mean my mum and your dad didn't tell you the good news? You're looking at your new housemate."

"No." My breath catches, because this is the worst thing that can possibly happen to me.

Almost as bad as that night.

"You're kidding?" Oakley hisses. "You take off at the beginning of summer, ghost us, ignore our calls and texts, and then turn up without warning and think you're going to live here? Over my dead fucking—"

"Oakley." Dad's voice ripples through the hall. "Reese, we weren't expecting you until tomorrow."

"You knew?" My head whips around to him, and he blanches.

"We planned to discuss it with you tonight over dinner."

"Oh, this is pure gold," Reese chuckles darkly. "And exactly what had you planned to tell them, *Dad*?"

"Reese, that's not—"

"Not what? Appropriate? Like how you were fucking my mum behind my dad's back all those months? Or how you ruined my family?"

"We should talk," Dad says, somehow managing to keep his composure. But then, it's his job. He defends some of the worst criminals in the country and does it with a smile.

"So let's talk." Reese folds his arms over his chest and cocks a brow. "Did you fuck her over the desk at work, or did she get on her knees and—"

"Enough!" Dad booms. "I will accept your anger and disrespect toward me because I understand there are things we need to talk about, but what I will not tolerate is hearing you talk about your mother that way."

Reese steps forward, blind fury rolling off him in thick, angry waves. "My mother is a lying, deceitful whore."

Fiona's gasp echoes through the hall and we all turn to find her standing there, unshed tears clinging to her lashes.

"Reese, you're early."

"Quite the set-up you've got here, Mum," he spits. "A nice little happy family."

"Reese, please."

Fiona Brown is a formidable woman. Sharp-tongued, driven, and a force to be reckoned with in a town ruled by men. But she's also kind and compassionate, and she makes my dad happier than I've seen him in a long time.

It was a shock at first, when we found out about their affair. But anyone can see how happy they make each other, and despite Reese's reaction, Fiona and Reese's dad had been having marital issues for some time.

"I haven't seen you in over two months. It would be nice to talk, to catch up."

"Your mum is right, Reese." Oakley offers him a faint smile. "We should all sit down and talk."

"Go fuck yourself, Beckworth." Reese lunges for my brother, and the two of them slam into the wall in a blur of fists and insults.

"Christian, do something," Fiona yells, and my dad wades into the chaos, pulling the guys apart.

"ENOUGH!" he bellows. "This is my home, and I will not tolerate this. Oakley, go upstairs and calm down. And you," he pins Reese with a dark look, "you will go sit in the kitchen and talk to your mother."

"You can't tell me what to do."

"No, but you live under my roof now, and you will respect my rules. Or there's the door." Dad flicks his eyes past Reese.

"Whatever." He shrugs out of my dad's hold and cuts each of us with a cold look that sends a shudder through me. "I'm out of here."

"Reese, wait—"

But he's gone, blowing out of the house like a storm. The door slams behind him, and Fiona sucks in a sharp breath.

"Well," Oak says, still loitering by the stairs, "that could have gone better."

Reese didn't return.

The mood in the house was tense after he stormed out. Dad had ushered Fiona into the kitchen and told me to deal with Oakley. He'd gotten an impressive split knuckle from his scuffle with Reese, but it was nothing an antiseptic wipe and some skin closure strips wouldn't fix. When you have a brother who plays rugby, you become well versed in cleaning up cuts and bruises.

"Where do you think he is?" I ask Oakley as we veg out in his room. Reruns of *The Walking Dead* play on his television, but he's more interested in whatever's on his phone screen.

"Probably getting fucked up or straight up fucked. You know what he's like."

Don't I just.

I shake *those* thoughts out of my head. "I can't believe he's going to live here. They should have told us sooner."

"And ruin the last few days of summer?" He looks up at me and gives me a weak smile. "I want to punch him all over again."

"It won't help anything."

"No." He flexes his busted hand, the closure strip lifting slightly. "But it'll make me feel better."

"I still can't believe he ghosted you all summer."

"I'm not surprised. It's Reese. He's always had a chip on

his shoulder. Especially since all that shit with Judge Bancroft and Abigail. Fuck, I wish he'd talked to me before taking off like that." Oakley drops his head back against the giant beanbag seat and blows out a steady breath. "I kinda get why he did it."

"What?" I balk.

"It's different for him. His whole life is mapped out."

My stomach drops. "You really think she'll make him go through with it? Marrying Abigail?"

"Before the summer, I would have said one hundred percent. It was a signed and sealed deal. But now... I don't know."

I make a small, derisive sound.

Arranged marriages, for God's sake. It's the twenty-first century. But the arrangement between Fiona Brown and Judge Bancroft is no secret. Upon graduating, once they turn twenty-one, Reese and Abigail are expected to be married.

I can't imagine Reese Whitfield—as he prefers to be called, because a double-barrel surname is too pretentious even for a rich boy like him, apparently—in a serious relationship, let alone a marriage. But none of the Saints Cross Heirs live particularly normal lives. They're the descendants of some of the country's most powerful and successful men. Magistrates, lawyers, politicians, businessmen, and investors. The upper echelons of Saints Cross have been marrying off their sons and daughters for years. To strengthen families' positions, to merge assets, to breed the perfect offspring.

All Hallows' School and nearby Saints Cross University don't educate your average teenagers. They cultivate the leaders of the future.

And my brother and his dumb friends are next in line to carry the baton.

Oakley's phone vibrates again, and he chuckles at whatever the message says.

"Theo?" I ask.

"Group chat."

"Of course." I roll my eyes, flipping back onto his bed. "What do they think about the whole Reese-is-back-and-is-our-new-housemate situation?"

"Theo is still laughing, Elliot is... well, you know Elliot. He's already told me to rein it in."

"You don't always have to do what he says, you know."

He shrugs. "You know how it is. He's the lead Heir. He has the key."

The key.

Another ridiculous tradition bestowed to every new generation of Heirs. The key to the Chapel. A private residence in the oldest building on the All Hallows' School estate.

"Anyway, I'm not—"

A loud crash from somewhere downstairs makes me bolt upright. "What the hell?"

"I'm guessing Reese is home." Oakley rises from his chair, grim determination etched into his expression.

"What are you going to do?"

"Make sure he doesn't do something he'll regret."

"Oak—"

But he's already gone.

I hesitate, really not wanting to get involved. Not while Reese is so angry. But he lives here now; it's not like I can escape him.

I love my dad, I love him something fierce, but he screwed up, not telling us about Reese moving in. I get why they wanted to wait, but a little time to get used to the idea would have been nice.

Stepbrother.

The word clangs through me.

I had sex in the woods at the end of year party with not only my brother's best friend, but also my new stepbrother.

A shudder rips down my spine as I fight to block out the memories.

It was a moment of madness. Anger and alcohol are never a good combination. Throw in a lot of unresolved tension and frustration and you get one colossal mistake.

When Oakley told me Reese had upped and left town with his dad, part of me had been relieved. If he was gone, I didn't have to worry about what happened that night ever coming out. About those photos.

I would never—

"Fucking hell, Reese. Just work with me here," Oakley booms as another crash reverberates through the house.

With a heavy sigh, I slip into the hall and find Oak practically dragging a very drunk Reese up the stairs.

"A little help, Liv."

"What? No! Let him sleep on the stairs, for all I care."

Oakley levels me with a hard look and I roll my eyes. "Fine," I groan. "But you owe me."

Reese murmurs something as I grab his arm and slide it over my shoulder, taking some of his weight.

"Jesus, Whitfield, how much did you drink? You smell like a brewery."

"Olive... Olive... Olive..." he slurs, and I hope to God he's too drunk to say anything that might make Oakley suspicious. Because if my brother knew what went down that night...

It doesn't bear thinking about.

Between us, we manage to wrestle Reese into his new bedroom.

"Sleep it off," Oakley says, giving him a little shove. Reese lands face down on the mattress but turns his head toward me. "I'll grab a bowl and some water. Stay with him a second."

"But... fine." I concede, dropping my gaze to Reese's unmoving form. He's barely conscious, so it's not like he can cause any more trouble. "Just hurry."

Oakley rushes from the room, and I pace alongside Reese's

bed. Fiona brought most of his stuff from their old house when she moved in last month. It's all been here, waiting for him. But no one ever said he might actually come and live here.

It's my worst nightmare come true.

He's my worst nightmare.

And now, there's no escaping him.

3

REESE

I roll over with a groan and fall straight into a cool patch of drool on the pillow. Nice.

As I rouse, my head pounds harder until I swear I've actually invited a fucking brass band to take up residence there.

Flipping onto my back, my stomach churns as I rip my tongue from the roof of my mouth.

What the hell happened last—

"Fuck," I breathe, my eyes popping open to take in my surroundings.

Shit. It was real.

"Fuuuuck," I groan into my hands before combing my fingers through my hair and pulling it until it hurts.

My head spins with everything that happened yesterday, from Dad giving me little choice but to return to Saints Cross, to finding that motherfucking note on our front door, and then stepping straight into this fully functioning little family where my best friend actually defends my whore of a mother. But then, I guess it's easy for them. Their father hasn't betrayed anyone. At least, no one important to them. Their mum died years ago, and as far as I know, Christian has been single ever since.

But of all the women, why my mum?

Why lie, cheat, and deceive my dad, the one person who held the key to breaking me free from the prison I've been locked in my entire life? He'd promised me that the day he left, he'd take me with him. That we'd get to start over together, somewhere far away from Saints Cross.

Was that all just as big a lie as their relationship must have been?

Footsteps pad down the hallway outside the room I must have been dumped in last night. I don't remember getting back here. I do remember swiping a bottle of whisky from the shop and heading down toward the Rock with the intention of drowning my sorrows.

I'd sat there for hours, drinking and wishing I was anywhere but back here as I rested on the old rock, the place where all the legends and rituals of this town stem back to, and looked out over the forest in the distance.

It's said that anyone who comes out here and touches this thing is cursed. But I'm long past worrying about that kind of shit. It sure is fun to tease those who truly believe it though.

Looking to my side, I have to blink a couple of times to make sure I'm not seeing things when a glass of water and a packet of painkillers appears before me. I can only assume it was Mum. Although why she'd bother after the way I spoke about her when I got here yesterday, fuck only knows.

It sure as hell wouldn't have been Oak or Olivia.

Lifting my hand, I rub at my jaw where Oak landed his impressive blow. He's been training while I've been gone. It makes me wonder if the others have too, and if they'll have a similar opinion about my sudden return.

Hindsight is a great thing, but I truly believed that the day I drove out of town would be the last time I would ever show my face here.

I thought I was severing all ties, and I thought going cold turkey and allowing them to get on with their lives as if I never existed was the best thing to do. At no point did I think about how they might react when I came back. Because I wasn't coming back.

Not ever.

I swing my legs over the side of the bed and quickly swallow the pills.

My head pounds as I stare at my bare legs. Whoever got me in here last night was apparently kind enough to ensure I was comfortable.

My mind wanders to Olivia, and a smirk curls at my lips. I bet she'd have had a good look. She sure wanted more of my cock on initiation night.

Thoughts of that night cause my anger to reignite deep within me. I reach for jeans and shove my hand into the pocket, wrapping my fingers around my phone and pulling it out.

It accepts my battered face and unlocks for me, and in only seconds, I'm staring down at the photos I took of her that night.

I've memorised each one of these images over the past couple of months to the point they may as well be painted onto the back of my eyelids. And like every other time, desire swirls with my anger. My temperature soars and my cock swells.

It would have been so easy to take more from her that night. I craved it, fuck. Her cunt was so tight, so fucking wet for me. Pulling out of her and denying something that I'd imagined for... way too fucking long was torturous. But I knew it needed to happen. I couldn't leave this place without letting her know what I really thought of her.

My mum, her dad. They might be the liars, the cheaters. But she's no fucking better. And I'm going to make goddamn sure she knows it too.

Dropping my phone to the bed, I finally scan the room I've been dumped in.

Confusion pulls at my brows as I take in all the things I'm surrounded by. The shelves are lined with familiar rugby trophies. The photos are of the boys and me over the years. The speakers, the books, even the computer. It's all... mine.

My heart rate increases as reality settles within me. Mum really has moved us in here. This is... this is my new room.

Pushing to my feet, I pad toward the door at the other side of the room and pull it open. There's a massive bathroom, and to the left, a dressing room that I'm sure Kim Kardashian would be proud of which is full of all the clothes I left behind.

"Jesus." This is really happening. Mum really is expecting me to live here. To become a part of this family as if there's nothing wrong with the fact that she's been fucking Christian behind all our backs.

With a pained groan, I stumble forward and toward the shower. I turn the water on as hot as I can stand, shove my boxers down my legs, and step under it.

The dirt from hanging out in a dusty field the night before washes down the drain as I stand there with my head hanging and my shoulders lowered.

Reaching for my shower gel, I don't even react to the fact that it's my brand. The one that, no matter how many times I demanded Mum buy for me, she would always fuck up and get a different one. How did she suddenly get it right?

I wash, scrubbing at my skin until it hurts in the hope that I'm still dreaming and I'll wake up back by the beach with Dad.

I hated it when we first got there. Although not as much as I did this place. Dad said it was temporary, and that once he'd got a few things in place, he'd find a real home and start over.

I didn't understand it. He had money, that much was obvious. Even if Mum was the big earner in our house. But he seemed content, and I was happy to be free of all the things that were expected of me here. I figured that as long as we were together, I'd follow him wherever he wanted to go.

If only I knew that he'd planned on kicking me back here before the new school year started. That all the promises he'd made were nothing but lies.

Has everything my parents ever told me been nothing but total fucking bullshit?

My fists curl as I silently make my way down the stairs to the sound of happy chatter in the kitchen.

"Have you got everything you both need for Monday?" Mum asks, sounding more concerned than I'm sure I've ever heard her before about the beginning of a school year.

When I was a kid, that was my nanny's job. And in more recent years, I sorted out my own shit and got on with it, since she was always too busy working. Unlike most of the founding families of Saints Cross, it's my mum who carries Heir blood. She wasn't allowed to be initiated, but she set out to prove my grandfather and everyone in this town that she had what it took to be just as good as them. It's why I have a godawful double-barrel surname—because she refused to take my old man's name.

"Yes, I think so." Olivia's soft voice washes over me.

"You don't need to worry about these two, Fi. They're the most organised kids I've ever met," Christian laughs.

"Oakley might be. Not sure I can claim that title," Olivia jokes.

If things were different, I wouldn't be able to disagree with her. Oakley's need for order and tidiness is fucking unbearable. But it's the least of my worries right now.

I come to a stop in the doorway. The sight before me makes my chest ache and my stomach knot.

They look like a real family. Like the one I've always wanted but never had.

Mum notices that Olivia's glass is empty and stands, reaching for the jug to refill it while Christian offers her the last pancake on the plate in the middle of them all.

"Well, well, well," I say, announcing my presence when they all fail to notice my arrival.

Four sets of hesitant eyes turn on me as I step into the room.

"This looks... cosy. Seems I missed the invite."

Stepping between Mum and Olivia, I reach for that pancake, fold it in half and stuff it in my mouth while Olivia bristles beside me.

"We weren't expecting you to roll out of your pit yet," Oakley spits, watching me through a swollen eye.

"It would probably serve you well not to underestimate me, Oak. You know how much pain I can cause, after all." My eyes dart to the split in his lip as he pushes his chair out.

"Oak, don't," Olivia warns.

"Yeah, Oak. Be a good boy and listen to your sister."

"Reese," Mum breathes. "Come and take a seat. I'll get you some food."

"It seems you've already eaten it all," I mutter, looking around at their half-empty plates.

"It's no problem to make more," Christian says. "If we knew you were up, we'd have—"

"Given me some warning? Forgive me, Christian, but that doesn't seem to be your style."

The second Mum stands from her chair, I drag it toward me, ensuring I'm close enough to Olivia to make her uncomfortable and sitting my arse on it.

"I'd like a coffee, and a whole stack of those pancakes," I say without looking at Mum.

She hesitates before she reaches the kitchen island.

"The man you're fucking isn't the only change with you,

huh?" I mutter. "It seems you learned to cook as well. The only thing I remember coming out of your kitchen when I was a kid resembled charcoal."

"That's enough, Reese," Christian snaps.

"Is it, though? Is it really?" I sneer. "I'm pretty sure after what you two have done, it barely scratches the surface."

"You don't have to follow his orders, darling," he says to Mum, who's standing in the middle of the kitchen with glassy eyes as if she's about to burst into tears.

The sight should probably affect me, but it doesn't. She deserves a little pain for the amount she's caused me over the years.

"What the hell has he done to you, Mum?" I ask, studying her. "The woman I remember would never have broken down so easily."

"It's complicated, Reese," she whispers.

"And here I was thinking that you're barely able to understand the simple things. Like only fucking the man you're married to."

"Enough," Christian booms, slamming his palms down on the table and pushing to stand. "We've made mistakes, Reese. We've hurt those we love, and we'll forever be sorry for that. But we're happy. Happier than we've ever been. And we want our family, our kids, to be the same."

"And you think that's possible after lying to us... for how long, exactly?"

Mum shoots a look at Christian, confirming that their affair started long before I figured it out.

"Those pancakes aren't going to cook themselves."

"Your mother isn't your slave, Reese," Christian barks, his face beginning to turn purple with frustration.

I've never known him to be anything but calm and collected. Even after we had a party last year and managed to get almost the entire house trashed, he was able to keep his cool. But it seems that my mother could be a very touchy subject to him, because one insult and he looks like he's about to blow his lid. "While you're under this roof, you're going to treat her with the respect she deserves."

"What are you going to do? Kick me out? Because it seems to me that for some fucked-up reason, you both want me here."

Tension ripples around the room as everyone bites back the words that are on the tip of their tongues.

Turning toward Oak and Olivia, my eyes bounce between the two of them.

"So tell me, Olive," I say with a smirk. "Did undressing me last night give you a thrill, or are you still an uptight bitch?"

4
―――

OLIVIA

His words ring through me as I grind my teeth together.

Don't take the bait.

Don't take the bait.

Smiling sweetly, I say, "We're family now, Reese. The way I see it, I was helping my new stepbrother out."

I almost gag on the words, but I don't let him see that. He thinks he's so fucking smug, sitting there, making things awkward and uncomfortable.

"Can we just have breakfast, please?" Dad implores. "Without trying to kill each other?"

"Now there's a thought," Reese murmurs, and I shoot him a hard stare.

'What, sister?' he mouths.

This isn't going to work. I can't see him every day of my life for the foreseeable future. It's been less than twenty-four hours and I already want to strangle him with my bare hands.

"What are your plans for today?" Fiona asks, keeping one eye on her son. "I thought maybe we could—"

"No."

"Reese, work with me here." She lets out a heavy sigh. "School starts on Monday, you must need some new—"

"I think I'll manage." He throws his cutlery down on his plate and stands abruptly, making the tableware clatter. "I'm going out."

"Out? Out where?"

But he walks off, ignoring her.

"Reese, come back here," she yells after him, but Dad pats her hand.

"Let him go, darling. It's going to take time."

"Time?" My brow lifts. "He's never going to accept this."

"Well, he doesn't have much choice." Her expression gutters.

"I'll talk to him," Oakley says. "When he's calmed down, I'll talk to him."

"Thank you, Son. We know this isn't easy, but Reese is a part of this family, and we all need to find a way to co-exist."

A shudder runs through me.

Family.

As if I need any reminder that we're now as good as stepbrother and sister.

God, if anyone ever finds out about what happened that night...

They can't.

I need Reese's word that he won't ever tell anyone about it.

The sudden trill of my mobile phone startles me, sending my centre of gravity off course. I slide down the wall into a breathless heap. Damn it. I've been working on the handstand scorpion for weeks, but I still haven't progressed to moving away from the wall for balance.

"Hello?" I bark, annoyed with the interruption, although it's my own fault for not silencing my phone.

"Hey, it's me," my friend Charli sing-songs. "What are you up to?"

"Yoga."

"Riveting," she deadpans.

"There's nothing wrong with wanting to improve my strength, balance, and flexibility. It's also great for relaxation." And God only knows I'll need some of that now Reese is living here.

"You know what else is good for relaxing, Liv? Sex. Sex is good. I swear multiple orgasms is the new meditation."

Charli is... a handful.

She got expelled from All Hallows' the year before sixth form. Now, she attends the public school in Huxton. But we still hang out occasionally. She doesn't care that my brother is an Heir, never has. It's why I've always liked her. The girls at school only care about using me to get to my brother and his friends.

"Did you want something, or did you only call to traumatise me with all your sex talk?"

"No, bitch, I was calling to ask if we're partying tonight."

"I hadn't planned on it."

"Well, a little birdie told me that there's a big party at Elliot's house tonight, and I think we should go."

Of course there's a party at Elliot's house. It's the last weekend before school starts. But that doesn't mean I plan on going.

"No. No way."

"And why the fuck not? It's been ages since I partied with you and the Heirs."

"Charli, come on. I have to live with Oak and—" I stop myself.

Crap, I didn't mean to say that.

"And what?"

"Nothing, it doesn't matter."

"You know I won't quit until you tell me..."

"Fine. Reese is back."

"No shit," she breathes. "Wait a minute, does that mean—"

"You guessed it. We have a new housemate."

"And stepbrother, by all accounts." I hear the smirk in her words and groan.

"Ugh," I clamber to my feet. "Can't we do something else? I could come over and we could—"

"I need to party, Liv. Things at home are... well, they're a fucking mess. I need to get fucked up, and nobody parties like the Heirs. Please come with me."

"Charli, I really don't—"

"Please, please, pleeeeease. We haven't hung out properly in forever, and I can't turn up without you."

"Gee, thanks."

"Come on, don't be like that," she whines. "We can get drunk and make fun of all the Heir chasers."

A smile tugs at my lips. Watching the girls of All Hallows' fall over themselves trying to get their shot with Oak and his friends is one of my favourite pastimes.

"Fine," I concede. "We can go for a little bit."

"Yes. Thank you, thank you, thank you! I owe you."

"It's fine. You want me to swing by and pick you up or meet there?"

Ever since Charli's mum was run out of town after a local scandal, Charli has kept me at arm's length. And I know her mum's boyfriend is a right creepy wanker, so I suppose going to the party is the least I can do for her.

"I'll meet you there, say seven?"

"Yeah, okay."

"Wear something sexy." She chuckles before hanging up.

I throw my phone down on my bed with a huff. The last thing I want to do tonight is party with my brother and his friends, but Charli's right.

If I'm going to do it, I'm going to do it in style.

"Holy shit, Liv. You look... if I didn't like dick so much, I'd be all over you."

My brows bunch together as I roll my eyes. "And you look... as slutty as ever." I say, taking in her black leather halter dress, fishnet tights, and biker boots.

Charli has always marched to the beat of her own drum, and her outfit choices have always been like a giant fuck you to the upper echelons of Saints Cross.

"Why thank you, bitch." She swishes her pink-streaked, jet-black hair off her shoulder and shoots me a salacious grin. "Ready to cause some mayhem?"

"I'm ready to watch you cause some mayhem."

"Hell to the fuck yeah." Grabbing my hand, Charli yanks me toward Elliot's house.

The long, sweeping driveway is already crawling with cars, but none stands out more than Elliot's custom paint matte black Aston Martin DB11. It makes the collection of Range Rovers, BMWs, and Audis look like child's play. Even Oakley's custom-built BMW X5 doesn't have a patch on the beauty that is Elliot's baby.

Lucky bastard.

Although no surprise given his father is Johnathon Eaton, one of the wealthiest men in Oxfordshire.

"Let me guess... you're imagining fucking someone on the bonnet of that car."

"One: that's Elliot's car, so no, that's gross. He's like my brother. And two: what is wrong with you?"

"I'm horny, and that is one sweet-ass ride."

Laughter peals out of me. "You're crazy."

"I need a drink." She grins. "Come on."

A couple of girls check us as we enter Elliot's house, sneering at Charli. She ignores them, but I bristle at their blatant disapproval, staring them both down.

Bitches.

I should be used to it by now, but I'll never get over how awful girls can be to one another. And all in the name of climbing the social ladder.

It's why, aside from Charli, I gave up trying to make friends a long time ago.

"Charli Devons, is that you?" My brother's voice rings out over the music, and I smother a groan. I was hoping to avoid them for a little while.

"Looking good, Oak." She saunters over to him and Theo as they hold court at Elliot's huge kitchen island. Big enough to seat at least sixteen people, it's topped with shimmering black marble the same as the other kitchen tops—a stark contrast to the pristine white walls. But I would expect nothing less from Johnathon and Julia Eaton.

"Theo," she clips out.

"Charli."

"Always a pleasure."

"Don't mind Theo," my brother smirks, "he's still sulking that Reese aka his competition is back. "

"Fucking idiot." He pins Oakley with a dark look. "I'm pissed because he's a fucking prick."

"So he's not here?" I ask, relief sinking into me.

"Nope. And hopefully he knows better than to turn up uninvited."

"Do I sense dissension in the ranks?" Charli asks. She might not be a student at All Hallows' anymore or even live in Saints Cross, but she knows the deal. And the guys give her somewhat of a free pass, given that she's my friend.

"He left us," Theo huffs, downing his drink and slamming it on the counter. "Fill me up, Beckworth."

"Now why did that get my blood pumping?" Charli chuckles. "Have the two of you ever thought about—"

"Fuck no," Oak grumbles. "Not cool, Charli. Not cool."

"So touchy, Oak. How can you be so adamant you don't like something unless you've tried it?"

"What are we trying?" Elliot appears, running an assessing eye over Charli. There's no lust in his gaze or even mild interest. But then, there rarely is where the Heirs' formidable leader is concerned.

Elliot is a glacier when it comes to letting people in. I've known him years and feel as if I've barely scratched the surface.

"See something you like, Eaton?" Charli teases, brazenly checking him out. There's no denying Elliot looks good in his ripped jeans and black Paul Smith rugby top, but his eyes are an icy warning to stay well back.

"You're not my type," he says flatly.

Most girls would recoil at his rejection, but not Charli. She simply throws her head back and laughs. "Oh, I've always liked you, Eaton. Now someone pour us girls a drink, and make it strong."

Oakley grabs two empty glasses and makes us each a vodka and coke, heavy on the vodka.

"Now we're talking." Charli lifts her glass to mine, clinking it. "Here's to getting fucked and getting fucked up."

"Are you sure she's not one of us?" Theo murmurs, watching with equal parts disgust, pride and awe as Charli downs her drink in one.

"Packing the wrong anatomy, I'm afraid," she says.

"I don't know. I reckon you've got a dick down there," Elliot taunts.

"Care to test that theory, Eaton?"

They launch into a debate about the fairer sex, but something catches my attention over by the door. A ripple of awareness goes through me as the air shifts.

"Wha—"

Reese appears, cutting through the crowd and heading straight for us.

"Motherfucker," Oakley whispers under his breath.

Reese doesn't acknowledge anyone as his legs eat up the distance between us. My heart pounds wildly in my chest as I'm caught in his intense, dark stare.

Oh my God.

This can't be happening.

It can't—

"You've got some fucking nerve showing up here," Theo spits, the entire kitchen hushing to witness the reunion between the Heirs and their absent member.

"Nice to see you too, Theo," Reese says coolly.

"You couldn't have called?" Elliot asks, arms folded over his chest as he leans back against the counter.

"Didn't know I needed permission to be here."

"I see the time away didn't deflate your ego."

Reese snorts at that, helping himself to a drink. "Charli Devons," he smirks, "didn't expect to see you here."

"I could say the same thing about you, Whitfield." She doesn't miss a beat, more than willing to verbally spar with an Heir.

Everyone is watching, their eyes like lasers in my back.

"Touché." He smirks at her, and something inside me tightens. "Anyway, this has been fun and all, but I didn't come to talk. I came to get fucked up." Lifting his drink in the air, he runs his gaze over each Heir. "Cheers, boys."

And then, he walks off like he didn't just drop a bomb at their feet.

5

REESE

The eyes of the entire sixth form burn into me as I make my way outside.

I knew it was going to happen. There was no chance of me turning up at this party out of the blue and slipping into the background. The boys and I have never been in the background in all our lives.

"Reese," a sickly-sweet voice says, and when I look over, I find Darcie Porter fighting her way through the crowd to get to me.

"Great," I mutter under my breath as she closes the space between us with an excited smile on her lips.

"It's so good to see you," she sings, not stopping until there's zero space left between us and she's shamelessly running her hands up my chest.

"Uh..." I grunt, unable to return the sentiment.

My skin burns with the attention of those I walked away from. I don't need to look up to know that the worst of those hate glares is coming from Olivia.

She hates Darcie with a passion that's almost as strong as what I'm sure she feels for me. It's why Darcie has always been the perfect bait. Especially since she's the headteacher's daughter and more than willing to do whatever she can to prove she's not the prim and proper star pupil her father makes her out to be.

A few other girls follow her, all their attention locked on me as if I've come back being suddenly interested in them.

Spoiler: I have not.

My opinion on the shameless Heir-chasing sluts of All Hallows' hasn't changed.

They have their uses, sure. Fuck knows, I've used them more than a few times. But that doesn't mean I'm going to return and suddenly lock one of them down. Hell, they all know that's never going to happen with me. Everyone knows that my future is mapped out. But still, they sniff around like strays, hoping to get a boost up the social ladder.

"How about we take this welcome home party to the dance floor?" I suggest, looking each of them in the eyes.

Unsurprisingly, they all agree excitedly. Darcie and one of her friends grab my arms and drag us deeper onto the patio where everyone is grinding it up to the beat.

Right before we get swallowed by the crowd, I shoot a look over my shoulder.

A smirk pulls at my lips when I find my boys, Olivia and Charli all standing in a line, glaring at me. Okay, so Charli is looking more amused than anything else. But I'm pretty sure Olivia, Oak, and Theo are each about to pop a blood vessel, while Elliot stands as stoic as ever.

I nod in their direction, my smirk growing as I'm dragged farther away from them.

I catch Oak lean over to whisper something in Theo's ear before they vanish from my sight and I'm once again surrounded by my admirers.

FILTHY JEALOUS HEIR: PART ONE

I have no idea how long we dance, but a few songs pass me by and I get more than a couple of drinks delivered thanks to some terrified soon-to-be lower sixth student, and rugby team hopeful, who literally tripped over himself to make me happy. Pretty sure he'd have dropped to his knees and sucked my cock should I have suggested it.

The buzz I've got going on and the hands that are trailing over my body are enough to almost make me forget where I am. Almost. But it's impossible when I feel their attention. Even when I can't see them. I feel it.

We've always been tight. Oakley, Elliot, and Theo are like the brothers I never had. Over the years, I've come to know them better than I know myself, so I'm more than aware that they're not going to let this go without having it out with me.

I'm amazed it hasn't happened already.

I was expecting it the second I walked into this house. But I guess they've decided to bide their time.

"We should take this upstairs," Darcie purrs with her lips against my throat.

The thought of that makes my dick want to shrivel up inside my body. My grip on her waist tightens, and I'm about to push her away when the crowd parts before me.

"Oh shit," someone cries before people start to move back, obviously able to read the danger emanating from both Oak and Theo.

"Reese," Darcie whispers, a quiver in her voice that makes me want to laugh.

Oak and Theo would never hurt her. Despite how much they might want to, they never would—not physically, anyway.

"You need to leave," Theo growls, his voice slurred and his eyes glassy. "You're not welcome here."

I look him up and down. He's exactly as I remember, only he's bulked out a little over the summer. It was our aim to do so as a group, to hit it hard, ready for the new season. Looking at the three of them, I'd say they took that challenge seriously. I, however, had other things to deal with than worrying about our next match and finishing our time at All Hallows' with a championship win under our belts.

"Pretty sure I am. Right, Darce?" I growl, grabbing her and pulling her back into my side before she scurries away like a scared little mouse.

"They don't get a say," Oak growls.

"And if I'm right, neither do you. Where is your fearless leader, anyway?" I ask, looking around for the final piece of our puzzle.

I don't spot Elliot, or Olivia for that matter, and I fucking hate that I keep searching. I shouldn't care where they are. Or what they're doing.

"It doesn't matter where the fuck he is, he doesn't want you here either."

Ripping my eyes from Theo's, I focus on my best friend's. "And you agree, do you?"

Oak snarls, closing the space between us. "You betrayed us, Reese. What did you expect? That we'd welcome you with open arms?"

"What I wasn't expecting was to find your dad still fucking my whore of a mother," I hiss.

His brows pinch. "Still?"

My fists curl and I take a step forward. "I always thought your dad had taste, and that was why he never dipped his dick into any of the whores in this town. Clearly, I was wrong. He's as bad as—"

Crack.

A feral growl rips from my throat as pain explodes from my jaw. "Motherfuck—"

"Wait," Elliot barks, jumping into the space between me, Oak and Theo.

"What the fuck are you doing?" Oak booms. "I know you want his blood as much as we do."

"Not like this," Elliot snarls, his voice low so that only the four of us can hear him.

His eyes hold theirs for a beat before he turns to me, his top lip peeling back. It's the only reaction he has, but it's all I need.

"Get in the cage," he demands, his tone deadly. "I won't have anyone else caught up in the middle of this bullshit. But you might as well give them some entertainment."

"Fine," I spit, shoving his hand from my chest and storming toward the end of the garden where the Eatons' tennis courts are—also known as the cage.

Excitement and anticipation buzz behind me as the crowd follows.

The second I get to the open door, I reach behind me and pull my polo shirt off, abandoning it in a heap on the ground.

I don't look back—I don't need to. I already know that they're following me with hunger and retribution in their eyes.

Oak might have got a few solid punches in yesterday, but it barely took the edge off.

We need this.

If there's going to be any way of moving past this anger between us, then this needs to happen.

Elliot knows it too. It's why he's allowing it.

I don't even flinch as the door is slammed closed, the entire metal cage around us rattling ominously.

Shadows move around me as the crowd fights to get the best view, but I don't hear their taunts or pleas for us to start as blood rushes past my ears.

"Face us, you fucking coward," Theo barks.

Sucking in a deep breath, I spin around as Olivia breaks through the crowd, her eyes finding mine.

'Don't do this,' she mouths, her attention flicking to Oak in concern.

Shaking my head at her, I roll my shoulders and crack my knuckles.

Sorry, sweet cheeks. This needs to happen.

The crowd's roar of excitement gets louder as both Theo and Oak shed their tops and step toward the centre of the court where the net should be.

"Two against one, huh?" I ask cockily, sizing them both up.

"You suggesting you don't deserve it?" Oak taunts.

"Fucking bring it on. I could take you both in your sleep and you know it."

Theo shoves me in the chest, taking me by surprise, and I stumble back.

"Oakley," Olivia screams. "Please, don't do this."

"Go home, Liv," he calls back. "We need to handle our shit."

"If you can't take the heat, Olive, you need to get out of the kitchen."

"Fuck you, Reese," she screams back, dragging my eyes from the two bulls getting ready to charge before me.

I look her up and down, a suggestive smirk playing on my lips. "Maybe later, sweet cheeks. You can help me celebrate taking these two motherfuckers down."

"Don't fucking look at her like that," Oak booms, shoving me again.

"What the fuck is this?" I ask, shoving his hands away. "You forgotten how to fight? Or are you too fucking pussy to try and take me?"

I'm too busy taunting Oak that I don't see Theo's fist flying toward my stomach.

All the air leaves my lungs on a groan as I bend over, pain surging through my body.

While I'm bent over, Oak takes another swing, proving that he's got more than what it takes for them both to have me on the floor.

But fuck that. I'm not letting them take me down.

I've got just as much to fight for as they have.

They might think they own this motherfucking town, but they're forgetting a quarter belongs to me too. And now I'm back, I intend on claiming every fucking inch that is mine.

My eyes find Olivia over his shoulder and I smile.

Every motherfucking inch.

I held my own for longer than everyone probably expected. But let's be honest, the odds were never in my favour. I might be able to take Oak and Theo individually, but together, they're a force to be reckoned with. And they were fucking relentless to go with it.

But by the time they were done with me, all three of us were covered in blood. Knuckles, lips and brows were all split from the brutal punches we'd thrown and our bodies littered with fast-emerging bruises.

With the fight over and me half dead on the floor, the crowd who were once hungry for blood quickly turned away to restart the party, melting away from the tennis courts as if I wasn't even there.

So much for being one of their fucking kings.

The only person who lingered was Olivia. And I quickly discovered that that had nothing to do with me. The second Elliot dragged Oak out of the court, she rushed toward him, her eyes taking in each of his injuries with a scowl on her face.

I didn't want to be amused when she joined in and smacked him in the shoulder, but I couldn't help but snort a pained laugh which made my ribs smart.

They hurt, but I was pretty confident they weren't broken.

We were fucked if they were—something Oak and Theo were more than aware of. They might not want me here, but they need me. The fucking team needs me, and they know it.

After smacking Theo upside the head, she turned her back on me as if I didn't even exist.

Her dismissal shouldn't have hurt. I shouldn't have fucking cared.

The house is in darkness as I stumble my way up the driveway.

It's the second night in a row I've barely been able to control my own body as I've fallen into the front door, praying that it's unlocked for me because I still haven't been given any keys. An oversight, I'm sure.

Yeah fucking right.

My head spins from the vodka and my body aches from the beating, but none of it can top the pain that slices through my heart as I tumble into the house.

My new home.

I scoff at my own thoughts as I stumble toward the stairs.

Movement at the top drags my attention from my feet, and my eyes widen at the person sitting up there.

"Worried about me, sweet cheeks?"

6

OLIVIA

I'm surprised I haven't worn a hole in the floor as I pace back and forth, keeping one eye on the door.

It's ridiculous—he deserved it.

Reese deserved every scrap of pain my brother and Theo delivered tonight. But when I'd seen him lying there, broken and bloody on the ground...

God, why can't I be a cold, heartless bitch? Why can't I go up to bed and go to sleep instead of staying down here, waiting for him to come home?

If he comes.

The guys partied on like they hadn't beaten the shit out of him. But I saw how much they drank, as if they were trying to chase their regrets away. They were a mess by the time I left.

Admitting defeat, I finally climb the stairs and head to bed. Wherever Reese ended up, I'm sure he'll be okay.

But something crashes against the front door, startling me, and I glance back, frozen as the door handle rattles.

Lowering myself to the top step, I sit there, waiting. Once I've seen with my own eyes that he's okay, I'll go to bed.

I'll go to bed and—

A dark figure stumbles toward the stairs, cursing under his breath.

Even from up here in the dark, I can see the cuts and bruises marring his face. He's a mess. But he's alive, and that's all I wanted to know.

Grabbing the handrail, I start to pull myself up, but his eyes snap to mine, a ripple going through the air.

"Worried about me, sweet cheeks?" His mouth curves.

"Just wanted to make sure you weren't dead," I spit as I stand.

"Unfortunately for you, I survived."

"You are such an arsehole."

"And yet, here you are, waiting up for me. Did you want to kiss me better?" He lifts his face into the stream of light and my breath catches.

His injuries are far worse than I realised. One of his eyes is practically swollen shut and there's dry blood crusted over his bottom lip.

"What?" he growls.

"There's a first aid kit in the bathroom."

"I'm touched you care, but all I need is a bottle of Daddy dearest's best whisky and I'll be set."

"Seriously?" I hiss. "What is wrong with you?"

"Pretty sure your brother and Theo tried to kill me with their bare hands."

I roll my eyes at that, stomping back down the stairs.

"Come to finish the job, Olive?"

"I asked you not to call me that." I brush past him and head for the downstairs bathroom.

When he doesn't follow me, I glance back and lift a brow. "Coming or not?"

"Where are we going? Because if you want to play nurse, I can think of much more—"

"Stop, just... stop." I let out a heavy sigh. "I know what you're doing and it won't work, Reese." He goes to respond, but I cut him off. "I stayed up because I'm a decent human being. Something you clearly know very little about."

Something flashes in his eyes, but I ignore it. "Now I'm offering to clean you up. You can either take my help or risk getting blood all over your new sheets and—"

"Fine. Lead the way."

Silence envelops us as we move through the house to the bathroom right at the end of the hall. I hit the light switch, bathing the room in a soft amber glow, but when I catch Reese's eye in the mirror, I suck in a sharp breath.

"Gruesome, huh?" he deadpans.

I shrug. "I've seen worse."

His mouth twitches at that.

"Sit." I motion to the small bench running along the wall next to the shower. To my surprise, Reese follows orders, but not without a pained groan.

"What hurts?" I ask, collecting everything I need and placing it on the marble counter.

"Everything," he admits.

My gaze drops down his body, noticing the way he's shielding his side protectively with one arm.

Gently, I tug his arm away and lift his polo shirt, wincing as the huge, mottled angry bruise comes into view.

"Do you think they're broken?"

"Not much anyone can do if they are."

"Reese, I—"

"Are you going to patch me up or not, Oli—"

I glare at him, and he chuckles, adding a small, "Olivia."

It feels far more of a victory than it should.

"This might sting," I say, folding an antiseptic wipe in half and bringing it to his face.

"Fuck," he hisses as I swipe it over his brow.

"Poor baby." I chuckle. "I can't do much for your eye. You should try and ice it before you go to sleep."

"Gee, I hadn't thought of that."

"Why'd you do it?"

"What?"

"Turn up at the party... bait them into the fight..."

"Why do we do any of the things we do?"

"Riddles, nice." I flash him a droll look as I fold the wipe into itself and continue cleaning the dried, crusted blood from his face.

"Your mum is going to lose it when she sees the state of you."

"Like I give a shit." He inhales a sharp breath when I move to his lip, dropping his head back against the wall. Our eyes collide, and I'm swallowed whole by the intensity burning in his gaze.

Memories slam into me one after another. His mouth on my skin, teeth and tongue. The huge tree at my back, his body pressed up against me, caging me in as he pushed inside me.

Heat curls in my stomach and I swallow.

"You're thinking about it, aren't you?" he asks, one of his hands sliding up the back of my thigh. "You're remembering how it felt to have my dick inside you."

"Reese," I breathe shakily as his fingers move higher, toying with the hem of my sleep shorts.

"I bet I could make you beg again. I bet I could make you—"

"Stop."

The word has the same effect as a bucket of ice-cold water and his hand falls away. I inhale a sharp breath, forcing the memories out of my head.

"That was a mistake." I press a fresh wipe to his mouth, a little too forcefully, and he hisses with pain.

Good.

Silence falls over us as I finish cleaning him up. I can't work miracles, and he still looks like he went ten rounds with Tyson Fury, but at least he won't get blood all over his fresh new sheets.

I discard the dirty wipes and cotton balls and tidy everything away before handing Reese two strong painkillers and a glass of water.

"Here, you'll need these."

He eyes the pills in my hand. "Maybe I want it to hurt."

"Suit yourself." I shrug, going to put them back. But he snags my wrist and takes them without so much as a thanks.

After downing the glass of water, Reese stands and glowers at me.

"What?" I snap, hating the trickle of awareness my body has at his close proximity.

He doesn't answer as he continues staring at me. The air crackles around us, mimicking the flutter of my heart.

"Reese, what are you—"

He turns on his heel and heads for the door, not sparing me so much as a thank you or goodbye.

Prick.

But he pauses in the doorway, glancing back at me. His eyes glint with something that makes me shudder as he drawls, "I'm going to enjoy breaking you."

The next morning, I wake to the sound of arguing.

With an irritated groan, I throw back the covers and trudge out into the hall, hardly surprised when I hear Oakley and Reese's raised voices downstairs.

"Will you both just calm down," Fiona shrieks right as I reach the kitchen.

"Seriously, did you not work out your issues last night?" I ask, heading for the coffee machine.

Oakley smirks at me while Reese glares at him.

"You knew about this?" Fiona asks. "Didn't you think to, I don't know... stop them?"

"You've lost your mind if you think I was about to get in

the middle of them." I shrug. "Besides, maybe it'll have knocked some sense into them."

Reese coughs 'bitch' under his breath, and Oak snorts.

"If this is what we can expect all term, you can go and live with your grandparents in Oxford." Fiona pins Reese with a look that would make grown men cower as she threatens him with his father's elderly parents.

"Fuck that, you can't send me there. They're old and—"

"So. Stop. Acting. Out. I know you're angry. I know you blame me. But you don't know all the facts. You don't—"

"Yeah, whatever." Reese blows past her and storms out of the kitchen.

"That boy will be the death of me." She shakes her head.

"He started it."

"Oakley, not helpful."

"Sorry," he murmurs.

My brother's face isn't as messed up as Reese's, but he has a split lip and a nasty looking bruise under his eye.

"Where did you get to last night?" I ask, knowing for a fact he didn't come home, given that he's still in last night's clothes.

"That's for me to know and you never to find out." He grins.

"I hoped you wrapped it. The last thing we need is an Heir chaser claiming you knocked her up." I smile sweetly, and Fiona almost chokes on her bagel.

"It's too early for this," she grumbles. "I'm going to find your father."

We watch her leave and Oakley smirks. "She's such a contradiction."

"She makes Dad happy." I shrug.

"Yeah, but where does this all end? Reese is... he's different." He lets out a heavy sigh, and I see the pain in his eyes.

Reese leaving Saints Cross affected Oakley most. He and

Reese were best friends. They shared everything. And then he left without so much as a warning.

My brother might not ever admit it, but it cut him deep.

"Us all living here," he added, "under the same roof... it has disaster written all over it."

"You were best friends once."

"Yeah, well, things change. He abandoned us, Liv. I won't forget that in a hurry."

"So what... you're going to beat the crap out of each other every morning over breakfast?"

"Since when do you care about Whitfield?"

"I don't," I rush out, hoping he doesn't catch the slight tremble in my voice.

Because I don't care. Reese is a selfish, entitled, arrogant twat. But when he touched me last night, I had felt something.

Jesus.

Oakley is right.

This is a disaster. Except not for the reasons he thinks.

I can handle Reese living here. What I can't handle is the strange effect he has on my emotions, my body.

I should hate him—I *do* hate him.

But there's something else too.

Something I never ever want to acknowledge.

7

REESE

I stand staring at myself in the mirror. It's an image I never thought I was going to have to see again. Here I am in my black All Hallows' uniform, ready to dive straight back into my old life as if I never even left.

The summer almost feels like a dream at this point.

The days I spent away from here, chilling on the beach, pretending that I didn't have a care in the world seem a million miles away now. Instead, I'm back in the one place I don't want to be, looking like shit.

Coach is going to bust a nut when he sees the state of us later.

Oak looks better than I do after our fight Saturday night, and I can only assume Theo looks similar, seeing as I wasn't invited to hang out with them yesterday like we always used to do on Sunday afternoons. Instead, I locked myself in my room and tried to pretend the world—the girl—outside my door didn't exist while I worked on my plan to get the hell out of here.

I need money, and I need to get my hands on it in a way Mum won't notice—well, not instantly, anyway. And I need a place to go, a new town to start over in and call my own.

Lifting my hand, I press my fingertips to the cut on my lip, still able to feel her touch as she cleaned me up. I should have refused her offer. Really, I didn't give a single fuck if I got blood on the pristine sheets. In fact, I'd happily get them dirty if only to piss my mum off. But I couldn't turn down her offer.

The need to see if my proximity to Olivia still affects her in the same way it did that night was too much to deny. Plus, I'd had a pretty shitty night. It would be nice to be able to pass out thinking about the way her body reacted to my touch instead of the unbearable pain thumping through my body.

I was fucking right too. The second I laid a finger on her, her entire demeanour changed. Her eyes darkened, her cheeks reddened, and her fucking nipples hardened through her tank.

How I held myself back from acting out on all the things that were running rampant in my imagination, fuck only knows.

Pretty sure I deserve a fucking medal or something for that shit.

She might not have confessed to it, but I know the whole time we were in that bathroom, she was thinking about initiation night. About how good I felt inside her for those few minutes. Just how desperate she was for me to fuck her in a way she knows I'm capable of.

She's heard the rumours. Probably listened to the bragging rights of the Heir chasers in the girls' locker room. Hell, she's walked in on the four of us up to shit we shouldn't have been enough times over the years to know what we're like.

All she's gotta do is ask for it.

No.

Beg for it.

And I might even give her what she's been craving since I walked away from her that night.

Or I might not.

A smirk pulls at one side of my mouth as I push my hand through my hair.

I meant what I said to her when I walked away.
I'm going to ruin her...
And it's going to be so much fun.

By the time I finally emerged from my bedroom, Mum and Christian were long gone, and Olivia had already left for school. Oak didn't stay here last night; he and the other two Heirs spent their first official night in the Chapel. I tried not to care that I wasn't invited to the sanctuary the four of us now had the keys to, but I failed. Badly.

It's the first time I've been in the house alone since I returned, and I can't deny that the urge to burn the place down is strong.

I can almost picture the four of them watching the embers as I stand, hidden in the trees that surround the property with an empty box of matches and a smug-as-fuck grin on my face.

Fuck with my life? Watch as I bring yours to its fucking knees.

In the end, I decide against doing something quite so drastic. Yet, anyway.

I hate the drive to school, the familiarity of everything I was more than willing to walk away from. I hate the attention that turns on me the second I step out of my car and the whispers that follow as I make my way inside.

I'm late. Later than I ever usually would have been.

We always had breakfast together with Scott, Evan and Liam in the Chapel. And I can only assume that's where they are now.

Eyes and whispers follow me all the way down to my tutor room. Most students jump out of my way, but some, mostly girls, edge a little closer despite the more than obvious 'stay the fuck away from me' vibes surrounding me.

Swinging the classroom door open, I scan the empty desks, my eyes landing on the back row.

Our row.

I hesitate, autopilot telling me to move there, to claim my seat, my position in this school. But the rational side of me, the part that's still in agony after Saturday night, is telling me to go elsewhere.

Excitement outside pauses my decision making, and when I look back, I find Oak, Theo, and Elliot marching this way with deadly expressions on their faces.

Damn near half the sixth form follows behind them, probably hoping that they're about to witness me get my arse handed to me again.

The bell rings out as they file into the room. Theo and Elliot both pass me as if I'm not standing here, while Oak slows.

I startle when his hand lands on my shoulder, and I curse myself for it.

"What the fuck are you waiting for?" he barks. "The bell rang."

He shoves me forward and toward the seat that has been mine for the past year at the end of our row.

"I... uh..."

"Just sit the fuck down, Whitfield," Elliot demands.

"S-sure."

Following orders like a good—albeit confused—little Heir, I drop my bag to the floor and fall into my chair as the rest of our class moves inside and takes their seats.

Oak leans over, obviously sensing my confusion. "You fucked up this summer," he states, his voice cold and hard, any of the friendliness I'm used to from him long gone. "But you're still one of us. And we stand together here."

Mr. Waters, our tutor group teacher walks in, his eyes scanning the class before they land on me.

Great. Even the fucking staff know what's going on.

"Missed you, Reese," Tasha, one of Darcie's irritating best friends purrs as she drops into my lap at lunchtime.

Sitting at our usual spot in the common room, it really is like the summer never happened. It's a massive head fuck.

To the outside world, to the Heir chasers, the lads might appear to be cool with having me back. But every time I catch one of their eyes, I see the truth within them.

They're doing this because it's expected of them, of us. They're not doing it because they missed me and want me to be a part of their group again.

Movement over by the door catches my eye right as Tasha smooths her hand down my chest, resting her palm on top of my abs.

A smile pulls at my lips when I find Olivia standing there, watching with her eyes narrowed in anger.

"Hey, stranger," another female voice says behind me before Lauren appears at my side.

The guys might be lapping up their own attention from the girls, but none of them are getting the kind of welcome back that I'm receiving. It's pissing them off more with every second that passes. Not that I can say I'm overly enjoying myself.

Or at least, I wasn't until I got to witness Olivia's reaction.

Twisting around to look at our newest arrival, I let a fake-arse smile pull at my lips.

"Hey, Lauren. How's it going?" Wrapping my arm around her waist, I pull her onto my other thigh, letting them both pet me as if I'm a fucking dog.

There is something really wrong with the girls in this school and their undying need for attention.

I don't need to look back in Olivia's direction to know that she's still watching us. I can picture her face all screwed up in disgust. I've seen it enough times when the four of us have girls hanging from every limb.

"Liv, get over here," Oak calls, spotting his sister and shoving his adoring fan aside so she can join us.

"Nah, you're all right. I don't want anyone thinking I'm a part of club desperate."

"You're only saying that because you know that none of our boys would touch you with a barge pole," Tasha adds helpfully once she realises that Olivia is talking about her.

"Oh yeah," Olivia mutters. "That's my issue. I want all of them so badly I can hardly think straight." She rolls her eyes so hard I can't help but wonder if it actually hurts.

"Ew," Lauren says. "You can't have all of them, Oakley is your brother."

"Oh, is he? Shit, I forgot about that."

"Liv," Oak growls, trying to get her to behave. You'd have thought he'd have learned by now that it's not so easy.

"I think I'm gonna go and— Oak," she cries when he jumps up, wraps his hand around her upper arm and drags her to the table.

"Sit. Eat. Be nice."

She snarls at him but drops her food to the table and does as she's told.

"So, tell us what you've been up to this summer, Reese," Lauren whispers in my ear.

"Oh, you know," I mutter, keeping my eyes on Liv. "This and that."

"You missed out here, baby. The parties have been wild."

"She's not wrong there," Theo agrees, downing his drink and throwing the bottle into the bin on the other side of the room like a pro.

"The hockey team is having a party Friday night. You should come," Tasha suggests.

I'm assuming because she doesn't think I'll be welcome at the Heirs' party. Hell, even if I'm not, I wouldn't be caught dead hanging out with the fucking hockey team. Her hand drops over my waistband as if a quick rub through my trousers is going to be enough to make me agree to anything.

Reaching for her wrist, I stop her before she makes contact with my less-than-interested cock.

"Might as well just lie on the table with your legs open," Liv mutters, staring down at her sandwich like it's personally offended her.

"What was that, Olive? I don't think my friends quite heard you."

Her eyes find mine, narrowing in anger. "No, they were too busy trying to give you a hand job under the table. Excuse me," she says, shooting out of her seat. "I seem to have lost my appetite."

She's gone before Oak has a chance to do anything, and I watch with a smirk as she marches out of the common room in her short silver, black, and green tartan skirt.

"What the hell is her problem?" Lauren mutters.

"Ah, you know what it's like when you don't stand up to the competition."

Thankfully, Oak's attention has been captured by an Heir chaser with her tits damn near falling out of her shirt so he doesn't hear my words, or notice when I shove them both from my lap.

"It's probably because Mr. Jenkins has left. I know I don't want to do PE without him," Tasha says, mentioning the student teacher all the girls were lusting over last year.

"Excuse me. I need to take a piss," I say, finally untangling myself from them and getting to my feet.

No one bats an eyelid as I walk away. I mean, the guys don't really want me there, so it's probably a relief as I take off in the direction I watched Olivia disappear only minutes ago.

If I'm lucky, I might just catch up with her.

8

OLIVIA

I hurry down the hall and duck into the girls' bathroom.

Damn Reese to hell.

Arrogant, smug bastard with his cruel taunts and wicked smirk.

I can't keep letting him get to me like this, but he was purposefully baiting me back there. And in front of Oakley and the guys, no less.

Argh.

Inhaling a sharp breath, I force myself to calm down. I've been dealing with boys like Reese for years. As long as I keep my wits about me, I'll be fine.

The bathroom door swings open and I look up, expecting to see a group of girls piling in, but instead—

"You." The blood drains from my face.

"Miss me, sweet cheeks?"

"You can't be in here."

"And yet, here I am." Reese smirks, running his eyes down my body—a slow, intense perusal as if I'm here purely for his entertainment.

"I'd forgotten how good this uniform looks on you."

"Pig."

"Now, now, Olive." He steps closer, taking the air with him. I inch back one step and another, until my back hits the wall and a small gasp escapes my lips.

Interest sparks in his eyes as they narrow with predatory intent.

"Reese," I warn. "I'll scream."

"Oh, by all accounts, do. It'll make it so much sweeter." He takes another step closer and my heart ratchets.

I glance toward the row of cubicles and, without hesitating, dart toward the end one. His deep chuckle echoes around the bathroom as I lock the door and press my hands against it.

"Seriously, you think that's going to keep me away from you?"

"What do you even want? You have plenty of girls more than willing to—"

"Careful. You're starting to sound jealous."

I snort. "Don't flatter yourself. I'm not jealous, I'm pissed. You followed me in here like some unhinged stalker. It's not—"

The door lock rattles and I watch with horror as it clicks open.

"Reese, don't you dare." Blood roars between my ears, an overwhelming whirring as I push with all my might to keep the door closed.

But it's futile. Reese is at least half a foot taller than me, and he's strong. Really damn strong. He has to be to play fullback for the All Hallows' Saints rugby team.

The door flings open as I inch back, glaring at him.

"Get. Out."

His lips twist with amusement as he lets his eyes sweep down my body. His pupils flare and something I refuse to acknowledge curls in my stomach.

"I don't think so. I think I want to play a game." He closes the door behind him and slides the lock into place.

A lick of fear goes through me, but I know Reese won't

hurt me. Humiliate and ruin me, sure. But physically hurt me, never.

My brother, Elliot, and Theo would end him if he ever laid so much as an unwanted finger on me.

Maybe even a wanted one.

The thought makes me smile, and he frowns.

"What?"

"I'm just thinking about all the ways my brother and the guys are going to kick your ass when they find out you're harassing me."

Another chuckle. Only this one rumbles through me, making my chest flutter.

I need to have a serious word with myself later about how I must not be so easily affected by Reese and his tiresome games.

He's one of the most gorgeous boys I've ever laid eyes on, but his redeeming qualities end there.

Reese Whitfield is one hundred and ten percent arrogant wanker, and I have no intentions of letting him—

He steps closer and I have nowhere to go, not if I don't want to end up a heap on the toilet.

"Reese," my voice quivers. "What the fuck are you doing?"

"Hmm, say that again." He reaches for me, trailing a single finger down my neck, dipping it over my crisp white blouse and between the valley of my breasts.

I'm not breathing. I can't breathe as he holds me captive, trapped in his dark grey eyes.

"You were jealous, earlier in the common room."

"No, I really wasn't."

"I think you're lying."

"I think you're full of bullshit." It comes out saccharine but full of bite.

His eyes flare again, a silent storm swirling in his inky depths. "Pretty little liar," he snarls. "I wonder if Oak has any idea how easily you lie."

"Reese..." I breathe.

"Hmm, you sound so fucking hot when you beg." His thumb strokes back and forth along my pulse point.

"Someone could come in here," I remind him.

"They won't. Tell me. Tell me you were jealous, sweet cheeks, and I'll let you walk out of here right now."

"What could I possibly have to be jealous of? I'm not an Heir-chasing whore." I smile sweetly.

"Care to wager that?"

"I..." I press my lips shut, because it's hard concentrating when he's touching me like this. My traitorous, fickle body likes the way he touches me. The possessive flex of his fingers along the side of my neck.

I really shouldn't like it, but God help me, I do.

Not that I'll ever admit it out loud.

Over my dead body.

"Tell me, Olivia. Say it and I disappear."

"Why?"

"Because," he leans in closer, his mint-scented breath fanning my face, "I know you, and you wanted it that night in the woods, just like you wanted it the other night in the bathroom. You want me and—"

"You're deluded."

"The photographs would suggest otherwise, sweet cheeks."

My blood turns to ice in my veins. "Is that a threat?"

"No, consider it... a promise."

"You bastard," I spit, anger saturating my insides.

"So feisty. You know they say angry sex is the best sex you'll ever have." His brow quirks up. "I'm game if you are."

"In your dreams."

"Oh, you already live there, Olive. The way you begged for me to fuck you... So needy and desperate." His fingers slide around my throat, my pulse thundering under his touch.

"Get. Your. Hands. Off. Me." I shove my palms into his solid chest and catch him unawares. Reese stumbles back against the door but snags my blazer, pulling me with him. We crash into the damn thing, his laughter an irritating buzz in my ear.

"Shit, Olive. This is going to be so much fun." He gazes down at me, and for a second, I imagine we're here under different circumstances.

Stupid, stupid girl.

This is all a game. A game I don't understand or want to play, but one Reese seems intent on playing regardless.

"W-what?"

He backs me up against the cubicle wall, caging me there as his hand dips under my skirt.

"Reese," I warn, clenching my thighs together. "Don't you—"

I smother a whimper as his fingers glide over my underwear.

"My, my, what do we have here?"

"Reese!"

"You're wet for me." His lips curve with smug satisfaction.

"Never."

His eyes light up at my denial. "Such pretty lies." Hooking my knickers to the side, he glides two fingers through the wetness there, passing over my clit enough times to make me moan.

"Fuck, yeah."

"I hate you." I seethe.

But I also hate myself because damn him, it does feel good.

"This." He pulls his fingers away, lifting them between us. "Suggests otherwise."

They glisten with the truth—Reese Whitfield does affect me. But I'll never say the words. Because clearly there's something very, very wrong with me.

"Mmm." He makes a big spectacle of sucking them clean, smirking at me while he does. "Delicious."

"You make me sick."

"Don't you mean I make you wet?"

I press my lips together, choosing silence as my answer.

"I should probably get back to Tasha. Pretty sure she's up for giving me a blow job before class. But thanks for the chat. See you around, Olive."

Glaring at him, I silently watch as he unlocks the door and slips out of the stall as if it's business as usual.

Exhaling a shaky breath, I drop down on the toilet lid and run a hand through my hair.

This is bad.

Really fucking bad.

But it's not like I can tell Oakley. Reese is an Heir. He's one of them. Not to mention the fact that Reese is promised to Abigail Bancroft.

Even if I wanted to explore this strange attraction we have to one another—and I don't, ever—it could never be anything more than sex.

I wait for Reese to leave and then wait some more. There's no way I can go back out there yet.

But I linger too long and the bathroom door opens, footsteps sounding beyond my stall.

Crap.

Inhaling a deep breath, I smooth my skirt down and step out of the stall.

"Oh, sorry, I didn't realise anyone was in here."

"Abigail?"

Talk about bad timing.

Guilt churns in my stomach.

"I'm sorry, did you need me to go?"

"What, no. You have as much right to be in here as I do. I was surprised to see you is all. How are you?"

Surprise flashes in her pale hazel eyes and I realise how weird I must sound.

Abigail Bancroft and I aren't friends. We aren't even really acquaintances. She's quiet, really quiet. A small, skittish thing with big hazel eyes, long, reddish-brown hair and heart-shaped lips. She reminds me of an ethereal creature, some red-haired fairy from the myths and stories we studied in English Lit last year.

But like everyone else at All Hallows', my eye doesn't go to her delicate features. It goes to the wicked looking scar running down her face.

She catches me looking and quickly smooths her wild curls over it.

"Shit, sorry. That was rude," I say.

"It's okay," she says, her voice barely louder than a whisper. "After a while, you get used to it. You're Olivia Beckworth."

I nod. "In the flesh."

"So you know Reese..."

"I... yeah." A heavy weight settles in my chest.

"He's back, then. I didn't know..."

"Yeah. He got back a few days ago."

"And now he lives with you and your brother."

"That's right."

Her lips twist. "I'd hoped..." She sucks in a sharp breath that seems to evaporate the air from the room. "It doesn't matter. Anyway, I need to—" Her eyes flick to a stall.

"Oh, yeah. Sorry."

I watch as she hurries into a stall and locks the door.

It feels wrong not to say more, to try and ease some of her obvious discomfort. But I don't know her, not really. And I'm not sure she would want to know me if she knew what I was doing in here five minutes ago.

So I wash my hands and slip quietly out of the bathroom. But I can't help think that if Reese has the power to ruin someone like me...

He'd destroy someone like Abigail Bancroft.

9

REESE

"Ugh," I grunt as I'm slammed into from behind before I quickly crash to the ground in a heap.

"Whitfield, get your arse back up," Coach Walker barks when he finds me down again.

"Fucking liability," Theo mutters from behind me, clueing me in to who took me out this time.

This whole practice session has been the same.

One after the other, they've been landing digs on me. Elbows in my ribs, fists in my gut when Coach isn't looking, and brutal tackles when he is.

I knew this first week back at training was going to be tough. I might have worked out over the summer, but nowhere near as much as I should. I knew it was going to show. But not this fucking bad.

"Get up, Whitfield," Oak taunts, coming to stand beside Theo.

"Leave him alone," Elliot says, finally joining the fray, and I stupidly breathe a sigh of relief. "Clearly he forgot his balls when he rolled back into town."

"Fuck you," I hiss, pushing myself up.

Every inch of me is in agony. The pain of the beating I took at the weekend has barely lessened. I did not need this.

"Ladies, get with the fucking program," Coach barks.

The man is a tyrant. But he's also about the only member of staff who demands our full respect here at All Hallows'. An ex-Rugby Union player, he has enough experience behind him to be training a team better than us. He constantly walks around looking like someone has popped his favourite ball with his lips twisted in frustration and his eyes dark with anger. He's also built like a brick shithouse and could probably crush each of us like flies if he so wished.

I finally make it to my feet. My ribs smart, making my eyes water as my muscles pull.

"Oi, three stooges, get fucking running. You're not getting off this field until you're crying in pain."

"Lucky for Whitfield, he's almost there," Oak taunts.

"Go," Coach barks, and unlike you'd see from any other order around this place, the three of them take off.

"You wanna talk about it, kid?" Coach offers.

"Nothing to talk about, sir," I state, attempting to stand a little taller in response.

"You need to get your shit together, Whitfield. We want results this year, and if you're bringing us down, then you might find yourself in the dance studio practising your pirouette instead of in a scrum with your teammates."

My argument is right on the tip of my tongue, but one stern look from him and I manage to swallow it down.

"Go and hit the showers," he barks. "I'm expecting more from you from here on out. This is your one and only warning."

"Coach." I nod, grabbing my water bottle from the sideline and marching toward the locker room, keeping my head high and using the pain surging through my body to push me forward.

Twisting the lid, I empty what's left over my head.

Pushing my fingers into my hair, I drag it back, stopping it from dripping into my eyes.

The familiar scent hits me the second I stumble through the door, but it doesn't have the effect it once did.

This place used to be my home, the place I always used to feel most like myself. But that's gone. Ruined the day I got in my car and followed Dad out of town, vowing never to come back.

"ARGH." My water bottle flies across the room, colliding with the tiled wall with a less-than-satisfying bang. "FUCK," I roar, my fist slamming into the wall, instantly opening up the cuts on my knuckles and making my body ache like a motherfucker. "Fuck. Fuck. Fuck."

I lean forward, pressing my brow to the cold tiles.

Why am I back here? What the fuck am I doing?

My fists curl as my chest heaves, trying to tamp down the fury that's burning me up inside.

You're here because despite everything he's ever said to you, your dad doesn't want you, and this is the only home you have.

And you need to them to understand just how much it fucking hurts.

I scoff at my own thoughts.

Home.

This isn't home. It's hell.

The only thing that makes it bearable right now is her.

That inkling of fear in her eyes is quickly extinguished by desire the second I get close.

I shouldn't have followed her earlier. I know that. But the urge to see her stare up at me with those big brown eyes, to hear her defiance falling from her lips all the while her body arched toward me? Yeah, it's fucking addicting.

And the only good fucking thing I've got going on in my life.

She's a liar and a traitor. And by the time I'm done with her, I'm going to make sure everyone knows it.

My cock swells as my twisted desire for both her and the vengeance we all deserve burns through me like a wildfire.

The sound of chants from outside the door tells me that my time alone is coming to an end, and I force myself to move.

It takes more effort and causes more pain than it should, pulling my shirt over my head. I feel like a total fucking pussy grunting in pain as I undress, but the noises fall from my lips without instruction from my brain.

What I need is my little nurse.

My teeth sink into my bottom lip as I make my way into the showers, wondering if it got bad enough that she'd even dress up for me. Nah, fuck that. She could strip off. Having those tempting tits in my face while she cleaned me up sure would make me feel fucking better.

I'm rocking a semi that I desperately need to sink before the guys appear when I finally slam my hand down on the button for the shower. Ice-cold water rains down on me for a few seconds before it starts to warm.

I hang my head, letting the water wash the mud and dirt from our extra-long training session from my body.

It's only fucking Monday, a little voice says in my head.

I wince. I can barely walk now. What the fuck is it going to be like by Friday?

Thankfully, I have myself back under control when the ruckus of the others fills the locker room. They all laugh and taunt each other, happiness at being back out on the field together after a long summer bouncing off the walls.

But it doesn't seep into me. It sends me deeper. Further into that twisted place that I've discovered lives inside me.

"Fuck me, Whitfield. You're a bit of a mess, huh?" Theo asks, the three of them hitting the showers first, as is always the case with the ruling Heirs.

I grunt in response, not having any inclination to discuss anything with them right now.

"Now that's not very friendly, is it?" Elliot growls, his voice low enough not to carry to the others.

I've figured out what they're doing.

They're keeping up appearances, letting me slot back into my life in public after that fight at the weekend. But really, deep down, I'm nothing but a virus that's infiltrated their group now. They can't be seen to cut me out. I am an Heir, after all. And no matter what, we stick together.

I bet they're fucking hating those old motherfucking rules right about now.

Spinning around, I hold Elliot's eyes. Hatred so strong I'm surprised it doesn't light him up pours from my eyes.

"Fuck friendly," I hiss, my adrenaline working to cover the pain and convince me that I could survive another round with these dickheads.

"And to think, we were coming over to check you were heading to the Chapel after this."

A sneer curls at my lips.

"It's tradition. First day of the year under new leadership."

"I know the fucking traditions," I scoff. They've been forced onto me by everyone my whole life.

"Good, then you'll be there after here. Everything is organised."

The smile Elliot gives me is pure malice before the three of them give my body one last look of disgust and turn toward their own showers to clean up.

And it's not until we're done and heading back to our benches that the rest of the team is allowed to enter the showers.

Despite hating the world and everything around me right now. I'm still filled with a sense of power as I watch the rest of them move.

It was easy to forget how much control and respect we have here while I was living an entirely different life over the summer.

Easy to forget that I was a god who'd fallen from his kingdom.

Well, I'm back now, and it seems my throne is still waiting for me.

At least publicly, anyway.

We walk out of the locker room side by side, as if nothing had ever happened.

It's a front that I'm not sure I've got the energy to be putting on, but one that I know I have little choice but to go along with.

There's a part of me that aches as I stand next to the boys who have had my back almost since the days we were born.

I know I was the one who ruined things. I abandoned them, ghosted them when I should have at least reached out.

I know all those things.

But it still doesn't stop me from missing them, despite it all being my fault.

It's just over a five-minute walk to the Chapel, the sacred building that Elliot was given the key to the night we were initiated as the reigning heirs.

The sun is still high enough in the sky to lick my skin with warmth. It makes me crave easier days when we all hung out here with Scott and his boys, drinking beer, fucking the chasers, and generally not giving a shit about life.

That's what our final year here should be about. And I guess, for them, it will be. Nothing has changed, other than they now have an untrustworthy traitor in their ranks.

I let out a sigh as the ancient chapel appears in the trees before us. It's the oldest building on the school grounds. The one with all the history, the traditions, the legends.

The air surrounding us darkens as we approach.

The guys have already made this place their home.

They've spent all summer fixing up the mess that Scott and his boys will have left behind. It pains me that I wasn't here for it. Making this place ours has been something I dreamed about for years. But turns out, I was never destined to get the chance.

Elliot pulls the coveted key from his pocket and pushes it into the giant lock in the colossal double front doors.

They're good enough for a king, so it's only right that they're the way into our kingdom. Or... their kingdom.

Any familiarity I had with the outside is gone the second I step over the threshold.

All of the fancy white marble from Scott's reign has gone, and in its place is black, dark grey, and silver. It's... incredible. Creepy, gothic, totally fucking fitting for all the debauchery that will no doubt happen here over the coming months.

I bite my tongue, not wanting to tell them all what a stunning job I think they've done of the place as we walk deeper inside.

It's been years since the building was converted from its original purpose to living—partying—quarters for Saints Cross elite.

It's almost impossible to see its old life, but there are a few relics that have lasted the test of time.

The lectern still stands front and centre, only it's used less for worshipping now and more for the king to reign over the masses.

Memories of Scott standing up there, kicking off a night of depravity, flicker through my mind. It's hard to imagine Elliot doing the same, but I guess he will in a few hours. Traditions and all that.

The three of them come to a stop in front of me once we're standing in the middle of the vast, open-plan room with an impressive staircase leading to the first floor balcony and, beyond that, the bedrooms.

Each set of eyes drills into me. But I don't cower. I hold my head high and glare right back.

"You don't belong in here anymore," Elliot tells me coldly. "Your room is untouched and the key is safely locked away. On the outside, you're one of us. You will uphold the tradition of being an Heir. You will do what is expected of you.

"But in here, with just us, all of that is stripped away."

"You're nothing," Oak adds, disgust dripping from his words.

Ignoring the venom pouring from their eyes, I plaster a smile on my face.

"So when do I get the grand tour?"

10

OLIVIA

"You're coming tonight, right?" Oakley whispers as we sit in class listening to Mr. Piper drone on about this year's coursework.

"No," I say.

"But it's our housewarming at the Chapel."

"Housewarming?" I almost choke on the word. "It's a glorified orgy and we both know it."

"Jealous you won't be getting any, Sis?"

My brows furrow as I inhale a calming breath.

I love my brother dearly, but sometimes he really is a clueless idiot.

"If I want some, I'll get some, thank you very much." I straighten in my chair and flip my hair over my shoulder.

"The fuck." He grabs my arm, pulling me back down. "Who?"

"Oak!" I hiss.

"Who are you fucking? Because I swear to God, Liv—"

"Let's get one thing straight," I grit through my teeth as the class goes on around us. "You are my brother, not my keeper. Who I fuck is none of your concern."

His eyes flicker with anger, but the fire quickly gutters.

"Shit, sorry. I just... I don't want some wanker to try and get to me and the guys through you."

"I can look after myself, Oak."

"I know you can. But I'll still always want to protect you. You know that, right?"

"Yeah, I know. It sucks you won't be at the house much now."

"You can come stay at the Chapel whenever you want, you know that."

"Never going to happen," I scoff.

I know exactly what they'll be doing in their new digs. The fact that All Hallows' still allows the Heirs to keep their private residence on the school estate is really testament to how deep the traditions and power run.

I let out a small sigh and Oak nudges my arm. "What's wrong?"

"Everything's changing," I whisper.

"Change can be a good thing. Speaking of change, have you thought about uni applications yet?"

"No, and I'd prefer it if you didn't get on my back about it."

"You need to make a decision, Liv."

"I know."

I'm not an Heir, so my career path isn't all laid out for me the way it is for Oakley. But that isn't to say Dad doesn't have expectations for me.

He wants me to apply to Saints Cross University, like Oak and the guys. But I'm stalling. Do I really want to survive another three years of them? To have them constantly breathing down my neck and thinking they can get all up in my business?

I don't. But the idea of starting over where everything is new and I don't know anyone isn't exactly appealing either.

"You know—"

"Oakley Beckworth, what a surprise." Mr. Piper clicks his

tongue. "Something you'd like to share with the rest of us? Please, the floor is all yours."

"Twat," Oak murmurs under his breath, flashing Mr. Piper a blinding smile.

"Well?"

"I think I'm good, sir. But thanks for checking in."

A couple of nearby girls snigger and I roll my eyes. Of course they'd find this kind of thing attractive. It's Oakley. He's an Heir and one of the All Hallows' Saints star players. It elevates him to celebrity status.

The biggest shock here is that Mr. Piper actually dared to say anything about the fact that we're blatantly sitting here, having a full-on conversation and ignoring every word he says.

One of the girls whispers something to her friend and scribbles on a page in her notebook. Tearing off the note, she folds it and leans over, dropping it on my brother's desk.

He shoots her a knowing smirk as he smooths it open and reads her message.

Want to go somewhere after class? You look a little tense, and I'd love to help you unwind.

"That is... wow," I say, peering over his arm.

He shrugs me off and grins. "Jealous?"

"Yes. Because it is my life's goal to fuck as many of our classmates as possible."

"Might help remove the stick from up your arse."

I flip him off behind my textbook and he chuckles before turning his attention on the blonde.

"It's a date," he says. "And bring your friend. I'm sure we can have a party for three."

The girls practically fall over themselves at his offer.

I roll my eyes, angling myself away from Oakley slightly.

He might be my brother, but it doesn't mean I have to like him all the time.

I headed straight home after school. Talk of the 'housewarming' has taunted me all day. At least with the guys moving into the Chapel, I won't have to deal with Reese being around as much. The house has become unbearably small with him here. Even when he's not all up in my face, I feel his presence.

This is a good thing.

The guys will spend most of their nights at their new fuck pad, and I'll be able to sleep easier knowing I'm not going to run into Reese on a late-night trip to the kitchen.

I should be elated, and yet, there's a strange pang in my chest.

Oakley has always been one of the Heirs. He's always been surrounded by a group of people all vying for his attention. But he's never made me feel less than part of his life.

Things are changing now, though. I can feel it like a shift in the air when a storm approaches.

I don't like it, but there isn't a damn thing I can do about it.

It's almost nine now, and the house feels desperately empty. Dad and Fiona are at some work thing, so I made some pasta and then did some homework. But I'm restless, trying not to think about the housewarming at the Chapel.

Oak begged me to go but stopped texting me about an hour ago. I guess he's distracted now.

Refusing to wallow, I grab my running shoes and my earbuds, slip on a lightweight hoodie and head out for a run.

It's dark out, a thick band of wispy clouds concealing the moon and stars. But it doesn't bother me, I'm used to being out here alone.

I like the quiet.

That time when the town begins to sleep and everything falls silent.

My legs pound the asphalt as I take the roads leading past the houses in our neighbourhood. Big, ostentatious houses that scream wealth and power.

My mind flickers back to the housewarming. I could have boarded at All Hallows' this term—Dad offered to pay. But it seemed silly to board when we live so nearby. Besides, I like my space, my home comforts. And with Oakley and Reese gone now, I'll have plenty of that.

I keep a steady pace, focusing on breathing, as I make my way around the perimeter of the town. But as the imposing silhouette of All Hallows' comes into view far in the distance, I slow.

I don't want to be there, watching a bunch of desperate Heir chasers fall over themselves for their shot with my brother or Elliot or Theo.

Or Reese.

Just his name does things to me.

Unwelcome, unnerving things.

He's under my skin, I can't deny that. But it doesn't matter. Reese Whitfield despises me and the feeling is mutual.

And yet...

No, Olivia. Don't go there.

Don't even think it.

I spot a flat rock through the trees and smile. Perfect.

Switching my music track to something more chilled, I climb up on to it, slip off my trainers and hoodie, and take a deep, calming breath.

Drawing my hands together, I slide my left foot up my opposite leg and hold it to a count of ten. Then, I repeat with my other leg. The tension begins to seep from my body, leaving me with every slow exhale. I move through the tree pose into standing backbend and then a chair pose, and down into a standing forward bend.

"Well, well, what do we have here?"

My heart ratchets in my chest as I shoot up and turn, searching for him in the trees.

Reese steps out of the shadows, hands casually shoved in his pockets, a sly smirk plastered on his unearthly handsome face.

I narrow my eyes, anger boiling my blood. "Stalker much?"

His shoulders lift in a small shrug. "Last time I checked, it's a free country, sweet cheeks. And this is the way home."

"What do you mean, way home?" I sit down to put my trainers back on. "I thought—"

"That I'd be staying at the Chapel?" His expression wavers a little. "Turns out Elliot has decided to confiscate my key until..." He trails off, and it hits me.

"Until they trust you again." Smug laughter bubbles inside me. "Ah, poor baby, must suck being the outsider."

"And yet, here you are, Olive. All alone, practising your yoga shit on a rock."

"I like my own company."

"Sure you do." He stalks closer, every step reverberating inside me.

"What are you doing?"

"Why, scared?"

Yes.

"No," I lie.

I'm not scared of him, not really, but I am unnerved by how easily he affects me.

Blood pounds in my ears as he comes closer and closer, until his palms fall either side of my thighs and he pushes his face right in front of mine. The bitter scent of whisky lingers on his breath. I should hate it.

I don't.

The initial anger in my veins dissipates into simmering heat. He's close. Too close. But I don't move.

I can't.

"You didn't come to the party. Why?"

"I didn't want to."

"You and me both, sweet—"

"Don't call me that."

"I'll call you whatever I want," he breathes. "Olive. Sweet cheeks. My pretty little slut."

"Reese," I hiss.

"Yes, Olivia?" He smirks, and I want to punch him right in the face.

"Get the hell out of my way and leave me alone." I shove him hard and he staggers back a little, giving me enough room to hop down and take off toward the path.

He falls into step beside me, a quiet storm.

"What?" I bark up at him, aware of him watching me.

"Way home, remember?" His brow arches with amusement, but I catch the flash of regret in his eyes.

Reese cares that he's been sidelined by my brother and the guys. He's just too arrogant to ever admit it.

"We don't have to walk together, you know."

"But it's so much fun," he chuckles darkly.

"Reese," I whirl on him, "what are you doing?"

His eyes are dark, so dark it sends a shiver rolling through me.

"Just thinking about all the fun we're going to have."

"We're not... that's—"

His hand snaps out, collaring me, his thumb brushing over my pulse point. He leans in, his mouth brushing the shell of my ear. "Tell me you don't want me. I can practically smell your pussy."

"Reese." I inhale a shuddering breath. It rolls through me like thunder, matching the violent beat of my heart.

"What do you say, Olivia?" he drawls. "Want me to finish what we started before summer? Want to me to fuck you so hard you'll feel me imprinted on your soul?"

Heat engulfs me. I'm angry, livid that he thinks he can talk to me like this. But I'm also trembling, the throb between my legs refusing to abate. Because despite the hatred between us, there's something else.

A fire that refuses to burn out.

And Reese knows it.

But I still can't figure out why...

Why he's trying to bait me into this game we're playing.

"What happened to you, Reese?" I whisper, aware of his fingers flexed around my throat.

"You, Olive," he growls. "You happened."

11

REESE

Tasha sits on my lap once again, her arse grinding down on my less-than-interested dick as she talks animatedly to one of the two girls Oakley is entertaining. I recognise them both as girls in our year. Hell, they could even have been in my classes in the past... I could have fucked them, but fuck if I can remember who they are.

"This place is so much more than I could have imagined," the redhead gushes. She might be talking to Tasha, but her eyes are locked on Oakley as he shamelessly stares down her dress. I mean really, she may as well not be wearing it for how little it's covering.

"Just wait until I get you downstairs."

The desperate whore purrs in response before threading her fingers in Oak's hair and shoving his face into her tits. I mean, if I had to suffocate to death, then I guess going by a pair of tits would be right up there.

"Are you going to take me downstairs, Reese?" Tasha purrs in my ear as her hand slips under the fabric of my shirt and she drags her hideous pointed nails down my abs.

"Unlikely," I mutter under my breath.

"I'm desperate to see what you've all done to the place.

When I was down there with Evan last year it was— ow, what the hell, Reese?" she whines like a little bitch as she hits the solid walnut floor on her pert arse.

"Whoops. I need another drink," I mutter, pushing to my feet and leaving Oak and his two hussies behind.

My eyes scan the space around me as I move toward the kitchen. There are people drinking, dancing, and enjoying themselves in every inch of the space.

A loud moan rips through the air, overpowering the music, and when I glance down the hall, I find Theo on his knees, his head under some girl's skirt as she screams for God.

Fuck my life.

I used to dream about having this. I was desperate for the status, the respect, the girls.

But I feel like a fucking whore in a convent right now.

I've never felt so out of place somewhere I should belong.

My boys are here. This should be my home, my lair. Yet all I can think about it is walking out of that monstrous front door and never coming back.

"Reese Whitfield, to what do we owe the pleasure?"

Hands grab my sides and my skin prickles in a way that makes me want to rip it off.

Spinning around, I find Melanie Brian. She was one of last year's Heir chasers. I'm pretty sure she spent most of her final year on her back with either Liam or Evan between her thighs.

"You back for another go at snagging an Heir, Mel?"

Her smile falters a little. "Nah, I'm all spoken for now, Reese," she sings, holding up a giant-arse engagement ring as if I should be impressed by it.

"What stupid motherfucker knocked you up?"

Her cheeks heat as her lips purse.

"Right, well..." I take off just in time to hear her laugh off my comment, but seriously, who the fuck would want to tie that down?

I finally make it to the kitchen after only being groped by a couple wandering hands.

"What's it to be, Whitfield?" Zayn Hickman, a new member of the team who has a fucking lot to prove right about now asks as I come to a stop in front of the array of bottles.

"Strongest bottle you got."

"You got it."

He reaches out for a bottle of whisky—not my usual choice, but I don't really give a fuck right now.

I need the oblivion it promises.

"Cup?" he asks, clearly misreading my body language.

"No." Reaching out, I snatch the bottle from his hand, twist the top, and flick it at him. It hits him right between the brows and he pales. "Want some advice?" I ask, although I have no intention of waiting for an answer. "Open your fucking eyes. They'll eat you alive if you're this fucking clueless all the time."

"U-uh, y-yeah sure," he stutters like a pussy, and I swear to fuck, a little sweat beads on his brow.

Fuck me, where did Elliot find this bellend from?

With the heat of the whisky burning down my throat and warming my stomach, I leave the party behind and burst through the front door.

Multiple voices call after me, but I don't stop to even look to see who it was. I don't give a fuck. The only thing I can think about is getting away from all this bullshit.

It's fake. All of it.

The power they hold, the bullshit traditions they uphold. The futures that have been mapped out for them.

They all act like it's a privilege, but really, it's nothing more than a noose around their necks.

A noose I'm no longer willing to accept.

Fuck my mother's expectations of me. Fuck the life, the marriage, she expects me to have.

What about the life I want to lead?

FILTHY JEALOUS HEIR: PART ONE

The bottle is already half empty as I stumble through the trees. We've spent years scaring the shit out of girls in these woods, so even with the moonlight illuminating the space through the thick leaf cover above, I can navigate it with ease.

Twigs crack under my feet and old leaves rustle, but there's nothing else out here. I can't even hear any animals.

Peace. Fucking finally.

Once I'm so deep that all I can see around me is darkness, I tip my head toward the sky and roar out my frustrations into the dead of night.

I keep going until my throat is raw and some of the tension in my shoulders has lessened. Then, I take another swig of the whisky and keep going toward the rocks on the other side which will lead me home.

Thoughts of that place, the Beckworths', doesn't do anything for my current state of mind. The only positive from that house is the girl in the room opposite mine.

The second I emerge from the cover of trees, movement up on one of the huge rocks catches my eye.

She moves so smoothly, so elegantly, that I find myself captivated by her for a few minutes as she switches from pose to pose.

I've never really understood Olivia's love of yoga, but I sure as fuck enjoy watching her do it. Especially those times she used to do it first thing in the morning in her tiny booty shorts and sports bra in the back garden.

Thank fuck Oak has never been an early riser, or he'd have caught me getting up at sunrise and watching his sister show her arse to the world.

Her body has the same effect on me now as it did back then, and my cock swells as images of bending her over, ripping her leggings down, and fucking her from behind fill my head.

Fuck this girl.

Fuck this beautiful, sexy, filthy little liar.

I palm my dick through my trousers, trying to ignore the fact that no other girl tonight has made it so much as jerk let alone harden. Leaning against a tree, hidden in the shadows, I watch her, swallowing a shot of whisky every time she moves.

It's not until she seems to come to a stop that I finally make my presence known, and fuck am I glad I do when her eyes widen and shock covers her face a second before her anger sets in.

Oh yes, game on, Olive. Game fucking on.

She hops down from her rock, her defiance and smart mouth only making me harder and more desperate for a repeat of initiation night.

She wants it, too. As we spit insults back and forth at each other, our irritation and obvious desire fuelling our hate-filled words, her eyes darken, her breathing increases and her blush deepens.

"What happened to you, Reese?" she whispers, causing my grip on her to tighten and her pulse against my fingers to race.

"You, Olive," I growl, loving the way her eyes narrow in anger at that nickname. "You fucking happened."

"But I never did anything. Nothing changed. One day you were just Reese, my brother's annoying frien—"

"Hot friend," I correct. "Don't even pretend that you never used to make any excuse to get into Oak's room when I was there to check me out."

"And then you turned into this vicious, hate-filled demon."

"Demon, huh?" I ask, leaning in closer, stealing her air.

"Reese," she begs.

"Fuck, I love it when you do that," I confess, my eyes flicking between hers and her tempting lips.

Her tongue sneaks out, running across her bottom lip as a wanton moan rumbles deep in her throat. A moan I think she assumes I don't hear.

But I do. And it hits me right in the cock.

"You're a filthy little liar, Olive."

"I've never lied to you."

My lip curls up in an accomplished smile. "You just did. And you're about to do it again." Her brow quirks. "Tell me how wet you are for me right now."

"Fuck you," she hisses predictably.

"Yeah..." I say, releasing her throat in favour of copping a feel of her tits. "I think I might. Just to prove a point though."

"And what would that be?" she asks, desperately trying to keep her voice level as I pinch her nipple through her bra.

I lean into her again, my lips brushing the shell of her ear before I breathe, "That you want me. That all you can think about is how I stretched you open and made you feel better than you ever have in your life."

I sense her hit coming a mile off, and I catch her wrist long before it connects with my cheek.

"Careful, sweet cheeks, or I'll start to think you get off on the pain."

"Fuck you," she hisses again.

"I thought we'd already cleared that up. I'm more than willing to find out how badly you want me."

"I hate you," she spits.

"The feeling is mutual. But doesn't it make it that much hotter?"

"You need to let go," she demands.

"I need to? Right. I'd love to hear your reasoning."

Her eyes narrow and her lips purse. "If Oak finds out you left a bruise on me, he'll kill you."

I can't help but laugh. "Your dear brother is in no state to protect your virtue right now, sweet cheeks. When I left, he had a girl on each thigh and his face in one of their tits."

A shudder of disgust rips through her.

"Jealous, Olive? Is that where you'd rather be right now? At the Chapel with an Heir on their knees for you?"

"Let. Me. Go," she seethes.

"Okay," I concede. "I'll let you go, and I'll even give you a head start."

"W-what?"

"I'll give you ten seconds. But you can be damn sure that when I catch you, all bets are off. So I suggest you run fast, little Olive."

"I-I don't—"

"Run," I whisper in her ear.

"What?"

Releasing her, I take a step back. "Ten. Nine. Eight," I start counting, and her eyes widen in realisation. "Seven. Six. It's almost like you want me to catch you."

"Fuck," she barks, before darting into the darkness and vanishing from my sight.

A laugh rips from my lips as the first real excitement I've felt since returning to his hellhole trickles through my veins.

"Five. Four. Three. Two. One," I say in a rush. "Ready or not, Olive. The big bad wolf is coming for you."

12

OLIVIA

I stumble into the trees, the overgrowth crunching and cracking beneath my feet.

"Ready or not, Olive. The big bad wolf is coming for you." His voice echoes around me, his dark chuckle sending shivers skittering down my spine.

Reese can flip a switch on his personality so quickly it gives me whiplash. It's disarming.

He's disarming.

And I know that if he catches me, he'll make good on his promise.

My heart drums in my chest, blood roaring between my ears as I run faster.

Luckily for me, I know these woods like the back of my hand. But it doesn't stop my heart rate from spiking as I hear something crunch behind me. I don't glance back, refusing to be distracted.

Reese wants to play cat and mouse? Fine. I'll make him work for it.

A smile tugs at my lips. I shouldn't like this—him chasing me through the woods at night like a predator hunting its prey

—but I can't deny that something else fizzles inside my stomach besides fear.

God, what is wrong with me?

This isn't normal.

If I heard about Oakley doing this to some poor unsuspecting girl, I'd give him hell for it.

Bursting through a thicket of trees, I hiss when a branch snags my shoulder, slicing through my skin. It's enough to make me ground to a halt and try and catch my breath.

"Don't make this easy for me," Reese calls from somewhere behind me.

Shit.

I dart behind a huge oak tree, pressing my back against the rough bark. Warm blood trickles down my arm, my heart crashing violently in my chest.

"I know you're here," he drawls, his footsteps slow and steady. "I can feel you."

Pressing my lips together, I try to remain utterly silent. Part of me wants to tell him to go fuck himself. Reese might be a bastard, but he's an eighteen-year-old boy. This is a game to him. A power play. A way for him to remind me that he's an Heir and I'm nothing but a young woman trying to survive in a man's world.

So why does the other part of me want to get caught?

Silence echoes around me as I listen for a clue to his whereabouts. But there's nothing.

Has he gone?

Is this all part of his plan to spook me? Chase me and then abandon me out here alone?

As quietly as I can, I slip out from my hiding place behind the giant oak, ready to make my way back to the house. But a hand snaps out from the shadows, grabbing my throat and pushing me back up against it.

"Going somewhere?" Reese growls in my face, his eyes glittering like two deadly orbs in the moonlight.

My own gaze narrows, silently seething at him as fear pulses through me.

"Something you want to say?" His fingers flex around my throat as he pins me there.

"Fuck. You," I spit.

"You'd like that, wouldn't you? If I finish what we started all those weeks ago. Tell me, sweet cheeks." He leans in, ghosting his lips over the corner of my mouth, eliciting a shiver from deep within me. "Have you let anyone else in here while I've been gone?"

Reese cups me possessively, grinding the heel of his palm against my clit.

A wanton whimper spills from my lips and his lips curve into a smug smirk. "You're so fucking responsive, Olive."

"Get your hands off me," I snap, trying to press my body into the tree trunk. But Reese cages me there, using his body to trap me in place. A heady mix of fear and anticipation races through me.

I shouldn't be excited by this and yet...

"Is that what you really want? Me to walk away? To leave you so hot and bothered?"

"I..." My voice quivers as I try and gulp a deep breath.

"I'll make you a deal. If you really don't want this, if I shove my fingers inside your leggings and you're not dripping for me, I'll walk away." Hunger flares in his dark gaze as if the very idea of touching me does things to him. "But if I find you wet, you have to let me get you off."

My stomach curls at his words.

"What's it going to be, Olive?"

I glower at him, because I've lost and he knows it.

He knew it the second I ran into the woods.

"Nothing to say?" His brow arches as he slowly, almost lazily rubs me through my leggings.

My head falls back on a defeated sigh. It feels so good.

Too fucking good.

"Right answer," he says, dipping his hand into my leggings and underwear. "Fuck, you're soaked."

Surprise coats his words as evidence of my body's betrayal coats his fingers. A moan rumbles through me as he pushes two thick fingers inside me.

"Reese," I choke out. "We can't do this."

"Sure we can." He crooks his fingers in a come hither motion and my knees almost buckle.

"Oh God," I cry, trying to bury my face in his shoulder. But he refuses to let me move, using his body weight to pin me in place.

"Not God, sweet cheeks. The devil. And I'm going to fucking ruin you." He pumps his fingers inside me, harder, deeper, while his thumb makes sweeping circles over my clit.

"This pussy is mine," he grits out.

"Yes... God, yes."

I don't know what I'm saying, too lost in the sensations crashing over me. Fisting his rugby shirt, I try to kiss him. But Reese hovers out of reach, watching me.

"Kiss me," I breathe. I need the intimacy, the connection.

"Oh, I'm going to kiss you, Olive. Just not on those lips." A wicked glint shines in his eyes, and before I can ask him what the hell he means, Reese drops to his knees and yanks my leggings down.

"R-Reese," I shriek, startled.

He grabs the backs of my thighs and forces my legs open as wide as he can, given the fact that my leggings are bunched around my calves, and he buries his face in my pussy.

"Reese." My fingers grab onto his hair as he aggressively licks me, spearing his tongue inside me. "Holy shit," I pant, riding his face, because I might hate him, I might despise everything that Reese Whitfield represents, but good Lord can the boy eat pussy.

Not that I have a wealth of experience to compare it to. But it feels amazing.

"More," I moan, scraping my fingers against his scalp.

"Fuck, Olivia," he murmurs, not bothering to come up for air, breathing the words onto me. Into me.

Using his fingers, he spreads me open and licks my clit, toying with it, sucking it into his mouth and grazing his teeth dangerously against it.

"Fuck," I breathe, unravelling.

It's too much. He's too much. And this whole thing is crazy. Completely, utterly wrong. But it feels too good to stop.

And deep down, maybe I don't want to stop. I want him on his knees before me, worshipping me, making me shatter.

"You taste so fucking good." He dives back in for seconds. "Why do you taste so good?"

"Less talking," I grab a handful of his hair, "and more eating."

His deep laughter rumbles over me, adding a new dimension to the sensations already wreaking havoc on my body.

More.

I want more.

And more.

And—

"Reese," I cry as my body begins to tremble involuntarily. He curls two fingers, rubbing that special spot deep inside me as he laps at my clit. Over and over and over.

Pleasure crashes into me, rolling through my body in overpowering waves.

"Fuck yeah," he says with smug satisfaction as he licks me through my orgasm, drawing out every last drop of pleasure. I gaze down at him, lust-drunk and sated, and he stares up at me like a fallen prince.

"What?" I whisper.

"You taste like victory."

And just like that, the world comes crashing down around me.

"Get off me." I shove his shoulder and he stumbles back, quickly shooting to his feet.

Grabbing my leggings, I yank them up my body.

Laughter rumbles through him again as he watches me, slowly sucking his fingers clean. "Mmm, looks like I was right, sweet cheeks."

I straighten myself, wincing as the cut on my shoulder smarts.

"Shit," Reese says, noticing the streak of blood down my arm. "Are you okay?" He takes a step forward but catches himself and draws to a stop. "You're bleeding."

"No shit, Sherlock." I inspect the cut. It's a little deeper than I first realised, but nothing I can't clean up myself.

"Do you need—"

"Don't pretend you care," I scoff, annoyed at myself. "We both know you don't."

Storming past him, I head for the house.

And this time, Reese doesn't follow.

What have I done?

That's all I can think as I lie in bed, staring up at the ceiling.

The second I'd gotten home, I came straight up to my room, stripped off, and took a shower before dressing the cut on my arm.

I heard Reese get back, his heavy footsteps in the hall beyond my bedroom door. Part of me wondered if he would knock.

He didn't.

Reese ignites a fire inside me, but it's a dangerous game we're playing. Because one of us will end up burnt, and something tells me it won't ever be him.

Filthy little liar. That's what he called me. But it doesn't make any sense. I've never lied to him. Not once.

Okay, that's not entirely true. I have kept some things to myself, but only because I don't want to give him any more power over me than he already wields.

Christ, I need to stop this... Whatever this thing is simmering between us. He doesn't want me. He wants to toy with me.

To ruin me.

He said it himself.

But why?

Why me all of a sudden?

It doesn't make sense. But then not a lot does when it comes to the Heirs and the world they inhabit.

My mind flickers back to my run-in with Abigail Bancroft at school, and a wave of guilt washes over me.

She's promised to Reese. The girl their families expect him to marry. But no one talks about it. Not Reese. Not his mum or my dad.

It's another expectation. Another burden to shoulder.

They're not together, but one day they will be, and it shouldn't matter. I shouldn't care. Because this—whatever Reese and I are doing—isn't serious. It's a game. A battle of wills. Nothing more.

Reese Whitfield isn't boyfriend material, and he sure as hell isn't husband material.

So why do I feel a stab of jealousy, knowing that he's promised to another?

That one day, he'll be hers...

And there isn't a damn thing I, or anyone else, can do about it.

13

REESE

I sit in the middle of my bed, staring down at my phone screen.

I should be moving some more money, finding somewhere to live. Anything other than getting lost in memories of watching her fall.

Something shifted in me tonight.

I'm not sure if it was when I truly discovered how much I'd been outcast by the three best friends I've ever had, or if it was the moment I swiped my tongue against her pussy and got a mouthful of her addictive taste.

But suddenly, things started to make sense to me in a way they haven't before.

I knew as I drove back into town that I needed revenge. That I needed to make those pay for fucking up my life and taking everything that I've ever wanted and making it their own. But I never quite grasped how I was going to do it.

Until tonight…

Until she gripped my hair so tight that I thought she was going to rip it clean from my head.

A wicked smile tugs at my lips.

Everyone loves Olivia Beckworth.

The Heirs see her as a sister, whether they're related by blood or not. And she's even got my mum wrapped around her little finger now they're living under the same roof.

She's my answer. I see it more clearly now than I did when I first drove past the 'Welcome to Saints Cross' sign, returning to my old life as if I'd been on holiday and nothing more.

The minutes tick by as I force myself to think over my plans. It's something I've been doing every free second I've had since Dad told me I had no choice but to return.

It seemed like a pipe dream then. But now I'm here, setting things into motion. I know it's possible. And now I've got close to her once again, I realise that it's going to be easier than I ever thought it would be.

Olivia seems to be holding true to her roots, lying to the most important person in her life. Oakley has no idea that anything has happened between us. She's kept her mouth shut, and I suspect she will continue doing so.

Confident that it's been long enough, I climb from my bed, dropping my phone into my pocket as I do, and pad toward the door.

Mum and Christian were already in bed when I got back, so I can only hope that they'll remain hidden in their room and not catch me slipping across the hall to creep on my new stepsister.

My heart thumps as I press the door handle down and step onto the thick carpet beyond the threshold. The room is in darkness. I can only see where I'm going thanks to some glowing fairy lights Olivia has hanging from her bookcases. But it's all I need to be able to see her sleeping, tucked under her covers with no fucking worries.

I know she sleeps heavily. I've been in here enough times with Oak over the years, playing practical jokes on her in the middle of the night. She never once woke up. She also proved the theory of people pissing themselves at night if their fingers were in a bowl of water wrong a few times too, much to our disappointment.

Pulling the chair from her desk, I roll it beside her bed and sit down, spreading my thighs wide as I watch her.

She looks almost angelic in her sleep. It makes it almost hard to believe she's got such a deceitful tongue hiding behind her full, tempting lips.

Rubbing my hands down my thighs, I rest back, letting my imagination run wild. I lick my lips, as if I'll still be able to taste her on them.

I watch her for the longest time, stealing all the little whimpers and noises she makes in her sleep, wishing I could get into her head to find out what she's dreaming about.

My cock aches, precum leaking into my sweats with my need for release. Teasing her, tasting her. It left me fucking aching for her.

"You're a fucking tease, little liar," I breathe, pushing my hand beneath my waistband and squeezing the base of my cock.

My eyes shutter as I fight the need to give in to temptation.

It makes me wonder how badly she'd freak out if she woke to find me here, getting myself off to the sight of her.

Or would she enjoy it?

Would she wake up burning for me and help me out? Take me in her mouth and…

Before I know what I'm doing, my hand is moving up and down my length and my muscles are bunching up in my need to let go.

Her lips part as my speed increases and she shifts in the bed, a little moan spilling from her mouth as I come in my pants like a fucking pre-teen.

Heat rushes up my cheeks, colouring them both in

reaction to my much-needed release and the embarrassment of how quickly it took to achieve it.

My chest heaves, my body relaxing as the release loosens my muscles and forces me to let go of a little bit of the tension I've been walking around with since the other day.

I pull my hand free, some of my own jizz covering my fingers, and I act before I think better of it.

Gently, I trace the fullness of her bottom lip, coating it in the evidence of my visit, before I stand back and appreciate the sight of her. Dragging my phone from my pocket, I clear all the notifications of messages and missed calls from my dad that I've been ignoring, and I take a quick photo to add to the others in my wank bank.

After pushing her chair back where I found it, I let my eyes linger on her for a second longer before leaving her room. The last thing I want is to get caught on my first visit. Especially as I'm planning on spending plenty more nights here, corrupting my little liar.

The boys don't want to let me move in with them, then fuck it. I'll make my own fun.

There's plenty to be had here, after all.

Just like the morning before, the house is in silence as I make my way down the stairs in my uniform with my bags thrown over my shoulder.

I head for the kitchen to grab a coffee before making my way to school.

I was ordered by King Elliot to join them at the Chapel at seven AM, ready for breakfast.

Well, despite my good intentions to move forward with regaining my old life, I seem to have failed at the first hurdle, because it's already five past and I haven't even left the house.

Whoops.

I never was great with my timekeeping. They can't expect me to suddenly be on top of shit.

"Oh fuck," I breathe as I step into the kitchen and find my mum sitting at the breakfast bar as if she's waiting for me. "Sorry, I'll just..."

"No, wait. Please, Reese. I only want to talk."

"Yeah, well I've got nothing to say to you."

I turn to leave but make the fucking stupid mistake of catching her eyes before I go.

"Please, Reese. Even if you just stay long enough for me to apologise."

My head tells me to walk out, to leave her and her stupid fucking apology behind. But my heart, my naïve little heart, begs me to at least hear her out.

"Fine," I spit. "But it better be good. I'm not sure any excuse will be enough to make me forgive you for fucking around on Dad."

"Reese," she breathes. "Things aren't always as they seem. Did you even let him explain while you were away?" I glare at her, letting her see the answer in my eyes.

"If this is your way of trying to tell me that you never loved him and my whole life was a joke, then you could go a better way around it."

"What? No. I've always loved your father. I *do* love your father."

I throw my hands up, indicating the house we're currently in.

"I know, I know. But things between your dad and me... they were complicated and—"

"Try harder, Mum. Right now, I'm starting to think your clients must be wasting their money getting you to defend them."

"Your father and I haven't been in love for a long time. But we both agreed that we wanted to keep our family. That meant we both had to make sacrifices for the greater good."

"Which was?" I ask.

"You, Reese. Always you."

"I'm sorry, but I'm struggling to understand how me walking in on you getting railed by my best friend's dad was for my own good."

She gasps, blood draining from her face as I reveal that little fact.

"Christian is a good man, Reese."

"A good lay, you mean?" I scoff.

She blows out a long breath as if she'll find some sense of calm by doing so.

"Life isn't so black and white, Reese. There's this whole heap of grey in the middle of it that is sent to try us, to test us. And sometimes, yeah, we make mistakes. But I promise you, I never hurt your father in the way you think I did."

"You mean, he knew you were fucking around?"

She gives me a weak smile, and it's all I need to answer that question.

"Motherfucker," I grunt, my fist slamming into the wall beside me.

"Our priority was always you, Reese."

"That's rich, seeing as neither of you were ever actually there for me. I can't see it would have made any difference to my life if you went your separate ways."

"In hindsight, maybe not."

"Why didn't you?" I ask, sensing there's more here than her need to give me some kind of normal life. "Why did you fake it for so many years?"

"For—"

"Do not say for me again. I know you, Mum. I know there's more. So please, for once, just be fucking honest with me. I promise you, it's not going to make me hate you anymore."

"Your grandfather."

A bitter laugh falls from my lips. Disbelief floods me that I didn't figure that out earlier.

"So good old pops died and you decided to give in and fuck your way around Saints Cross."

"We all have things that are expected of us in life, Reese. Sometimes, you have to roll with the punches and find happiness wherever you can."

"Roll with the punches. Like my arranged marriage?" I blurt, anger forcing the words from my lips.

I never talk about the fact that this woman standing before me on the verge of tears promised me to Judge Bancroft's daughter when we were nothing more than kids, and actually thinks we're both going to follow through with it.

Abigail is the opposite of my type. There is no way Mum or Judge Bancroft can think for even a second that putting us together is a good idea.

"Abigail is a good girl, Reese. She's—"

"Yeah, that's my point. Not exactly my perfect girl. I need mine a little more... rough around the edges. Experienced."

"She needs someone like you. Someone who can protect her from all the snakes in this town."

"Then sign me up to be her sponsor, not her fucking husband."

"It's out of my hands."

"It wasn't the day you signed my life away though, was it?" I spit back.

"I need you to trust me, Reese. I'm trying to do my best here."

"Well, try harder. The only people who are falling for it are those who actually belong in this house."

I storm away, her pleading voice following me down the hallway.

"Sometimes, we need to be selfless beyond all else, Reese. Sometimes, putting other people first and playing this game is all we have."

"This game?" I ask, regretting being sucked back in.

"Yeah, life. And in case you didn't already know,

happiness and love are it. The end goal. Maybe you should stop trying to push everyone who loves you away and focus on the good they can bring to your life instead."

I slam the door behind me the second she's stopped talking. But her advice doesn't leave me the whole way to the Chapel, where I'm sure I'm probably going to walk straight into the middle of another fucking argument.

14

OLIVIA

It's weird, heading into school by myself. But with Oak staying at the Chapel and Reese gone before I even managed to drag myself out of bed, I have no choice but to drive in alone again.

Darcie and her friends all gawk at me as I climb out of my car and smooth my pleated skirt down my thighs. I narrow my eyes at them, and they go back to their conversation.

Stupid bitches.

No doubt they're talking about the party last night. Who got with who and who made a fool of themselves.

A shudder runs through me as memories assault my mind. Reese. The woods. His ridiculously skilled tongue and fingers.

Ugh.

Get a grip, Olivia.

He wasn't that skilled, and he practically assaulted me. But I know I could have escaped if I had really wanted to. I could have screamed for help or kneed him in the balls or punched him right between his stormy grey eyes.

The truth is, I liked the chase. And more than that, I liked being caught.

I give a little shake of my head. There really is something very wrong with me.

Heading into the building, I run over the day's classes in my mind. But the second I enter the corridor, I freeze.

Gareth Franklin, a first year new to town, has Abigail Bancroft cornered in the alcove under the stairs leading to the first floor. I can't hear what he's saying, but terror glitters in her eyes as he crowds her further into the shadows, taunting her, if his devious smirk is anything to go by.

I make a beeline for them, anger zipping up my spine. "Get away—"

Reese appears out of nowhere and grabs the boy, shoving him away from Abigail. "What the fuck do you think you're doing?" He gets all up in Gareth's face.

"We were only talking." He stands his ground. "Isn't that right, baby?"

Abigail blanches, cowering in the alcove.

"Who the fuck are you?" Reese grits out. "I don't recognise you."

"I'm new. Just moved to Saints Cross from—"

"Don't give a fuck." Reese fists his shirt, dragging him close enough that they're almost nose to nose. "Maybe you didn't get the memo, or maybe you need to be reminded, but this is our school, and we don't tolerate little pricks like you preying on our girls."

Our girls.

My chest squeezes at his words.

But I guess he's right—she is his.

"Shit, dude." Gareth finally has the sense to look scared. "We were only talking."

"Dude? Do I look like I'm your fucking dude?" Reese slams him up against the wall, knocking the air clean from his lungs. "Want my advice?"

"W-what?"

"Keep out of my fucking way, and if I catch you sniffing around Abigail again, you're a dead man."

Reese releases him with a hard shove and Gareth practically slides down the wall, fear radiating from him. He clambers to his feet and all but runs down the corridor.

Abigail steps out of the alcove and gazes up at Reese with a weak smile. "Thank you." I see the whispered words form on her lips.

Reese goes rigid and glares are her. "Whatever," he says. "I didn't do it for you."

Her expression is crushed as he spins around and walks away. She glances down the corridor, her gaze snagging on mine. A silent question simmers in her eyes, but I don't engage.

I'm not sure I have any of the answers she wants.

So I take off in the opposite direction, putting some space between us. But that sickly, unnerving sensation lingers, and I don't like it. Because I know what it is.

Jealousy.

I was jealous seeing Reese defend her.

Christ, he's under my skin in a way I hadn't expected—or wanted.

Reese Whitfield isn't a good person. He's arrogant and smug, and a little bit messed up inside.

Yet, I want him. My body wants him.

I whip out my phone and pull up my chat history with Charli.

> Olivia: What are you doing tonight?

> Charli: Dinner with my mum and wankstain, why?

Crap.

> Olivia: I need to get out of Saints Cross for a bit.

> Charli: Things that bad?

> Olivia: They're... complicated.

> Charli: Sounds intriguing. I can't get out of tonight, but tomorrow? We could go to the Spire. It's karaoke Wednesday. I know the new barman, he's cute and will definitely be down for sneaking us a few drinks if I ask nicely.

> Olivia: I'm in.

I need to put some distance between me and Saints Cross. Me and Reese.

> Charli: Yes!!! I'll text you tomorrow and we can make plans. Wish me luck for tonight, something tells me I'm going to need it.

> Olivia: Good luck. You can always stab Dan with your fork if it goes sideways.

> Charli: DON'T tempt me. Laters. x

A soft chuckle escapes me, but it's quickly followed by a gnawing sensation. I miss Charli. I liked having her around. Being an Heirs sister is a lonely place to be sometimes.

And something tells me this year is only going to get worse.

By lunchtime, my suspicions are confirmed. Oakley texted me earlier, asking me to have lunch with them in the Chapel, but when I spot him, Elliot, and Theo heading out of the building with Reese in tow, I decline.

That place isn't big enough for the both of us, and Reese's

little white-knight routine from earlier seems to have gotten him back in their good graces.

So I head for the refectory to grab some lunch, but the second I step inside, I almost collide with Abigail.

"Sorry," she blurts out, her cheeks pinking. "I... I wasn't looking where I was going."

"It's fine."

Her eyes dart around the room. "This place is really busy. I try to avoid it, but I forgot my packed lunch." She's all wide-eyed and surprised as a couple of students rush past us in a hurry.

"Yep, it's... something, all right." I scan the sea of bodies all jostling to find a table and in the lunch queue.

I should probably ask her if she's okay after earlier, but the words teeter on the tip of my tongue. Abigail stares expectantly at me, as if she senses I want to say something. But when I don't, she says, "Well, I suppose I should brave the queue. Are you—"

"Actually, I'm meeting somebody," I lie.

"Oh, okay." Her expression drops, sending a bolt of guilt through me. But I can't make friends with Abigail.

It's weird.

I'm... whatever I'm doing with Reese. It feels icky, unease trickling down my spine.

I know they're not together; they barely even acknowledge each other around school, but one day, she will be his.

Whether he likes it or not.

And it isn't in my future plans to be someone's dirty little secret.

My chest tightens. I guess that's what I am now. Reese hasn't told anyone about me, and I don't want him to.

What we're doing is... wrong.

Messed up.

I need to put a stop to it.

But I'm not sure I can.

Reese ignites a fire inside me, and the heat between us is addictive. But the thing about playing with fire...

Someone always ends up getting burned.

"Liv." Oakley waves as I enter English Lit. Reluctantly, I traipse over and drop down into the chair next to him.

"Where were you at lunch?"

"I told you, busy."

"Yeah." He nudges my shoulder. "Busy doing what?"

"I had a thing."

"Bloody hell, Liv, why are you acting so weird?"

"I'm not."

"Is it because I stayed at the Chapel? You know—"

"Believe it or not, Oak, I do have a life outside of you and the Heirs."

His brow lifts, an amused smile tugging at his mouth. "Yoga does not constitute a life, Sis."

"Piss off." I swat him away, annoyed at how much his words affect me.

"Seriously though, you good? Because I know things are going to be different this year. But you're welcome to hang out at the Chapel any time. I already told you that."

"I'd rather not hang out at your little fuck pad."

"Jesus, Liv." He chuckles, running a hand down his face. "You make it sound like that's all we do."

"Isn't it?" I quip, and he elbows me in the arm.

"I'm still your brother. I'll always make time for you."

"Aw, I'm touched." My eyes roll as I chew the end of my pen, trying to ignore the giant knot balled in my stomach.

We don't keep things from each other—that's always been our mantra. But now, it feels like nothing but secrets exist between us.

I hate it, but I don't know how to fix it. Because if Oakley finds out what Reese did, what I've been doing... he will lose his shit.

There's already enough animosity between them, and I do not want to end up the middle of it.

"Did Whitfield make it home last night?"

"What?"

"You know. Reese, our new housemate." His eyes crinkle. "Future stepbrother."

"Don't you mean, *my* new housemate."

"Come on, Liv. Don't be like that. You always knew I'd be moving out come second year."

"Yeah, I know." But I didn't know I'd be stuck living with Reese then. "You're going to let him back into the fold eventually, right?" I ask.

"He fucked up, Liv." Oak shrugs. "Part of me gets it. It's different for him, and then this shit with his mum and dad. But he could have talked to me, he could have—"

"Good afternoon, people." Mr. Piper strolls into the class and drops his leather satchel on the desk. "Sorry I'm late. Hopefully you've all been spending the time productively."

"He's still one of us," Oakley whispers, "but trust isn't rebuilt overnight, Liv."

"Yeah."

A shiver runs down my spine. If Oak discovers the truth about me and Reese, any fragile trust rebuilt between them won't only crack. It'll shatter.

I can't do that to my brother.

I won't.

Whatever Reese and I have, it has to end.

A hollow feeling goes through me.

But that's silly.

You can't lose something you never had in the first place.

Reese Whitfield isn't mine.

And he never will be.

15

REESE

I didn't make a conscious decision to defend Abigail when I rounded the corner and found that first year prick getting in her face and scaring the shit out of her. It was just an ingrained reaction.

That's what the Heirs do.

We rule this fucking school.

But that doesn't mean we just lord it over the rest of the students and throw kick-arse parties. It means we take on the hard jobs too. And punishing those who hurt a fellow student of the school is right up there.

We don't put up with bullies on our turf, and anyone who tries to push people around will eventually find themselves with the four of us breathing down their necks. And unlucky for Gareth fucking Franklin, he's managed to land his name first on our list this year.

Now we need to ensure the lesson we teach him is loud enough to send ripples through the rest of the school that we mean fucking business.

There's always unrest when the key changes hands.

Scott and his boys have ruled this place for two years. Everyone knew where they stood, mostly.

But we're new. Everyone might know us. We might already have a reputation around the school halls. But we haven't had a chance to exert our power yet.

Well, today, that is going to be changing.

I knew they were watching as I threw that stupid prick against the wall. Their intrigued stares burned into my back as I spelled out quite simply that no one, even the pussy fucking new boy, even thinks about taunting one of our girls.

I half expected one of them to drag me away and take over the punishment themselves. But they never did. They stood with the rest of the crowd that had gathered and watched the show.

The only disappointment about the whole thing really was that pussy little Gareth didn't piss his pants.

That would have turned my day right around.

There's always time. Something tells me the boys and I will be seeing more of Gareth before he gets the chance to run back to wherever he hides at night.

With any luck, he boards at All Hallows'. That will give us round-the-clock access to him. Should we need it, of course.

From the arrogant glint in his eyes as he stared up at me, I'd be tempted to say that scaring the shit out of innocent girls is the least of what he's capable of.

"Up the pace, ladies," Coach barks as my fingers touch the white line at the end of the pitch.

All of us are covered head to toe in mud, but apparently, our performance during our training wasn't good enough, so instead of practicing new plays, he's got us running fucking drills as punishment for our piss-poor effort.

"Is he trying to fucking kill us?" Oakley grunts beside me, his fingers touching the ground less than a second after mine.

"Pretty fucking sure, yeah."

A pained groan rips through the air as another of our new year twelve teammates collapses in a heap on the ground.

"You're not going to be winning any matches this year with dedication like that, princess."

"Motherfucker," Elliot grunts as he appears at my other side. "That's Middleton."

"Oh shit," Oak pants.

Elliot doesn't need to say any more. The surname is enough.

Middleton is one of the next Heirs who will take the key from us after our year at the top. There is no fucking way he should be rolling around on the ground right now like a pussy.

"Eaton, get back in line," Coach barks as Elliot darts right, fisting the back of Middleton's shirt and dragging him back to his feet.

"You don't fucking quit," Elliot growls in his ear before shoving him back into line.

To my shock, when I look up, I find the punk I threatened at the party last night still on his feet. Although his face is damn near purple.

Coach doesn't let up for the longest fucking time, and when he finally does blow his whistle to bring the torture session to a close, almost everyone who's still standing falls to the ground.

All bar the four of us.

Our eyes connect as we stand there fighting to get our breath, an understanding passing between us as we exert our strength and power.

None of them said anything about my show earlier, but there was a shift in the air. Following the unwritten rules of being an Heir has bridged something between us, and I can only hope that it continues. Because Mum was right this morning. Sometimes, we all have to sacrifice things for the greater good. And that for me right now is figuring out a way to bring everyone in this motherfucking town to its knees. And the way to do that is to force myself back into the life I thought

I'd left behind and earn their trust once more. And when I've got that back… boom.

"What the fuck is so funny, Whitfield?" Theo barks as a sadistic laugh slips from my lips.

I glance around, my eyes tracking each of our teammates half dead on the ground.

"Those fucking pussies. We've got our work cut out making sure they're up for this."

Both Oak and Theo rub their hands together in excitement as wicked ideas fill their minds.

We've been planning initiation tasks for fucking years. And even I can't deny that the thought of finally being able to watch them play out ignites a fire inside me.

"I expect you all on better form tomorrow night, ladies. Maybe leave your tiaras at home, yeah?" Coach barks after ripping all the guys on the ground new ones.

He nods in our direction before stalking back toward his office.

"Let's move," Elliot demands. "We've got a little rat to go and sniff out, after all."

"A rat?" I ask.

"Yeah, that cunt you marked earlier. I think a louder message might need to be given. We're not starting the year off allowing anyone to think we're soft."

Oak and Theo both agree as we march toward the locker room.

"Where is he?" I ask, knowing nothing about the prick other than that he likes to prey on innocent girls.

"Out there." Elliot jerks his chin toward where the football team is training. "They're about to have their session cut short," he states.

"Oh?" I ask, curious as to what he's schemed up.

"Their coach is about to get a call that's going to ensure he leaves. So that prick will be heading our way any minute."

Just before we get to the door to the locker room, we all

watch as their coach blows his whistle, bringing his session to an end before talking to his players animatedly.

The second he dismisses them, he takes off running in the opposite direction.

"How the fuck did you do that?" Oak asks, shock and pride laced through his voice.

Elliot chuckles. "The rat is heading into the trap, boys. You ready to start this year properly?"

"Damn, I thought that was last night while two girls were sucking my— ow," Theo hisses when Elliot slaps him hard across the head.

"Get your head in the fucking game, Ashworth."

We head into the locker room as the rest of the rugby team finally stumbles after us, and the football team also heads this way.

Hunger and the need for this fight burn through me something fierce.

The four of us stand in the open space in the middle of the huge room. Pained voices head our way, but the second they step foot inside, their words falter and silence falls. Anticipation ripples through the air as the rest of our team look at each other, fear etched into their features.

They probably think we're gunning for them after that poor show.

To be fair, we are. But not right now.

Our new recruits will be put through their paces soon enough. Right now, we've got our sights set on our first victim.

When we don't make a move to pull anyone forward, they all edge around the room, still looking at each other as they wait for the other shoe to drop.

More male voices fill the air as the football team gets close and understanding seems to wash through the room.

The year thirteens are first inside, and the second they take us in holding court, they instantly pale. They know the deal—they've witnessed the Heirs in action before. Although, not us, which adds an element of unease to this whole situation.

No one is aware of how we're going to handle our business yet.

Every new generation of Heirs plays it differently. Some opt for pure pain. Others, like Scott, go for mind games. Even I'm unsure of how Elliot is going to play it this year. He might not be as vindictive and ruthless as his older brother, but I'm not naïve enough to think he doesn't have it in him. He is, after all, an Eaton. And his father's reputation precedes him.

"What the fuck is going on?" some dumb-arse year twelve barks as everyone slows in front of him.

"Shut the fuck up, dickhead," someone mutters as danger and fear ripple through the room.

I search the new boys standing behind the ones we've gone through All Hallows' with, hunting for our target.

The second my eyes land on his, he tilts his chin up in defiance.

Fucking stupid prick.

Clearly, no fucker has clued him in as to how things work in this school since I tipped him off earlier.

A couple of his teammates are clearly quicker than him, because some helpful guy shoves him from behind.

Caught off guard, Gareth cuntbag Franklin stumbles through the crowd and quickly finds himself standing right before the four of us.

Both teams stand shoulder to shoulder around us, stopping him from running, if he's stupid enough to even try it.

He squares his shoulders and stares each of us dead in the eyes.

"Gareth Franklin," Elliot starts, spitting his name as if it's poison. "Day two... You made it to day two before landing yourself at our feet. Some might say that's a fucking stupid thing to do."

Gareth laughs as if this is all one big joke. "Who the fuck

do you lot think you are?" Mirth dances in his eyes. But when he's only met with silence and the growing threat of violence, it soon starts to diminish.

"Who? Us?" Elliot asks.

"We're your worst fucking nightmare," Theo adds.

"Judge, jury, and motherfucking executioner," Oak sings, making the dude's brow wrinkle in confusion.

"You step out of line at All Hallows', you answer to us."

"Fuck off," he scoffs. "You don't have that kind of power," he states confidently, but when no one agrees with him, his smirk begins to falter.

"Are you sure about that?"

He looks between the four of us once more, his confidence levels weakening with every passing second.

"What?" Elliot taunts. "Do you think mummy and daddy will have something to say about it?"

Gareth's lips part to answer, but Elliot doesn't give him a chance.

"As far as I can tell, she's too busy sucking her boss's cock to pay much attention to what her little prince is doing."

His face turns a shade of red that I'm not sure I've seen before.

"Whitfield. Care to finish what you started earlier?" Elliot offers.

To everyone watching us, it might seem friendly. But I hear the challenge in his voice.

They want to know I'm with them. That I really want to reclaim my place. This is the start of me earning my way back into their circle.

And I'm going to take it.

Gareth might know it's coming, but that doesn't stop him from flying back into the blood-hungry crowd the second my fist collides with his jaw.

"Fuck you," he spits when he's shoved back into the fray roughly.

"Oh, dude. There's only one of us who's getting fucked up right now."

To give him credit, he tries to fight back. But as is usually standard when it comes to bullies, he's all fucking mouth, and before long, he's on the dirty tiled floor, bleeding and crying like a little bitch while the four of us stand over him with accomplished smirks pulling at our lips.

"Anyone else wanna try us?" Theo taunts, but unsurprisingly, no one replies.

"What the fuck are you lot doing?" a deep voice booms from behind the crowd before it parts, revealing Coach with his arms crossed over his chest.

His eyes find ours before they collide with the pained ones of the pussy at our feet.

"Sir, they came at me. Th-they—"

"Enough," he booms. "Get your filthy arses in the showers. And you," he spits, looking down at our prey, "get the fuck up and stop dirtying up my floor."

"B-but—"

"Now, arseholes. Move." He claps impatiently, and everyone shuffles to find their piece of bench, ready to wait for their turn in the showers.

As he walks past us, he claps Elliot on the shoulder, much to Gareth's horror.

Fucking hell, maybe being back isn't that bad after all.

16

OLIVIA

By the time Wednesday evening rolls around, I can't wait to get out of Saints Cross for the night.

Avoiding Reese and my brother is hard work. But I manage it.

Reese has been oddly absent too, although it probably has something to do with the fact that he's back in with the Heirs, the four of them prowling the corridors of All Hallows' like merciless kings.

News soon spread about Gareth and his unfortunate broken nose.

I don't condone violence, but part of me knows he deserved some of what was coming to him.

Checking my reflection one last time, I fluff my hair and throw my bag over my shoulder, heading for the bedroom door. Charli has promised me a night of drinks, hot guys, and ear-splitting karaoke, and I can't—

"You." I grind to a halt, glowering up at Reese as he takes in my outfit.

"Hot date?" he deadpans.

"None of your business." I barge past him, but not before he grabs my arm, yanking me back.

"You're avoiding me."

"And you're going to make me late for my date." I flash him a smug smile.

"Don't push me, Olive. You won't like what happens."

"Fuck you, Reese." I shove him away and take off down the stairs. He follows but keeps a safe distance.

Wanker.

Of course he had to be here tonight, right when I'm leaving the house.

"Olivia, is that you?" Dad calls.

"Yeah, I'm about to leave."

"Okay, sweetheart. Have fun and say hi to Charli for me." He appears around the kitchen door. "And try not to get into too much trouble."

"I think you're telling the wrong twin." My lips twist with amusement. "Bye, Dad. Reese," I clip out as I grab my keys and head for the door.

His eyes follow me the whole way, but I don't spare him a second glance.

But when I climb in my car and glance up at the house, I don't expect to see him still standing there, his big frame eating up the doorway.

For a second, I think he might give chase. He doesn't, though. He stands there, staring.

Done with his games, I fire up the engine and peal out of the driveway, ready for a night without the Heirs looking over my shoulder.

Or Reese Baron Whitfield breathing down my neck.

The Spire is packed with not an All Hallows' student in sight.

It's perfect.

"Wow, they grow them good over in Huxton Academy." I grin at Charli, watching a couple of boys from her class stalk past us. One of them gives me a cheeky wink, and she chuckles.

"Olivia Beckworth. I didn't know you had it in you."

"I don't... yet."

"Oh my God." She falls about laughing, slurping the rest of her vodka Coke down. "I'm so glad you came. I didn't know if..." Charli trails off, her eyes darting to the floor.

"We're friends, right?"

The word sounds strange on my lips, but I mean it. Outside of Oak and the Heirs, Charli is the closest thing I've ever had to a friend.

"Oh my God, yes. The girls at Huxton are so not my people. It's funny." She lets out a soft sigh. "I never really fit in at All Hallows', but I don't think I fit in at Huxton either."

"If you ask me, fitting in is overrated."

"I'll drink to that." She flags down the roving barman and orders us two shots each of cherry sours.

"You do know it's a school night," I remind her.

"School schmool. I need this, and something tells me you do too."

She isn't wrong there.

I sniff the bright red liquid and retch a little. "That is—"

"A means to an end, my friend. Now drink up." She clinks her plastic glass against mine and tips her head back, downing it in one. Not wanting to be outdone, I follow, retching again at the godawful burn as it sluices down my throat.

"Oh shit." Something catches Charli's eye, and I turn slowly to see a group of lads enter the bar.

"Is that—"

"Dale Starling, yep."

"He's... filled out."

"That's one way of putting it. Word on the street is he's pumping steroids."

That would explain his new beefed-up appearance then.

Dale Starling is the fly half for the Huxton Harriers, and the Saints' bitter rivals.

My brother hates him with a passion.

"Oh shit. Shit. He's coming over here." Charli tries to act aloof, but it only draws more attention to us.

"Do I know you?" His leering gaze sends spiders crawling under my skin.

"I don't think so." I smile.

"She with you?" he asks Charli.

"What does it look like?"

"You know, I'd really like to fuck the attitude right out of you, freak."

"Don't speak to her like that."

"Or what, beautiful? What are you going to do—"

"Leave the girls alone, Dale," one of the barmen shouts.

"We're only talking."

"Actually, we're not," I reply loudly enough for our section of the bar to overhear.

"What's your name?" Dale asks, looking impressed.

Not what I was going for.

"Sarah." I smirk.

"Want a drink, Sarah?"

"I'm good, but thanks." I flash him another saccharine smile, but it doesn't deter him.

I can't help but wonder what Oak would say if he knew I was here, cavorting with the enemy. What Reese might say.

"Well, ladies, we'll be over there," Dale points to a cluster of tables, "if you feel like joining us later."

A small nod is my only answer while Charli toys with the ends of her curled hair, making no attempts at hiding her blatant appraisal of Dale's dark-haired friend.

"You're right. Huxton does grow them good. It's a shame they're complete tossers."

"I'm beginning to think all boys are."

"You know what we need? A trip to Saints Cross U. Check out some of the older lads."

"And run into the Scions? No thanks." A shudder goes through me at the thought of ever having to see Scott Eaton again. Some of the shit he got up to in his reign of All Hallows', makes Oak and his friends look like children.

"Ooh, the karaoke is about to start."

"Please tell me I don't have to sing." I balk.

"Nope." She flashes me a knowing smirk. "We can sit back, relax, and enjoy the show."

"Are you going to answer that?" Charli asks me sometime later. Karaoke is in full swing and the drinks are going down far too easily. But I haven't felt this relaxed in forever.

"It's probably Oak."

"Well, if you checked"—she snatches my phone off the table—"you'd know. It's Oak."

Charli hands out my phone and I take it, opening our message thread.

> Oak: Reese said you're in Huxton with Charli...

> Olivia: So what if I am?

> Oak: Come on, Liv. It's Harrier territory.

> Olivia: Nobody knows me here except Charli. Stop worrying.

> Oak: I'll always worry where you're concerned, sis. So what exactly are the two of you up to tonight?

A smile tugs at my lips. I want to be pissed at him, a small part of me is. But I also like that Oak still cares. That even as he's pulled more and more into the Heirs world, he'll always be there for me.

> Olivia: That's for me to know and you never to find out.

I add a winky emoji for good measure and switch my phone off. He's probably too busy with his hand up some Heir chaser's skirt to be that worried about me and what I'm doing.

"Dale keeps looking over here," Charli says from the corner of her lips.

"He can look all he wants. I'm not interested."

"And that would be why exactly?"

"I don't know what you mean."

"So Reese is—"

"Seriously, that's... gross. He's an Heir and my new stepbrother, or whatever you want to call it."

"I don't know how you do it. Living with Oakley and Reese."

"Charli, they're my family."

"Okay everyone," the compère says, "let's give it up for Charli Devons."

"You're going to sing?"

"Surprise." Her eyes twinkle with excitement. "Make sure you cheer for me."

"Oh, I will."

Laughter bubbles in my chest as she hurries to the stage and takes the microphone. I don't miss the judgemental stares thrown her way. But at least Dale and his friends seem to be impressed that she got up there.

The whole place joins in as Charli regales us with her best version of 'Like a Virgin'. She looks so carefree up there, her smile wide and content. But I see the cracks. The pain behind her eyes.

She lost everything when she moved to Huxton.

"Here." Dale appears out of nowhere and slides me a drink.

Arching a brow. I say, "I'm good, thanks."

"That's a bit rude."

"Yeah, well, I don't accept drinks from strangers."

"Come on now, beautiful." He sits down on the banquette beside me. "I haven't spiked it or anything."

"Good to know." Disbelief coats my words. I glance back at the stage, but Charli is too caught up in the performance of her life to notice me and Dale.

Crap.

"So I figured it out."

"W-what?"

"Where I know you from." His lips twist into a smirk, sending my heart into freefall.

"You go to All Hallows'."

"So? I didn't realise there was a Huxton-only policy here."

"Oh, there isn't." He moves closer, his big body blocking my view of the bar. Fear snakes through me as I glare at him.

"But everyone knows there's no love lost between the Harriers and the Saints."

"I'm not a fan of rugby, sorry."

Where the hell is Charli? The song ended at least ten seconds ago, but there's no bloody sign of her.

"That's not all though, is it, beautiful?" His eyes dance with delight as he reaches for my arm, toying with the cap sleeve of my shirt. "You're not just any girl, are you, Olivia?"

Shit.

"I—"

"What's going on?" Charli finally appears, cutting Dale with a hard look.

"Just getting acquainted with Olivia. I've never met an Heirs sister up close and in person before. Figured they kept you all on leashes or something."

"Get off me." I seethe, swatting his hand away. "I'm not here to cause any trouble."

Dale snorts at that, as if the idea is ridiculous.

"You can run along now," Charli hisses. "She's not interested, and I'm sure there are plenty of girls willing to be your plaything for the night."

"Relax, I'm going." He slides out and stands, raking a hand through his hair. "Send your brother my love." His dark chuckle makes my stomach dip.

"Oh, shit." Charli flops down beside me. "He recognised you."

"Apparently so." My lips thin.

"Are you going to tell Oakley?"

"Why the hell would I do that? Nothing happened."

Except, something did happen. I'm pretty sure there was a threat in there somewhere.

"Because Oak will lose his shit if he knows Dale was harassing you."

"He wasn't harassing me, Charli. He was... trying to exert his power. Either way, he doesn't scare me."

Reese makes Dale Starling look like a teddy bear.

"I'm going to go on record and say I think it's a bad idea."

"If I tell him, he'll come here. Probably with his friends. That is a bad idea."

"Yeah, you have a point. Maybe we should go?"

"No way. We came here to have fun." To get away from Saints Cross. "And fun we're going to have. Ignore Dale and quit talking about my brother."

"Do you know what we need?" A devious smile tugs the corner of her mouth. "Shots. We need shots."

My eyes flick to Dale and he smirks again.

Shit.

But I refuse to be intimidated, glaring right back at him. So I'm Oakley Beckworth's sister? Big deal. Dale glances away first and a smug satisfaction washes over me.

"Liv?" Charli tugs my arm and I look at her, grinning.
"Shots," I say. "Shots it is."

17

REESE

"Oh, yes, Oakley," a voice cries from behind me, making my teeth grind so hard in my mouth I'm surprised I don't chip one. "Yeah, baby. Just like that."

Jesus fucking Christ.

I slump lower down on the sofa, my eyes locked on my dark phone screen. The only notifications on there are once again courtesy of my dad.

Elliot told me after practice that I was coming back here tonight. That I could hang out. Very generous of him.

It all sounded good. Things have been better since I beat the shit out of Gareth and proved I wanted my place among them.

But if I'd have known that hanging out would have included them with a girl each and me sitting here with little choice but to listen to the moaning and groaning, seeing as they refuse to take the girls downstairs, then I wouldn't have fucking agreed.

I'm being punished, I get it. But fucking really?

I glance up at Elliot, who's on the opposite sofa with a blonde between his legs.

"You're so big," she praises after he helps her free his cock.

I can't help but roll my eyes at her over-the-top excitement.

Yeah, okay, the four of us haven't only been given more money and power than we know what to do with. We're pretty fucking lucky in the junk department too. But I really don't need to hear about how fucking hung Elliot is.

Elliot holds my eyes, and they crinkle at the corners in amusement.

As if he can read my thoughts, he grabs a fistful of the blonde's hair and growls, "You think you can take it all, beautiful?"

Her head bobs like a fucking nodding dog before she lowers down, proving her worth.

Elliot's eyes shutter as she goes to town on him, slurping like he's her favourite flavour lollipop.

My lips peel back in disgust. He might be lording it over me, but I'd put any money on that being one of the worst fucking blowies he's ever had.

"Easy, beautiful," he growls, dragging her off a little. "It's not going to disappear. There's no rush."

A laugh falls from my lips as I continue watching them. "You're gonna need to try harder, Eaton." I gesture to my flaccid cock that's grateful to be hiding behind my sweats. "Not even an inch of jealousy right now. You can keep slurper all to yourself."

Pushing to my feet, I swipe my empty beer bottle from the table and head for the kitchen, quickly discovering why Oak's girl was moaning so loudly.

He's fucking her on the kitchen counter, her bare arse rolling back and forth on the black granite.

"I hope you're gonna sterilise that once you're done," I comment with a smirk, knowing that talk of cleaning is going to put Oak right off his game.

He's a neat freak who's always within ten feet of a

packet of anti-bac wipes. The thought of her arse crack planted exactly where he preps food is going to sink that boner faster than finding the brunette impaled on his cock is his sister.

Thoughts of Olivia slam into me, and my blood finally starts to heat a little.

Memories of watching her sleep, of keeping tabs on her all day at school today while she was completely oblivious run through my mind.

But all of that quickly morphs into the image of her walking out of the house earlier, looking hot as fuck and heading into enemy territory.

Olivia isn't stupid, even if I might make her head spin to the point she wonders if she is.

I've got to believe that she wouldn't put herself in the middle of Harrier territory.

"Oakley," Counter Arse wails as he ups his pace.

I swallow down the growl of frustration that wants to erupt from my throat as I rip the fridge open.

"You can join in too," a hoarse, needy voice calls, and I still.

"No, he fucking can't," Oakley barks. "You're mine tonight."

"Fuck, yeah," she cries.

"Play with your tits for me, baby."

She immediately does as he demands, having zero fucking concern about me standing here, like this is fucking normal. Although to be fair, in this house, it pretty much is.

An angry growl rips around the room, cutting through the cries and moans of Oakley's girl. Theo's is equally as fucking irritating, but at least I can't see them behind the fucking island.

"Just fucking give up, yeah?" Elliot barks, shoving the girl off him and tucking his cock back into his pants.

"B-but, I was getting to the good bit."

I can't help but bark a laugh. I knew he wasn't enjoying a second of slurpy lips.

"It should have all been good," he seethes. "Get out," he demands, pointing toward the front door as he glares at her with nothing but the promise of pain if she refuses.

"I-I-I'll let you fuck my arse."

"Jesus," I mutter in amusement.

"Desperate doesn't look good on you."

"Didn't stop you earlier," I quip.

"Shut the fuck up, Whitfield."

I raise my hands in surrender, although I don't avert my eyes from the drama for a second.

"Just go. And if you intend on ever returning, you might want to up your skills."

Her cries fill the air as she finally makes a run for the door.

"You sound stressed, baby. Come over here and I'll show you how it's really done," Counter Arse purrs.

Elliot meets Oakley's eyes, a silent understanding passing between them.

It guts me, because it's the exact kind of connection that Oak and I used to have. But that's gone now. And I know it's all my own fault.

I shouldn't care. But these boys were always the best part of my life here, and I can't help but miss them at times.

Elliot stalks over as Oak rips the girl's arse cheeks from the counter, placing her on her feet and spinning her around.

"I thought she was yours?" I ask, a little more dejection than I'd like lacing my tone.

I don't want her. And I certainly don't want to share her. But that's not the fucking point.

"Different rules, man," he mutters.

Gripping the back of her neck, he forces her to bend over, filling her from behind as Elliot steps in front of her and shoves his trousers around his hips.

Not willing to stand there and watch as the pair of them

spit-roast her, I walk out of the kitchen, kicking Theo's foot as I pass the island and disappear in the direction of the bathroom.

The slam of the door echoes through the building before the silence of the room beyond engulfs me.

Falling back against the door, I press my hands to my knees and breathe for a few minutes as confusion reigns in my head.

I don't want to be here playing this game with them, ruling the school like we were born to. Yet, at the same time, I do.

I want my best friends back. I need them.

Being here while they cut me out, punish me, and force me to earn their respect and trust back fucking hurts.

"ARGH," I roar, confident that the heavy wooden door at my back and solid brick walls will contain my frustration.

Dragging my phone from my pocket, I open the gallery I've got her photos hidden in and stare down at her. Finally, my cock wakes up, but even more frustration quickly follows.

Where is she right now? And was she actually going on a date? Because if she was going on one with a fucking Huxton kid, then she has to know that we'll be paying him a visit the second we find out.

I take a piss, wash my hands, and waste some time in the hope that they will have all made use of their girls and sent them packing back the time I get back out there.

And thankfully, only a few minutes later, I find that I'm right.

"Ah, here he is. The pussy who'd rather jerk off in the bathroom than party with us."

"Fuck off. If I remember rightly, I wasn't actually invited to participate, just spectate."

I swipe one of the bottles from the coffee table and drop down onto the sofa beside Oak, happily ignoring the one that Theo is laid out on with his hand stuffed in his boxers.

"You already suffering from whatever that ho gave you, Theo?" I ask

"Nah, man. He's clean as a whistle. Just keeping him warm."

At his mention of the word 'clean,' I glance over Oak's shoulder at the kitchen, finding no evidence of any activity on the counter.

"He cleaned it already," Elliot says. "Barely put his cock away before he was scrubbing."

"Fuck you, man. Like you wanted her juices all over your fucking counter."

"Didn't stop you smothering your cock in them."

"I showered," he grunts.

Fuck. How long did I lock myself in the bathroom for?

"Right, well. You figured out what your sister is up to yet?" I ask, hoping it's nonchalant enough that no one will pick up on the seriousness of the question.

Oak pulls his phone out and opens his tracking app while Theo scrolls through options on Netflix before landing on something.

"We're not fucking watching that," Elliot complains, although I don't look up to see what it is. My eyes are locked on Oak's screen.

"It's meant to be hot and full of sex."

"Then put on fucking porn. I'm not watching some sappy romance shit."

"Get that fucking stick out from up your arse and experience something different for once," Theo mocks.

"I should have kicked you out with the girls. And go and put some clothes on, you look like a fucking hobo."

I finally shoot a look over at Theo, and honestly, I can't even argue. His hair is all over the fucking place, he's got bite and scratch marks all over his chest, and— "Is that a hole in your boxers?"

He beams at my question while Elliot bristles.

"Yeah, bro. She was that fucking desperate for my man, D down there. She—"

"She's turned her fucking family tracking app off," Oak spits, anger coating each word.

"Just message her, I'm sure she's fine. She's not a kid anymore," Elliot instructs.

"You don't get it," Oak mutters.

"Just do as he suggested and message her," I encourage, as desperate as he is to know she's okay.

"Fine."

He taps at the screen while Theo offers up other options on the TV, all of which Elliot refuses.

"Fine, you choose something then, our almighty fucking leader," Theo grunts, throwing the remote at Elliot and hitting him right between the eyes.

"You fucking—"

Elliot dives for him as Oak continues tapping away.

"She says she's fine and no one knows who she is."

His words don't settle anything inside me.

Theo's grunt of pain fills the air as the pair of them roll off the sofa and hit the floor with a dull thud.

"Careful, man," Oak says, finally looking up and watching the two of them brawl. "The one-eyed snake might sneak out of his hidey-hole and get you."

"Ugh, get the fuck off me, wankstain," Elliot grunts, using Theo's chest to push himself up. "Go and shower. You smell like cheap perfume and pussy."

"My favourite scent," Theo says with a smirk as he also gets to his feet.

"If she causes us fucking trouble with the Harriers, I'm gonna—"

"Gonna what?" Elliot asks, falling back into his spot while Theo stalks off like a kid who's been sent to his room.

"I dunno, lock her up in Dad's house to keep her out of trouble."

Oh yeah.

Because she's totally safe under that roof...

18

OLIVIA

I'm drunk.

Not white girl wasted, but I've got a good buzz going. Enough that I let Charli persuade me to get up and dance on the makeshift dance floor while people get up and sing about sweet Caroline, living on a prayer, and summer nights.

It's wild, messy, and I haven't had so much fun in a long time. I've almost forgotten all about Reese Whitfield.

Almost.

But apparently, vodka makes a girl horny, because I'm desperately trying to fight the urge to text him and ask him to come and pick me up.

I won't, though.

I won't ever give him that kind of satisfaction.

"Hotties, over by the bar." Charli tips her head in their direction and my eyes collide with a cute blond.

"They look like surfers."

"In Huxton?"

"Maybe they're visiting."

"Maybe we should go and say hi." She grabs my hand and

starts tugging me in their direction, but a wave of nausea rushes through me.

"Liv?"

"Toilet. Now."

"Oh no." She cackles as I spin on my heel and hurry through the crowd. But by the time I reach the bathroom, I feel okay.

"False alarm."

"Maybe you should get some water and think about calling it a night."

"What time— shit, it's that late?"

"Time flies when you're having fun."

"Yeah, I need to call a cab. My dad will shit a brick if I'm out later than one on a school night."

We head to the bar and ask for two bottles of water to go. But the second we step outside of the pub, my good mood vanishes.

A wicked glint ignites in Dale Starling's eyes as he pushes off the picnic bench and rises to greet us. "Well, well. What do we have here."

Charli squeezes my hand, stepping forward slightly. "Don't mind us," she says, full of fire and fight. "We're just leaving."

We try to move around him and his group of friends, but Dale steps in front of me, smirking as he lets his hungry gaze drop down my body.

A violent shudder rolls through me as fear spikes in my blood.

"What's the hurry? Stay. Talk."

"I don't think so. Our taxi is going to be here any second."

The one I haven't ordered yet.

Shit.

"Come on, Liv." Charli tugs on my hand, but Dale snatches my arm, pulling me back toward him.

"Get off me, tosser."

"Feisty, I like it." His friends all explode with laughter as he reaches for a strand of my hair, toying with it. "Question is, do you suck dick as good as you look like you do?"

I press my lips together, refusing to let him bait me.

Guys like Dale—like Reese and my brother and their friends—thrive on power. On lording it over other people to make themselves feel better.

At least, that's one thing they have in common.

His eyes flare with anger. "What? You think you're too good for me or something?"

"Dale, don't be such a dick." Charli lunges for him, but one of his friends catches her by the waist and pulls her out of reach.

"Relax, Devons, I'm only having a little fun. Isn't that right, Olivia." He drawls my name like it's something dirty. "Yeah." His fingers flex around my neck. "We could have all kinds of fun, you and me."

My teeth grind together as I snarl at him.

"Starling, man," someone says quietly. "We're a little exposed out here."

"Yeah, yeah, Jack, keep your hair on. We're almost done here." Leaning in, Dale's lips brush the shell of my ear. "I'll see you soon, beautiful."

He releases me and I jerk back, putting as much space between us as possible.

"If you ever touch me again—"

"You'll what? Run back to your prick of a brother and tell him?"

My lips twist into a grim line.

Because that's the last thing I plan to do.

It would be like throwing gasoline on an already burning fire.

"Come on, Liv." Charli shoves out of Dale's friend's arms and grabs my hand. "Let's leave these arseholes to it."

We take off down the street, my body trembling.

"Are you okay?" she asks me quietly, and I nod, too overwhelmed to reply.

"Maybe we should call Oak—"

"No. He can't know about this," I breathe.

"Yeah, you're right. I can't imagine him and the Heirs letting it slide if they knew Dale had his hands on you." Guilt coats her words. "I swear I didn't know they would be there tonight. It's not usually their scene."

"It's fine. I'm fine."

But as we hurry away from the Spire, I don't know who I'm trying to convince more.

Her?

Or myself.

I wake to a bass drum in my head. Obviously, the pint of water I downed before I went to bed didn't help neutralise all the vodka in my system.

Rolling onto my back, I stare up at the ceiling, replaying the night over in my head. Dale Starling aside, it was fun hanging out with Charli and being a reckless eighteen-year-old.

Life in Saints Cross is different. Especially if you're an Heir's twin sister.

Part of me wondered if Reese and Oakley would be here when I got back last night, waiting up to grill me about my non-existent date. But there was no sign of either of them. So I guess Reese is back in the fold properly, or he found somewhere else to sleep for the night.

I ignore the twinge of jealousy inside me. I'm not an idiot. I don't expect anything from him. He's an Heir. It's practically synonymous with the words 'casual sex'.

Forcing myself out of bed, I throw myself in a tepid shower and try to wash away the stain of last night.

I made Charli promise never to breathe a word of what happened with Dale to anyone. Especially not anyone who might run off and tell Oakley.

I don't relish the thought of keeping yet another secret from my brother, but I also don't want to be responsible for starting a war between All Hallows' and Huxton Academy.

Throwing on my uniform, I drag my hair into a loose plait over my shoulder and head downstairs.

"Morning, sweetheart." Fiona greets me. "Rough night?" A knowing smile tugs at her mouth.

"Things got a little messy."

"Well, so long as you were safe and stayed out of trouble. We were all young once."

If only she knew.

"No Reese this morning?" I keep my voice light.

"He stayed out."

No shit.

"How are things going with him?"

"S-sorry, what?" My heart crashes in my chest as I gawk at her.

"With school, I mean. He'll barely talk to me."

"Oh, oh. Uh, fine, I think."

She lets out a small breath. "I didn't mean for it to happen like this, you know. He's so angry with me. Maybe we went about it all wrong."

"Morning," Dad breezes into the kitchen. "Do I even want to know?" He eyes me across the breakfast island.

"Probably not."

His brow flicks up. "You look like you could use a strong coffee."

"Thanks."

"I can make breakfast—"

"No, thank you," I murmur as my stomach roils at the thought of food. "I don't think I could eat."

"It sure feels empty without Oakley and Reese around,

doesn't it?" Dad slides a coffee across to me. "I remember my first week in the Chapel. It was a crazy time."

"Seriously, Dad. I'm not sure me or Fiona need to hear about your college sexcapades."

"I'll have you know I was an angel."

"Yeah right, tell it to someone who believes you." I chuckle, groaning as my head pounds. "Can I go back to bed?"

"No," he and Fiona say in unison.

"Fine. Maybe I can sleep in class."

"Olivia!"

"Relax, Dad. I wouldn't dream of cutting class."

"That's my girl." He walks over and presses a kiss to my hair. "You're a good girl, Liv. I definitely got lucky with you."

"Thanks, I think."

Although I'm not sure he'd feel the same if he knew what I let Reese do to me in the dark.

Draining my coffee, I check my phone. "I'd better make a move."

Leaving my car at Charli's seemed like a good idea last night, but now I'm regretting it. A mile walk to All Hallows' is the last thing I need, but maybe the fresh air will do me good.

It sure as hell can't make me feel any worse.

But before I make it into the hall, the front door opens and Oakley's voice fills the house.

"Let's go, Liv. Your taxi is here."

"What?" I gawk at Dad and he smiles. "Figured you might need a ride."

"Seriously?" A low groan rumbles in my chest. I appreciate the sentiment, I do. But riding to school with Oakley quizzing me about last night is not what I had in mind.

"You could at least pretend to be grateful." Oak leans over and pinches my arm, keeping one hand on the steering wheel.

"I am, I'm just hungover."

"Do we need to talk about the fact that you and Charli were out, alone, getting drunk?"

"Do we need to talk about the fact that you're my brother, not my dad?"

"Jesus, you're a bitch when you're suffering."

"I feel like something crawled in my stomach and died."

"Where did you say you were again?"

"Just some pub in Huxton." I shrug, pressing my forehead against the tinted glass.

"Why are you being weird?"

"I'm not being weird."

"Yes, you are. There are only four pubs in Huxton, so which one were you at?"

"Why do you care?" I pin him with a hard look.

"Because you're my sister. Because Huxton is Harrier territory. Because I don't like the idea of some townie prick putting his hands on you."

"You do know I'm a person, right? Not a doll you can keep locked up in a glass cabinet."

"Come on, Liv. I'm only looking out for you. You're too good for anyone from Huxton."

"You can be a real dickhead sometimes," I hiss. "If you must know, I went out with Charli to escape this place."

"What the fuck is that supposed to mean?"

"Forget it. Forget I said anything."

"No, Liv. What does that mean? Escape this place? Why the fuck would you need to escape?" He grabs my wrist and my eyes snap to his.

"If you have to ask, Oak, then you really are a dumb shit."

"What, I... are you on your period or something? Because you're acting fucking crazy."

"And you're acting like a territorial, over-the-top arsehole."

Tension ripples through the car, and Oak's hand tightens on the steering wheel.

"Fucking girls," he mutters, and a bolt of anger goes through me.

But I don't try to fill the silence.

I have nothing to say to him right now.

Nothing he'll want to hear, anyway.

19

REESE

I wake with a bitch of a sore neck and a thumping in my brain that can only be blamed on the empty bottles and shot glasses that littered around me when I finally crack my eyes open.

I should probably feel pleased that the Heirs allowed me to crash on the sofa after they fucked me up in one of our old drinking games, one of which I knew they'd rigged the second Theo started dealing the pack of cards.

I knew it was going to be painful. I knew I was going to regret it. But I also knew that I couldn't exactly refuse when my number one mission right now is reclaiming my place.

Twisting onto my side, my stomach rolls as the room around me begins to spin again.

The Chapel is in silence, but with the sun streaming in through the small windows that line the wall opposite me, I know it's time we should all probably be moving our arses.

I've still failed to force myself to move when a dull thud from upstairs sounds out, followed by a series of doors closing.

I look up at the exact moment they all appear on the balcony that runs around the upper floor and groan when I find them dressed, ready for school and looking as if last night never happened.

Of fucking course. There was probably water in their vodka bottles last night.

"Oh, Whitfield," Oak taunts, leaning over the railings to study me. "You've looked better."

"Fuck off," I grunt, finally managing to find the strength to roll to a sitting position.

"Just be glad we took pity on you and didn't shove you out on your arse. Just think what kind of position you could be in right now," Elliot points out.

"Yeah, yeah. I need to go home and—"

Clothes rain down on me from above. "Just go and get ready," Elliot demands.

Gathering everything up, I push to my feet and stumble in the direction of the bathroom. By the time I get there, the boys hit the bottom of the steps, their eyes all assessing me closely.

Fuck knows what they're looking for, and I have even less clue if they find something they like or not, because their expressions are blank.

Well, that's not entirely true, because concern lingers in Oak's eyes.

"I've got to go to the house to get Olivia. Apparently, last night wasn't quite as uneventful as she led me to believe."

"Of course it wasn't," I mutter. "What did she do?" I ask, hoping that I come across as nosey instead of my concern levels matching his.

"Came home wasted without her car."

"They'll have had that thing up on bricks before she even got out of Huxton," Theo states, walking away from us in favour of the kitchen.

"I'm gonna fucking kill her for that stunt," Oak promises, shoving his hand angrily through his perfectly styled hair and instantly messing it up.

He blows through the Chapel like a storm, only pausing in

the kitchen for a moment before he leaves the echo of the front door in his wake.

"Should we warn her?" Theo shouts, although he sounds much more amused than concerned.

"Nah, she has to know it's coming. Maybe it'll make her think twice before she heads into Harrier territory again."

With one more assessing, irritated look, Elliot turns away from me, dismissing me as if I'm not even here.

"Breakfast will be in fifteen minutes. You will be at the table."

I roll my eyes at his demands as I continue toward the bathroom, more than ready to wash the scent of last night that's still clinging to me down the drain.

By the time I re-emerge, Elliot and Theo are at the table with breakfast sitting before them. And there's a third plate and an empty seat.

I remember watching Scott and his boys sitting there like fucking kings of the world every morning, with their fancy-arse breakfasts made by the cook Mr. Eaton pays to feed the Heirs and keep his mouth shut about what goes on in the Chapel.

The scent of bacon hits my nose and my stomach grumbles, my hangover vanishing into nothing as my hunger takes over.

"I told you not to be late."

"Keep your frilly fucking knickers on, Eaton."

My eyes feast on their plates as I move closer, but everything soon crashes down around me when I realise mine is different.

I don't have salty bacon, sweet pancakes and the freshest fruit All Hallows' can get their eyes on.

I have granola.

Dry.

And some gross, green-looking smoothie thing which I don't even want to know the contents of.

Motherfuckers.

"What's wrong?" Elliot drawls. "Not hungry?"

"I hope this power trip helps you sleep at night, knob."

"I sleep perfectly fine. Thank you for your concern, Whitfield."

"He's lying," Theo offers. "He doesn't sleep a wink, because he refuses to take that crown off his head long enough to rest."

I snort a laugh as I can't help but agree with his assessment.

"You want the rabbit food too, Ashworth?"

Theo stares at him, a silent threat rippling through the air.

I force my less-than-desirable breakfast down, knowing that it won't be worth Elliot's wrath not to do so. A couple of days ago, I'd have thrown it over his head. But things are different now. I'm playing the long game.

That means swallowing down his bullshit and playing his games.

Surprisingly, my stomach had settled a little by the time we headed out, and I hated Elliot for that almost as much as I was grateful.

I follow Theo into our class before lunch, my head now clearer and my stomach growling for more food as we make our way to our seats at the back.

The second my arse hits the chair, something forces me to look up, and fuck am I glad I do, because I find Olivia walking in with her head down, hiding behind her hair.

"Feeling rough, Beckworth?" I bark, ensuring that every set of eyes in the room turns her way.

Her eyes instantly find mine. They're dark with exhaustion and her lingering hangover. Apparently, she didn't get a shot of that gross green shit to sort her out this morning and is burning with hate.

'Fuck you,' she mouths, moving deeper into the room.

Miss Fletcher notices her hesitating. "Just go and sit next to Mr. Whitfield, Olivia. You're making the place look untidy."

She sucks in a sharp breath, her lips pursing with frustration.

But when she looks around at the room for another option, she quickly comes up short, because while she paused, everyone else filed in behind her and every seat has been taken.

"Come on, Olive. I won't bite... hard."

Theo chuckles at the rabbit-caught-in-headlights look on Olivia's face.

"Looks like your new stepsister is a real fan of yours, Whitfield."

"I'm sure I can warm her up."

"Don't let Oak hear you say that."

My lips part to respond, but I forget whatever my comeback was going to be when Olivia finally moves and drops down beside me.

Her sweet scent fills my nose, making desire burn through me in an instant.

Leaning over, I breathe her in before whispering in her ear. "You were a bad, bad girl last night, Olive."

She stiffens, locking down her real reaction to my closeness and the way my breath tickles over her skin.

"And I think you need to be punished."

Her entire posture changes at those words, her chest moving more dramatically as her heart rate picks up.

"You'd like that, wouldn't you?" I ask as Miss Fletcher starts introducing whatever the fuck we're meant to be doing for the next hour.

"Fuck off, Reese."

She schools her features and reaches down to grab her books and pencil case from her bag.

With the rest of the class, and even Theo distracted thanks

to the fact that Miss Fletcher is on his end of sixth form bucket list, I reach between us and drag Olive's chair closer to me.

"What are you doing?" she hisses as our thighs touch.

"Keeping you safe, Olive. We have no idea when you might go running off into enemy territory again."

"I can assure you that it won't be in the middle of class."

"Can't take that chance, sweet cheeks. Oak would never forgive me if I let anything happen to you." I regret the words instantly, and when Olivia's eyes flare with excitement, I know she didn't miss it either.

"He's already never going to forgive you. And the second I tell him what you're doing to me, he will probably kill you."

"Can't say I've got all that much to live for right now, little Olive. So I think I'll take my chances."

"I think your future wife might have something to say about that," she mutters, and I take a sharp breath as her words hit exactly as she intended.

"You don't need to worry about her, Olive. But I must say, jealousy looks good on you."

She bristles but doesn't respond. Probably for the best, because I'm not sure she could say anything that could convince me that my words weren't true.

Olivia might hate me, might wish me all the pain in the world from what I did to both her and Oak this summer. But beneath that, she wants me. Her head is yet to catch up with her body on that.

It'll happen, though.

And when it finally does, I'll get every single thing I need to right the wrongs, to hurt those who hurt me, and to finally break free of the shackles holding me to the goddamn town I no longer want to be in.

Once again, I'm the last to the Chapel for the lunch Elliot demanded I attend.

They all turn to look at me from the dining table, and I internally groan as I wonder what delights they've got to eat and what mine will be in comparison.

The scent of cheese hits my nose, but I don't allow myself to believe it might be coming from my plate.

"What time do you call this?" Elliot barks.

"Lunchtime," I grunt.

Truth is, I ran into a couple of year twelve boys who were about to go at it in the middle of the hallway over some slut they apparently both banged over the summer. Safe to say that the black eyes they're both sporting aren't courtesy of each other.

I clench my fists as I move toward them, something Oak doesn't miss. "Oh wow, this looks nice," I praise, ignoring the steaming bowls of pasta they all have and focusing on my dull-as-fuck cheese sandwich with shitty white sliced bread.

"Even asked chef for the special cheese."

"Great. My favourite," I lie. This is going to be like eating fucking rubber.

Once again, I swallow down my need to argue and suck it up. It won't be forever. They'll forgive me eventually, and then I'll be one step closer to shattering their perfect little worlds.

My lunch is dry as fuck, and the lukewarm water Elliot also ensured I had wasn't exactly a great help.

We're almost done when Oak's phone vibrates on the table.

Dropping his cutlery, he reaches for it. A deep frown forms on his brow as he stares at the screen.

"What is it?" Elliot asks.

"Motherfucker," Oak booms, shoving his chair back with such force it topples to the floor with a loud bang.

"Wha—" Elliot snatches his phone, pressing play on the video that's filling his screen. My blood turns to ice as I stare down at Dale Starling leaning into Olive as if he's about to fucking kiss her.

"I'm going to fucking kill him. But only after I've killed her."

"I'm assuming she lied to you about this?" I ask, trying and mostly failing to keep the smug lilt from my tone.

Thankfully, Oak is too angry to recognise it as he takes his phone back and storms toward the door, ready to go and have it out with his sister.

"Oak, wait. We'll—" But it's too late. He's gone.

The three of us look at each other, a silent agreement passing between each of us as we rise from our seats.

I'm sure there's a slim chance of it happening, because Oakley and Olivia have the freaky twin connection and all that, but we really need to find her before he does, for her own good.

And possibly mine, if I'm able to pull some magic out of my arse in the next few minutes.

20

OLIVIA

I'm minding my own business, eating lunch in the refectory when Reese appears, his dark gaze searching the room for—

Me.

Crap.

He zeroes in on me and I instantly know something is wrong.

Hardly in the right state of mind to deal with his games today, I grab my lunch tray and take off in the other direction, hoping to slip out of the door leading to the outside courtyard.

But as I weave through the tables, someone says, "Olivia, hi."

I whirl around and find Abigail standing there. She smiles and adds, "Want to join—"

"I can't right now, sorry." I glance back to find Reese fighting his way through the lunchtime crush, his expression as dark and stormy.

Abigail glances over to where I'm looking and frowns. "Is he coming—"

"Sorry," I rush out. "I really need to go."

Shouldering the glass door, I spill outside and dart around

the side of the building, hoping to lose him. But Reese is annoyingly quick, and as I reach the end of the building, his voice ripples through the air.

"We need to talk."

"No thanks," I call over my shoulder.

"Olivia, I swear to fucking God. Would you just slow the fuck down?"

"Go away, Reese." He grabs my bag and yanks hard enough for me to stop. I whirl around and scowl. "I am not doing this—"

"What happened last night?"

"W-what?" The ground goes from under me. "I don't know what you're talking about."

"Starling sent Oak a video. We know you were with him."

Crap.

Double crap.

I fight to compose my panic, lifting my chin in defiance. "With him... you think... wow. Just when I think you can't get any lower, Whitfield. Not that I need to justify anything to you, but you can call off your bloodhounds. I was with Charli at the Spire. Dale Starling turned up out of nowhere and recognised me."

"So you didn't kiss him?"

Kiss him? What the actual fuck?

"Excuse me?" I hiss.

Reese crowds me against the wall, caging me in with his hand beside my head. "You heard me, sweet cheeks. Did. You. Kiss. Him?"

Oh, this is pure gold.

Reese Whitfield, the guy who claims not to care, is pissed because I might have kissed another guy.

"Maybe," I sass, giving him a little half-shrug.

"Olivia..."

"Reese..." My lips curve with amusement. "If I didn't know, I'd say you were jealous."

"Fuck off, I'm not—"

"Keep telling yourself that. Now, if we're done here..." I go to move around him, but he shoves me back against the wall, pressing the entire length of his body into me.

"What happened, Olivia? You're not walking away from me until you tell me." Something akin to fear flashes in his eyes, but surely, I must be mistaken.

Reese doesn't care about me. He cares about taunting me, about the push and pull that exists between us.

"Noth—" His fingers dig into my hip, and I narrow my eyes. "Fine. He recognised me and tried to spook me, happy?"

"Did he touch you?" he seethes, his body vibrating with anger.

"Drop the caveman act, Reese. I'm fine."

"Why didn't you tell Oakley this morning?"

"Because I'm not some damsel in distress. I can handle the likes of Dale Starling."

"Oak is pissed."

"Oak can go fuck himself." Irritation coats my words. "He's not my keeper."

"Oh, that's it, is it? Acting out to upset big brother?"

"Twin. *Twin* brother. And like I said, I didn't know Dale was going to be there."

"You went into Harrier territory—"

"Oh my God," I shriek. "Listen to yourself."

"If he touched you—"

"What? You'll what?" I seethe, getting all up in his face, anger saturating my veins.

I should have known that Dale Starling wouldn't leave it there. That it was all part of some plan to bait the Heirs. But I didn't know he'd recorded it, that he'd send it to Oak.

"You can't let Oak do anything stupid, Reese."

"I'm not Oak's keeper," he smirks, throwing my words back at me, and I want to wipe it off his stupidly gorgeous face.

Voices pierce the air and Reese bolts away from me, dragging a hand through his hair.

"Found her," he says, right as Oak, Theo and Elliot round the corner. "Was just about to text you."

"Prick," I hiss under my breath.

"What the fuck, Liv?" Oakley says. "You were with that bellend Starling?"

"Oh my God, I wasn't with him. He turned up at the pub we were at."

"Looked like you were getting pretty close, if you ask me," Reese adds.

"No one is asking you," I snap.

Is he for real?

I cut him with a deadly glance, but he only smirks again.

"Why didn't you tell me?" Oakley's brows pinched. "You should have called me."

"Like you would have been in any state to come and get me."

"Liv—"

"No, Oak. You've got to stop doing this. We're not kids anymore. I don't need you all up in my business, acting like I need your permission to live my life. It was a few drinks at the pub with Charli. Dale Starling is all bark and no bite. Clearly, he only wanted some leverage over you. Which, by the way, is exactly why I didn't tell you. Nothing happened. I'm fine. Everything is fine."

My chest heaves as I stare at my brother.

"Are you done?" he asks quietly.

"Are you going to go after him?" His jaw tics and I shake my head. "Oak, nothing happened. He isn't worth it. He's trying to bait you."

"Fine. We won't go after him this time."

"You won't?" My eyes narrow.

"No. But stay away from Huxton, Liv. I mean it. Or next time, he's a dead man."

"So dramatic." I roll my eyes as I barge past my brother and Elliot and take off down the path.

But his voice gives me pause.

"Party at the Chapel tonight. I expect you to be there."

Overbearing arsehole.

I glance over my shoulder and shoot them all a saccharine smile, and reply, "We'll see."

After I spend the rest of the afternoon avoiding Reese, Oak and the Heirs, I head straight home and lock myself in my bedroom.

Who the hell do they think they are?

Annoying, infuriating, entitled pricks, that's who.

God, I'm so angry at Oak.

At Reese.

Especially Reese.

My phone buzzes, and I read Charli's latest text.

> Charli: We should totally gatecrash their party tonight.

> Olivia: Have you lost your goddamn mind? I don't want to be anywhere near them.

I'd called her on the way home to vent. Of course, Charli thinks I should play them at their own game. It's totally her style. But I don't want to give Reese any more ammunition.

> Charli: Come on, it will be fun. You can ignore them, flirt with some guys, show them you won't take their overbearing Heirs-rule-the-world bullshit.

> Olivia: I don't think it's a good idea.

I don't want to go. I don't want to be anywhere near that

place or the debauchery that happens inside the Chapel's brick walls.

But do I want to spend my last year at college hiding from them?

From him?

> Charli: We're going. Be ready for eight. I'll pick you up on the way.

My lips twist. She's so bloody persistent, but maybe I need that sometimes. Maybe I need someone to push me. I roll onto my back and lift my legs in the air, stretching them.

> Olivia: I'll think about it.

> Charli: See you later… and Olivia?

> Olivia: Yeah?

> Charli: It's okay to live on the wild side occasionally.

If only she knew.

21

REESE

"Keep fucking moving," Elliot growls at the bound and blindfolded guys we're shoving deeper and deeper into the woods.

The sun is beginning to set through the trees. By the time we get to the starting point of this game and give them their instructions, it'll have sunk beneath the horizon, plunging us into darkness.

There's a loud cry as someone stumbles before a body crashes to the ground.

"Get the fuck up, Middleton," Theo barks. "Or do you just like being in a pathetic heap on the ground? It seems to be your favourite fucking position. If you wanna make the most of it, you could always open your mouth and—"

"Enough," Elliot grumbles.

Oak leans down and pulls Middleton up by the back of his shirt and places him on his feet.

Silence falls around us again as we continue directing the new rugby team recruits through the woodland.

The four us stand in line as one unit together. It's as it always should have been, and for that moment, I wonder why I ever wanted to leave this behind.

All my life, my boys have been everything to me.

Glancing over, I meet Oak's eyes. Anger and the need for retaliation still burns through him from that video from Dale earlier.

I get it. Hell, I more than fucking get it.

Fury and jealousy collided so fucking hard within me, both as I watched it play out on his screen and then when I found Olivia and she dared to taunt me over it, allowing me to think that she might have kissed the motherfucker.

She wouldn't. Deep down, I knew that. She would never betray Oak like that.

But still, the thought of her wanting that cunt's attention didn't fucking sit right with me in any fucking way.

My lips twitch at the corners, the promise of pain and retribution for that swipe he took at them more than evident in my own dark eyes.

Oak nods as if he can read it within me before I look beyond him to Elliot and Theo.

Elliot is as focused and stoic as ever, but I know deep down he's as excited about this as the rest of us, while Theo has a wide-arse smile on his face like this is the best day of his life.

Fond memories of us completing this task along with the rest of our year thirteen teammates fill my mind. It was hell. It was hammering down with rain, the woods were slick with mud, and by the time we made it back to the Chapel to claim our win, we were covered from head to toe. The only benefit of that was that no one could really tell we were butt naked.

We have to pick up a few more fallen soldiers before we make it to the clearing where this challenge starts.

We bring them all to a stop in a beam of orange light that filters through the leaves, and they all seem to breathe a sigh of relief.

Fuck knows why, though. They already know what's coming next, and they know it's going to get a hell of a lot worse. This challenge gets talked about by every student at All Hallows' from the day they start.

"You boys think you've got what it takes to be an All Hallows' Saint?" Elliot asks, his voice deep and haunting.

A less-than-impressive yes comes from our blindfolded victims.

"You're going to need a little more enthusiasm and determination if you're going to survive the next hour of your lives, knobheads," Theo happily announces, crossing his thick arms in front of his chest to look even more terrifying—not that they can see him.

"This is your first initiation task, boys. You pass this, you may continue training with us. You fail, and you can head on over to the dance studio and don a tutu instead. Is that understood?'

A roar of agreement sounds out, their adrenaline picking up at last.

"When your wrists are freed, you can go ahead and strip. We want all your clothes thrown in front of you. Blindfolds will remain on until we tell you to remove them.

Theo, Oak, and I pull our flick knives from our pockets and walk around behind the guys, cutting through their bindings one by one.

As each one is released, they immediately follow orders, shedding their clothes and throwing them into the mud.

Anticipation ripples through the air as the three of us keep going.

"Ow," my guy complains, flinching as I accidentally catch his wrist with my knife.

"Don't be a pussy, Ainsworth," I hiss. "A little scratch from me will be the least of your worries by the time the end of this night rolls around."

"You already know the rules. But for the sake of tradition, I'm going to lay them out for you again, just in case anyone has suffered a blow to the head recently and forgotten anything.

"We will release you from here, and you must follow the marked route back to the Chapel. There will be no shortcuts, no cheating, or trying to find an easy way out. We have eyes in every inch of these woods, and we will know long before you get back if you've fucked this challenge up.

"We will be waiting for you at the other end, and if you're really lucky, we might have vodka and clothes for you. If you're not, it might be a hose and ice-cold water."

Fists clench in anticipation, and others move from foot to foot as the chill of the early autumn air breezes past their balls.

"After three, you may remove your blindfold. You turn around and you take off. Just remember, you need to take this seriously. Because none of you want to be the last one back."

Elliot falls silent, and we stand and watch them like hawks waiting to dive for that poor, innocent little mouse.

Then, throwing them off guard, Elliot shouts, "ONE."

The three of us laugh as they trip over their own feet to get a head start, more than a couple of them slipping in the mud we ensured was waiting for them on the start line despite the dry days we've had recently.

"Ah fuck, this is going to be epic."

A loud wail rips through the trees only a minute later, making our laughter grow.

"Looks like they've found our first trap."

We weren't lying. We have the rest of the team dotted through the woods wielding paintball guns, water bombs and rotting food. As much as I'm looking forward to watching them all stagger back to the Chapel, there's a big part of me that wishes I was hunting them through the trees.

"Let's go and get the party started, boys. We've got some retaliation to deliver."

Turning in the opposite direction to where our victims ran off, we take the short trip back to the Chapel.

The party has already started inside. The music booms

and the girls immediately turn our way, their eyes lightening up as their kings return home.

"Tonight is going to be epic," I announce as someone pushes a glass of neat vodka into my hand.

"You know the plan, yeah?" Elliot asks me as we form a circle, cutting everyone vying for our attention off.

"Yeah. I'm good for it," I agree.

"I still don't understand why it can't be me," Oakley complains.

"You need to be here. If Olivia notices your absence, we're fucked," Elliot says for what must be at least the tenth time since we came up with this plan. "As soon as those motherfuckers get back and distract everyone, you do what you need to do."

I nod, more than ready to head to Huxton to pay Dale fucking Starling a little visit—although thoughts of how I'm going to get my alibi make my blood run a little cold. But needs must, and there is no fucking way I'm letting that cocksucker get away with being anywhere near Olivia.

"Just fuck it up a bit, yeah? Don't go over the top."

"Yeah, yeah. I'm not a complete moron."

They all look at me with raised brows, which makes fire lick at my insides.

"I can fucking handle this. Trust me, yeah?"

They all nod, and in only seconds, our little huddle has fallen apart as the girls get impatient and get their hands on us.

"Hey, Reese," Darcie purrs at me, her hands running up my chest.

Her touch feels like tiny daggers slicing my skin wide open, but I don't stop her. Not tonight. I need her.

A smirk curls at my lips as I stare down at her.

"You look like you've had a long day, Darce. We should get you a nice strong drink."

I swear to God, her eyes turn into little hearts like a

fucking cartoon character the second I respond to her shameless flirting.

"I'm more fun when I'm drunk," she confesses, one of her hands descending south.

I catch her wrist before she makes it past my waistband. I need her to think I'm interested, and one brush of my cock is going to show her just how little affected I am by her body. Even if her tits are pushed up under her chin and her skirt is so short that I'm sure it will show the world the overused goods should she bend over.

Twisting her around, I place my hand on her lower back and push her toward the bar.

With more than a few shots warming my stomach, I scan the crowd, looking for Olivia. Oakley made her promise that she'd be here earlier. And although he's convinced she'll come, I can't say I'm feeling quite so confident.

She's made it more than clear that she hates this place and everything that happens inside. Hell, a part of me doesn't want her here either, watching as the girls paw at us, at her brother, like they own us.

But also, if she's here, then we know she's safe. We know she's not running off into enemy territory again and getting herself into trouble.

With Darcie's hand reluctantly locked in mine, I less-than-gently drag her toward the sofas where Elliot, Oak, and Theo are sitting surrounded by girls.

"You want some?" Oak asks, holding a little baggie in front of him. His eyes are blown, making it more than obvious that he's already started his night.

"Nah, man. I need to be sober for what I have planned." I run my eyes over Darcie, trying as hard as I can to look at least a little bit interested in what she has to offer.

Unsurprisingly, she buys my crap and throws her leg over my waist, letting her dress ride up enough to gift me with the unfortunate sight of her bare cunt beneath.

"I think you forgot something tonight, Darce," I growl in her ear, still feeling absolutely no desire for her even when her bare pussy is grinding down on me.

"It's a gift." Is it fuck. "This way, you can have me whenever and wherever you want me."

"Wow, how generous of you."

Thankfully, she's already drunk enough not to hear the sarcasm in my tone. Oakley doesn't miss it though, and throws his head back as if I'm the funniest fucker on the planet.

The girls on either side of him take advantage of the situation and begin kissing up each side of his neck.

"Hell, yes. Tonight is going to be epic," he bellows, earning a round of cheers from the rest of the room.

"Any news yet?" I ask Elliot.

He shakes his head. "Another ten minutes, by the looks of it," he says, glancing down at his phone.

Darcie leans forward, her lips brushing my ear.

"Just enough time for what I want to do."

Her fingers find my waistband and I move on instinct, forgetting about what I'm meant to be doing tonight. She lands in a heap on the floor, her dress lifting so that she's flashing everyone who might be looking.

"Whoops, sorry, Darce. Let's go and get you another drink, yeah?" I offer, hoping it's enough to pacify her and make her forget why she's got a bruise on her arse in the morning.

22

OLIVIA

"I can't believe I let you talk me into this," I groan at Charli as we walk into the Chapel. Music pumps out of hidden speakers, reverberating through me.

"We could always go hang out with Dale and—"

"Bitch," I hiss.

"But you love me." She flashes me a blinding smile. "This place is the tits."

"It's disgusting."

"Someone sounds a little jealous."

"Jealous? Of this... it's practically a rich boy's brothel." Tipping my head over to where one of Oakley's teammates has his hand shoved up a first year's skirt as she writhes against him, I add, "Case in point."

Charli makes a beeline for the bar and orders herself a drink. Because of course there's a bar with a bartender.

I really, really hate this place.

Everything it stands for, the traditions and values it upholds. But when my eyes land on Oakley and I see him holding court with a small group of girls, mischief twinkling in his eyes as he laughs, my expression softens a little.

He's waited his entire life for this, and he looks so happy.

Of course, I'm sure all the attention and sex offered up on a platter is a huge part of the draw, but I also know my brother and I know how important it is for him to continue the family legacy. He wants to walk in our father's footsteps and become a lawyer.

"This was a bad idea," I hiss as I join Charli at the bar as she shamelessly flirts with the bartender. He is kind of cute, although I wonder what he must think of all this.

"What do you want?" she asks me, but I decline.

No way I'm letting my guard down here.

We move to one of the leather sofas and sit, watching the chaos unfold around us.

"Look at them all," she says. "Heir chasers en masse. I mean, part of me gets it. They're good-looking lads. But a dick is dick. So long as a guy knows how to use it—"

"Oh my God, Charli. I do not want to be thinking about my brother's dick."

"Yeah, but if you had to choose one, who would it be? I think I'd go for Elliot."

"Elliot?" I balk.

"Yeah. It's always the brooding, silent types that are the kinkiest in the bedroom."

"That's... wow."

"Oh, come on, like you haven't thought about what he's hiding under all that ice and arrogance?"

"He's like a brother to me, Charl. They all are."

"Yeah, I guess that's a bit of a fantasy—"

A loud cheer goes up around us as three guys stagger into the room, butt-naked and covered in mud, paint, and... what is that?

"What the fuck is that smell?" Charli dry heaves as we watch more of them pour into the room.

Elliot climbs onto the ornate coffee table and lifts his glass in the air. "Looks like we have our winners. Get yourself a drink ladies, and then go get a fucking shower. You reek."

"Where are the rest of you?" Theo asks, smirking as he watches the first-year players squirm on the spot, trying to cover their junk.

"Initiation," Charli breathes, and I nod, fighting the urge to roll my eyes.

"A couple of lads got hurt, we left them."

"You left them?" Elliot snarls, his eyes darkening. "Is that how you treat your teammates, Middleton?"

"W-what? I thought... you said it was the first one to make it back—"

"But I didn't say anything about leaving anyone behind. We're motherfucking Saints. If one of us falls, you'd best believe the rest of us will be there to pick him back up."

"Fuck," the guy hisses. "It's a fucking death trap out there. You're not seriously—"

Elliot jumps down off the table and prowls toward him. A ripple goes through the air, the room bathed in silence as everyone waits to see what Elliot will do.

"You want to play on my team? You want to be a Saint?" The guy nods, fear glittering in his eyes. Elliot's lip curls up disgust. "So the get the fuck back out there and go get your teammates."

"Jesus, he's scary," Charli whispers.

"Y-yeah, okay." The guys backtrack out of the room, and Elliot mutters, "Fucking pussies."

Laughter bounces around the room as someone turns the music back up and the party goes on like it's business as usual.

And I guess where the Heirs are concerned, it is.

"Oak seems to be enjoying himself." Charli says as we watch a girl grind down on his lap.

As if he hears us, he glances in our direction and his smile grows when he notices me.

Excusing himself, he rushes over to me and drops down beside me. "You came."

"You can thank Charli. She coerced me." Oak grins at me, his pupils blown. "Are you on something?" My brows pinch.

"Just a little pick-me-up." He winks.

"Oak," I hiss.

"Don't worry, Liv. It's good shit. I feel in-fucking-credible."

"Jesus, Oak." My brows furrow and he pouts.

"Nooo, don't go all fun police on me. It's a party, we're celebrating."

"Olive." Reese appears, looming over us. "Didn't expect to see you here."

"Reese, always a pleasure."

Oak groans. "Can the two of you at least try to get along? You used to be friends."

"That was a long time ago," Reese spits, sending a violent shudder through me.

"Okay, this was fun and all, but we didn't come to watch you and the slut squad in action, so we'll be around." Far, far away from them.

I stand, grabbing Charli's hand and tugging her away from them.

"Stay out of trouble tonight, Sis," Oak calls, and I flip him off over my shoulder.

His deep rumble of laughter follows me, but it's the heat from Reese's heavy stare that penetrates some of the ice around my heart. When we reach the big ornate doors leading out of the room, I risk peeking back, and sure enough, Reese is watching me.

A devious glint in his eye.

A silent message that looks a lot like: I'll be watching.

"You know I'm surprised Oak didn't go after Dale," Charli says as we sit outside, the party still raging on inside. We've managed to avoid Oakley and Reese and the other Heirs.

"I made him promise."

"Yeah, but come on, Liv. It's Oak and the Heirs. They're not exactly known for playing nice."

"You think they'll go after him." My heart sinks.

"I think Dale knew you were the perfect bait..."

"Ugh. Sometimes, I really bloody hate this place."

"Come on, let's go." She stands, brushing her hands down her cut-out jean shorts. "I need to pee, then you can give me a ride home."

Thank God.

I am so over tonight.

But the second we go back inside the Chapel, my stomach drops.

"Oh my God, is that Darcie Porter?" Charli points to where Darcie is draped over Reese like a cheap throw.

"Yeah." My teeth grind as I take in her outfit, or lack thereof.

"She looks like the entertainment."

"She likes the attention." I shrug, hardly surprised when she runs her perfectly manicured nails up his chest, nipping his jaw.

God, I hate her.

I hate that he's touched her. Kissed her.

I hate that he hooks his arm around her waist and draws her near, flicking his dark gaze to mine. Taunting me. Daring me to do something about it.

But I won't.

I won't play his games—not anymore.

"You okay?" Charli asks and I nod, my teeth grinding together behind my lips. "We could stay?" she asks. "Play him at his own game?"

"W-what?" My eyes snap to hers and she smirks.

"You're not fooling anyone."

"I don't know what you're talking about."

Charli rolls her eyes. "Of course you don't. Come on. One dance for the road." She stands and offers me her hand.

"I'm not sure this is a good idea," I protest.

"Sure it is. Sometimes you have to fight fire with fire. Give him a taste of his own medicine, Liv. What's the worst that could happen?"

The second she says the words, my stomach twists. Because where Reese is concerned, I'm not sure.

We make our way to the middle of the room and Charli starts swaying her hips, rolling her lithe body to the beat. "Come on, dance like no one is watching."

But they are watching.

He's watching.

Charli grabs my hands and weaves them in the air between us, her head thrown back with a smile. She looks sexy, so carefree... I envy her. Because I'm strung tighter than a bowstring.

Reese hasn't taken his eyes off me. But he hasn't taken his hands off her either. He lifts her slightly, dropping her on his lap so she's fully straddling him as his fingers tuck underneath her halter top and graze the sides of her boobs.

"Holy shit, he hasn't stopped looking at you," Charli whispers. I can't look at her.

I can't tear my eyes off Reese as he drops his mouth to the crook of Darcie's shoulder and kisses her there. She grinds down on him, lopping her arm around his neck to leverage herself.

A hollow pit gnaws inside me as he keeps his eyes on me and his lips on her.

"Maybe we should go," Charli says, stepping in front of me and breaking the tense connection between me and Reese.

"No," I snap. "I want to dance."

Glancing around, my eyes land on a cute guy I recognise from my history class. His eyes widen as I crook my finger at him. With a small nod, I flash him what I hope is a seductive smile. He drains his beer and makes his way over.

"You're Oakley's sister, right?"

Not Olivia... Oakley's sister.

Irritation skitters through me, but I force it down. "Dance with me," I breathe.

"Uh, I'm not sure. Your brother—"

"Dance with me." I loop my arms around his shoulder and press my body up close to his.

"Y-yeah, okay." He audibly swallows but curves his hands around my waist and starts moving to the beat.

I tug him closer, moving us around in a half circle so I'm facing Reese. So he can see my eyes as I rub my body against the poor, unsuspecting guy.

Reese's eyes flare with anger, his grip on Darcie's waist tightening. If she notices, she doesn't let on, too busy trailing her tongue up his neck.

It's a dangerous game I'm playing. Especially here, in my brother's territory, but Reese Whitfield is under my skin. More than I care to admit.

The guy's hands glide down to my arse, and for a second, I think Reese is going to march over here and put an end to my little display. But he doesn't. He lifts Darcie off his lap, grabs her hand and starts pulling her toward the double vaulted doors.

The doors I know that lead to the staircase. The staircase I know leads down to their basement.

He doesn't look back. He doesn't challenge me to stop him. To intervene.

And it occurs to me...

Maybe he doesn't want me to.

23

REESE

Bile stirs in my belly, quickly burning up my throat as I lead Darcie down to the basement.

This isn't my first time down here, far from it.

But it is hers.

And from the way her eyes are glittering with excitement, I'd say she's been looking forward to a visit for longer than we've given her credit for.

The heavy doors slam closed behind us, rattling through me and making me question this part of our plan.

Elliot was adamant that Darcie was our girl.

He's probably right. He usually is. And I can't deny that this little part of our revenge plan sure fits right into mine with Olivia.

The jealousy that darkened her eyes as she watched Darcie grinding down on me on the sofa makes a smirk curl at my lips.

She can pretend that I don't affect her as much as she likes.

We both know that she's a filthy liar.

She can try and make me jealous with any motherfucker in this place, but we know that there is only one person she's imagining between her thighs, only one cock thrusting inside her until she forgets her own name.

Images of what that might look like fill my head and my cock swells. Although, it sinks faster than I thought possible when Darcie turns into me and looks up with her hungry, dilated eyes.

She's taken something. Probably the shit that Oak is riding high on.

I have to hope it makes her more compliant, and if I'm really lucky, lowers her libido. Although, that seems pretty unlikely from what I've been forced to endure so far tonight.

"This place is even better than I imagined," she purrs, running her hands up my chest as we step down the final few stone stairs.

A shiver rips down my spine from the temperature change, but she doesn't seem to notice, despite the fact that she's basically wearing nothing.

The hallway down here is practically untouched, and it looks much like it did back in the day when it was actually a functioning chapel. The rooms behind the next set of doors are an entirely different matter, and I can't deny that I want to see that kinky shit the guys have filled the place with.

The clang of the lock echoes around the empty space as I slide the key that Elliot gave me purely for this task past the old metal.

Darcie squeals in excitement and darts forward the second I push the door wide.

"Oh my God, Reese. This place is insane."

I follow her, looking around at the vast room with wide eyes.

Holy shit. She is not wrong.

There is a huge—and I mean huge—bed filling the centre of it, and that is about the only normal thing in here.

"I don't even know what some of this is for. I think I need to get reacquainted with Christian Grey again if we're going to be spending time here. I want to try it all," she breathes hungrily, running her finger along what looks to be a whip.

Jesus, Eaton.

"I think we should go somewhere a little more private," I say, making a beeline toward one of the doors to the rooms beyond.

"I'm more than happy for people to watch."

"Why doesn't that surprise me," I mutter under my breath. "I'm not really into that, Darce."

"Oh, you'd rather have me all to yourself," she says excitedly, bouncing over to me.

Jesus Christ.

The moment I have the door closed behind us, she's in my space and attempting to drag my shirt up my body.

I stand frozen and stare down at her. But she's too distracted with trying to get me naked to sense the danger in the air.

"Sit down, Darcie," I state, my voice so cool and detached that I'm sure Elliot might even be impressed.

"W-wha—"

Pressing my hand to the centre of her chest, I force her to back up and she stumbles toward the bed when I give her a less-than-gentle shove.

"You want me to strip for you?" she offers in a breathy, desperate voice.

"No, I really fucking don't. I've got a deal for you."

She pushes herself to sit on the bed and blinks at me as if I told her that I'm really an alien who doesn't possess a cock.

"A... deal?"

"Yeah. I need an alibi, and you need the bragging rights of being with an Heir to take a few steps up the social ladder. So what do you say? Wanna help each other out?"

She continues to stare at me as if I've suddenly started talking in a different language.

"So you didn't bring me down here to fuck me?" she asks, I swear to God blinking back tears.

Jesus, this girl is really fucked up.

"No, Darcie. You're not really my type. No offence."

I realise my mistake with those words the second her bottom lip starts to quiver.

Fuck me. I do not need this shit.

"Look, I'm sorry, okay. I just... I know that you're trustworthy enough to help me out with this," I say, hoping that a change of angle might help. "I could have asked any girl up there, but I knew you were the one for the job."

Thankfully, her demeanour completely changes.

"So you're going to what... leave me down here, go and do something you shouldn't be doing, and then I get to claim that you showed me heaven all night long or something?"

"See, you're cleverer than you look, Darce," I praise through gritted teeth.

She smiles at me, but I can practically see the cogs turning behind her eyes as she considers my offer.

"And I can tell everyone that you did anything to me down here."

"Anything," I agree, cringing hard. "So long as you follow the rules."

"The rules?" she confirms, but there's no way she needs me to lay them out for her—every Heir chaser knows them like the back of their hands.

"Yeah, you know. You can't talk about the details of the dungeon. That's for us and our chosen ones to know about." I wink, and she eats it right up.

"Where are you going?"

"You don't need to know about that."

She considers me for a moment before I turn to point at the cupboard behind me.

"There are drinks and food. The TV works. Have a little private party for one while you let your imagination run wild about what I could have done to you." My stomach churns, already considering the kind of bullshit I'm going to have to go along with to make this plan work.

It's going to be fucking worth it, though.

"How long will you be?"

"Two hours, tops."

"Plenty of time for multiples O's from your talented tongue then."

"That's the idea. So, we've got a deal?"

"I mean, it's not quite as sweet as it could be." She lets her eyes drop to my body, but she doesn't say any more.

"That's a yes?" I confirm.

"Sure thing. Lucky for you, I've got a really, really vivid imagination."

"Fantastic. See you in a bit then."

She calls for me as I step out of the room, but I don't bother hanging around to hear what she wants to say. Instead, I flick the lock and take off through the hidden back door toward my car.

The drive to Huxton is fast, and in no time, I'm pulling up at the end of the street where Elliot told me Dale's beloved orange Ford Focus RS would be.

Flipping down the glovebox of my Subaru BRZ, I stare at the extras I packed for tonight's job before quickly slamming it closed. The Heirs need me toeing the line right now. I need to follow orders.

With my fingers wrapped around my knife, I step out of the car, pulling my hood up as I look up and down the street to ensure there are no witnesses.

I duck between the other boy racer cars that line the street to their favourite hang-out in the middle of their shitty estate.

A devilish smile pulls at my lips as I come to stand beside Dale's baby. This thing is his life. His socials are full of him posing like he thinks he's all that on the thing.

It's pathetic. Especially because if you were to actually lift the bonnet, anyone would discover that this isn't a legit RS, just a pretty paint job and an extra couple of stickers. Fucking wannabe bell piece.

Even if he didn't deserve this for touching Olivia, he would for being an arrogant waste of oxygen.

Lifting the knife to his back door, I press it into the paintwork.

"Touch what belongs to us, and we'll come right back at you, motherfucker."

I scratch right down the side before dragging it all the way back, making sure it's deep as fuck.

I do the same on the other side, keeping an eye on the street to make sure no one appears before sinking my blade into each of his tyres.

The sound of them deflating feeds the beast that lives inside me, and I smile like a fucking maniac as I admire my handiwork.

Pocketing my knife, I walk back toward my car, but I stop when I get to my door as the video that motherfucker sent us with Olivia fills my mind once more. It blurs into what school is going to be like for the next few weeks as Darcie fills everyone's eager ears with bullshit about our night together.

Anger bubbles up inside me for this prick and the events he's put into place that led me here.

Ripping open my passenger door, I flip open my glovebox and follow through with my own little mission.

Elliot told me to fuck his car up but to leave it standing.

Well, fuck him and his fucking God complex.

With everything I need, I march back toward dickwad's car and wrench open the petrol cap.

Because he's an arrogant motherfucker who thinks he's untouchable, he hasn't even locked it.

In only seconds, I have the scarf I stole from Mum covered in lighter fluid and stuffed down into the car with my lighter ready.

"Fuck you, motherfucker," I roar, probably way too loudly considering I'm meant to be being discreet, but fuck it.

Adrenaline is flooding my body, and my need to see this little bitch's car go up is the only thing I can think about as I spark the lighter and hold it beneath the fabric.

"Fuck you, Dale Starling. Fuck everyone who's trying to control my goddamn life. FUCK YOU."

I stand there long enough to be confident that it's going to burn all the way down, and then I hightail it out of there.

Flooring it down the street, I'm in the next one over when a loud, earth-shaking boom rips through my car.

"Fuck yes," I bark as an accomplished smile stretches wide across my face.

I don't go back to the party—I can't while I stink of kerosene—so I swing by home for a quick shower and a change of clothes before I head back to free Darcie from her prison. Shame really, life would be so much fucking easier without her trying to cling onto me like a fucking limpet. I can only imagine that she's going to get so, so much worse after this little stunt she helped me pull tonight.

Fuck it.

Knowing that little bitch is going to be crying over his lost baby right now makes it more than worth it.

24

OLIVIA

"Good morning, sweetheart," Dad says as I enter the kitchen. "How was the party?"

"Well, there's every chance one or two of the first-year rugby players are still out in the woods, naked and covered in God knows what..."

He chuckles. "Ah, good times. I remember it well."

"Seriously, Dad, it was gross."

"Oh, come on, Olivia. Boys will—"

"Be boys, yeah. I got the memo, Dad." My eyes roll dramatically. "But you know that can't always be a cop-out for plain stupid. It's the twenty-first century. Don't you think it's time the Heirs moved with the times?"

Shaking out his morning paper, he folds in in half and lets out a heavy sigh. "Tradition is important, sweetheart. The foundations of society are built on them. Sixth form is a chance for the boys to expel all that restless energy before things get serious."

"Lucky for them." I make myself a strong coffee, relieved I didn't break my no-drinking rule last night.

Even after Reese disappeared with Darcie. Charli and I had left not long after that. I couldn't be there, knowing he was with her, touching her the way he'd touched me.

I felt stupid, thinking that something more existed between us. Reese isn't capable of feeling. He's spoilt and arrogant with layers of ice encased around his heart.

They're welcome to each other.

Liar.

I ignore the little voice and drain my coffee, hoping it might burn some sense into me. I am not going to wallow over Reese Whitfield and his man whoring ways.

"What are your plans for the weekend?"

"Workout, homework, the usual."

"You know, Olivia, it wouldn't hurt you to get out more. Enjoy life."

"I enjoy life, Dad." Just because I'm not a Darcie Porter of the world, doesn't mean I don't have a fulfilling, content life.

A strange current runs through me, but I shake it off.

"Good morning." Fiona appears, looking as perfectly polished as she does during the week.

She picks up the television remote from the table and turns on the widescreen hanging on the far wall, and the news reporter's monotonous tone fills the air.

"Another day, another political scandal," she tsks, switching on the coffee machine.

I'm only half tuned in when the next announcement catches my ear.

"The explosion in Huxton is thought to be the work of vandals. Mr. Starling is offering a reward from anyone with information pertaining to the damage to his son's car. Police confirmed that it happened around eleven PM last night."

Icy dread floods my veins.

No, it can't be...

They wouldn't.

"Starling... why does that name sound familiar?" Dad asks, and I tense.

"He... uh, attends Huxton Academy. He's a Harrier."

"Yes, that's the one." He goes back to his morning reading as if arson is a regular occurrence in Huxton.

It isn't.

And while I want to believe my brother and the Heirs have nothing to do with it, my gut is screaming at me that they did.

Damn it.

They were at the party all night. I saw them, right there. But that isn't to say they didn't orchestrate the entire thing.

Bloody idiots.

Excusing myself, I hurry upstairs to my room and slam the door shut behind me.

Grabbing my phone, I locate Charli's number and hit call.

"Hello." Her groggy voice fills the line.

"It's me. Did I wake you?"

"Yeah, it's fine. What's wrong?"

"Someone blew up Dale Starling's car last night."

"What?"

"I saw it on the local news. Mr. Starling is offering a reward to anyone with information."

"Crap. Do you think it was them?"

"Do you?"

"I mean, it's one hell of coincidence if it isn't. But they were at the party. When we left, they were all right there."

"I know. I guess they could have paid somebody to do their dirty work."

"Shit," she hisses. "That makes sense. What are you going to do?"

I know what I'd like to do, but something tells me Oak and his friends might object to being strung up on the rugby goal posts by their balls.

"I haven't decided yet." I bristle.

"There might be another explanation," she says, but I hear the doubt in her voice.

Charli warned me last night that Oak wouldn't let it go...

And it looks like she was right.

An hour.

I last an hour before I send Oakley a text demanding to know what happened.

> Oak: I don't know what you're talking about.
>
> Olivia: Seriously, Oak. It was on the local news.
>
> Oak: I don't know what to tell you Liv, but I swear to God I had nothing to do with it. We were at the party, you know that.
>
> Olivia: You promise?
>
> Oak: Cross my heart, hope to die. Stick a needle in my eye.

Soft laughter bubbles out of me at the silly childish rhyme we used to say to one another when we were younger.

Another text comes through before I can reply, making my brows pinch.

> Oak: Do I need to worry about Ben?
>
> Olivia: Ben?
>
> Oak: Yeah, the lad you were dancing with…

Oh.
Ben.
Right.

> Olivia: Uh, no. It was an experiment.

God, why did I say that?

> Oak: Sounds kinda odd.

> Olivia: Long story. But let's just say you don't have to worry about Ben again.

> Oak: Thank fuck. Because I'm not ready for you to get with anyone.

> Olivia: Seriously? Do you think I'm a nun?

> Oak: I try not to think about my sister as anything else...

> Olivia: Wow, that's... wow. You need to get over yourself, Oak. I don't know whether to be flattered or slightly concerned that you still think I'm a virgin.

"Ugh." I slam my phone down and heave a ragged breath. My brother can be so sweet and understanding, and then sometimes, he can be such a clueless twat.

Grabbing my yoga mat, I unroll it on the floor and take a deep, calming breath. But as I get in the cat position to warm up, stretching my shoulder and back muscles, the anger doesn't dissipate. In fact, it swirls like a storm inside me. Because deep down, I know Oakley would lie to me. If he thought he was protecting me, he would lie.

And I hate it.

I hate that I live in a world where men get to decide what a woman can and can't handle.

It's why I still haven't filled out my application for Saints Cross U, why I have a stack of brochures for universities outside of Oxfordshire hidden in my desk. Oakley would never forgive me if I do it, though. If I break away and try to make a life outside of Saints Cross.

I roll my shoulders, dropping my body down into cow position. But it's no use. I can't find my zen. Not with too many thoughts running around my head.

Flopping onto my back, I stare up at the ceiling, picturing Reese's smirk last night as he groped Darcie.

A game.

That's all I am.

He's out to hurt me. To ruin and break me. And I still don't know why.

But Reese Whitfield has never needed much in the way of a reason to do anything.

Ugh.

I need to stop obsessing over him, over this toxic thing between us.

He showed me his true colours last night when he went off with Darcie. He knows how much I hate her.

Damn you to hell, Reese Baron Whitfield.

I spend the day cleaning. My room, then the kitchen and bathrooms. Dad and Fiona insisted I didn't need to, we have a cleaner for that, but the mindless activity is a good distraction.

Once I'm done, I grab my laundry basket and take it down to the utility room. Unlike Theo's and Elliot's families, we don't have help around the house. After Mum died, Dad didn't want us to be 'those' kids raised by a nanny and housekeeper. He wanted us to pitch in and be a family. The kind who pulls their weight and gets on with it. It builds character, apparently.

There's two baskets of freshly laundered clothes, so I move them to one side and add my laundry to the washing machine and set the program.

I'm about to leave when my gaze snags on one of the

baskets. It's Reese's. Before I know what I'm doing, I scoop it up and head upstairs to his room.

He'll kill me if he finds me in here, but temptation is too hard to resist. Dropping the basket on his bed, I take in his space. Although Fiona had it decorated for him—hoping that one day he'd come back—it's all Reese. Dark grey walls with splatters of royal blue that match the thick curtains and bedsheets. It reminds me of a storm at sea. The angry swell of water. Dark thundering clouds. My lips twist with amusement. If a space ever perfectly captured someone's personality, it's this room.

There are photos of him with the guys on the shelves, but I already know he didn't decorate the place with them. That was Fiona in the hope he might feel at home here.

The basket of laundry taunts me. I should leave it, or even better, douse it all in itching powder. God only knows, the arsehole deserves it.

Darcie Porter.

How could he?

He knew how that would make me feel.

Because he doesn't care.

Reese isn't a good person. He isn't—

Something catches my eye in the corner of his room. It's his laundry bin, identical to the one in my room except it's dark grey and mine is light blue.

My heart crashes violently in my chest as I move toward it. The black hoodie hanging half in, half out of it. It's only a hoodie.

Before I can stop myself, I reach for it and pull it out. The faint smell of kerosene assaults my senses and I frown.

Why would—

No.

No!

It makes no sense. I saw Reese at the party. I saw him lead Darcie out of the room. Saw the lust in her eyes. The desire.

A huge pit gnaws my stomach as I clutch the hoodie. I know what it means. I know I'm holding the item of clothing Reese wore to blow up Dale Starling's car.

But why?

Did he do it for Oakley and the other Heirs?

Was it part of some task to get back into their good graces?

Or did he act alone?

And if he did...

I shut those thoughts down.

It doesn't make any sense.

None.

Dropping the hoodie back into the laundry basket, I hurry out of Reese's room and slip into my own, closing the door behind me.

Either Oakley is telling the truth and Reese went on a one-man mission to destroy Dale's car, or my brother is lying, and they're all in on it.

And I don't know which is worse.

25

REESE

A loud bang rocks through me, forcing my eyes open.

The Chapel is bathed in light, the morning sun long risen. I blink a few times to clear my vision. My head swims with the amount of... I can't even remember what it was I drank when I got back last night.

Having to spend the rest of the party with Darcie's hands all over me like she owned me to make it look realistic was the last thing I fucking needed. But, as much as I might have wanted to pick her up and launch her in the direction of the dorms to get fucking rid of her, I knew I needed to play the game. For a little bit at least. Everyone needed to believe I really did take her downstairs to show her the time of her life, or my alibi is fucked.

Leaving my fate in the hands of Darcie fucking Porter really doesn't sit great with me. But it's the best we could come up with. Elliot was convinced by his decision, and heaven forbid I go against our control freak of a leader.

The pounding of feet on the stairs reminds me of why I'm suddenly awake when I should still be sleeping off the effects of the previous night before a furious Elliot rounds the corner and makes a beeline straight for my position on the sofa again.

With a pained sigh, I haul myself up so I'm sitting and not at such a height disadvantage. My back pulls and my neck aches.

"What the ever-loving fuck did you do last night, Whitfield?"

I stare up at him, trying and failing to keep a smirk off my face as I take in his dark, angry eyes and the pulsating vein that looks like it's about five seconds from popping at his temple.

"Payback," I say simply, sensing that he probably expects me to answer that question despite the fact that he clearly knows what I did.

"We told you to fuck it up, teach him a lesson. Not fucking destroy his car and end up on the local fucking news, you prick."

I shrug. "Keying it didn't seem like enough. I got creative."

"You fucking blew it up. And two of the cars either side of it, if the fucking news report is to be believed."

I push to my feet as he stares down at me, doing his best impression of a fire-breathing dragon.

Reaching out, I rest my hand on his shoulder. "You really need to calm down, E. I think you're about one outburst away from an aneurism."

An angry growl rumbles deep in his throat before he knocks my hand from his shoulder. He charges at me with the force of a bull, and I have little choice but to let it happen.

We both crash onto the sofa, but with Elliot's force and our combined weight, the whole thing flips back, crashing down on the old flagstone floor behind us.

"You motherfucker," he roars, recovering faster than me and planting his fist into my stomach. "You had one fucking job. Orders you were meant to follow."

I don't fight back for a few minutes. Instead, I let him burn off some of his frustration.

Over the years, the three of us have learned how to deal with his outbursts.

It takes a lot for Elliot to crack, but when he does, he needs to expel it for a few minutes, let the red haze lift a little before he's a worthy opponent and aware of what he's actually doing.

Shoving his shoulders, I manage to roll him off me before pinning him to the floor and throwing my fist into his jaw.

"What the fuck are you two doing?" Theo bellows, heading toward us leisurely and staring as if we're two crazed animals at the zoo.

I glance over my shoulder at him, finding his hair sticking up in every angle and his hand lost in his boxers.

Elliot uses my moment of distraction to take another swing at me, and his fist collides with my eye before I crash to the floor beside him.

"Fucking cunt," I mutter, pressing my hand to my eye as Elliot stands, smoothing down his t-shirt and sweats before walking toward the kitchen as if that never happened and he didn't let his inner monster take over for a heartbeat.

"Does someone want to tell me what's going on?" Theo looks between us, but eventually he settles his eyes on me, because who else could have fucked something up here? Surely not our almighty leader. "What did you do to wake the devil?"

I roll my eyes at Theo but accept his hand when he offers it to help me up.

"You mean you haven't looked at your socials yet this morning?" Elliot barks.

"No. I was woken by you two fucking animals going at it."

"He started it," I mutter, although loudly enough for Elliot to hear me.

"I swear to fucking God, Whitfield—"

"What? You swear to God what? You gonna make me sleep on the dining table next? Or outside maybe? You do know that you're not actually fucking God around here, right?" I spit. "I did what was needed of me last night. I did everything—" Almost. "That you said. I've even let the entire fucking school think I shoved my cock in that slag, not to mention listen to her brag about how much I enjoyed it for the rest of the year. Is that not e-fucking-nough to prove my loyalty?"

"He's got a point, man," Theo agrees.

"He blew up Starling's fucking car," Elliot seethes, making Theo still in shock.

"I thought you were just going to key it and slash the tyres."

"Yeah, didn't we fucking all. Where the fuck is Oak?" Elliot barks, changing the subject without even taking a breath.

"Last I saw of him, his head was buried between some bird's thighs."

"Jesus fucking Christ. He'd better have got rid of her," Elliot snarls, abandoning his coffee and storming toward the doors that lead to our basement.

Theo and I are hot on his heels.

I think Theo is probably going for Oak's protection, whereas I'm all about the entertainment should that room be littered with girls.

I'm not the only Heir who can break the rules from time to time.

Doors slam and the anticipation grows as Elliot makes his way downstairs. But when he throws open the doors to the main room, his shoulders sag in relief when we find Oak passed out naked in the middle of the massive bed.

"What are you doing?" Theo asks when Elliot marches toward the bathroom and then reappears only two minutes later with a jug of what I can only assume is cold water.

Amusement floods me as I stand shoulder to shoulder with Theo and watch as Elliot throws the contents over Oak.

"Dad, no. I wasn't even going to—" His words falter as he opens his eyes and finds the three of us staring at him. "You fucking cuntbags," he groans, not giving two single shits about the fact that he's laid out like a starfish. A starfish mauled by a shark, that is.

"Who the fuck tried to eat you last night?" Theo asks, clearly tracking the multiple bite marks across his body as I am.

"Fuck knows. They were good, though."

"They?" I ask, kinda disappointed I missed the best bit of last night's party while I was pretending to be Darcie's fuck of the year.

"Yeah, man. It was fucking epic. Best night ever," he sighs with a satisfied smile playing on his lips.

"Sorry to burst your bubble, Casanova, but you need to get up. We've got an issue."

"It's not an issue. I made sure nothing can be traced back to us. You need to chill your fucking tits, man."

Oak pushes his hair back and finally sits up. "You made sure what can't be traced back to us?" he asks ominously.

"Cover your fucking cock up, brush your teeth, and then we'll talk. You look like a well-used whore right now."

"Jealous, Eaton?"

"Fuck you. Just do as you're told." He turns and marches out of the room.

"Sure thing, boss." Oak salutes his back before falling to the bed once more. "Everything hurts. I think I'm dying," he whines.

"You gonna tell him, or should I?" Theo taunts, looking up at me.

"What did you do, Whitfield?" Oak asks with his eyes closed.

"Blew up Starling's car."

Oak's eyes pop open in shock before a smirk twitches at his lips. "On purpose?" he asks, excitement sparkling in his eyes.

"What the fuck do you think? That cunt deserved it for using Olivia to taunt us."

"Too fucking right he did. He's gonna regret the day he

decided to go up against us," Oak promises. "I guess we'd better go and talk Elliot off the edge and figure out our next move."

Oak slides to the end of the bed, swinging his legs over the side and placing his feet on the floor.

"You seen my clothes?"

The three of us all look around. The place is fucking trashed. But I don't spot any male clothes amongst the girls' underwear and used condoms.

Fucking dogs.

"They probably stole them to sleep in to remember your night together."

"They're fucking welcome to them. They already know there won't be a repeat."

"How would you know?" I ask. "You can't tell me you remember any of the girls you fucked last night."

"I'll know," Oak disagrees, giving up on his search and marching to the door that leads to the stairs with everything still hanging out.

We're halfway up the stairs when a high-pitched voice rips through the air, the familiarity of it making me wince.

"So you just thought it would be okay to use me in this?" Darcie screams. "I could be an accessory to arson."

Shoving Oak out of the way, I move faster. I might not like the bitch, but she did us a solid by agreeing to be my alibi last night, and we really don't need Elliot going crazy psycho on her arse.

"How the fuck would it get back to you? You were downstairs having your brains screwed out by Whitfield. How was that, by the way? As mind-blowing as you always imagined? His cock is hella small, right?"

"Shut the fuck up, prick," I grunt, marching straight over to a red-faced Darcie.

"You," she seethes, pointing right in my face. "You left me down there while you went to blow up that idiot's car. Do you have any idea what that could do to my reputation?" Her eyes shift to something behind me, and when I glance over my shoulder, I find Oak standing there with his hand cupping his junk.

"Beckworth, I told you to go and get some fucking clothes on."

"You don't need to do that on my account," Darcie purrs.

"And you're worried about your rep?" I scoff, marching into the kitchen to finally get some caffeine.

"Beckworth," Elliot booms, and after a dramatic roll of his eyes, Oak heads up to his bedroom, Darcie's eyes feasting on his arse until he disappears from sight.

The second he's gone, her demeanour completely changes.

Crazy fucking bitch.

"You should have told me what you were really doing."

"You're not the only one," Elliot mutters under his breath.

"I should go and tell my Daddy about this. He won't have an arsonist attending All Hallows'."

Elliot stares at her blankly as if her threat means nothing to him. "Feel free, Darcie. But be aware of what we'll offer up in return."

Her brow creases, confusion filling her features. "What are you talking about?" she demands.

"You're not going to talk to anyone about what did or did not happen last night aside from what was agreed between you and Whitfield."

"Oh yeah, and why is that?"

Elliot makes a show of pulling his phone from his pocket. He finds something before turning it around.

We all knew he had a card up his sleeve. It's why he was so confident that Darcie was the one to help last night. But he never let on as to what it was. Although, as a wanton moan rips through the air, we're clued in pretty quickly.

"No," Darcie cries, surging forward as if she's going to grab the phone from Elliot's hands.

She doesn't even get close. Theo is too fast for her to even get a chance, wrapping his arm around her waist and pinning her to his solid frame.

"And who exactly is that fucking you like a dirty whore, Darcie? Did you want to fill my boys in for me?"

"Fuck you, Elliot."

His lip peels back as he runs his eyes down the length of her. "No, you're all right. I have some taste, and desperate, dirty whores aren't it."

"Who is it?" I ask, curiosity burning through me as he watches the show with a blank expression.

Elliot looks down at his screen again. "Darcie?" he asks.

Tears fill her eyes as she stares pure hate at Elliot, not that he gives a fuck. "M-my daddy's f-friend," she stutters, but something tells me that's not even the worst of it.

"Oh wow," I breathe. "That really is quite scandalous, even for you, Darce. I guess you really need this keeping under wraps, huh?"

"I'll do anything," she cries. "Please, promise me you'll delete it."

Elliot finally looks up at her again.

"Don't worry, Darcie. I'm not keeping this shit on my phone any longer than necessary, but rest assured, I have backup copies should we need them."

"You... you... wanker."

"Oh, Darcie," Elliot growls, pocketing his phone and stalking closer to her. "I'm so much fucking worse than that."

A yelp rips through the air as he grabs her by her hair and drags her toward the doors.

"Now, do us all a favour and fuck off, yeah? And keep your filthy mouth shut."

"B-but Reese said."

"Oh, you can tell the whole fucking world about your

night together. You can make that as creative as you like, just like you agreed. But anything else passes your lips and that video goes viral. Got it?"

She nods, a whimper falling from her lips before he finally shoves her through the door and slams it behind her.

"What the fuck?" Oak barks, finally returning in a tank and sweats. "Did I miss all the fun?"

26

OLIVIA

"I kid you not, Keeley, his dick was huge."

"Oh my God, what did you do?" Keeley Davis sniggers as I sit quietly in the bathroom stall, praying to God that they'll move it along soon.

I didn't intend on getting stuck with them in the girls' bathroom. But the universe clearly loves any opportunity to fuck with me.

"What do you think I did? Rode him like a champ." She smacks her lips together as if she's applying gloss. Bright red, no doubt.

"And..."

"And what? It's sex, Kee, use your imagination."

"I can't believe you fucked an Heir."

"Told you I'd make it happen this year. And Reese is... ugh, he's so bloody hot."

"I don't know, I think I prefer Oakley. I've heard he's a real freak between the—"

No.

No. No. No.

I press my hands to my ears. No one needs to hear a girl recount her sexual fantasies about your twin brother.

Their laughter fills the bathroom, setting my teeth on edge, but eventually they finish their gossiping and preening and leave.

Thank God.

I slip out of the stall and wash my hands, splashing some water on my neck. My heart is working overtime, making my stomach churn.

Darcie was with Reese. She said it herself. So how the hell did he manage to sneak out of the Chapel and go to Huxton?

It doesn't make sense. I'm missing something, I have to be.

Because it's the only explanation for his kerosene-scented hoodie, isn't it?

My phone vibrates and I dig it out of my blazer pocket, groaning at my brother's name.

All weekend he's bombarded me with messages, trying to worm his way back in my good graces, but I've mostly been avoiding him.

Reese committed arson, I know he did, and there's every chance my brother, Elliot, and Theo were in on it, and that is not okay with me.

Sure, there have been plenty of incidents over the years. Fights, drugs, vandalism, and trespassing. The Heirs of All Hallows' are lawless. Reckless and hot-headed.

Because society tells them that their money, their names and family ties place them ahead of everyone else. Dad was right about one thing—it's how it always has been and probably how it always will be.

Scanning the text again, I decide to ignore Oakley. I'm not ready to talk to him. I'm not ready to talk to any of them, and given how well they've settled into their roles as the new Heirs at school, it shouldn't be too difficult to stay out of their way.

"Liv," Oakley calls as I enter class, but I slide into an empty seat in a row near the front.

"Are you fucking kidding me?" he hisses. There's a commotion behind me, and then I sense him.

"Move," he growls at the lad beside me.

"Come on, man. This is my seat. I always—"

"I said, move."

I offer him an apologetic smile as he packs up his stuff and switches seats.

So much for avoiding him.

"Seriously, Liv. You're starting to piss me off."

"Me?" My eyes narrow with contempt. "I'm pissing you off? Go annoy someone else, Oak. I'm not in the mood." I stare upfront, dismissing him.

But of course, Oakley doesn't appreciate being ignored. Another prerequisite of being an Heir, apparently.

He drags his table and chair closer, leaning right in. "Look, I already told you, it wasn't us."

He lies so easily and it hurts. It hurts that he can look me in the eye and act as if I'm the one in the wrong.

"I don't believe you."

"Liv!" His hand slams down on the table and my eyes widen.

"Shit, I didn't mean... I don't like that we're fighting."

"I don't like that my brother is a lying tosser."

"I swear to God, Olivia. I am not—"

"Like I said, Oakley, go annoy someone else."

I stare ahead again, refusing to look at him.

"Hormonal bitch," he mutters under his breath, and I cut him with an icy glare.

He smirks, and I give him the bird right as Mr. Piper walks in.

"How lovely, Miss Beckworth."

"Sorry, sir," I mutter, much to Oak's amusement.

Anger explodes inside me at how flippant he's being. My

hand shoots up as I blurt, "Actually, sir. I'm not feeling so good. Please may I be excused?"

"The fuck, Liv?" Oakley hisses, and I flash him a saccharine smile.

"I'm sure you can manage, Miss—"

"Period cramps, sir. Really bad ones. I need some painkillers and a hot water bottle."

"Yes, well, that is... yes. You should go..." He flushes bright red, as if the word 'period' is the worst thing I could have possibly said.

Stuffing my things into my bag, I don't spare Oakley a second glance as I walk out of there and make a beeline for the side exit.

I can't be here, not today. Not with all this unresolved anger.

My phone vibrates. Once. Twice. A third time.

I don't even bother to read Oakley's texts. He can stew on his lies a little longer.

Deceitful bastard.

Guilt snakes through me. He isn't the only one lying. But it's not the same. My relationship with Reese, if you can even call it that, isn't illegal. It couldn't land us in jail. Not unless Reese pisses me off so much that I try to strangle the life right out of him.

Bursting out of the fire door, I almost run straight into a girl sitting on the steps.

"Crap, I'm— Tally?" I gawk down at her.

"Oh, hey."

"What are you doing out here?"

"The same thing you are, if the way you spill out of the door is anything to go by." She lifts her shoulders in a small shrug.

"Is everything okay?" I ask, sensing her emotions.

"Same shit, different day." She barely looks at me, and I don't blame her.

Me and Tally Darlington aren't friends. We aren't even acquaintances, all thanks to the names we both bear.

Beckworth and Darlington.

If my father is one of the best defence lawyers in the country, hers is the best prosecution lawyer. More than once, Dad has come up against Mr. Darlington in the courtroom, and there is no love lost between them.

Befriending Tally would be like befriending the enemy, a move neither my father nor brother would appreciate.

Maybe that's all the more reason to do it.

My lips curve.

Tally glances up, noticing. "What?"

"Nothing."

"Are you planning on staying out here or..."

"Don't worry, I'm not staying." I skip past her.

"Wait, Olivia."

"Yeah?" I look back at her.

"Sorry, that was rude. I'm just having a really bad day." Something flashes in her eyes, but I'm all out of sympathy today.

I've got enough of my own problems without inheriting a girl I've barely spoken two words to my entire life.

"Don't worry about it," I reply before taking off down the path leading back around the building to the car park.

It's times like these I miss Charli. At least when we were at school together, I had someone to turn to.

Climbing into my car, I slam the door shut, flinching at the sound. A quick check of my phone says I have two texts from Oakley.

> Oak: What the fuck Liv?

> Oak: Seriously, stop acting like a drama queen and come back to class...

Tears of frustration prick the corners of my eyes. He doesn't get it.

Why would he?

I spend the afternoon studying in my room. It's hardly the rebellious act I felt like committing as I fled All Hallows', but it's the safest. Oak won't come back here and pick a fight, not with Dad and Fiona already home.

They got back an hour ago, their voices drifting up to my room. But I haven't been down to say hello.

Eventually, my grumbling stomach gets the better of me, and I venture downstairs in search of some food—only to come to a sudden halt at the scene before me.

"What is going on?"

"Sweetheart, you're awake."

Awake?

I frown.

I was never asleep.

"The boys thought it would be nice for us all to eat together."

"I'm not hungry."

My stomach growls at the smell of Chinese food, and they all look at me.

"Sounds like you're ravenous." Reese smirks, and I want to throw something at his head.

I've never been a particularly violent person before, but he sure has a way of bringing that out in me.

"Come on, Liv. It's your favourite." Oak smiles, apology glittering in his eyes.

Damn him.

He's too good at this—manipulating people to his own ends.

But neither of them is aware that I know the truth. Well,

some of it. Because I still haven't figured out how Reese pulled it off.

"Fine," I snap, joining them at the table.

"How are you, sweetheart? Oak said you weren't feeling so good this afternoon."

"I'm fine, thanks."

"I got you some things."

"Things?" My eyes slide to Oakley's.

"Yeah. You know, painkillers, chocolate, women's things."

"You brought me sanitary products?"

Dad almost chokes on his spring roll while Reese stares at us, confusion crinkling his brows.

"Yeah." Oak shrugs. "It's no big deal."

He bought me guilt tampons.

Oh my God.

"That is... I really don't know what to say."

"Such a sweet, thoughtful thing," Fiona says. "You're lucky to have each other."

Lucky.

Sure.

I load my plate with some prawn toast and wontons and give my brother a thin smile. "I'm sure Dad and Fiona don't want to hear about my... issues. You should fill them in on the party."

"Oh yes, was it fun?" Fiona asks, completely oblivious to the ripple of tension that goes through the room.

"Nothing to tell." Reese stiffens, studying me.

"Oh, come on, there's always a tale or two from a party at the Chapel. I heard that you and Darcie Porter were getting cosy."

His eyes narrow, anger rolling off him in vicious waves.

"Darcie Porter, the headteacher's daughter?" Fiona frowns.

"Relax, Mum, we're not... it's not serious."

Oak sniggers, and I pin him with a hard look.

'What?' he mouths.

Fiona's mobile starts ringing.

"Crap, I'm sorry," she says, checking the caller ID. "It's Krystal, I told her to call tonight."

"Aunt Krystal?" Reese asks. "I haven't seen her in years."

"We still catch up now again. I'll tell her I'll call back later." She gets up and goes to take the call, slipping into the hall.

"I didn't know you have an aunt called Krystal," I murmur.

"Oh, Krystal isn't really Reese's aunt, sweetheart. She was my best friend in high school. She used to come around a lot when Reese was a little boy, and he took to calling her auntie." Something passes over her face, but I don't ask her to expand.

I don't know why I said anything in the first place.

We all eat in awkward silence for the next few minutes. Reese watches me watch Oak. What are they playing at, trying to ambush me like this?

I don't like it—the two of them in cahoots again. It feels... weird.

After I've devoured my prawn toast, I take a sip of my water and sit back in my chair. Everyone's enjoying their food. A rare memory of peace between the five of us.

I clear my throat, earning their attention.

"Something wrong, sweetheart?" Dad asks when he realises I've stopped eating.

"No, Dad. The food is great. I was thinking about what happened over in Huxton."

"Huxton?"

Oak straightens, his eyes going to mine while Reese barely looks up.

"Yeah. Has anyone come forward with any information yet?"

"I don't know, sweetheart. But I'm sure they'll catch whoever did it. Someone will have caught them fleeing the scene on CCTV or a Ring doorbell."

"True. It's a bit scary to think there's an arsonist on the loose. Charli lives right up the street from the Starlings."

"I'm sure it was an isolated incident," he adds with a tone that suggests this line of conversation is over.

But Reese makes a small sound of disapproval and says, "If you ask me, the prick deserved it."

27

REESE

"Must we talk rugby rivalries over the dinner table?" Mum sighs, taking her seat at the table again, as Olivia's hate-filled stare burns into the top of my head.

"What exactly does that mean?" she asks, completely ignoring Mum's request.

"That he's an entitled dick. He's had something like that coming for years with the way he lords it over everyone."

Olivia snorts a mixture of disbelief and amusement that finally makes my head lift from my food.

"What?" I ask, confused by her outburst.

"You're accusing someone else of being an entitled dick. Fuck, Reese, you lot all own that title to the point I'm surprised you don't actually have trophies to prove it."

"Enough, Olivia," Christian growls in annoyance.

"You're defending them?" she asks, although I have no idea why.

Christian has made it quite clear time and time again that he fully supports us. He was an Heir back in the day, and then a Scion at Saints Cross U—why would he be against it? He knows how much fun having the power is. He wants that for Oak, and in turn, he wants it for me and the other two.

"It's all part of being an Heir," he reasons, and these kinds of disputes are great for Oakley's future career.

"Of course you only see the good in this stuff," she mutters, letting out a huff that tells everyone in that she doesn't have the energy to go up against her dad. Who does? He's formidable.

A ripple of tension goes around the room while Olivia seethes and Oakley bristles next to me.

I have no idea what they're fighting about really. He's barely said a word about her all weekend, but I know it's eating at him. He didn't need to bring up the fact that he dragged me to the shop for fucking tampons to pacify her to tell me how much he hates fighting with her.

It's always been the same. It's like she has the power to flip a switch in him that only she can turn off again. I used to hate it when we were kids. I'd do anything I could to cheer him up, but it was never enough. He didn't need me. Just her. It fucking killed me.

"So how are classes? Do you like your new teachers?" Mum asks naïvely. She's putting this shit on to pretend that we're all one big, happy family, and I hate it almost as much as knowing my best friend is hurting.

"Yeah, it's great," Oak mutters, stuffing his mouth full of noodles.

"Excuse me, I just need…" Olivia trails off before taking her plate to the dishwasher and disappearing out of the kitchen. No one speaks until the sound of her slamming her bedroom door ripples through the house.

"What have you two fallen out over? I'm assuming this is more than hormones," Christian says.

"It's nothing," Oak says with a shrug. "Thank you for this, it's been… great."

He follows Olivia's move, cleans off his plate, and dumps it in the dishwasher.

"I've got homework to do. I'm gonna stay here tonight if that's—"

"Of course, sweetheart. You don't even have to ask."

"You coming?" he asks me, but I hesitate. Fuck knows why.

"Fine, well, you know where I am if you need me."

He's gone before anyone gets to say anything, and I'm left with Christian and Mum staring at me like they're about to impart some parental advice.

Safe to say, I bolt as fast as fucking possible.

Being here and sleeping in a bed might be preferable over the Chapel's sofa, but only just.

Everything is quiet as I make my way up the stairs, and I smirk, imagining them both sitting in their rooms with their faces twisted up in anger over whatever bullshit fight they're in the middle of.

I stop when I get to my door, my eyes firmly locked on hers. I wonder what she's doing right now. If she's thinking about me.

Doubtful, but it doesn't stop me from abandoning the idea of my bedroom in favour of hers.

I've missed her the past few nights, but with the parties raging at the Chapel, I could hardly sneak off in favour of watching my soon-to-be stepsister sleep.

I expect her to say something the second I open the door, so when nothing comes, I assume that's a suitable invite and close the door behind me.

Stepping forward, the sound of her breathing hits me in the silence, letting me know that she's here before I turn the corner and suck in a breath.

Holy fuck, I've walked into heaven.

Olivia is bent in half, her arse pointing right at me in a tiny pair of shorts, her long legs on full display.

My fingers curl into fists as I rest my shoulder against the wall and watch her. But she doesn't do anything. She stays there, probably with her head filling with blood, exactly like my cock.

Reaching down, I rub myself through the fabric of my trousers, imagining what it might be like to take her like that.

A groan rumbles deep in my throat when she pushes up, this time literally bending her body in half as she wraps her hands around her ankles.

Jesus fucking Christ.

Unable to stop myself, I push from the wall and step right up behind her.

I lower my hand, letting my fingers trail up the back of her thigh.

The second she notices my touch, she shrieks and stumbles forward, but I'm ready for her and clamp my hand around her hip, dragging her arse back against my aching cock as my other hand wraps around her throat, forcing her to stand upright.

"Reese," she growls, but there's no heat behind it, and as she rubs her arse back against me, it loses any seriousness.

Releasing her hip, I pluck the white AirPod from her ear, moving it to mine. The dulcet tones of some random dude spewing meditation bullshit spills from it, and I quickly flick it away, sending it flying across the room until it bounces across her desk and falls behind it.

"What the fuck?" she barks, flinching as if she's about to fight against my hold. But the second I tighten my grip on her throat, she stills.

"I can think of something much more therapeutic for your anger right now, Olive."

"You need to get out of my room. Oak is—"

"Oak is pissed at you. I can't see him storming in here any time soon."

It's a lie. Oak is a big puppy dog when it comes to his sister, and I wouldn't put it past him crawling in here on his hands and knees and begging for forgiveness. Fucking pussy.

"Reese, you—" she starts again, but I cut her off.

"Are you wet for me, Olive? I know the period story is bullshit."

She tenses in my arms, and this time when she fights me, I let her go. Getting her fired up will only serve me better in the long run.

"How the fuck could you possibly know that?" she seethes, walking to the other side of the room before she spins around and gifts me the sight of her low-cut sports bra.

Fuck, her tits look insane.

"My eyes are up here, knobhead."

I let my gaze slowly roll up her body, not missing the way her chest is heaving and her cheeks are flushed. Granted, that could be from her being upside down when I walked in, but I can lie to myself well enough.

Her hands land on her hips as she continues to glare at me.

"So?" she prompts.

My brow lifts as I admit that I've forgotten that there was a question.

She huffs in irritation. "How do you know it's bullshit? You track my cycle or something?"

"Nah, I barely know what day it is, let alone that shit. I just... know. I can tell by looking at you."

Her eyes narrow.

"You're so fucking full of yourself," she scoffs.

"So prove it."

"P-prove it?" she parrots.

"Yeah." I smirk.

"Fuck you, Reese. I don't have to prove anything to you."

"You're right," I agree, prowling toward her. "You don't. Because I don't care. Even if I'm wrong, it won't stop me."

"Jesus. Are you even hearing yourself?"

I don't stop moving forward, and when she realises that I have no intention of pausing, she backs up until she bumps against the windowsill.

"Uh-oh, you seem to have run out of space to escape, sweet cheeks." Lifting my hand, I brush my fingers down her cheek.

For the briefest second, her eyes shutter at my gentle touch. But everything changes in an instant as fire blazes within them and she knocks my arm away.

"Get your filthy fucking hands off me. I know where they've been," she seethes.

"Oh?" I ask, tilting my head to the side, loving this jealous side to her.

"Not only am I not interested in anything you have to offer, Whitfield. But I certainly do not want Darcie Porter's cast-offs. To be honest, I'm surprised your fingers and cock are still attached to your body after dipping them into such a poisonous creature."

A smirk pulls at my lips as I lift my hand and hold the two fingers in question between us. Her top lip peels back in disgust as jealousy flares in her brown eyes.

It makes me fucking burn for her.

"They look okay to me, sweet cheeks. Did you wanna check my cock for damage too? Because I'd love to see you on your fucking knees for me right now."

My hand darts out, my fingers twisting in her hair as if I'm about to force her to the floor, putting her at eye level with my dick.

My teeth grind as my boner presses against the fabric of my trousers. There's no fucking hiding it, and if she were to look down, or better, comply with my demand, then she'd see exactly what she does to me.

"Seems to me that I had my fingers in you first, Olive. So there's probably an argument that Darcie got your sloppy seconds."

"Didn't sound like there was anything sloppy about your

performance on Friday night, from what I've heard," she mutters under her breath.

"Oh? Care to share?"

"Like you haven't heard her praising your massive cock like it should be fucking cast in stone and turned into a Saints Cross relic."

I snort a laugh as the prospect of a statue of my cock placed in the town square pops into my mind. I've sure had worse images in my head.

"Sounds to me it's something you should be worshipping right now."

"In your fucking dreams."

"Yeah, actually," I confess. "I often wake up hard as fuck, thinking about what it might be like to push my cock past your full lips, to feel your tongue licking up the length of my shaft, tasting me."

Her eyes darken and her lips pop open in shock.

"I want to know how deep you can take me. I want to see tears streaming down your cheeks as I fuck your mouth and listen to you moan as you take me like the dirty, filthy whore you are, Olivia Beckworth."

A bang comes from the other side of the room and we both still, waiting to see if Oak is going to come crashing through their Jack and Jill bathroom.

When nothing else follows, I use her moment of panic to my advantage and shove my non-poisonous hand into her shorts, not stopping until I get the answer to the question I first asked when I announced my presence.

"Oh, sweet cheeks. You really wanna suck my cock, huh?"

"Reese, no," she warns, but it soon turns into a moan when I sink two fingers inside her soaking pussy.

"Tell me you're a liar, Olivia," I demand as I begin finger-fucking her harder.

Her jaw locks and her eyes blaze with hate.

When it becomes clear that she's not going to say a word, I rip my hand from her shorts and hold my fingers between us.

"Liar," I breathe before wrapping my hand around her throat again, dragging her from the window and throwing her down on the bed. "And do you know what liars deserve?"

"Reese," she half warns, half moans as I tuck my fingers beneath the waistband of her shorts and drag them down her thighs.

"Punishment."

28

OLIVIA

This cannot be happening.

The four little words flutter through my mind but don't linger. Because although I know it's wrong, although I know nothing about this is normal or right or logical, it feels too damn good to stop.

Jesus, what the hell is wrong with me?

Reese hovers above me, his eyes as dark as the night as he brazenly cups me, sliding a finger right through my folds and pressing it inside me.

"Oh my God," I breathe, my lungs constricting as he goes deeper.

"Admit it. You want me, Olive."

Anger flares inside me at his taunt, but I don't take the bait. I'm too lost in this moment of madness, the risk and anticipation.

My brother is right on the other side of the bathroom. But for a second, I want to be found. I want him to know what it's like to be constantly on the periphery of things.

I'm not an Heir—I never will be.

So as close as the two of us are, I'll never truly walk in his world. And part of me resents that.

Hates it even.

But this, messing around with Reese, letting him touch me like this, it feels like my own personal fuck you to a society built to keep women one step behind.

"Say it, sweet cheeks." He leans down, ghosting his mouth over mine. Touching but not. Breathing his mint-flavoured breath all over me.

"Say. It."

"Never." I bare my teeth and his smirk grows, that cocky glint in his eye intensifying.

"Fine, have it your way." He presses another finger into me, stretching me as his thumb rolls over my clit, making a cry lodge in my throat. I swallow it down, trapping it behind my teeth as he finger fucks me with vicious intent.

His touch isn't sweet or tender. He's brutal, forcing my body to bend to his will.

"I can't wait to fucking get inside you."

"Never going..." A moan rumbles in my throat as he curls his fingers, rubbing that magic spot deep inside me. "To happen," I pant, bowing off the bed, seeking more.

More... more... more.

"I'm going to enjoy watching you beg." Reese smashes his mouth to mine, stealing my breath and every ounce of my lingering anger as he kisses me like he wants to devour me.

My arms loop around his neck, pulling him closer as I ride his hand, needing more.

Needing everything he's willing to give me.

I don't understand why it feels so good, but in this moment, I don't care.

I only care that he doesn't stop.

"Are you going to come for me, Olive?" His lips move to my neck, caressing the skin there, teeth nipping and biting. "Let me feel your pussy soak my fingers."

"Reese," I cry, an intense wave building inside me.

"Your brother is right next door. Imagine what he'd say if

he knew you were letting me get you off, begging me to let you come."

"Please…" I choke out, pleasure saturating every inch of me. It's not enough, though. I need more. I need him to get me there.

"Please what, Olive?"

He stares down at me with an intensity that makes my heart stutter. His fingers slow, teasing me, gliding in and out.

"Please, I'm so close…"

Reese tears away from me and I blink up at him, confused. "What are you doing?" I hiss.

He stands over me, bringing his glossy fingers to his mouth and sucking them clean. "Mmm, tastes like desperation."

"Excuse me?" I grab the bedsheet and pull it over my exposed body as I sit up.

"Admit it and you get to come."

"Reese…"

"Admit. It." He curls a hand around my jaw, tipping my head back so I have no choice but to look at him.

The pleasure evaporates as I glower at him, refusing to say the words he so desperately wants to hear.

"Such a filthy little liar." He tsks.

"You're one to talk."

His eyes widen before narrowing as he studies me, no doubt trying to figure out what I mean.

"Something you want to tell me, sweet cheeks?"

"I know what you did," I spit.

"And what exactly is it that you think I did?"

"It was you. You went to Huxton and you blew up Dale Starling's car. But what I can't figure out is why. Did you do it for my brother and the Heirs? To try to win back their trust…"

I hesitate, trying to swallow my next words. But I can't do it.

I have to know.

"Or did you do it for me?"

His expression darkens as his mouth twists with wicked intent. "That's an interesting theory." Slowly, he begins to inch backwards to the door. "But you're forgetting one thing."

"What's that?" I take the bait, right as his hand reaches for the handle behind him.

"I spent the night balls deep inside Darcie."

My stomach sinks as I clutch the sheets tighter. "You bastard."

"Aww, did you think you were special, Olive? Did you think I marched off to Huxton to defend your honour?" He snorts. "I don't know what you think you know, but if you need proof that I was otherwise engaged, ask Darcie for a play by play. I'm sure she'll be happy to recount how thoroughly fucked she was by the time I was done with her."

"Get out," I seethe quietly, rage and shame vibrating through me.

"Or what?"

"Or I'll scream. I'll scream so fucking loud Oak won't be the only one running in here. My dad and your mum will, too."

"Don't play games you can't win, Olivia." My name is a dangerous whisper on his lips. "Or have you forgotten about the photo evidence I have of you from that night?"

"Why do you hate me so much?"

Because I see it as clear as day in his eyes. He wants me, I don't doubt that. The thick bulge in his grey sweats is telling enough. But his lust is laced with hatred, the two emotions woven tightly together.

I should know, because I feel it too.

"I—"

"Hey, Reese?" Oak calls out, and icy panic floods my veins.

"Shit," I mutter, smoothing my hair down and grabbing my shorts. "Distract him," I snap. "And don't you dare say anything."

"I don't exactly have a death wish," he growls back.

Reese smooths down his t-shirt and pulls the door open, stepping into the hall. Thankfully, he keeps it pulled almost closed, so I can quickly get dressed and try to calm myself down.

"What's going on?" Oak asks. "Where's Liv?"

"She's in there."

"Yeah, but what were you doing in there?"

Blood pounds in my skull as I strain to listen.

Please don't come in here. He'll know. One look at me, and Oakley will know something is up.

"What the fuck do you think I was doing?" Reese grumbles. "Checking she was okay."

"Since when did you grow a heart, Whitfield?"

"At least I wasn't sulking in my room like a child."

"Fuck you, man. I wasn't sulking. Is she... okay?"

"You should ask her. She wouldn't say much to me."

Relief slams into me, but it's short lived when there's a knock on the door.

"Liv?"

"Go away, Oak," I yell.

I can't see him like this. My lips are still swollen from Reese's aggressive kisses, my skin still flushed from his possessive touch.

"Come on, Sis. Don't be like that. I want to know you're okay."

"I'm fine. You don't need to check in on me."

"You let Reese in."

I detect a trace of jealousy in his voice.

I want to tell him that I didn't let Reese do anything, but that will only lead to more questions, so I swallow the words down.

"Oak, serious—"

The door bursts open and my brother appears, looking so wounded I have to smother a laugh.

"Really?" My brow quirks with annoyance.

"I don't like it when you're pissed at me."

"I don't like it when you're lying to me."

"How many times do I have to tell you, I'm not—"

"Just go," I sigh. "I'm not in the mood."

Oakley stares at me, and I wonder if he spots it. But then an arm drops over his shoulder and Reese says, "Come on, Oak. Let's leave Little Miss Perfect to her PMS." He sticks his head inside, smirking over Oak.

God, sometimes I don't know whether I want to kiss the smug expression right off his face or murder him with my bare hands.

Probably a bit of both.

How can someone you despise get so deep under your skin?

It doesn't make any sense.

All I know is that since that night at the end of school initiation party, something ignited inside me. Something that reacts every time Reese is within close proximity.

Part of me wonders if all we need is to fuck the tension out of us. But I'd rather stick pins in my eyes than admit that out loud. Especially after he got with Darcie at the party.

A shudder runs through me. I can't believe I let him touch me after touching her.

"Friends?" Oakley asks with those stupid puppy dog eyes of his.

"Whatever," I murmur, barely meeting his eyes. "Can you leave me alone now?"

"You sure you don't want to come watch scary movies with me and Reese?"

"We're doing that?"

"Hell yes we are, Whitfield. Liv should come too, right?"

"Yeah, she should definitely come."

Heat licks down my spine at the low, gravelly quality to his voice.

"See, even Whitfield wants you to come hang out."

"No." I get up and pad over to my bedroom, grabbing the door handle.

"Liv, come on—"

"Goodbye, Brother." I slam the door in his and Reese's face with a smug smile.

Eventually, I'm going to have to fess up about finding Reese's hoodie. But not tonight.

Instead, I need an escape plan. Because there's no way I can be in the house with Oakley and Reese after what just happened.

So I grab my phone off the desk and text Charli.

> Olivia: Hi, I know it's out of the blue, but can I come over? I need to get out of the house.

> Charli: Fuck yes! Want to stay the night? Arsewipe is away on business, so it's just me and Mum.

> Olivia: Sounds good. I'll be there soon.

Grabbing my bag, I shove a clean uniform, my phone charger, and my toiletry bag inside. Once I have everything I need, I glance at my bedroom door and let out a weary sigh.

Now for the difficult part—escaping the house without my brother and Reese noticing.

29

REESE

"She knows," Oak blurts the second I follow him into his room.

He throws himself onto the bed with a groan, and my eyes shoot to the door that will lead me straight back to Olivia.

My cock still aches for her, but thankfully, Oak's sudden appearance helped to sink my boner sharpish.

I swallow nervously. He's right. She does know.

But how?

We covered our tracks. My alibi is watertight to the point that the entire school knows exactly where I was at the time, thanks to Darcie's big, slutty mouth.

A shudder rips up my spine, and I wonder for the millionth time why I had to be the one lumbered with that bullshit.

Oak or Theo could have taken on the leech.

But then you wouldn't have been able to get payback for Dale fucking Starling touching what's yours.

I banish that little voice from my head, but another quickly pops up in its place.

"Did you do it for my brother and the Heirs? Try to win back their trust... Or did you do it for me?"

"Fuck," I hiss under my breath, the image of her laid out beneath me with her legs spread playing out in my mind.

"What?" Oak asks, not missing my muttering.

Scrubbing my hand down my face, I walk deeper into the room and fall onto Oak's beanbag chair. I'm instantly swallowed up by it. But I can't help thinking how much I'd rather have something else wrapped around me... Olivia's thighs.

Fuck.

I tug at my sweats as they begin getting too small again.

"How?" I finally ask when my silence on the situation begins to get uncomfortable.

"I don't know. Fuck. FUCK," he bellows, his feet slamming down on the bed in frustration. "I fucking hate lying to her."

So don't, sits right on the tip of my tongue.

Oak can trust her. She wouldn't sell him out and willingly get him tangled up in this shit. She might, however, sell me down the river to get rid of me.

"She's got me by the fucking balls, and now she'll barely even talk to me."

"She'll get over it," I mutter, more than aware of how good a grudge that girl can hold. Especially when it comes to Oak.

"Everything is changing, man." He sits forward and threads his fingers through his hair and rests his elbows on his knees. "We've got everything we've always dreamed of. Elliot has the key; the Chapel is ours. The power, the girls, the parties. I knew it meant that I'd be out of the house more, and that things would be different, but not like this.

"The distance between us is growing, and I feel like a pussy, but I don't know. She's... she's a part of me, and I want her to be in my life, but she's pulling away faster than I thought, and holding on to her is like trying to hold sand."

I stare at him unblinking as he opens himself up and lets his pain bleed all over the bed.

Guilt twists up my insides because I know I'm playing a big part in Olivia not wanting anything to do with us as a group, or to hang out at the Chapel.

But then I think back to the beginning of the summer and focus on the fact that Olivia was lying to us all, even Oak.

The truth burns through me like acid. I should tell him what she was hiding, the betrayal she was covering up. But then where would that leave me?

And selfishly, I want this. I want her. That lust-filled hatred she shoots my way every time our eyes connect.

I'm not ready to give that up yet. Not until I've done what I came here for.

Not until I see her and those who wronged me twisted up in pain and regrets.

"I know I can't understand because I don't have a sibling, let alone a twin, but all of this is kinda inevitable. It sucks. But you were never gonna be as close as adults as you were as kids. Life, other people, they're all going to get in the way."

"I know. Fuck. I know. I just... I fucking hate it."

"You're gonna have to get used to sharing her, man. One day, she'll meet someone and—"

"Don't," he warns, finally lifting his head and shooting me a deadly look.

"Don't pull that *no one can ever touch her* bullshit when I know for a fact you were with multiple girls on Friday night."

A wicked smile pulls at the corners of his mouth as he predictably relives what he can remember from that night. "Man, it was crazy," he says, rubbing his jaw, deep in thought.

"Sure sounds like more fun than what I was doing," I mutter.

"Fuck off. You loved every minute of that. You wouldn't have gone as far as you did if you hadn't."

"Maybe," I mutter.

"Anyway, Darcie sure has made it sound like you had the time of your life."

"Hasn't she just. Do you know how many girls I've had come up to me since, wanting to know if the rumours are true about the size of my cock."

Oak snorts a laugh.

"Why the fuck haven't you forced them to find out with their mouths?"

I squeeze my eyes shut, the image of the only girl I want on her knees for me filling my head.

"I can confirm that most of them do a decent enough job."

"I don't want my cock sucked by some decent-ish whore."

"Oh?" Oak asks, curiosity burning through his eyes. "Is there something I don't know?"

"What? No, of course not. I forgot how fucking desperate the All Hallows' girls were while I was away, and it's such a fucking turn off."

Anger twists at his features as I mention my absence, but he quickly recovers.

"Okay, so indulge me. What kind of pussy did you find this summer that's made you so fucking fussy?"

My lips part, ready to shoot something back, but the truth slams into me with force.

The only action I saw this summer was my right hand and those photos I took of Olivia.

Fuck me. When did my life get so pathetic?

As promised, Oak finally put on some horror film I've seen advertised but paid little attention to once he stopped bitching about Olivia.

Part of me revelled in the fact that there was a divide

between them. It's what I wanted. To rip everything away from her and expose her as the lying, traitorous whore she is. But there was another part, a part of me that was desperate to be the kids, and the friends, we once were who wants to do anything I can to fix them. To fix us.

The boys—and Olivia, because she and Oak come as a package deal—used to be everything to me. My brothers. My family.

Walking away from them this summer was hard, but I had the promise of something better on the horizon, and I was a stupid, bitter boy who thought the grass would be greener.

Hell, I'm still that hopeful boy, because I'm still craving that green grass. But being back here, slotting back into my old life, sure makes me question everything more than I expected to.

I had a clear plan. All I had to do was play the game until I could get what I needed, then I would let off the atomic bomb I was working on and run into the sunshine.

Because all I need in life is myself, right?

A soft snore comes from the bed, and when I look over, Oak has slumped down so low that he's almost vertical.

Pushing from his beanbag, I find the remote that's hiding in the sheets and turn the TV off, plunging the room into darkness seeing as we watched the film with the lights off like we did as kids.

Slipping from the room, I have to blink a few times as the light from the hallway sears into my eyeballs like lasers.

The house is silent. I have no idea if Mum and Christian have gone out or are in bed, and to be honest, I don't really give a shit. The less I think about them, the better.

I have every intention of going to my room, I really, truly do, but it seems that my legs have a different idea, because when I reach for a door handle, it's the one that leads me to the room opposite mine that I have zero right walking back into.

But when the fuck did I care about what I should and shouldn't be doing?

My heart races, my cock hardening as her scent hits me the moment I push the door open.

That image of her on the bed earlier fills my mind once again, and I move faster, imagining dragging the sheets from her body and continuing exactly where we left off, only with my head between her thighs instead of my hand.

Adrenaline pumps through me as I surge forward, but I come to an abrupt halt when her room opens up before me and I find her bed suspiciously empty.

I spin around and throw the bathroom door open in the hope that I might find her mid-shower. I already know I won't. Something deep down inside me knows that she's not here. It doesn't stop me from wishing for the best and checking the room in case. But it's empty.

Dragging my phone from my pocket, I pull up our chat.

> Reese: Where are you?

Her message shows as read almost immediately, but she doesn't reply.

> Reese: Olive.

Nothing.

> Reese: Are you so scared of admitting what you really want that you'd rather run away from me?

I can picture her teeth grinding as her eyes flash with that defiance that brings me to my knees every time I see it.

> Reese: Pussy.

> Reese: Are you still wet for me?

I walk back out of the bathroom and look around her room. Flicking on her bedside lamp, I bite down on my bottom lip as ideas flicker through my head.

> Reese: Guess where I am right now?

I pull open her top drawer, disappointed when I find socks. Boring.

The next one is full of her lacy bras. Better.

"Bingo," I breathe, reaching into the third drawer and pulling out a pair of pink lace knickers.

Lifting them to my nose, I inhale the scent of fresh laundry mixed with whatever that unique Olivia smell is. My cock jerks as I crawl back on her bed with my loot twisted in my fingers.

My phone buzzes, and a wide smirk stretches across my face.

"Gotcha."

> Olive: Get out of my room.

> Reese: No can do, sweet cheeks. I love your lingerie collection. Very sexy. I particularly like the pink set with the little heart charm hanging from the lace.

> Olive: KEEP THE FUCK OUT OF MY STUFF.

A chuckle falls from my lips as I imagine her face getting all red and cute with anger.

Lifting my shirt up to reveal my abs, I half shove her underwear beneath the waistband of my sweats. Switching to my camera, I snap a picture and send it to her.

What I really want to do is send her one of my face with

her knickers in my mouth, but that seems like a fucking stupid thing to do, and the perfect ammunition to come back at me with for the ones I'm holding of her.

The difference here is that I'll never share those photos of her with anyone. But something tells me she'd happily spread any shit about me around school faster than Darcie gets on her knees.

> Olive: I'm going to kill you in your sleep.

> Reese: And I'm going to come on your pillow. Isn't this fun?

30

OLIVIA

"So are you going to tell me the real reason you needed to escape the house last night?" Charli asks as I plait my hair into a loose braid over my shoulder.

"I already told you, Oakley was annoying me."

"Oakley, right."

"What is that supposed to mean?" I glance over at her and she arches a brow.

"So it had nothing to do with your new stepbrother?"

"He's not my stepbrother, Charl. He's... nothing."

"You are a terrible liar."

I press my lips into a thin line, and her soft laughter fills the room. "You know, I am an excellent reader of people. And you, Olivia Beckworth, are hiding something."

"I don't know what you're talking about."

"So what was that at the party? With Brad—"

"Ben," I correct, grabbing my bag and shoving the last of my things inside. I need to get going if I don't want to be late for class.

"Brad. Ben. He could be called Bertie for all I care, but don't even try to deny you were only dancing with him to make Reese jealous."

"No comment."

"Seriously, you're going to pull that shit with me? Your friend?"

Giving her a little shrug, I grab my keys and say, "If we leave now, I can give you a lift on my way."

"Thanks, but I'm taking the car. Mum lets me borrow it when Dan the Dickwad isn't here."

"That's a new one." I chuckle.

"Just trying it on for size. It's so much easier when he's not around."

"Your mum still not budging on that?"

"Nope. She thinks he 'makes our lives better'."

"I'm sorry."

"Don't be. As soon as I'm done with school, I am out of here. You know, you should come with. We can hitchhike across the world, surviving on nothing but drinks from hot men and the clothes on our backs."

"Yeah, I'm not really sure that sounds like my idea of fun."

"Boring." She snorts, touching up her lip gloss. "I'm going to buy the cheapest flight out of Heathrow."

"And what does your mum think about your great escape plan?"

Charli shrugs, slipping on a diamanté embroidered hoodie. "I haven't told her yet. She doesn't give a shit though. So long as she's got precious Dan the Wanker."

"Charl, she loves you," I say.

"Yeah, well, she has a funny way of showing it." She glances at her phone and balks. "Shit, is that the time? You're going to have to step on it or you'll be late."

I make it to All Hallows' with two minutes to spare, but it's probably a good thing. Less chance of bumping into my brother—or even worse, Reese—in the corridors.

Unease still ripples through me from his messages last night, that photo of his abs and my stolen knickers still burned into the backs of my eyelids.

Oakley tried to call me first thing this morning, but I ignored it.

I'm tired of the way they try to bulldoze over my life time and time again. I made him promise they wouldn't do anything stupid where Dale Starling was concerned, and he broke it. Because reputation and appearances and exerting their power over anyone they deem a threat will always be more important to the Heirs than anything else.

It's patriarchal arrogance at its finest, and I'm stuck in their world, whether I want to be or not.

As I hurry down the corridor to class, something snags my attention on the sixth form noticeboard. Ugh. The first rugby game of the season is this Friday, which means All Hallows' is set to become a battleground as the Saints go head-to-head with their opponents with hopes of progressing to the county cup.

If my brother and the lads were unbearable before, they'll be insufferable once the season starts. All that testosterone and aggression. It doesn't help that Coach Walker is a drinking and golf buddy of Dad, and Elliot and Theo's fathers. It's why he's all too happy to turn a blind eye to the Heirs and their reckless behaviour.

With a heavy sigh, I hitch my bag up my shoulder and slip into class, mumbling an apology for being a tad late. The teacher throws me a disapproving glance and silently ushers me into my seat.

Of course, this class is the only one I share with Darcie Porter and her air-headed friends. She whispers something as I drop into my chair, and they all snigger. Glancing back, I pin her with a hard look and mouth, 'Problem?'

"Nothing." She gives me a saccharine smile, and I want to rip her perfectly styled hair out of her skull.

God, she and Reese really bring out my violent streak.

The teacher begins to lay out the topic for the day, a riveting dissection of life in Tudor England. I take some notes, distracted by the low din of Darcie and her friends' incessant chatter.

"Can you three shut up?" I hiss over my shoulder.

"Rude, much. We're discussing the work."

"Of course you are, and I'm running for Head Girl."

"Against Tally Darlington?" Darcie scoffs. "You'll never win."

"I was..." I shake my head. "It doesn't matter. Just please try and keep it down."

Thirty seconds.

They manage a whole thirty seconds before they start dissecting the size of Reese's dick.

"Grower or shower?" Tasha asks.

"Both," Darcie sniggers. "I swear he was so big, he hit my cervix every damn time."

"So lucky," her friend murmurs, and my stomach roils.

They continue like that for the next ten minutes. How many times he made her come, how loud she screamed, the scratch marks she left on his back.

My ears perk up as I glance back again.

"What?" Darcie sneers.

"How bad was it?"

"What?" she asks.

"Reese's back?"

"Ew, why do you want to know?"

I shrug. "Your nails are practically weapons..." My eyes drop to her talons, and for a second, I imagine her raking them down Reese's skin while she cries out with pleasure.

Stop.

I shake the unwanted and rather disturbing thoughts out of my head.

"You're not jealous, are you?" Darcie smirks. "Because

you know Reese would never touch you in like a million years. You're Oakley's sister and you're... not exactly Reese's type."

Bitch.

Smug. Vain. Bitch.

Taking a deep breath, I face the front of the room again, giving Darcie and her friends the cold shoulder for the rest of the class. As soon as the teacher dismisses us, I dig out my phone and open up my chat history with Reese.

> Olivia: Meet me before lunch?

> Reese: What? Why?

> Olivia: You'll have to meet me to find out.

> Reese: You seem to have forgotten, sweet cheeks, I make the rules.

So predictable. I roll my eyes as I file out of class.

> Olivia: Fine. Don't meet. No skin off my nose.

> Reese: Behind the gym. Come alone.

> Olivia: Oh, I plan on it.

A smirk curls my lips. Reese thinks he's so fucking smooth.

Well, if my suspicions are correct, I'm about to bring him down a peg or two.

Reese makes me wait seven minutes and twenty seconds.

I know, because I timed him.

The smug wanker appears around the corner, looking every bit the posh bad boy that'll buy you Louboutins without so much as blinking and then fuck you in nothing but the red-soled heels.

"You're late," I snap, and he smirks.

"Feeling a little restless there, Olive?" He crowds me against the wall, pressing his hand onto the bricks beside my head. "You ran last night."

"You call it running, I call it regrouping."

"Is that so..."

"It is." I slide my hands up his chest and bat my eyelashes.

His eyes narrow in return as he captures my wrists in his big hand. "What game are you playing?"

"Actually, I was thinking we could call truce." Yanking my hand back free, I drop it to his trousers and brazenly stroke his dick through the stiff material.

"Fuck," he chokes out. "You're playing with fire..." he warns, but I keep stroking, applying more pressure to keep him distracted as I slip my other hand around his back and underneath his shirt.

"What are you doing?" His brow lifts.

"I want to feel your skin." I pout. Sweet and seductive.

I run my fingers up his back, stroking every inch of his smooth, warm skin. There isn't so much as a scratch on him. At least, it doesn't feel like there is.

"Fuck, that feels good," he groans.

I lean closer, brushing my lips over his jaw, letting them hover over the corner of his mouth. "Take off your shirt, Reese."

"W-what?" He blinks at me, confused.

"I want to taste you. All of you. But not unless you take off your shirt."

Suspicion dances in his eyes, so I quickly unbutton his trousers and slide my hand inside, grasping him firmly.

"Jesus, shit, Liv," he pants.

"If you want my mouth around your dick, I suggest... You. Take. It. Off."

"Yeah, shit, okay." He starts shifting out of his blazer and loosening his tie. Then, he's unbuttoning his shirt and pulling everything off.

I give him a coy smile, letting my eyes trail over his toned, muscular body. So much tanned skin. Perfectly smooth, scratch-free skin.

"Let me," I whisper, still stroking him as I step into him and kiss his shoulder, his chest and pecs, running my other hand all over him as I feed his lust. Moving around his big, imposing body, I smile triumphantly the second I see his back. The skull inked on his skin taunts me, a reminder of his obligations—his destiny. But I shove down those feelings and focus on the task at hand.

Pulling my hand free of his trousers, I keep moving until I'm behind him.

"Come on, Liv. Don't keep me waiting. I want you on your knees, your mouth wrapped around—"

"You lied." I spit the words.

"The fuck?" He spins around, cutting me with an icy glare.

"You didn't fuck Darcie. She's your alibi. You made me and everyone else think you were with her all night so you'd have an airtight alibi. It was you. You went to Huxton, and you blew up Dale Starling's car. And I want to know why."

He stares at me, the air crackling around us. "You don't know shit."

Reese grabs his shirt and blazer and pulls them back on.

"I found your hoodie."

"What?"

An icy cold tremor goes through me at the hostility in his voice. But I refuse to cower now.

"You heard me. I found your hoodie."

"You were snooping in my room?" His hand shoots out and grabs me around the throat, spinning me around until I'm pressed against the wall.

"You're not the only one who can play this game, Reese." Another violent shudder runs through me as he stares at me, through me.

I'm right.

It was him.

Reese did it, and he's using Darcie as his alibi.

"Fuck. *Fuck*." He releases me and staggers back, jamming his hands into his hair and tugging the ends.

"Reese, come on, just talk to—"

"Fuck you, Olivia." He gets right in my face again and bares his teeth. "I swear to fucking God, Beckworth, if you tell anyone about this—"

Laughter and voices cut through the air and Reese releases me again, moving away.

"Reese," I start, but he shakes head, loops his tie around his neck and takes off down the path.

I sink against the wall, wondering when life got so fucking complicated.

31

REESE

I take off down the path in a rage. The laughter that had filtered into my lust-filled mind has faded away once more as I fight the red haze of anger that's taking hold of me faster than I should allow it to.

I knew that Olivia knew, but she really *knows*.

Fuck.

She knows that all the bullshit that's spilling from Darcie's creative lips are lies. She knows I didn't take her down to the basement to fuck her six ways from Sunday, and she knows I was the one to blow up Starling's car.

But worse than all that...

I let her play me like a fool.

She offered herself up on a platter in a move that was a complete U-turn to anything she's done since I got back to town, and I fell for it the second she reached out and ran her fingers over my cock.

Fuck, I'm such a fucking idiot.

She doesn't want me. She hates me. So why would I think she did?

Because you're a fucking fool.

Your desire for her, your need to claim her is beginning to overrule anything else.

"Fuck," I roar, the door to the locker room right up ahead.

The few guys that are littered around doing lunchtime clubs jump out of my way and quickly scarper when they see me coming.

The door crashes back against the wall as I blow through into a space where I feel able to let it out.

What I really need is to go back to the Chapel, but seeing as those motherfuckers still haven't given me my key, I have little other choice.

"GET OUT," I boom, when I find a couple of guys staring at me as I stand in the middle of the space like a raging bull. "GET THE FUCK OUT."

Half dressed, they share a concerned glance before bolting toward the door.

"FUUUUCK," I bellow before the door even slams closed. My fingers thread into my hair, and I pull until it hurts so bad it makes my eyes water. "FUCK. FUCK."

Surging forward, my fist collides with one of the lockers that lines the wall, leaving a fuck-off dent in it that Coach will want to rip me a new one for, but I don't give a fuck.

I hit it over and over. My knuckles split and pain shoots up my arm, but I barely feel any of it. I'm too lost in my haze, my anger, my frustration.

I let her play me.

I let her have all the fucking power, and she got exactly what she wanted.

That isn't how this game is meant to be going.

I'm the one in charge. I'm the one with the power, with the plan, with the need for revenge.

Me.

My chest heaves, my body covered in a sheen of sweat as I finally fall back against the busted lockers.

But everything I was feeling pales into nothing when I

glance at the door and find Olivia there, watching me as if I'm some caged fucking animal at a zoo. She's gnawing on her bottom lip, her brow knitted in concern as she stares at me with wide eyes.

"Reese, I—"

"No." I surge forward, twisting my fingers in her blazer and dragging her deeper into the room.

"Reese," she cries, her small hands locking around my arm to try and stop me, but she's got little chance of that happening.

"You played me," I growl, continuing to back her up.

"You lied to me. You let me think..." She cuts herself off, still refusing to admit the truth. To admit that she wants me.

"I let you think that I fucked Darcie?" I growl, my voice low and dangerous as I drag her so close that our noses brush.

The taste of her is still on my lips, the memory of her tongue moving against mine still so fresh. It makes a whole new kind of fire burn through me.

Her lips slam shut, her teeth grinding behind them until I'm convinced she's going to crack one.

"Yeah, I let you think I fucked Darcie," I confess. "Do you know why?"

She sucks in a breath but doesn't say a word, just shakes her head, although the move is so minimal that I'd probably miss it if I weren't right up in her face.

"Because that motherfucker needed to pay." I release her blazer in favour of her throat as we continue to cut through the locker room.

She gasps, her eyes locked on mine.

"He touched something that belongs to me. And there was no fucking way I was ever letting him get away with that."

"Reese, I— REESE," she screams, cutting off whatever she was about to say when I finally get to our destination and slam my hand on the button for the shower. "What the fuck? Let me go," she demands, her hands flying, making contact with me anywhere she can as ice-cold water rains down over both of us, soaking us in an instant.

"Reese you can't—" I step into her body, taking hold of both of her wild wrists and pinning them against the wall above her head.

"Yes, I can, Olive. I can do whatever the fuck I want. Didn't you get the memo? I fucking own this school."

"A quarter of it," she seethes. "And when Oak finds out about this he'll..."

"He'll what, sweet cheeks? Beat my arse for ever touching his precious little Olivia?"

"You prick. You fucking—"

My words are cut off when my self-control shatters and my lips slam down on hers. Whatever she was about to spit at me gets lost in our kiss, in our desire.

Hitching one of her legs up around my waist, I grind my aching cock against her pussy, making her moan in delight.

"You did this," I growl without breaking the contact of our lips. "You did this, Olive. Just remember that when I've got my cock so deep inside you that you no longer remember how to breathe."

"Oh fuck," she pants, her hips happily rolling in time with mine, the sensation of her burning cunt making my cock weep for her.

I may have threatened it, but I didn't actually come on her pillow. Fucking wanted to. But knowing I was holding off for this makes it so fucking worth it.

"I'll give you everything you need. All you've got to do is tell me you want me."

"Argh." Her frustrated cry rips through the air as she still fights me.

"I think it's more than obvious right now how much I need you, so why is it so hard to say the words? You know the truth. I didn't dip my cock in that fucking bitch, so what's the issue?"

The water still rains down on us, only now, it's warm.

Every inch of both of us is sodden. Olivia's hair is plastered to her face, her dark make-up washed down her cheeks.

But fuck... it only makes her look hotter.

"Are you wet for me, Olivia?" Her eyes flash with realisation that I've used her real name before she surprises me once again.

"I think we both know I'm soaked right now." But then her eyes flash with amusement, and I drag myself out of the depth of my lust for this girl.

"I should fuck that smart mouth right here, Olivia. Find out what good it can be used for when you're unable to talk."

Her eyes narrow, but not before flashing with heat.

Fuck. She wants it.

My trousers barely contain my cock as it fights to break through the fabric to find her pussy, her hand, her fucking anything that will help relieve the pressure that's building up in me faster than I can control.

I squeeze my eyes closed for a beat to try and get myself in check before I do something I'm going to really regret. But it's hard, so fucking hard—pun intended.

"Tell me. Tell me you want it."

But she still fights it. The words are right there, swimming in her eyes, on the tip of her tongue, but still... nothing.

"Fine. But don't forget that you chose this."

Fisting her hair, I force her to her knees before me. "Take my cock out," I demand. "You were so keen for it earlier."

Hate flashes in her eyes, but instead of refusing like I expect her to, she shocks the fuck out of me and reaches for my waistband.

In seconds, my sodden trousers and boxers are around my hips, my cock jutting out between the two of us, needy and desperate.

"Darcie was wrong," Olivia states, her eyes locked on my length as it twitches in desperation, starved of her touch.

"Oh yeah?" I grit out.

"I've seen bigger."

"Fuck you, Olive." My fingers return to her hair and I force her forward, pushing the head of my cock between her lips as a wild, feral roar rips from my throat, echoing around the silent locker room.

Her heat, the softness of her lips... fuck, her tongue as she swipes it up the underside of my shaft.

"FUCK."

My fingers tighten, pulling her back and setting a frantic pace as my need to blow my load in her mouth consumes me. Reaching out, I plant my hand on the wall, hoping it's enough to hold me up as my knees threaten to buckle.

The sight of her on her knees for me, her brown hair dark with water, her tiny hands resting on my thighs...

Fuck. All of it fucking wrecks me in a way it shouldn't.

My balls begin to draw up embarrassingly fast. I rationalise that this has been a long time coming and try to put any male pride to one side as I focus on my end goal—Olivia being able to taste me for the rest of the day.

"Oh fuck. Your mouth is fucking sin, babe."

Her eyes shoot up to mine, hate and desire colliding so fiercely, I'm almost sure she pulls away just to spite me.

Sadly, I don't get a fucking chance to find out if she's going to be a good girl and take all of me or not, because the locker room door slams open before a voice that sends ice through my veins booms through the deserted space.

"Whitfield, you in here?" Oakley booms.

Olivia's eyes widen so far, I'm amazed they don't pop right out of her head and roll across the floor.

Reluctantly, I pull her off my cock and drag her to her feet.

"Hide behind that door," I hiss, pointing across the shower block. The door leads to the toilets. She can lock herself in a cubicle until I figure out a way around this.

Fuck.

What the fuck was I thinking?"

She looks around, ready to argue, but then Oak calls again and she takes off running, water dripping from her as she goes.

In a rush, I tuck my sad cock away and turn my back to the entrance of the shower. Pressing my palms to the tiles, I let the water crash against my back as I wait for him to find me.

And only three seconds later he does.

"Reese, what the fuck?"

I suck in a breath, preparing to turn around and face him. Three. Two. One.

Concern fills his eyes as I spin around and find them.

"I need the key to the Chapel, Oak," I say in a voice that I hope sounds desperate enough.

"Uh... what the fuck is going on?"

"Please," I beg. "I just need to get out of here. I need—"

"Fine. But you can answer to Elliot when he freaks the fuck out over this."

I take off, leaving the shower running behind me, snatch up my bag that I hadn't even realised I'd dropped, and take off out of the locker room with Oakley hot on my tail, my mind spinning for an excuse for my bizarre behaviour.

32

OLIVIA

The door slams shut, reverberating through me, and I slip out of the toilet stall.

What the hell am I going to do? I'm soaked to the bone with make-up smeared over my face.

There's no way I can risk going back to school like this. I need to get out of here.

Panic rises inside me as I creep into the changing room and scan the place for something to cover myself up with.

Bingo.

I spot an All Hallows' hoodie hanging on one of the coat pegs. Yanking it down, I slip out of my blazer and pull it on over my saturated shirt.

Reese Baron Whitfield is going to be the death of me.

I didn't follow him back here to finish what I'd started. I only wanted to talk.

Stupid girl.

A boy like Reese doesn't talk.

But part of me wanted to hear him say it. I wanted him to admit that he went to Huxton for me.

I got more than I bargained for, though.

Bringing a finger to my mouth, I touch my lips, remembering what it had felt like to be on my knees for him.

But the fantasy is ruined when I hear voices beyond the changing room door. I need to get out of here, and fast. Instead of going out the door leading to the corridor and the rest of the building, I slip out of the door leading to the sports field. No one is out here. No one except—

"Abigail?"

She's sitting there, staring out at nothing.

"Is everything okay?" I ask, approaching her.

She finally looks up at me and frowns. "What happened to you?"

"Nothing, I'm—"

"I saw you, Olivia." She gives me a weak smile that sends a bolt of guilt through me.

"Saw me?"

"Go into the changing room after Reese."

"I wasn't... that's not... it's complicated."

"I'm not jealous, if that's what you're thinking. Reese is... he scares me."

"He's an arsehole."

Her mouth quirks up. "He is. But you two are—"

"Nothing. We're nothing." The words sour on my tongue.

"Are you sure you're okay? If he hurt you—"

"He didn't, but I need to go home. I can't stay at school like this." I motion to the state of me.

"I could give you a lift?"

"Oh no, you don't have to do that."

"It's fine. I wasn't planning on staying much longer anyway."

"Don't you have class?"

"Yeah, but nobody will miss me." Abigail stands and gives me a strange look. "My car is only over there." She motions to the smaller car park at the back of school.

Unlike my own car, which is parked outside the main entrance, right in plain sight of a lot of the A Level classrooms.

I have a choice.

Risk going to my car and being spotted by half my year, or going with Abigail and finding out more about the girl promised to Reese.

"Uh, sure," I say. "If you don't mind."

"It's no problem, really."

She takes off down the path and I fall into step behind her.

"So, do you want to tell me what happened?"

"Not really," I whisper, aware that I must look like a drowned rat.

"But Reese was somehow responsible?"

"Like I said, it's complicated."

"Do you like him?"

"I... I shouldn't," I admit quietly, the truth of the words making my chest ache.

"Hey, maybe if the two of you fall in love, it'll get me out of the stupid arrangement our parents seem insistent on following through on." Despite her soft words, there's fire in her expression that surprises me.

I don't know Abigail Bancroft, not really. But like everyone else at All Hallows', I see enough to know that she's a shy, reserved girl.

She leads me over to a matte black Lexus SUV and I let out a low whistle. "Nice."

"I think my dad would call it efficient and reliable. Get in," she says.

Once we're both inside and belted up, I ask, "It's just you and your dad?"

Abigail nods. "My mum died in the accident that—" She indicates to her face.

"I'm sorry, I know how hard it is to lose a parent."

"It's been just the two of us for a long time." Her voice cracks.

"Abigail?"

"Sorry," she swipes at her eyes, "you don't want to hear this."

"No, I do. It's okay, you can talk to me."

"He's sick. My dad is sick."

"I'm sorry."

"Me too."

"What's wrong with him, if you don't mind me asking?"

"He has Huntington's disease. He got diagnosed eight years ago, right after the accident."

"I'm sorry," I repeat, because what is there to say? I don't have tons of knowledge about the disease but enough to know that the prognosis isn't good.

"It isn't your fault. I just can't imagine a day where he isn't there for me, you know?" She gives me a strained smile.

"Thanks for this," I say, wanting to lift the heavy mood. "I really appreciate it."

Abigail has no problem finding my house, not that I'm surprised. Most people in Saints Cross know where Christian Beckworth lives.

"Pretty house," she says as she pulls into the long, winding driveway.

"Like you don't live in a house just as big and beautiful as this." I flash her a smile.

I like her.

Maybe that's a weird thing to say, considering she's to one day be married to the boy I'm fooling around with.

"I guess you've got me there. I'll see you around, Olivia."

"Actually, would you like to come inside?"

The blood drains from her face and I add, "I don't bite, promise."

"I... I'm not really used to—"

"What? Hanging out? Raiding the fridge for leftovers? I'm sure you can come inside for ten minutes? Reese and Oak are at school and then they have rugby practice. The house is all ours."

Abigail hesitates, chewing on her bottom lip. "Fine, okay."

"Great."

Reese would flip his lid if he found out I was doing this, but he can go to hell right now for all I care.

He hasn't even texted me since he fled the boys' changing room like he was leaving the scene of a crime.

Arsehole.

I let myself into the house, beckoning Abigail to follow me. She's nervous, tugging on the hem of her skirt, her big hazel eyes glancing around the place. It's hard not to look at her scars. To wonder if they hurt. But unlike a lot of kids at school, I don't see them as anything to ridicule.

In fact, a strange emotion bubbles up inside me as I think of all the times I've watched kids mock her or taunt her about them.

"You're staring," she says, and I begin to stutter out an apology. "It's okay, you can ask me if you want."

"I was wondering if they hurt."

Her finger traces the biggest scar running from her jawline to right above her ear. "Sometimes they pinch, like the skin is stretched too far. It's hard to explain it."

"I'm sorry."

"You say that a lot."

"I guess I do. It was a car crash, right?"

She nods. "It's how we found out about my dad's disease. He had a seizure and lost control of the vehicle. Turns out, he'd been ignoring the symptoms for years."

"That must have been hard." I motion for her to sit at the breakfast counter while I grab a container of homemade cookies.

"He still blames himself now. But I know it wasn't his fault."

"How is he now?"

"Struggling, but he's a stubborn old fool and doesn't like to make a fuss. His symptoms have been well managed for the last couple of years, but I'm starting to notice a deterioration in his health. He hides it well, but I see the signs." Her eyes fill with emotion. "He and my mum were older when they had me. I know he worries about... leaving me." She swallows over the words. "It's one of the reasons he made that stupid arrangement with Mrs. Whitfield-Brown." Anger coats her voice.

"One of the reasons?" I arch a brow.

"There's more to it. There has to be. I'm his only daughter, the apple of his eye. I can't believe he'd willingly hand me over to someone like Reese. He'd eat me alive."

"Maybe he knows that Reese and his family can protect you. Reese is—"

"Dangerous?" Abigail stares at me.

"He isn't scared to get his hands dirty, no. And the world can be a cruel place for—" I stop myself, realising how I sound.

"A girl like me? Scarred and damaged?"

"That's not what I mean. I'm sorry, I shouldn't have said that."

"No, I get it. You're only speaking the truth. Our world chews up and spits out anyone who doesn't fit the mould. I know that. I've lived it for the last eleven years."

Strained silence falls over us as I stuff half a cookie into my big mouth. I didn't mean to make her feel less than she is. Something tells me Abigail Bancroft possesses an inner strength most of us at All Hallows' don't have. But I don't say any of that, because the last thing I want to do is patronise her when I know how difficult it is for her to be here, in my house.

"We should hang out," I blurt, swallowing the last of my cookie.

"Hang out? Together?"

"Yeah. I mean, we're kind of doing that now."

"I'm not sure I fit in with you and your friends."

"What friends?"

"Your brother... the Heirs... Reese.

"You just named my brother and his friends. I'm sure you know me well enough by now to know that I don't exactly have a huge social circle at All Hallows'?"

"Why is that? You're Olivia Beckworth. Life for you should be—"

"Easy? I scoff. "You have met my brother, right? Overbearing. Overprotective. An alpha-arsehole of epic proportions. I love my brother dearly, but he has never made life easy for me. Somewhere along the way, it got easier not to be wary of people's motivations rather than trust they didn't want to use me as a stepping stone to Oak and his friends."

"That sounds kind of tragic."

"It is. Which is why you and I make the perfect twosome."

"Oh, I don't know." A skittish expression washes over her. "I can't step into your world, Liv. It'll eat me alive."

"Not if I don't let it."

I like her.

I've decided. And we all need a friend now and again. Even if that friend is the future wife of the boy you're trying hard not to fall for.

Shit.

I am.

I'm falling for Reese.

I like his filthy, crass words and the way he doesn't handle me with kiddy gloves. I like the way he makes my body sing and heart race.

I like him.

And I think, that maybe, beneath his mean, cold, doesn't-give-a-fuck exterior, he likes me too.

But there are two very glaring problems with this realisation.

One. My brother will never accept it. I'm his sister. Off-limits.

And two, Reese doesn't belong to me.

He belongs to Abigail.

33

REESE

The heavy door of the Chapel slams against the wall the second after Oak unlocks it for me and I storm forward, needing to get the fuck away from him and the questions filling his eyes.

"Reese, wait," he calls, and damn it, my steps falter at the concern in his tone. "You wanna check out your room?" This time, there's a smugness in his voice that tells me he knows he's got me.

I spin around, finding him coming up behind me, holding his set of keys in front of him.

"M-my room?" I ask like an imbecile.

"Come on," he says, scrubbing my wet hair like he's my fucking father before taking off toward the stairs.

Since I've been back, the only stairs I've used in this place are the ones to the basement. The upper floor has been off-limits to me.

Until now, apparently.

I follow behind Oak, grateful that he's not questioning me as to why he found me falling apart in the locker room.

Silence fills the space between us as we walk past the first two doors and come to a stop in front of the third.

"Elliot has the one at the end, obviously," Oak mutters, rolling his eyes.

The room at the end stretches the entire width of the building and is the biggest and most elaborate master bedroom I've ever laid eyes on. Or at least, it was that one time Scott let us check it out before it became out of bounds unless you were personally invited. "That's mine," he says, pointing to the door next to us. "And that's Theo's." He nods across the hall.

A million questions sit on the tip of my tongue, like asking how they decided this was mine. I know it's not the smallest, so how did I end up with it when they all hated me?

"Theo lost a bet," he mutters as if he can hear my unspoken question.

The click of the old lock rattles through me before Oak swings the door open and gestures for me to head inside.

I was expecting it to be trashed. To have been left exactly as Scott and the others will have left the entire place so that I could have my taste of that part of the initiation that I missed.

But that's not what I find as I step inside and my sodden shoes sink into the grey carpet.

"What the—"

"We hoped you might come back," Oak admits quietly behind me. "So we... yeah." When I look back, he's rubbing at the back of his neck nervously. "Hope you like it."

His smile guts me as pain flickers through his eyes.

I really hurt him, all of them, when I disappeared from their lives without a second thought. Or at least, that's what I allowed them to think.

Truth is, I missed them every fucking day. But it wasn't them I was running from, not really. It was this life, the expectations, the betrayal.

Guilt burns through me as all the times I've got close to Olivia flash behind my eyes.

It's going to wreck Oak when he finds out what I'm doing, what I'm planning.

But is that enough to stop me from revealing the truth?

No fucking chance.

He deserves to know it as much as everyone else does. And I'm going to be the one to give it to them.

Ripping my eyes from his, I look around my room once more. The sun is streaming through the stained-glass window, casting all kinds of colours across the light grey walls and oak furniture.

It's stunning, it really is. And it only makes the guilt knotting my stomach hurt more.

"I'll... uh... I'll leave you to it. Figure out how I'm gonna explain this to Elliot," he admits with an unamused laugh.

"I've got your back," I say honestly. "I needed this today."

Oak nods, backing up toward the door.

My lips part, and before I get the chance to suck the words back in, they spill from me. "I'm sorry, Oak. I'm sorry I abandoned you without—"

"It's okay. I... I get it. I think. This place. Our lives. They can be intense. I can't say that I've never thought about running a time or two. I just wish you'd have talked to me."

I nod because it's one of my biggest regrets too, although I'm not sure what it would have changed.

"I found out she was cheating on my dad a few weeks before initiation," I admit, feeling like I need to give him something, because the truth of how we ended up here today certainly isn't going to fall from my lips.

"Must have been a shock."

"When Dad said he was leaving town, all I saw was an escape. I needed away from the pressure, from... my future."

"Abigail?"

I wince as her name echoes around me and regret washes over Oak's expression.

"Shit, sorry," he whispers, realising he's broken one of my rules.

"It's fine, it's— go and grab us a drink or something. I'll

shower and we can hang. There's no point going back to class now."

"You got it." He hesitates as if he's going to ask me why we're even here in the first place, but thankfully he swallows down that demand and walks out of my room.

Years of friendship means we pretty much know each other inside out, and thankfully, that means he knows not to push me to talk. He knows that I'll open up when I'm good and ready. Thank fuck, because I still don't have a decent excuse for that earlier.

"Fuck," I hiss, squeezing my eyes closed as I think of Olivia.

Did she manage to escape okay?

I dig my phone from my pocket—thank fuck it's survived my impromptu shower with Liv—and pull up our chat to ask if she's okay.

But in the end, I close it back down and head for the shower.

I'm probably the last person she wants to hear from right now—and anyway, I'd rather see her in person to finish what we started than exchange a few angry messages.

"You're hanging out with Abigail?"

The words I overheard Oakley say on the phone to Olivia earlier haunt me as I finally lie on my own bed in the Chapel.

Predictably, Elliot was pissed when he discovered that Oak had caved and let me in here. But the gruelling training session we endured in the hopes of preparing us for Friday night's game sure helped to expel some of his anger, and he was almost over it by the time we got back here.

I didn't stop him sulking about it and locking himself in his lair soon after we'd eaten though. Control freak.

But his temperamental emotional state is the least of my worries right now.

Why the hell is Olivia hanging out with Abigail?

I've typed out at least ten different messages since I eavesdropped on their conversation earlier in the hopes of finding out what her excuse was for ditching the rest of the day. I get fuck all on that front, but the Abigail thing has sure thrown me.

The only thing I can figure out is that she's trying to get some dirt on me, trying to play games with things she has no right in poking her nose into.

Why else would she suddenly befriend a girl who I doubt is her kind of person?

I'm sure Abigail is lovely. But she's so fucking quiet, I have to doubt she has much of a personality. She just... exists. Almost like a ghost in the room that you're not entirely sure is there or not.

"Fuck," I hiss, my need to know what the fuck is going on becoming too much to ignore.

As per Elliot's earlier request, I should already be asleep. The game is approaching, and that means our wild, playboy lives get put on hold. The parties stop, the drink is banned, and we suddenly have to pretend that we're professional sportsmen for a couple of days.

The whole thing is bullshit if you ask me, but I'm not about to rock the boat now I've got a king-sized memory foam mattress instead of that concrete sofa to sleep on.

The Chapel has been in silence for well over an hour, Oak and Theo following orders like good little Heirs and going to bed at curfew, and I wonder if they'd hear anything if I were to...

My eyes lock on the door, then flick to my trainers that I kicked off after practice.

Not only did I not expect to find this room all ready for

me, but I also didn't think I'd find the cupboard full of all the shit I might need to live here, including condoms and lube in the bedside table, despite the fact that there's a no-girls-allowed rule up here. They sure did think of everything, those arseholes.

I push from the bed before I think better of it, shove my feet into my shoes, and silently pull my door open. Before I know it, I've escaped the old building without making a noise, and I'm in my car and heading toward the Beckworths'.

The streets are dead, and as I pull up to the house, I find it in total darkness.

I can't help but smile as excitement begins to stir, my blood heating as I remember how her lips felt wrapped around my cock.

"Shit," I hiss, palming my semi through my sweats. I really fucking need her to finish me off.

In only seconds, I'm letting myself into her room, my cock fully hard and tenting my sweats as I move silently through the darkness and pull her chair over.

Just like I hoped, she's peacefully sleeping, her cheek resting on her hand, her full and tempting lips parted, inviting me to take what I need.

My eyes drop down her body, which is exposed with the duvet bunched at her waist. If it were lighter, I have no doubt I'd be able to see the outline of her nipple through the thin fabric.

Just the thought of stripping her naked makes my cock weep, and I'm powerless but to push my hand into my sweats and fist myself.

A growl rips from my throat as I remember her tongue twisting around the head, lapping at my precum.

"Fuck," I bark, my release already in touching distance after she left me desperate earlier.

Reaching out with my free hand, I wrap my fingers around

her duvet and slowly pull it down her body, needing more of her.

It's a risk, but I figure that I don't really give a shit if she wakes.

She might still be refusing to admit how much she needs this. But I'm not. It's more than evident every time she's felt my hard cock pressing against her. Darcie might be a lying bitch, but she sure got something right—the size of my dick is kinda hard to miss.

A groan falls from her lips as the covers brush over her bare legs, leaving her exposed in a tiny pair of lace knickers that make me bite down on my bottom lip.

Abandoning the sheets, my fingers collide with her calf and I drag them up, loving the way her skin erupts in goosebumps at my touch. I trace over the edge of her underwear, and a moan spills from her parted lips before she rolls slightly onto her back, revealing more of her body to me.

With the light from the moon flooding the room, it's impossible to miss the way her nipples press against her vest.

Gliding my fingers up her toned stomach, I make it to her tits, circling her nipples, making her moans get louder and my cock even harder.

"Reese," she moans in her sleep, and I damn near come in my pants.

"You dreaming of me, sweet cheeks?" I murmur. "You imagining sucking my cock like a good girl again?" This time when I speak, she stills, and a smile pulls at my lips a beat before her eyes fly open.

Her lips part, ready to scream, but I'm faster, pressing my palm over her mouth and jumping on top of her, pinning her to the bed.

"Reese, what the hell are you doing?" she whisper-shouts, her eyes bouncing between mine and where my hand is still lost in my sweats.

"Finishing what we started."

Shifting, I shove my sweats down and expose myself, painting the tip of my cock over her lips.

"Gonna say it yet, Olive?"

34

OLIVIA

My heart crashes wildly in my chest as I stare up at Reese, completely and utterly at his mercy.

He's here, in my room.

Why does that send a thrill through me?

I should be biting his dick clean off at the fact that he's here, looming over me like some creepy stalker, not flicking my tongue over the tip as I gaze up at him.

"Fuck," he hisses, gripping the headboard behind me and forcing his dick past my lips. Not that I resist.

Reese thinks he holds all the power. Thinks that I'm under his spell. But he's the one who can't stay away.

"What?" he growls, pulling away enough for me to catch my breath.

"You're here." I smirk.

"Don't read too much into it. I'm here because I want you to tell me why the fuck you were hanging out with Abigail."

"Abigail?" My heart sinks. "You're here… because of her?"

"What are you playing at, sweet cheeks?" His hand slides to my throat, grasping me there.

"She gave me a ride home. I invited her in. It was no big deal."

"You two friends now or something?" His fingers flex around my neck.

"Does it matter if we are?" My brow lifts, defiance burning inside me.

"Stay the fuck away from her, Olivia. I mean it."

Jealousy surges inside of me. Irrational, illogical jealousy.

Except maybe it isn't.

Because maybe part of me wants to be his.

"What?" he growls.

"Know what I think?" I grasp his length and slide my hand up and down, pumping him slowly.

"Olive…" he warns, involuntarily moving closer, but I grip him tighter.

"I think you're lying. I don't think you came because of her at all."

"You don't know what the fuck you're talking about."

"Say it." I throw his words back at him. "Tell me you want me."

Something flashes in his eyes. "I want to fuck your pretty little mouth."

"Liar."

"Takes one to know one." His eyes darken, anger swirling around him like a storm.

We're at a stalemate, neither of us willing to admit what my heart already knows. Lines are blurring between us.

Maybe they've been blurred ever since that night at the party before the summer.

I shouldn't want him—I don't want to want him. But I can't help myself.

"Open up, sweet cheeks," he croons. "Let me in."

I part my lips, letting my tongue lick the tip of his dick again, savouring it like a lollipop. There's something about Reese that makes me want to be wild and reckless, and I can't get enough.

He rises up on his knees a little, pushing himself deeper. I swallow him down, hollowing my cheeks and breathing through my nose, refusing to let him win whatever game we're playing tonight.

"Fuck, Olivia, you suck me so good." His head drops back, his Adam's apple bobbing as a deep groan rumbles in his chest.

I work him harder, faster, dragging my tongue up the length of his shaft and then sucking him back into my mouth. His fingers slide into my hair, holding me right where he wants me as his thrusts become jerky, his breaths choppy and ragged.

"Fuck... Fuck," he groans, his entire body tensing as his dick thickens and hot, salty liquid hits the back of my throat. I swallow him down, greedy for every last drop.

"Fucking hell," he croaks, stroking his thumb down my cheek. "You are—"

The words never come.

Because he won't admit it.

He won't ever say it.

Infuriating prick.

"You got what you came for," I snap, trying to shove him away. "Don't let the door hit you on the way out."

Confusion flashes in his eyes, but then a wicked smirk tugs at his mouth. "You're not getting rid of me that easily." He leans back a little and grabs me by the thighs, flipping me onto my stomach.

"Reese—" I start to protest, but he yanks me back onto my knees and hooks my underwear aside, licking the length of me.

"God," I moan, trying to bury my face into a pillow. It's too good. His fingers curl around my hip, pulling me closer as his tongue spears inside me, stealing the breath from my lungs.

"More," I cry. "God, more."

His dark chuckle sends shivers running down my spine as intense waves build inside me.

"You taste so fucking good," he murmurs, and I wonder if he realises that he sounds bewitched. Desperate for more.

Desperate for me.

But when his tongue moves to my clit and two of his thick fingers slide inside me, all thoughts evaporate out of my head as my world contracts around us. At the dirty, filthy things he's doing to my body.

Something wrong could never feel this good, this right, could it?

He eats me like a man starved, lapping at my core like I'm his last meal. My fingers twist into the bedsheets, holding on as everything coils tight. Close, I'm so fucking close.

"Reese... Reese... Reese," I chant.

"Say it," he drawls, the words rough against his throat. "Say it and I'll let you come."

I push my arse into his face, refusing to bend but demanding more.

"I mean it, Olivia," he warns, his grip on my thighs almost vicious. I'll have bruises tomorrow, but I don't care. "Say. It." His fingers withdraw, leaving me cold, but I'm too close.

Just one more—

I slip my hand between my legs and rub my clit just the way I need.

"Don't you fucking da—"

My legs almost give way as my orgasm barrels into me and I cry out, cry his name, knowing it'll torture him that I came.

"Fuck," he hisses, and I wish I could see his face, the pure torture in his eyes as he watches me ride through the pleasure saturating my body.

Reese climbs off the bed and I lie down on my side, sleepy and sated.

"Everything okay over there?" I smirk, unable to resist taunting him.

"Olivia," he warns.

"I like it when you say my name. Like I'm in trouble. Like you don't know how to handle me."

His eyes narrow to thin slits, dark and deadly. He looks

like he either wants to fuck the air from my lungs or smother me with a pillow and drown out my words.

Maybe even both.

"You won't win," he says coolly, erecting that wall of ice between us again. But it doesn't feel as impenetrable as it used to. Every time we do this, the cracks grow, thawing some of the ice around his stone cold heart.

"So you're not staying then?" My brow arches and his scowl deepens.

"You're not fooling anyone, sweet cheeks." His cocky, arrogant façade slides back into place.

"The only person trying to fool themselves here is you, Reese. Shut the door on your way out." I turn over, close my eyes, and smile to myself.

The next morning at breakfast, I don't expect to find Reese sitting there, eating his cereal with Dad and Fiona.

"This is a surprise," I say, barely sparing him a second glance.

"Reese needed to pick up some textbooks for class," Fiona says.

"I bet he did," I murmur, remembering how it felt to wake with him pinning me to the bed, the tip of his dick painting my lips.

A bolt of lust goes through me and I squeeze my thighs together. Jesus, I need to get a grip.

But he's under my skin. And this game we're playing is building to something. We both feel it. He's just too damn stubborn to admit it.

"All set for tomorrow?" Dad asks him, trying to make small talk.

"Yeah, I'm ready. The team's ready."

"Well, we'll be there, cheering you on, won't we, sweetheart?"

Silence echoes around the room, and I glance up and realise Dad is talking to me.

"I... uh, yeah. Go Saints," I say drolly, shoving half a blueberry muffin in my mouth.

"Olivia. It wouldn't hurt you to be supportive."

"Oh, I'm sure she'll find her inner cheerleader tomorrow, Christian." Reese smirks right at me, bringing his spoon to his mouth and licking it the way he licked me last night.

Smug bastard.

Challenge glitters in his eyes. He thinks he can embarrass me into submission.

Well he's got another think coming.

I scan the kitchen and my gaze lands on the fruit bowl. Bingo.

Going over to it, I pluck a banana out and peel it slowly, holding his dark gaze as Dad and Fiona discuss the case she's working on over coffee and toast.

Reese leans back, eyes narrowed and jaw tense as I flick my tongue over the tip and then take it into my mouth. Slow, teasing licks, never once breaking eye contact. The muscle in his jaw tics, his hand curling into a fist on the table.

Power is such a fickle thing.

Wanting to show him he's not the only one with tricks up his sleeve, I push the fruit further past my lips, practically deep throating it.

"Shit," he blurts as his glass of juice goes flying, soaking him and the table. He leaps up and glowers at me.

"Problem?" I ask sweetly, biting the end of my banana.

"Reese, whatever is the matter?" Fiona asks him.

"Fly," he rasps. "I thought a fly landed in my cereal."

"A fly?" Dad chuckles. "You're going to need to hold your nerve a little better tomorrow on the pitch."

"I... I'm going to change."

I fight a smile as he gives me one last seething glance and spins on his heel, fleeing from the kitchen with his hand practically cupping his rock-hard dick.

Olivia: one.

Reese: zero.

Fiona lets out a weary sigh. "I worry about him," she says, and Dad pats her hand.

"He'll get there. It's a big adjustment for everyone. Sweetheart?" He frowns at me.

"Yeah, Dad?"

He gives me a knowing look. "What's going on with you two? I sensed some tension just now."

"Just Reese being Reese," I shrug, turning my back on him, hoping he can't see the flush to my cheeks.

Fooling around with Reese won't only destroy Oak. It'll hurt Dad and Fiona. But I'm not sure I can stop.

"Don't push him too hard, sweetheart," he adds. "He's been through a lot, and he's carrying a lot on his shoulders."

Fiona whispers something to him, and I glance back at them.

"Don't worry, Dad," I say. "I can handle the likes of Reese and his mood swings."

If only he knew.

But when my phone vibrates and I dig it out of my blazer pocket and see his name, a trickle of anticipation goes through me.

> Reese: You're going to pay for that, sweet cheeks.

I smile to myself as I text back.

> Olivia: Bring. It. On.

35

REESE

A deep, pained growl rumbles in the back of my throat as I violently fist my cock.

But like everything since the moment I walked out of her room last night, it's not enough.

Olivia Beckworth's fucking mouth has ruined me.

One hand presses against the cool tiles of my walk-in shower as the water rains down on me. Every single muscle in my body is locked up tight, yet it has nothing to do with our impending game and everything to do with the girl I can't get out of my fucking head.

All day... all fucking day, all I've been able to see every time I so much as blink is her with the fucking banana.

What the hell was she thinking?

It was obscene. It was... "Fuck." The growl of desire rips from my throat without permission as my balls begin to draw up.

But. It. Is. Not. Enough.

I haven't even come, and yet I know this release is going to be as unsatisfying as fuck.

In the past, the run-up to our games was never like this. Not for me, anyway.

The others might be doing their usual pregame ritual bullshit, but I've apparently been reduced to spending time with my right hand while rubbing one out to thoughts of my best friend's sister.

I always thought pregame sex was the second-best kind of sex there was. It was the perfect appetiser to the epic winners' sex that would undoubtedly be offered up from a number of the Heir chasers that follow our games in the hope of getting some action with us.

But since Olivia, I've realised all that is bullshit.

Because the best kind of sex is hate sex. If only I could mix that with the anticipation of the game or the thrill of the win.

Fuck me. It would be epic.

Just the thought of that is enough to have my cock jerking in my hand as my cum drops into the water swirling around my feet.

My cock barely softens, the orgasm hardly scratching the surface of the tension knotting up my muscles.

I need to get rid of it, or I'm going to be good as fucking useless tonight.

But how?

There's no fucking way I'm dragging some faceless Heir chaser down to the basement like I know Theo did the second we walked out of our final class of the day.

What I need is her.

But I already know where she's going to be.

Oak's pregame routine is set in stone. It always has been. And it always involves Olivia. I don't stand a fucking chance of getting anywhere close to her, let alone dragging her away.

"Yo, bro. You still here?" Theo's voice booms through my room a second before my bathroom door swings open and he strides in as if I fucking invited him to join me.

"What the fuck, man?" I bark as his eyes drop to my semi.

"Dude." His brows rise as if I'm the one in the wrong right

now. "I had enough to share, you know. You were more than welcome to—"

"Shut the fuck up," I hiss, turning the shower off and reaching for a towel to cover up.

"You haven't fucked anyone since you got back to town, have you?" he muses as I stalk toward the basin, pulling open the cupboard above and grabbing my deodorant, half tempted—fuck, more than half tempted—to spray it in his eyes instead of under my arms in the hope it makes him leave.

"Spit it out, Theo. I'm not in the mood for riddles."

"Just pointing out a fact. You're clearly up for it. What's the deal? You become a born-again virgin over the summer or some shit?"

I stare at myself in the mirror, inspecting the more-than-usual scruff I let linger on my jaw.

I had every intention of shaving it off before this game, but then the sound of Olivia moaning as it grazed against her thighs echoes through my mind again, and I forget about making the effort.

"No," I growl, reaching for some hair wax. "I'm not a fucking born-again virgin. I'm just..." I let out a sigh, my eyes catching his in the mirror.

Nostalgia hits me like a fucking truck as memories of us talking girls, sex, and everything in between come back to me from before I walked away from them. And not in a seedy, braggy way either.

The four of us, despite what I'm sure others assume, were a family. We shared, we talked. We were fucking it for each other. And I hate that I ruined that.

Not that I'd have ever be able to admit to any of them that the reason I haven't been sticking my dick in anything that wears a skirt was because of Olivia.

She's been off-limits. Hell, more than off fucking limits to us since before we were even interested in girls. Sister and exes —and not ex-fucks, actual ex-girlfriends, if any of us were stupid enough to have one—have always been a hard limit for all of us.

"You're just..." he prompts.

"Not fucking interested in your sloppy seconds," I grunt, storming across the room and shoulder checking him on my way out in the hope it stops him from continuing with this bullshit.

The second I'm back in my room, I drag the towel from my waist, pull on a pair of boxers, and then tug on my All Hallows' tracksuit that Coach expects us to turn up wearing.

"Since fucking when?"

"Since fucking now," I boom, surging toward him and getting right in his face, more than ready to prove my point with my fists.

"Whitfield," an ice-cold voice cuts through my room as my fists curl at my side. "That's enough."

My shoulders sag in defeat as I continue to hold Theo's, but he sees it and a smirk tugs at his lips.

"You're in the shit now. You fucked up his feng shui," Theo taunts, loud enough for Elliot to hear him.

"Shut your fucking mouth, Ashworth," Elliot seethes, "and go and wash your cock. I saw the girl you dragged down to the basement, and I wouldn't be surprised if you'll need antibiotics by sunrise."

My brow lifts in a 'told you so' gesture, but Theo doesn't give a fuck.

"I wrapped it. We're all good."

"Ashworth," Elliot barks once more, and finally he takes a step back and stalks toward the door like a good boy.

"I'll do as you say, but only because the scent of her pussy will put me off my game. Shame I can't say the same for the two of you, frigid fucks."

Elliot's eyes widen in surprise, but he wisely chooses not to respond.

"We lose tonight, and it's your fucking fault," Elliot spits.

"I was halfway through my routine and I—" He cuts himself off when a snort of amusement rips past my lips. "Fuck you, Whitfield. Fuck you."

He spins on his heels and marches from my room, although not before letting me hear his muttering about how I shouldn't even be in this room to distract him.

"Enjoy the rest of your routine," I call after him, chuckling. He responds by slamming his door so hard the floor beneath my feet vibrates.

Jesus fucking Christ. If this shitshow is anything to go by, then we're fucked tonight. And we can't fucking lose the first game of the season. The Harriers are going to be watching our every move, and we can't let them see any hint of weakness.

They've been suspiciously quiet since their beloved leader lost his prized possession, but we're not naïve enough to think they're not going to retaliate.

They never have taken anything lying down, and I certainly don't expect it to start happening now.

Grabbing my packed bag from the end of the bed, I throw it over my shoulder and head downstairs, needing an energy drink or two to get me ready for the night ahead, although I already know I won't find any.

Part of Elliot's game plan is insisting we all go on a health kick in the days leading up to every match. I already know the options are going to be limited to water or the blended-up green shit he pays our cook extra to concoct especially for us.

Lucky us.

I expect the place to be empty, so the sound of voices throws me for a loop when I get to the stairs. I assumed Oak was going to go home to get ready as he usually would, but apparently, he's brought temptation right to my doorstep.

"You're bluffing."

Her soft, amused voice cuts through me, making my steps falter the second they echo around the tall stairwell.

Fuck me, if I knew she was down here, I wouldn't have been jerking off in the shower to the memory of her.

"You letting him win, as usual, Olive?" I ask, jogging down the last few steps and turning around the corner to find them sitting at the dining table with cards in their hands.

"She doesn't let me win," Oak growls, his eyes not lifting from his hand while Olivia's shoulders tense with my arrival.

"Are you sure about that?" I mock, dropping my bag and walking up behind Olivia to check out her hand.

"Olivia has zero game face. She can't lie to me if she fucking tries," Oak states confidently.

Pressing my hand to the table, I blow out a breath, allowing it to race over Olivia's neck. Her grip on her cards tightens, and if I were to look, I know I'd find her skin covered in goosebumps.

"You've really got him fooled, huh?" I mutter, checking out her cards. A straight flush—impressive.

"Shut the fuck up, Whitfield," Oak growls, his eyes drilling into his sister as if he's going to see her cards reflected in them.

With him thoroughly distracted, I run my knuckles down Olivia's spine, delighting in the way she shudders against my touch.

"She's bluffing. Her cheeks heat when she's bluffing."

Olivia sucks in a sharp breath.

Oh yeah, that's the reason. Nothing to do with the way she burns up at my innocent touch.

"Reese," Olivia hisses. "I don't need your help."

"So I can see." Pushing to stand, I stalk toward the fridge, already dreading what I'm going to find as she demands for Oak to lay down his cards.

Silence crackles between them for a beat before Oak triumphantly barks, "Full fucking house, lil' sis. Read 'em and weep."

"Fuck," Olivia hisses, forcing me to turn around and watch

in favour of the disgusting shit waiting for me. "Two pairs. You got me."

She throws her cards face down so he can't see her lie before she gathers up the rest of the pack to hide the evidence.

"Fuck yeah. The king still reigns."

"Better luck next time, Olivia," I mutter, watching her through narrowed eyes.

Oak's smug-as-fuck grin falters when his phone ringing cuts through the air.

"Who the fuck thinks it's a good idea to call me now," he growls, his previous joy gone as if it never existed. "Dad," he mutters, looking torn between answering or ignoring him.

"Just answer," Olivia tells him. "He wouldn't call if it wasn't urgent. He knows how important this is to you."

"Fine," he mutters, shoving his chair out behind him and stalking toward the front door, letting it slam ominously behind him.

"And then there were two," I mutter, stalking closer to Olivia once again like a magnet unable to resist the pull.

"I'm leaving," she says, hopping up from her seat, but she doesn't get very far before I slam my palms down on the table either side of her hips, pinning her in place.

"Why'd you let him win?" I demand.

She shrugs. "Because he needs his pregame ritual to run smoothly. Going into a game already a loser isn't good for anyone's ego. Even one as big as yours."

"Ouch," I breathe, the smirk on my face proving how little that insult really touched me. "You know, I've got a ritual I need a little help with before we leave for the game," I confess, pressing my hips to hers and allowing her to feel what I need assistance with.

"Unfortunately for you, the only ego I'll be stroking tonight is Oak's. You can go fuck yourself."

She gasps when my hand collars her throat. "I already have, sweet cheeks. While remembering how it felt to have your lips wrapped around my cock. Problem is that my memory isn't as good as the real thing. And if I don't get what I need in the next..." I glance over at the clock, "thirty minutes, your brother is going to be walking out onto that pitch already a loser."

"Don't you dare pin this on me," she growls, her eyes narrowed in anger.

I lean in, brushing my lips against her ear, letting my breath race over her skin once again. "Time to pay up for that stunt yesterday morning, sweet cheeks."

"Reese," she warns as I drag her from the table and shove my hand into her pocket to find her phone.

"Text Oak. Tell him you left and that you'll see him after the game."

"No, I can't. I—" Her words cut off on a gasp as I push my hand inside her leggings and cup her pussy, delighting in how damp I find the lace that's covering her.

"Text him, Olivia, and make it convincing."

36

OLIVIA

Nervous anticipation hums in every inch of me. I slipped out of the Chapel without crossing anyone's path and took the track leading into the woods behind the school that joins All Hallows' with the rest of town.

Footsteps crunch behind me and my heart ratchets, but it's only Reese following me.

Right as he said he would.

The Rock looms up ahead and my pace quickens, his hungry gaze burning a hole in my thin hoodie.

"Good girl," Reese says, finally reaching me.

"How did you manage to escape?" I ask him, edging backwards until my back hits the weather-worn stone.

"Told them I had a pregame ritual I wanted to try out." His expression darkens as he reaches for me, sliding his hand possessively up my chest and flexing his fingers around my neck.

"I didn't think you'd agree to this." His thumb traces my bottom lip.

"I'm not some weak, spineless girl, Reese. You don't have to worry about breaking me."

His eyes flare again. "Is that so?" He smirks, but then his

resolve cracks a little. "I haven't been able to stop thinking about you and that fucking banana. I should punish you for that little stunt."

"Do your worst."

"Why?"

"You know why," I whisper.

I'm tired of this dance. The part where we both pretend there isn't more between us than these stolen, hate-fuelled moments.

"We don't have long... maybe this wasn't a good idea." He pulls back, raking his fingers through his hair.

"You're tense," I say, reaching for him. "Let me help. Let me be what you need."

His eyes darken as I run my fingers down his hard chest, desperate to touch him.

Reese's body trembles as he stares down at me. Intense. Unnerving.

"What's wrong?" I ask.

"It isn't supposed to be like this," he whispers before slamming his mouth down on mine. Questions hover on the top of my tongue, melting away when he plunges his tongue past my lips and devours me. His big, strong body pins me against the Rock as he grinds against me, showing me exactly how much he wants this.

Me.

"Hurry," I breathe, knowing we don't have much time. My hand slips between us, palming his already hard dick through the thin material of his tracksuit bottoms.

"Fuck, Olivia... fuck." He murmurs the words onto my lips, gently thrusting into my hand.

"How long do we have?"

"Not long enough," he replies, sliding his arms around the backs of my thighs and picking me up, laying me out on the flat edge of the Rock.

"This isn't going to be soft or gentle." His eyes glitter

with lust and dark, wicked things as he yanks my leggings down and pulls his bottoms over his hips, enough to fist his dick.

This is happening.

Oh God, it's happening.

But I'm so desperate for him.

Reese pumps himself a couple times, swiping the tip of his dick through my folds.

"I have dreamed about this." His eyes hold mine as he slowly pushes into me, inch by inch until he's seated fully inside. "You're so fucking tight, it feels like you're choking my dick."

I clench my inner muscles, watching with satisfaction as his expression turns feral.

"Fuck, do that again," he rasps.

So I do.

Holding him tight inside me.

I feel full, so stretched, but it isn't enough.

"Move," I say. "I need you to move."

"You want to get fucked by the big bad wolf?" Reese grins down at me, pulling back slightly and slamming forward.

"Yes," I cry, the surface of the Rock rough against my back as he fucks me like he hates me.

And maybe he does. Maybe underneath every perfect roll of his hips or every drag of his lips over my skin is a simmering hatred for me.

But something this good can't only be hate. The way he moves inside me, sliding his hands under my legs to lift me onto him, changing the angle and making it deeper, better... just more, is too damn perfect.

I fist his Saints hoodie and yank him down, needing his lips on mine and his tongue in my mouth.

"Christ, you're hot," he murmurs, kissing me hard and bruising, sliding his lips down my jaw and to my throat where he sucks on my skin.

"Reese, wait up—" But it's too late. There's no way he didn't leave a bruise.

He marked me.

Whether he meant to or not, Reese marked me and I like it. His hand comes to my throat, pinning me there as he thrusts into me, over and over.

"I need you to come first," he says.

"Such a gentleman," I sass and he growls at me, slipping his other hand between our bodies and touching the place where we're joined.

A small whimper falls from my lips when his thumb connects with my clit, adding an extra layer of pleasure that has my body shooting off like a rocket.

"That's it, sweet cheeks. Milk my fucking dick." His thrusts turn feral. Jerky and wild.

"God, Reese... I can't... it's..."

"You can and you will. Take my cum, Olivia. Take it all." He groans, his dick swelling inside me right as I shatter, crying out his name.

"Fuck... fuck." He pulls out and comes all over my pussy and thighs, smearing it over my skin with his fingers. I glance down and realise he isn't just smearing it, he's painting a word.

Reese.

"This body belongs to me now," he says, eyes so black they barely look human. A chill goes through me as I try to catch my breath.

I'm a mess, wrung out with Reese's cum all over me. Yet, I've never felt more alive. He needed this from me.

He wanted me.

He can spout about how much he hates me and that he thinks I'm a liar, but he's only fooling himself.

Reese Whitfield cares—I'm just not sure he cares enough.

"Don't you have a game to win?" I say, shoving him off me, suddenly feeling out of my depth.

This is what happens when you play in the lion's den. For a second, you think you've tamed the beast, only to realise that you're one wrong move from being eaten alive.

That's how Reese makes me feel every time I'm with him. I think I'm breaking down his walls, finally getting to the bottom of what makes a boy like him tick, only to stumble and realise there are so many more layers to uncover.

I push up on my elbows and stare at the mess he's made of me. I should feel disgusted, but I don't.

"You like it, don't you? My mark on you?" He strokes his jaw, watching me.

"You should go," I say, trying to clean myself up with a discarded tissue from my pocket.

If only Oak could see me now.

What would he say about this? About the things I let Reese do to me?

But this isn't about Oak or my father or Abigail or the other Heirs. It's between me and Reese, and although I know we're on a collision course for disaster, I can't seem to stop myself.

"So eager to get rid of me?"

"You're going to be late," I say, dragging my leggings up and hopping down off the Rock. "The lads will ask questions."

His eyes flash with something, but then he gives me an imperceptible nod. "You know what they say about this place?" he asks, his voice a quiet whisper that does things to me.

"What?"

Of course I know. Everyone knows what they say about the Rock, and the legends that surround it. But I've never believed in myths, and I want to hear him say the words.

"They say whoever touches the Rock will be cursed for all eternity." He hesitates, staring at me with an emotion I can't decipher. But then his lip curls into that familiar snarl and he adds, "What do you think happens if you get fucked on it?"

His words land their intended blow, and I flinch at the hostility back in his voice. My Reese is gone, replaced by the Reese who claims to hate me and the rest of the world.

I step up to him, refusing to cower even when my heart is in shreds. "I'll take my chances."

"You're fucking crazy," he murmurs, reaching for my hair and twirling a strand around his finger. Dipping his head, he leans in, and for a second, I think he might kiss me. My heart flutters, anticipation firing off around my body, but it doesn't come.

Instead, Reese hovers there, close but not close enough. "I'll see you around, Olive. Thanks for the ride."

He pulls away and saunters off down the path back toward the Chapel as if he hasn't just destroyed my body...

And taken another piece of my heart with him.

I attend the game, but only because my father and Oak expect me to be there. What I really wanted was to go home and lock myself in my room and figure out why I keep letting Reese do this to me.

I'm not stupid, I know that what we're doing is toxic, dangerous and reckless. But I can't stop.

I don't want to.

And the more scraps of attention he gives me, the more I want.

The Saints come out fighting, a well-oiled machine that commands the field with sheer skill and dominance. Their opponents barely stand a chance against Elliot and his soldiers. Because that's what they remind me of. An army clashing with their enemy.

Reese is something to behold, the way his long, muscular legs eat up the field as he charges with the ball tucked under his arm. The rest of our players guard him, giving him the space he needs to make it downfield.

The crowd goes wild, cheering and shouting for their beloved Saints as he slams the ball down past the goal line. The guys all rush for him, falling into each other as they celebrate their first five points on the board.

"Reese looks good out there," Dad says to Fiona, who beams as she clutches his arm. "Uh-oh," he quickly adds when it looks like Reese and one of the opposing team's players get into a scuffle.

My heart crashes violently in my chest as I slide my hand up my clavicle, watching as they get all up in each other's faces.

Walk away, Reese, I silently implore. *Walk away.*

Elliot wades in, shoving Reese away toward the rest of their team.

God, I can't take it. The thought that someone might hurt him. Or worse, ruin his season before it even gets started.

I'm not supposed to care.

He's not supposed to be the boy I can't take my eyes off, but he is. And it's a giant fucking problem.

Pulling my phone out, I text Oak, knowing he won't see it until later.

> Olivia: I don't feel well. Not coming to the party. But kick some Chiefs arse and enjoy your night. xx

"Sweetheart," Dad notices me. "What's wrong?"

"I... uh, I feel really sick, Dad. I think I'm going to head home."

"But the game..."

"Sorry. I already texted Oak and let him know. My stomach is hurting. Maybe I have a bug or something."

"Do you need me to—"

"No, Dad. It's fine. Stay, watch the game and tell Oak I'm proud of him. I'll see you at home later." I lean in and kiss his cheek.

And then, with one last glance back at Reese, I get the hell out of there.

37

REESE

"**F**UCKING YES!" one of the guys bellows the second we all crash through into the locker room.

"We're going all the way this year, boys," Elliot booms as we all throw ourselves into a huddle in the centre of the room, whooping and hollering, celebrating our first win of the season.

Fuck, I feel good.

Everything hurts but in the best possible way, and I revel in it.

Shoving bodies out of the way, I get deeper into the pile to find my boys so we can celebrate.

"The Saints fucking rule," Oakley yells when I find him. He pulls me into his body, hugging me in excitement as the lads around us begin chanting.

"We're gonna do it this year, man," he shouts in my ear before releasing me.

Despite the excitement and the thrill of the win, my stomach knots with the knowledge that I won't be here to see it if they do manage it. Or at least, that's the plan.

The second I get to the point where I can shatter Olivia's

heart, I'm gonna be heading straight out of town again, leaving them all to pick up the pieces of their pathetic little lives.

My chest aches at the thought of doing it, but I don't have a choice. I can't stay around here and watch Mum and Christian building their new life together, forgetting about how they lied to everyone. How they allowed Olivia to lie for them.

"Yeah," I say when Oak stares at me like I've got three heads. "Yeah, man. All the fucking way."

"Whatever ritual it was you went off for earlier, you gotta fucking do that again next game. You killed it out there."

Guilt eats at me, but it's quickly replaced by desire as I think back to my new ritual.

"I fully intend to, man," I say as everyone begins to get to their feet once more.

"Are you motherfuckers ready to party?" Elliot shouts.

"Hell yes," comes back.

"I didn't fucking hear you. I said... ARE THE SAINTS READY TO PARTY?"

"WE'RE READY TO FUCKING PARTY." The floor vibrates with the volume of the response before everyone slams their feet down and starts clapping their hands, chanting, *Saints, Saints, Saints*.

They're all still going as the four of us head for the showers first. Stripping out of my muddy kit, I slam my hand down on the button for the shower, memories from a very different time in here not so long ago filling my mind.

Fuck. I haven't had anywhere near enough of her tonight.

"Fuck, this feels good," Theo says as the water pours over him. "We're gonna be fucking champions. I can feel it in my bones."

"Hell yeah, but right now, I need booze and girls. And a fucking lot of them," Oak says, washing his junk in preparation for the night ahead.

"A-fucking-men to that," I add, instantly regretting that I didn't when Theo shoots me an inquisitive look.

"You actually gonna get your dick wet tonight then, Whitfield?"

"Keep it fucking down, Ashworth," Elliot snaps.

"They ain't fucking listening. And plus, Darcie has been more than descriptive enough for everyone to buy it. Pretty sure I heard her telling someone about a birthmark you've got on your inner thigh the other day."

"I don't have a—" I shake my head. "She needs to fucking tone it down. Anyone I've been with will start questioning her if she gets something wrong."

"Maybe it's time for another little chat with your favourite Heir chaser," Oak suggests with a smirk.

"I could think of better ways to celebrate," I mutter, reaching for the shower gel and squirting a more-than-generous amount into my hand.

"The girls are going to be all fucking over us tonight."

"Like they aren't any other night of the week," Elliot deadpans.

"Surprised you've got any juice left after the screaming Olivia and I heard coming from the basement earlier," Oak quips.

"Don't you worry about my juice. I got plenty in the tank."

"Fuck. I need alcohol," I mutter, turning the shower off and pushing my hand through my hair, letting the excess water run down my body.

Grabbing a towel, I wrap it around my waist as the others follow suit to allow the rest of the boys to hit the showers.

Just like every post-home game party, we're going to be spending the night in the clearing out by the Hideout. By the time we get there, the bonfire should be raging and the girls will be waiting to lavish attention on every member of the team. Although, our new little first years are going to have to wait to get their turn on a pair of perky tits. We've got a couple of extra games planned for them tonight.

We dress to the raucous chatter of the rest of the team and head out before them to swing by the Chapel to dump our shit and change out of our tracksuits so we can make a fashionably late entrance.

The second we're spotted emerging through the trees, a loud cheer goes up. It's fucking bizarre, but I'm totally here for it as girls descend on us and drinks are thrust into our hands.

"You were incredible tonight, Reese," Darcie purrs, pressing her tits against my chest and leaning in as if she's going to fucking kiss me.

Reaching out, I collar her throat before she gets too close. "What the fuck do you think you're doing?" I growl, low enough so that no one around us can hear.

"Just making it look authentic, baby," she purrs, making my dick shrivel. Talk about coming back to Earth with a bump.

Finally getting inside Olivia, winning our first game, and then putting up with this whore pawing all over me as if I'm her favourite pet is not what I had in mind for tonight.

A shudder rips through me, one Darcie stupidly mistakes for desire. I catch her wandering hand right before it makes contact with my dick. I forcefully shove her back, making her stumble in the grass on her fucking stupid heels and fall onto her arse.

"Whoops," I say innocently, while Elliot scowls at me.

But fuck him, fuck Darcie. Fuck everyone who thinks I stuck my dick in her. It was a means to an end, and she played her part. Now, it's time she fucked off and got obsessed with someone else. Someone on the football team ideally, so she can get out of my face.

"Whitfield," Elliot growls.

With a grunt of annoyance, I stick my hand out and offer Darcie help.

She stares at me. Her lips might be all twisted up in anger, but her eyes are still filled with desire.

After a beat and right before I change my mind, she slips her hand into mine and allows me to pull her up.

"Thanks, baby," she coos, dropping a kiss on my cheek and refusing to let go of my hand.

"Come on then, let's get this party started." Glancing over at Theo, I find him with three girls around him.

"Looks like you already have," I mutter.

"Jealous, Whitfield?" he quips.

"Nah, I only need one girl to get my dick hard, not three."

Dragging my hand from Darcie's, I march toward where a makeshift bar has been set up and grab a bottle of vodka.

Just like the last time I partied out here on initiation night, we get the good shit, while the minions get stuck with lukewarm beer. Fine by me.

"You're going to get found out if you keep pushing her away," Elliot warns as he and Oak follow me, leaving Theo behind with his fan club.

"She's had a week. I'm done now."

"So you're happy to let everyone know the truth, are you?" Elliot taunts. "Because as far as I can see it, Darcie's wandering hands seem like a better option than jail."

"Haven't you heard? My new stepdaddy is the best defence lawyer in the country. He could get me off."

"Whitfield," Elliot growls again, clearly not appreciating my joke.

"Dude, you need to go and get laid. You're too tense," I point out, much to his irritation. "That meditation isn't doing you any good. Maybe you should switch it up and try out the Kama Sutra instead."

"Fuck you, Whitfield. Fuck you." He grabs a bottle of vodka and disappears into the crowd, leaving me with an exasperated Oak.

"What?" I bark before sinking at least four shots one after the other and not bothering to come up for air.

"Do you need to keep baiting him?"

"Maybe if he pulls the stick out from his arse once in a while, he might actually get a joke."

"What the fuck is with you tonight? We won, man. You should be buzzing."

"I am." *Fucking buzzing to get back into your sister's pussy.*

I look around at the crowd, trying to seek her out, but I don't spot her brown hair anywhere.

"Where's Olivia? It's unlike her not to congratulate you on your win," I quickly add to look less suspicious.

"She went home," he murmurs, clearly not happy about it. "I had a message saying she was sick."

My stomach knots, guilt flooding through my veins. "That sucks."

"Right?" he says, disappointment darkening his eyes. "I need my post-game shot with my number one fan."

I stare at him, fighting to keep back my piss taking, but he must read it in my eyes.

"Fuck off, Whitfield. You don't understand."

"Nah, got no fucking clue, mate." *Big fat fucking lie. I get it now more than I ever have done. I need her as much as he does, just not in any kind of brotherly way.*

"I need to get wasted and fucked."

"In that order?" I ask lightly, passing the bottle of vodka to him.

"Yep," he announces, lifting it to his lips.

Movement over his shoulder catches my eye as Tasha and Misty descend on us.

"Well, you might just be in luck, my friend."

Hands slide around his waist before they both press their tits against his arms.

"Hey, Oak," Misty purrs. "You were looking good out on

that field tonight."

"Pitch. We play on a..." His words tail off as their hands begin to wander. They couldn't give a fuck if we play on a damn cloud. All they're interested in are the players.

"Right, well, I'll leave you to that then, bro. Just remember to wrap it this time. We don't want crabs in the Chapel again."

"Ew, Oak. Is that true?" Misty whines, the sound like nails on a chalkboard.

"Nah, baby. We're all clean as a whistle. We don't stick our cocks into anything, you know."

"Pfft."

Something hits the back of my head, and when I look down I find a bottle lid by my feet before a wide-arse smirk across Oak's face.

"Enjoy." I smile, flipping him off and walking away, trying to convince myself that it's too early to slink off and go and check on Olivia.

Pulling my phone from my pocket, I find our chat and come up with something to send.

> Reese: You can't hide from the big bad wolf, sweet cheeks. I need a celebratory fuck, and no other pussy will do.

Who says romance is dead?

"You look lonely," a familiar voice says.

"And you look and sound fucking desperate," I shoot back. Spinning around, I pin Darcie with a look that would make everyone else cower. But not this dumb bitch.

"I don't like seeing you sad," she says as if I never spoke.

She reaches for my waistband, and my fingers wrap around her wrist, stopping her. "Ow, come on, Reese. I want to know if all those rumours I've spread are true."

"I can confirm they are. I'm hung like a thoroughbred. The birthmark isn't so factual though, so you might want to squash that one in case anyone else I've been with has categorised them."

Her lips open and close like a goldfish, her grip on my belt tightening.

"It's not going to happen, Darcie. You can pout those dick-sucking lips all you like, but you're not wrapping them around mine."

"B-but I don't have a gag reflex."

"Good for you," I mutter dismissively. "In case you hadn't already noticed, I'm not interested." Ripping her hand from my belt, I push it lower, much to her delight. "You feel that. Not even a fucking tingle."

"I'm sure I could fix that in a heartbeat."

Shamelessly, she drags her strapless top down, freeing her tits.

But still. Nothing.

"Do you want some advice?" I ask, dragging her hand away from me. Her wide, hopeful eyes stare into mine. "This shameless whore act isn't sexy. It might have got your daddy's friend on his knees for you, but that's because he's a fucking paedo who molests children. If you can find some self-respect, you might stand a chance of getting a decent guy's interest. Now, fuck off and go and hang out elsewhere."

Spinning away from her, I storm into the trees.

Thankfully, she doesn't follow.

I don't stop until I get to the hideout. It's deserted, waiting for Elliot, Theo, Oak, or me to bring the private party back here.

Lowering my arse to the steps, I tilt my head toward the dark sky and once again try to convince myself to enjoy tonight.

But it's pointless. The only place I want to be right now is with her.

It's wrong.

So fucking wrong.

I'm meant to be using her. Playing her. Making her the pawn in my game of destruction.

I shouldn't be craving her this much.

My phone vibrating in my pocket finally drags me from my own head, my heart jumping into my throat as I imagine her on the other end demanding a booty call.

Finally, my cock stirs, the memory of taking her on that rock only hours ago the only thing I can focus on.

But the second I look at my screen, any hope I had withers and dies.

Mum's name stares back at me, and my thumb hovers over the cancel button.

I don't remember the last time she called me, and it's with that sad realisation that I swipe the screen and lift it to my ear.

She wouldn't call me for chit-chat. This is more serious.

"What?" I bark down the line, wanting her to think she's interrupting the best night of my life.

"Is Olivia at the party?" she demands without even bothering with a greeting.

"Uh... no, I don't think so, why?" I ask, pushing to my feet, my heart suddenly picking up speed.

"We don't think she came home, and she said that—"

"She was ill," I finish for her, not liking the panic in her tone.

"Oak isn't answering his phone."

"I'll get him. We're coming now," I shout, bursting through the trees and scanning the crowd. "OAK," I boom, but the music is too loud. "Fuck. I'll find him. We're coming, okay?"

I cut the call and push through the crowd, demanding to know where my best friend is.

"OAK," I shout, shoving my way through the crowd in my search for him.

Grabbing one of the first-year players whose name I haven't bothered learning yet, I drag him toward me, getting right in his face.

"Have you seen Oakley? Theo? Elliot?" I boom, making him pale.

"N-no, I-I—"

"Reese, what's wrong? Elliot barks, the crowd parting for him.

Releasing the first year with a shove, I spin on my heels. "Where's Oak?"

"I dunno. He disappeared into the trees with a girl a while ago. What's happened?"

"Olivia never got home."

"She probably changed her mind and went—"

"She was sick. She should be at home."

Elliot must read something in my face, because he instantly stops trying to argue with me.

"Christian has been trying to call him. He's not fucking answering."

"Hardly surprising," Elliot mutters as we storm through the crowd, who have all now turned to see what the drama is.

"Ashworth," Elliot booms, twisting his fingers in the back of his shirt and physically dragging him away from the girl who was trying to suck his face off.

She wails like a banshee, and when I look down, I realise why. Her hand is stuck in Theo's trousers.

"We need to find Oak. Now," he tells Theo, his tone leaving no space for argument as Theo stares at him, gawping in shock with his fly open.

"Uh... y-yeah. Sure. I think he went that way," he says, pointing toward the tree line.

The three of us run in that direction, Theo doing as he's told for once.

"OAKLEY," Elliot barks as we trudge through the trees, the twigs snapping beneath our feet.

"BECKWORTH. You'd better be close to blowing your load or we're about to ruin your night," Theo helpfully informs anyone who might be listening.

My phone buzzes as we continue searching, and when I pull it free, I find a message from an unknown number.

Swiping the screen, dread fills my stomach as I wait for the app to open.

> Unknown: I have something that belongs to you…

FILTHY JEALOUS HEIR: PART TWO

HEIRS OF ALL HALLOWS' BOOK TWO

1

OLIVIA

"Cat got your tongue, beautiful?" Dale Starling smirks over at me as he casually sips his beer.

"You need to let me go," I grit out.

"Let you go? But the fun is only just starting." He spreads his legs wide, brazenly running his hand over his crotch.

Disgusting pig.

"Come on, D, man. Maybe she's right, maybe we should—"

"Would you quit whining like a little bitch, Manford? We're just having some fun."

Dale's friend shoots me an apologetic glance but doesn't say anything else.

Coward.

I still can't believe he kidnapped me and brought me here to some abandoned building on the edge of Huxton. It's obviously where they come to hang out, since it's filled with typical bachelor pad things. An old sofa, a makeshift bar, and a slightly wonky pool table. But there's only the three of us here tonight.

"The Heirs won't—"

"Will you stop talking about the fucking Heirs?" he spits.

"The Heirs came into our territory and fucked up my car. Seems only fair we fuck up something that belongs to them."

A violent shiver runs down my spine, but I don't let him see the fear in my eyes.

"This is not a good idea," Manford says, his leg jostling as he perches on the roll arm of one of the mismatched chairs.

"Have a drink and loosen the fuck up. I don't remember you disagreeing when we spotted her leaving the game, ripe for the taking." A wicked glint flashes in Dale's eyes.

They'd been right there, waiting for the game to finish to no doubt start shit with my brother and the Heirs.

But they saw me first.

If only I hadn't fled...

I glance at my mobile phone on the coffee table beside Dale. They confiscated it the second they wrestled me into their car, but so far he hasn't tried to get into it.

But if I can get my hands on it, I can text or call Oak. Or the police, since Dale Starling has clearly lost his fucking mind.

I get that Reese blew up his car, but kidnapping seems a big step up from vehicle arson.

"You want a drink?" Dale asks me.

"Unbelievable," I murmur and his eyes narrow.

"What the fuck did you say?"

"I said, 'unbelievable'."

"I was trying to be polite."

"You really are crazier than I thought. You can't kidnap someone and—"

"I think I liked it better when you were quiet," he snaps. "Manford, get us another beer."

Oh good. He's going to get drunk before he does whatever it is he brought me here to do.

I assume I'm bait. A hostage he'll taunt my brother and the guys with.

"You do know who my father is, right?" I ask.

"Like I give a shit."

"You should. Because when he finds out you took me, what do you think he's going to do?"

"You won't talk," he says with pure male arrogance.

"You sound awfully confident."

"Oh, I am. Because after I'm done with you, you'll—"

"Dude. Not cool," his friend protests. "I didn't sign up for this shit."

"If you don't like it, there's the fucking door." Dale tips his head to the only door in or out.

"I'm out, D. This is... fucked up." He storms out, leaving the two of us alone.

"Pussy." Dale scrubs his jaw, draining the rest of his beer. "Although, I'm kind of liking that we're all alone. Now maybe we can do this the easy way."

"The easy way?"

"Yeah." Slowly, he stands and stalks toward me, sending my heart into a tailspin. He reaches for me, cupping my face as I try to recoil from him.

"Get your hands off me."

"Or what? What the fuck are you going to do, Olivia?" My name rolls off his tongue like silk, but it's edged with venom.

"Is your dick really so small you've had to resort to kidnapping an innocent girl to get your point across?"

Anger flares in his expression as he roughly grips my hair, pain exploding along my skull.

Shit, that hurts.

"Fucking bitch. You're going to pay for that." A dark smile curls at his lips. "Let's see what an Heir's sister really tastes like."

His mouth crashes down on mine as I struggle against him. He's too strong, his tongue plunging past my lips as I thrash, trying to claw at his hands and chest as he falls down on me, forcing me into the sofa cushions.

"Get off me, you piece of shit," I cry when he pulls away for a second. "Don't you dare touch—"

His mouth drowns out my cries as he kisses me again. But this time, I'm ready for him, biting down hard on his tongue.

"Fucking bitch." Blood sprays from his mouth as he backhands me so hard, stars swim in my vision.

I blink, trying to focus as he hacks a mouthful of blood onto the floor. "We could have done this the easier way, but I have no problem sending you back to them in tiny little pieces."

"You'll never get away with this."

"They'll all be balls deep in pussy right now, too fucked off their faces to even realise you're gone."

His words strike like bullets. Because he's right. They'll all be partying in the woods, surrounded by enough girls and booze and drugs to keep them distracted.

My heart squeezes at the thought of Reese with Darcie or some faceless girl. Part of me wants to believe he wouldn't go with someone else, but I know better than to assume what happened at the Rock meant anything.

Besides, part of being an Heir is about keeping up appearances. Playing a part. And everyone will expect their starting player to be front and centre of the celebrations.

My glossy eyes flicker to Dale's phone. I need to distract him. I need to figure out a way to get my hands on—

"It's a shame you're a Beckworth," he muses, running his hungry gaze down my body. "Such a fucking waste."

He roughly palms my breast and bile rushes up my throat.

This cannot be happening. All over a fucking stupid rivalry that got out of hand.

"Perky." He smirks. "Bet my dick would feel great fucking them. What do you say?"

"Go fuck yourself." Spittle flies from my mouth, and he hits me again—this time hard enough for tears to burst from my eyes.

"Kidnapping and assault." Anger and fear vibrates inside me. "My daddy is going to have a field day with you."

"Your family isn't the only ones with connections, bitch." He yanks me off the sofa by my hair and shoves me onto the floor.

"I'm going to enjoy this." His hand goes to his belt, unsnapping it as I try to shuffle away. But he drops to his knees right over me, trapping me there. Shoving his hand inside his black Calvin Kleins, he pulls out his semi-hard dick and fists it.

I retch, vomit rushing up my throat. "You sick fuck," I scream, trying to buck him off me. But he's too big. Too overpowering. He reaches over to the table and grabs his phone, filming me as he jacks himself off.

"Stop, you psycho," I growl, my anger boiling over.

He shuffles forward, smirking viciously as he groans and grunts. "You wanna lick me, beautiful? Suck a real man's dick?"

Blood roars in my ears as I try to move away, to avoid looking at him. Squeezing my eyes closed, I force myself to take a deep breath.

I'll get out of this.

I'll find a way—

The clatter of his phone startles me and then his hand is there, wrapped around my throat, forcing me to look at him.

"You're going to watch me come, bitch. And then I'm going to fuck you so fucking hard, you'll never forget I was there."

"No." It's a quiet plea as he chokes the air from my lungs, his fingers tightening around my skin.

"Fuck yeah, beg again... that's hot. That's so fucking—" He groans, coming all over his hand and my chest.

Shame washes over me, the last shred of my fight leaving my body. He grabs his phone and angles the camera at me as he swipes his finger through the sticky mess and pushes it toward my lips.

"N-no, don't... please—"

"Keep begging, beautiful." He forces his finger into my mouth and I retch around it. "Maybe I'll be gentle when I ruin your rich-as-fuck pussy."

"They'll kill you," I breathe, something inside me breaking apart. "When they find out what you've done, they'll kill you."

He climbs off me, and spits at me, "They can fucking—"

"LIV?" someone yells, and relief slams into me. "OLIVIA?"

Oakley.

Oakley's here.

"Fuck." Dale pales, glancing at me and then to the door, and it's my turn to smile at him.

"You're a dead man." I chuckle, a deranged, lifeless sound as tears track down my cheeks. "Any last requests?"

The doors burst open right as Dale tucks himself into his jeans...

And all hell breaks loose.

2

REESE

"Motherfucker," I bark, pure, unfiltered hatred dripping from every syllable.

"What?"

"Starling has her." My voice barely sounds like my own as I growl those words.

"Starling has who?" Theo asks as Elliot's face hardens in anger.

"Olivia."

"Oh fuck."

"Exactly. We need to find Oak now," I spit, taking off running through the trees.

With only the moonlight filtering through, we can't see all that much, but something tells me we'll hear them first.

And only a minute later, I discover that I'm right.

"Oh fuck, yeah. Oakley. You're a fucking king," some girl cries out. "Yes. Yes. Right there. Fuck yes. Your cock is everything. Give it to me."

"Jesus," Theo grunts.

If this were any other time, her over-the-top praise might amuse me. But right now, all I feel is panic.

Blinding fucking panic.

My heart races and my hands tremble as I pick up speed and head in the direction of the chanting. The second we burst through the undergrowth, I wrap my hand around Oak's arm, dragging him away from the tree and the girl he's fucking against it.

"What the—"

"Oakley," she cries as I drag him off her.

"Whitfield, what the fuck are—"

"Olivia," I pant as he tucks his still hard cock away. "Starling has her."

He stills at those words, and he doesn't react for a good twenty seconds as his brain tries to catch up with the fact that he's no longer about to blow his load into whoever the girl is and instead is about to go and cause Dale Starling some serious fucking pain.

"How?" he barks. "Where is she?" He looks between the three of us with a mixture of hope and despair warring in his eyes.

He wants us to say we're joking, but deep down, he knows we're not.

"Someone better start fucking talking," he demands, his panic beginning to set in.

"We don't know anything yet."

"Then how do you—"

I lift my phone for him to see.

"We got it too," Elliot confirms. "Just came through."

"Shit, he texted it to everyone?" I ask.

Makes sense I guess, since how else would he know that Liv is... whatever she is to me?

"Check yours," I bark. "Your dad has been trying to get hold of you. She never made it home from the game."

"Fuck. Let's go. Call him back. Find out where the fuck she is."

"Oakley," a shrill voice says from behind us.

"Fuck off, Misty," Elliot barks when Oak fails to say anything

"B-but—"

"He said fuck off," I snap over my shoulder before we leave her behind with her knickers around her ankles.

"He's turned his phone off," I hiss when it goes straight to voicemail.

"Motherfucker. How the hell are we meant to find her?"

"Because he wants us to. If he wanted her hidden, he wouldn't have reached out. Motherfucker wants the attention."

The party passes us by as we race toward our cars.

"Dad," Oak barks down the phone. "That piece of shit Dale Starling has her." Christian's panicked voice rumbles down the line. "We'll find her, Dad. And he'll fucking pay."

Dark figures appear in front of us before we get to the car park, making my hackles rise.

"Who the fuck is that?" Theo asks.

"Fuck," Elliot breathes. "It's the Harriers."

"Jesus fucking Christ. What are they playing at?" Oak barks.

"I think we're about to find out," I mutter as they walk toward us as fast as we are approaching them.

My fists curl and my pulse picks up in my need to cause these motherfuckers some pain for even considering laying a finger on Olivia.

The three of us stand shoulder to shoulder, more than ready to take them on despite there being more of them.

"Wait," the guy in the middle says with his hands up in surrender, "we're not here for trouble."

"Then why the fuck are you here?"

"We came for you, not for your sister, man."

Despite his words, Oak surges forward, fisting his shirt and getting right in his face. "Where the fuck is she?" he bellows.

"Oak," Elliot says softly, wrapping his hand around his

shoulder and pulling him back while I stand there practically vibrating with anger.

"She's at our hangout."

"I swear to God, if he's laid so much as a finger on her..."

The guy swallows nervously.

"Follow us, yeah?" one of the other guys says before they all turn back toward the car park.

I march forward to catch up with Oak, as desperate to get to Olivia as he is, but Elliot and Theo hang back.

"What the hell are you waiting for?" I shout, noticing they haven't moved.

"What if it's a set-up?" Elliot asks, ever the fucking rational thinker.

"And what if it's not?" I ask. "What if he's hurt her or wor—" I cut myself off, barely able to think about the possibilities of what he could do to her, let alone say it aloud.

"Are you really going to stand there and refuse to go? To put her at even more risk?"

When Elliot hesitates, a low growl rumbles in Oak's throat.

"Fine. Reese, let's go."

I turn away from Elliot and Theo, ready to dive into a car with the Harriers even if they have something less than pleasant planned for us. It'll all be worth it for the chance of getting her back.

"Fuck, wait. We're coming," Elliot calls, running up behind us. "I'll drive. I've barely drunk anything."

"Put your fucking foot down, Eaton," Oak growls as we dive into Elliot's Aston Martin and he rushes to follow the Harriers from the car park.

Unsurprisingly, they lead us into the heart of Huxton, before driving down the street where I torched that fucker's car.

My fists curl on my lap, my need to snap that motherfucker's neck burning through me.

"I'm going to fucking kill him if he's touched her," Oak promises.

You and me both.

Despite not saying the words out loud, or at least I don't think I do, Elliot's eyes meet mine in the mirror, his brows pinching in concern.

"I fucking hate that cunt," Theo mutters, thankfully stealing Elliot's attention.

"Dad will ruin him for this," Oak promises.

"If we don't snap his neck first," I hiss.

Brake lights glow around us and Elliot brings the car to a stop behind theirs before we all dive out, following them down to some abandoned warehouse.

There's a guy loitering at the corner of the building, and the leader of the little group of Harriers exchanges a couple of words with him before they all turn to us.

"She's inside," the guy says. "I'm so fucking sorry, I didn't think he'd—"

Hearing enough from the pussy who clearly followed that piece of shit Starling blindly into his suicide mission, I pull my arm back and swing as hard as I can. My fist collides with his cheek, sending him flying back into the dirt.

"Fucking pussy," I roar, diving for him, but a pair of hands grab my upper arms.

"Save it for the cunt inside," Elliot breathes in my ear, holding me back.

Unable to leave it there, I lift my foot from the ground and slam it into his stomach. He grunts in agony before puking all over himself.

"That's the fucking least of what you deserve for this," I growl.

"He doesn't know you're here. We won't get involved."

Oak shoves the Harriers out of the way and storms toward the door.

"LIV?" he shouts. "OLIVIA?"

He kicks the door open, and it crashes back against the wall a beat before we both run inside.

"LIV?" I boom.

"Oakley." Her soft yet terrified voice fills the air and we move faster.

"We're coming," he bellows, racing through the rabbit warren of a hallway, swinging door after door open in his need to find his sister.

"We're going to kill you, you fucking cunt," I bark, following Oak on his search with Elliot and Theo right on our heels.

"Olivia," Oak sobs when he swings the next door open and his eyes land on her.

Dale is still climbing from the floor, his hands at his waistband. My heart sinks into my fucking feet, and before I even get a chance to glance at Olivia. I fly at him, the beast inside me taking over.

"Motherfucker," I bark, colliding with him and slamming my fist into his stomach, forcing him to stumble back. "Don't you fucking run from us, you coward."

My fists rain fury down on him, fucking up his face in a couple of solid punches before Oak joins me, landing a few brutal blows of his own that send Starling crashing to the floor.

But that doesn't stop us.

And it's not until Olivia's sobs crack through the red haze that has descended over both of us that we pause.

"Oakley, stop, please."

He falls deathly still beside me, hanging his head and squeezing his eyes closed.

Turning around, I finally look at Olivia. Tears stream down her cheeks, her bottom lip trembling as she wraps her arms around herself as if she'll fall apart without them.

"P-please, Oak. I need you."

All the air rushes from his lungs and he spins, rushing toward her and gathering her up in his arms.

Her sob rips through the air as she clings to him as if the world is going to crumble around her without him.

He might be her brother, her twin brother, but jealousy surges through me as she cries into the crook of his neck.

"We've got you, Liv."

Elliot and Theo step forward, both placing their hands on her in support.

"You're safe, Olivia," Elliot breathes as I stand there like an outsider once more.

Pain carves through my chest as I watch, but it's nothing compared to the moment Olivia lifts her head from Oak's shoulder and her eyes collide with mine.

3
———

OLIVIA

"**G**et her inside," Fiona says, ushering Oakley into the house as he carries my trembling body in his arms.

"Maybe we should call—"

"N-no," I croak, clinging to my brother. "I'm okay. You can put me down now."

But Oak doesn't loosen his grip, marching straight through the house and up the stairs as Dad, Reese, and the guys stay downstairs.

"What the hell happened?" Fiona asks as we arrive at my bedroom door.

"Dale fucking Starling."

Just the mention of his name sends a violent shudder through me.

"Shh, I got you." Oak lowers me gently on the bed and perches beside me. "I'll kill him," he breathes. "I'll fucking kill—"

"I'm fine." The lie spills out because Oak needs to calm down, and I need to pull myself together. But Dale's touch is imprinted on my skin, and his cruel, vile words are ingrained on my mind. Not to mention the fact that I'm covered in his—

FILTHY JEALOUS HEIR: PART TWO

Vomit rushes up my throat, and I dart off the bed into my bathroom, making it in time to shove my head into the toilet.

"Shit," Oak mutters, following me inside. He gathers my hair off my shoulders and rubs my back. "I'm sorry, Liv. I'm so fucking sorry."

"I'll get her some water," Fiona says, leaving us alone.

When I've emptied the contents of my stomach, I pull the flush and sag into Oak's waiting arms.

"Did he—"

"No. You got there just in time."

Oh God.

Dale was going to rape me, he was going to—

"Hey, hey, you're safe now." Oak pulls me closer. "He'll pay, Sis. You know Dad won't let him get away with this."

"I need to get out of these clothes." I start tearing at my rugby shirt, panic flooding me.

"Shit, Liv. Wait, let me help." Oak helps me to my feet and carefully strips the soiled clothes from my body.

"Can you manage?" he asks, motioning to the shower.

I nod, too weary to reply.

"If you need anything, I'll be right outside the door, okay?"

"I'm fine." I wrap my arms around myself, feeling vulnerable. Oak's jaw clenches as he hesitates.

"Liv—"

"Just go, Oak. I can manage."

He leaves but doesn't look happy about it. The second the door closes behind him, I strip out of my underwear, stumble into the shower and turn on the water, barely noticing the temperature.

I'm numb. Hardly able to believe what happened. What almost happened.

As I press my palms flat against the tiles, the first tear falls, and another, until I'm sobbing into the stream of water, purging the fear and shame and embarrassment. But the more the tears fall, the worse I feel.

A loud knock at the door startles me.

"Liv, you good in there?"

It's Oak.

Relief pours into me as I turn the shower off and step out, grabbing my big fluffy robe and pulling it over me.

"I'm coming," I reply, refusing to look at myself in the mirror.

When I step out of the bathroom, Oak pales at the sight of me.

"That bad, huh?"

His fist clenches at his side. "Dad wants to talk to you, but I told him—"

"Oakley." I move closer. "It's okay. I'm okay."

If I keep saying it, maybe it'll stick.

Maybe he'll believe it.

Maybe I'll believe it.

"He touched you, Liv. He fucking put his hands on you... because of me."

"You couldn't have known he'd do this."

Oakley ushers me into bed, pulling the covers up over me. "I'm going to get Dad and Fiona. He'll fix this, Sis. He'll make sure Starling pays."

I nod, because what else is there to say?

I want him to pay, I do. I'm just not sure I want to know what my father and his connections will consider punishment enough.

Oakley leaves the room, and for a second there's nothing but silence. The blood whooshing in my ears. My heart beating in my chest.

"Olivia?" Dad peeks inside. "How are you feeling?"

"I... I'm okay."

It could have been worse.

I was lucky.

If they hadn't showed up when they did...

I swallow the words.

"Good God, sweetheart. I've never been so scared as I was when Oakley said Dale Starling had taken you. I know this world can be... difficult. But never in a million years did I think..." He stares off at nothing, smoothing the edges of his fraught expression. When his gaze finds mine again, I choke on a sob.

"I don't want you to worry about a thing, okay, sweetheart. I'll take care of this." He runs a hand through my hair and presses a kiss to my forehead. "But first, I'm going to need you to tell me exactly what happened. Do you think you can do that?"

I blink away the fresh wave of tears and nod. "I-I think so."

"Good." He smiles. "And Olivia, I need to know everything."

After I recounted everything to Dad, Fiona came in to clean up my cuts and bruises. That was hours ago, and I'm supposed to be sleeping. But every time I close my eyes, I see his face and panic.

I could text Oakley, but I heard him and Dad arguing earlier. I'm hardly surprised. Oakley is Oak. He probably wants to deal with Dale himself.

I haven't seen Reese, Elliot, or Theo since we got back to the house. But I know Reese is here, somewhere in the house. I've heard him.

I could text him too, but what would I possibly say? I saw him lay into Dale. The pure rage rippling off him, swirling around him like a storm. Reese was—

A quiet knock at my door makes my heart flutter.

"Oak?" I whisper, and the door creaks open.

"Hi." Reese steps inside, his features barely visible in the sliver of moonlight leaking in through the curtains.

"Reese?"

"I won't stay," he says, moving closer. "I needed to see you. To make sure..." He's close now, right by the edge of the bed. His lips press into a thin line as he runs his gaze over my face, the bruises there.

"Fuck," he breathes.

"I'm okay."

"Nothing about this is okay." He scrubs his jaw. "This is all my fault."

"We both know that's not—"

"Don't. Don't do that. If I hadn't blown up his stupid fucking car..."

"You're finally admitting it?" My lips curve, but he doesn't return my smile. "Reese, I'm fine. It looks worse than it is."

"He almost fucking raped you." He chokes on the words, and even in the shadows, I see the blood drain from his face.

"Lie with me?" I ask.

"What?"

"You heard me. I can't sleep. Every time I close my eyes, I—"

"I can't. I should go."

"Please, don't," I rush out, panic rising inside me again. "Just lie with me for a little while, until I'm asleep."

"Our parents—"

"It's almost three in the morning. Everyone is sleeping." Or at least, they should be.

Something passes over Reese's expression and I ask, "What?"

"Oak... he left."

"Of course he did." I let out a weary sigh.

"The lads went with him."

"Yet you stayed."

"I couldn't leave. Not until I saw you, until I knew..." He glances away again.

"I'll be okay when you lie down with me."

I'm not playing fair, but if he walks out now, I'm not sure I'll survive it. I need him. I need to feel his arms around me.

Torment glitters in his eyes, and for a second, I think he's going to leave me. But then he rasps, "Budge over," and climbs in beside me.

"Thank you." I nestle into his side, soaking up the strong, steady presence of him.

"I wanted to kill him," he whispers into the dark.

"I know." I swallow over the lump in my throat.

"It wasn't supposed to be like this."

Us.

He means what's happening between us.

"I know."

"But I saw him on top of you, and it snapped something in me, Olivia. Fucking shredded my insides."

"I know." Tears burn the backs of my eyes, but I refuse to let them fall. "For what it's worth, I don't blame you, Reese."

"You should." He pulls me closer, dropping his chin to the top of my head.

"Reese, I—"

"Shh, Liv. You should try and get some sleep."

"Yeah."

I don't want to sleep. I want to talk about us. About the way he makes me feel. About what happened out at the Rock. But as his hand drifts up and down my spine, my eyes grow impossibly heavy.

And, lying here in Reese's arms, sleep finally claims me.

The bright morning sun greets me as I peel my eyes open, but I wince with pain. Everything hurts. My cheekbone and jaw. My throat where Dale choked me.

But nothing hurts as much as realising Reese is gone, his side of the bed already cold.

I'm not surprised—he couldn't risk staying or us being discovered. But it still stings.

"Olivia?" Fiona calls from beyond my door.

"I'm awake."

She peeks inside. "How are you feeling?"

"It hurts."

"Oh, sweetheart." Slipping inside, she comes and sits on the edge of the bed, tracing her fingers over my injuries. "Gosh, I want to drive over to Huxton and teach that young man a lesson."

"I'm fi—"

"Don't you dare say you're fine. You were sexually assaulted, Olivia. If Oakley and the boys hadn't gotten to you in time, we'd be having a very different conversation."

"I know. Is Oakley back?"

Her expression drops. "No. But Elliot called your father. They've got him contained at the Chapel."

"Contained? What the hell does that mean?"

"It means that they know not to let him leave until your father has paid Mr. Starling a visit."

The knot in my stomach tightens.

"What will happen to him?" I ask.

"Dale Starling is a predator, Olivia." Her expression darkens. "And your father will make sure he's dealt with accordingly."

But not through the usual channels. Because the Beckworths and the Whitfield-Browns and the Eatons and Ashworths don't handle things like normal people. They use their connections, their money and power. And I know my father is about to deliver a whole world of hurt to Dale and his father's doorstep.

"Can I get you anything?" she asks, stroking the hair out of my face. "A drink? Something to eat?"

"Coffee, maybe."

"Of course. Reese is downstairs trying to make himself

useful. I'm meeting a friend for coffee soon, so I'll ask him to bring you one up and stay with you until I get back. I know he'll never admit it, but I think he's worried."

"He is?" The words slip out, but hearing her say that makes me all warm inside.

Fiona smiles. "Of course he is, Olivia," she says. "You're family."

Family.

The word echoes through my skull. But she's right, isn't she?

We are family.

And no one—not her or my father or Oakley—will ever accept the thing between us.

Because one day, she'll be my stepmum and Reese...

He'll be my stepbrother.

4

REESE

I sit at the table in Christian's kitchen with my fist curled on top of the worn wood. I can't hear Mum talking to Olivia, but I know she is. Jealousy burns through me, knowing that she's spending time up there, checking she's okay while I stay down here.

The guilt from knowing she was hurt last night because of me floods my veins. Because of my stupid revenge mission on Dale fucking Starling. If I'd have just done as Elliot had instructed and only fucked his car up a bit, then he might not have felt the need to go to such extremes to hit back at us.

I squeeze my eyes closed, desperately trying to rid myself of the image of Dale pinning Olivia to the ground as he—

"Fuck," I hiss, achingly aware of what would have happened if we hadn't got there when we did. I could see his intentions clear as day in his dark, evil eyes.

"Everything okay, sweetheart?" Mum asks as she marches into the room, startling me.

"Uh..."

"She's okay. You all got there just in time. You did good." She smiles at me as if she actually means that. As if she's not suspicious as fuck about all of this.

I can see the accusation right there in her eyes, but for some reason, she keeps it locked down.

Mum isn't stupid. Far fucking from it. I have no doubt that if she weren't born as a woman into this town ruled by men, then she'd have been in Christian's position right now instead of being his right-hand woman.

I've never once heard her complain about it, but I've seen the way other men have treated her over the years, even back when I didn't understand. But since getting close to Olivia, I've had a front-row seat to how she feels about living in this town and having to abide by the old-fashioned traditions we're ruled by. It's more than obvious how hard Mum must have fought to get where she is now.

"Yeah," I mutter, unable to agree with her previous statement. "I should head out. Go and check on Oak."

"Olivia is worried about him," she muses as she reaches into a cupboard for a mug before bringing the coffee machine to life. "I don't think I've ever seen him quite that angry."

"Rightly so," I mutter, feeling pretty close to the fucking edge myself.

"Elliot and Theo will keep him in check."

"Still, I need to head over." The last thing we need right now is Oak, or any of them getting suspicious.

"Actually, I need you to stay here with Olivia for a little bit. I'm supposed to be meeting Krystal. I'll only be gone an hour or so," Mum says, her voice soft in a way I'm not sure I've heard for a few years.

"Seriously, you need to meet Krystal? Today of all days?" I gawk at her.

"She's going through some things. I promised her we could get coffee. I won't be long." A refusal is on the tip of my tongue when she then turns toward me with Olivia's favourite mug in her hand. "Take this up to her, please. I think she'd much rather see you than she would me."

I really fucking doubt it. But I need her, and my selfishness is going to win right now.

I held off as long as I could last night, but the second it was safe to sneak into her room unseen, I was there.

I'd expected her to be asleep. I had every intention of watching her for a bit, getting enough to convince myself that she was okay and then to slip out again unnoticed.

The last thing I wanted was to see her big, scared eyes staring up at me as she told me she couldn't sleep because of that motherfucker. And I really wasn't expecting my presence, my embrace, to be soothing enough to send her to sleep.

My body begged for me to drift off with her scent filling my nose. But I couldn't. I couldn't risk Christian or Oak coming in to check on her and finding me there.

I guess I could attempt to convince them I was doing my step-brotherly duty of making sure she was safe, but I'm not sure it would have flown somehow. And not because Olivia had slipped her hand beneath my shirt to rest her palm against my abs.

My heart is in my throat as I make my way up the stairs toward her.

Slipping out from beneath her this morning pained me.

I was so comfy—and so fucking hard—that the last thing I wanted to do was leave her alone, especially when I knew she'd wake alone and immediately think of that piece of shit again.

But what else was I meant to do? Risk Oak walking in? He was already falling apart at the seams because Olivia had been touched by someone who never should have been anywhere near her. Finding me wrapped around her would have done very little for his mental state, I'm sure.

I knock, feeling more nervous than I have for a long fucking time as I wait for her to invite me in.

The second her quiet and hesitant voice hits my ears, I lower the handle and head inside.

"Hey, Mum said—" My words die on my tongue when I round the corner and find her sitting up in bed with the covers pooled at her waist and all her cuts and bruises on show.

Rage erupts within me and my hand trembles, sending coffee sloshing all over her cream carpet as it quickly bubbles over.

I'm going to fucking kill him.

"Reese?" she whispers, her voice hesitant and cracked with emotion.

She might as well have reached inside my chest and gripped my heart in her clutches.

"Uh... I-I—" I stutter like a fucking idiot.

"I'm okay," she lies, just like she did from the moment we found her yesterday.

"Bullshit," I spit, my voice harsher than I intended.

Her gasp of shock rips through the air, and I immediately feel like an arsehole. She tries to fight it, but I don't miss the tremble of her bottom lip or the way her eyes water.

"I brought you coffee," I say, surging forward, needing to focus on anything but how broken she looks. Broken because of me.

"Th-thank you. Where... um... where did you go? I woke up and you—"

"Did you want to be caught?" I growl, the thought of someone walking in and finding her wrapped around me like a fucking snake floating through my mind.

Her fingers twist in the sheets.

"N-no but—"

"Then there is no but, is there?" My voice is cold, hard. Completely at odds with the way I'm feeling as my eyes track each of her cuts and bruises.

"I need to go, I—"

"No, Reese. Wait," she cries, but it's too late. I'm halfway toward the door with the need to get the hell away from her before I do something stupid like strip off and crawl into bed with her once again.

Without allowing myself to think, I thunder down the stairs with my sights firmly set on the front door.

"Reese, what's the matter? Is Olivia ok—"

The door slams behind me, cutting off her words and her concern.

Throwing myself into my car, I jab my finger into the start button as movement in the hallway window catches my eye. I glance at Mum, but I don't look to see the concern and confusion that's going to be in her eyes.

Flooring the accelerator, I fly out of the driveway and turn toward All Hallows'.

The drive to the Chapel is shorter than I'm sure it's ever been. The tension in my shoulders and the guilt twisting in my gut haven't lessened one bit. The only thing about all of this that's making me feel better is that Christian will make sure that motherfucker Starling pays for this.

It might not be in blood, which is exactly what Oak wants right now, but I have no doubt that Christian will make sure he ruins that cunt forever for even thinking about touching his daughter.

Pulling my newly acquired key from my pocket, I take the path to the massive double doors before pushing it into the lock.

Silence greets me as I step inside, and my heart rate picks up that Elliot and Theo haven't been able to contain Oak and he's fucked off to Huxton to finish the job the pair of us started on that motherfucker.

But the second I look toward the sofas, I find my fears are unfounded, because they're all there.

Oak is sitting on one of the sofas alone. He's leaning forward with his elbows resting on his knees and his head hanging between his shoulders.

Elliot and Theo are both resting back as if everything is

right in their world, but the creases in their brows tell me everything their relaxed postures don't.

"What's going on?" I ask when they continue to ignore me.

"Nothing. Oak's—"

"Don't," Oak spits. "Don't fucking talk about me as if I'm not even in the room."

He surges to his feet, his eyes finding mine. Despair and pain war within them, and the guilt I was already struggling with only gets worse.

"How is she?" he asks, his voice void of any emotion.

"She's..." My words falter as I realise that I'm about to use the same bullshit statement she pulled on me. "She needs you."

Oak shakes his head.

"What she needs is that cunt wiped off the face of the Earth for thinking he could put his hands on her."

"Your dad is gonna take care of it, man," Elliot soothes.

"Not fucking good enough. It would already have been sorted if you two arseholes would let me out of this fucking place."

"They're doing the right thing," I say quietly.

Oak's posture hardens, his shoulders widening and his chest lifting, his eyes darkening with anger the longer he stares at me.

"You," he seethes, taking a step toward me. "All of this is your fucking fault. If you'd just done as you were told that night... Fuck it, if you'd never turned your backs on us and left, then none of this would have happened. Starling knows we're broken, and he's using it against us."

"Oak," Elliot says firmly, but it doesn't have the impact I think he was hoping for, because Oak continues to prowl toward me, his first curling in his burning need for a fight.

I hold my hands out at my sides, more than prepared to take whatever he wants to turn on me. Because he's right. This is all my fault, and I deserve the pain for it.

"Oakley," Elliot barks, now sitting on the edge of the sofa as if he's about to jump between the two of us. "Reese is as pissed about this as you are. We don't need to be turning on ourselves. If we do, he's won."

Elliot's eyes meet mine, an understanding within them that I don't like. He saw the panic inside me as acutely as he could see it in Oak last night. Was it too much?

"Oak's right, Elliot. I'm the one who caused this. I deserve —" *Crack.*

"Motherfucker," I grunt as pain explodes from my jaw where Oak landed his first punch.

"I said no, Oakley," Elliot growls, his voice pure ice as I recover from the hit.

When I look up, I find Oak being restrained by Theo and Elliot standing between the two of us.

"Get it fucking together. Your sister needs you," Elliot demands before closing the space between us.

There's something in his eyes that makes my heart jump into my throat.

"You need to watch your back, Whitfield," he warns so that only I can hear. "I can only protect you from so much."

With that ominous warning hanging between us, I glance over his shoulder at Oak before marching toward the front door once more, only pausing to grab a bottle of expensive whisky on the way out.

"Don't wait up," I hiss as I leave them behind, more than ready to find the promise of darkness that lingers at the bottom of the bottle.

5

OLIVIA

The bed dips behind me and strong arms slide around my waist.

"Reese?"

"Go back to sleep." The deep rumble of his voice rolls through me like thunder.

He tucks his face in the crook of my neck and tangles his legs with mine, pulling me as close as possible.

"What are you doing?" I whisper, smiling to myself.

He's here.

After fleeing my room this morning and disappearing for the day, he's here. In my bed. Holding me.

"Needed to see you." His warm breath brushes my skin, sending shivers down my spine. But I also smell the liquor on his breath, the overpowering scent of top-shelf whisky.

My spine goes rigid. "You're drunk."

"I might be a tiny bit drunk." He smiles against my neck, his fingers dipping under my pyjama top.

"Reese..." I cover his hand with mine.

"Shh, sweet cheeks." His lips brush my cheek. "I just want to hold you."

"You... Reese Whitfield... want to spoon?"

"Fuck yeah, I do."

I smother a chuckle, melting back against him as silence envelops us. Just when I think he might have fallen asleep, I whisper, "Reese?"

"Yeah?" he murmurs.

"Nothing." I chicken out from saying everything I want, swallowing the words on the tip of my tongue.

"Stop overthinking it."

"I'm not—"

He pulls away and pushes me onto my back, staring down at me. "I know you, Olivia. I know the way your mind works."

"You sound awfully confident." Reaching for him, I push the strands of hair from his forehead. His eyes shutter as he inhales a sharp breath at my touch.

"You care." My voice cracks.

"Even if I do... we both know this can never—"

"Shh." I press my finger to his lips. I don't want to hear about how we can't be together. Not now, in this moment.

The air crackles and shifts around us, his eyes dipping to my mouth.

"I want to kiss you so fucking badly." He reaches for my face, cupping my cheek and dusting his thumb over the ugly bruise there.

"So kiss me." My voice shakes, mimicking the way my body trembles beneath him.

"I... I can't."

"You can. I'm not glass, Reese. I won't break."

I anchor my hands around the back of his neck, pulling him down on top of me. He resists at first, letting out a heavy sigh as he tries to keep some space between us.

"Please," I beg.

"Fuck," he rasps, nudging his nose against mine, breathing me in.

"Kiss me, Reese. Just kiss—"

His mouth crashes down on mine, stealing the air from my

lungs. He hovers above me, careful not to drop all of his weight onto me. But I want to feel him. I need it.

"I don't want to hurt you." He pulls back, his chest heaving between us.

"You won't." I gaze up at him.

"He hurt you... because of me."

"So make it better."

"Fuck, Olivia. You don't know what you're asking me to do."

"I wouldn't ask if I didn't." I lift my chin in defiance. "Make me forget, Reese. Make me—"

He collars my throat gently, kissing me harder. Deeper. Our tongues tangle, his wrapping around mine, dominating me.

"Is Oak—"

"At the Chapel." Reese breathes the words against my lips. "But your dad and my mum are—"

"On the other side of the house. They won't hear us. I'll be quiet."

"Oh, you will, will you?" He pulls back to look me in the eye, but the heat there dims. "You're hurt—"

"I'm fine. Stop making excuses. I want this... I want you, Reese."

"Fuck," he hisses under his breath, and I can see the wheels turning in his head. He's at war with himself, tormented about whether or not to give me what I want.

"I'm not having sex with you," he says, making my heart tumble. I start to protest, but he pins me with a dark look. "You can't expect me to do that, not yet. Not after he—"

His eyes shutter again, but I rest my palm against his cheek, bringing him back to me.

When his eyes flicker open, what I see takes my breath away. But I don't have time to question it, because Reese rolls off me and tucks me into his side, my back pressed up against his chest.

"You seriously want to sle—"

His fingers splay against my stomach and slide downward, toying with the waistband of my pyjama shorts.

"I'm going to make you come," he whispers against my ear, "and you're going to be as quiet as a mouse."

Shoving his hand inside my shorts, his fingers glide through my soft curls.

"R-Reese," I choke over the air caught in my lungs.

"Quiet, remember?" He nips the skin beneath my ear. "Or I'll stop."

Oh God.

I'm not sure I can lie here, silent and still, while he plays with me. But I try my best, pressing my lips together to trap the moans building in my throat as two of his fingers slide through my folds and dip inside me.

"You're so fucking tight, Olivia. Imagine it's my dick filling you up, fucking you. I bet you'd like that, wouldn't you, sweet cheeks?"

I nod, focusing on the way he touches me, how expertly his thumb circles my clit as he pumps his fingers in and out of me.

His other hand collars my throat again, twisting my face enough that he can kiss me—dirty, wet kisses that leave me panting for more.

"You're so fucking beautiful like this." Hunger blazes in his eyes as he watches me while he pushes me closer and closer to the edge.

"Think you can take a third?" he asks, and I murmur some incoherent words, too lost in the sensations battering me.

"That's it, sweet cheeks. Let me in." He pushes a third finger into me, curling them deep and rubbing that spot deep inside.

"God," I moan, and his hand slides up my jaw and clamps over my mouth.

"Be. Quiet," he warns, working me faster, his thumb and fingers playing my body with perfect synchronicity.

It's too much and not nearly enough, but all too soon, my stomach coils tightly, pleasure pooling inside me.

"I'm coming." The words are drowned out against his palm and my legs begin to tremble, an intense wave cresting over me.

Reese doesn't let up though, wrecking me in the best possible way until I'm a breathless, sated mess in his arms.

"Think you can be quiet now?" he asks quietly, and I nod. His hand slips from my mouth, but he collars my throat again, tipping my head back. "You're fucking ruining me," he whispers, kissing me.

"I'm ruining you?" My brow arches and he chuckles.

"You got what you wanted, little liar. Now go back to sleep."

"You'll stay for a while?" I ask, not ready for this moment to be over.

He rolls his eyes at me, but I see the glint of possessiveness there. "Yeah, I'll stay. Now sleep."

Between the heat of his body cocooning mine and the post-orgasm endorphins saturating my body, my eyes barely close before I fall into oblivion.

"Olivia, sweetheart, how are you feeling?" A voice startles me and my eyes fly open. "W-what?"

"The fuck?" Reese grumbles from beside me right as Fiona calls, "Olivia," again.

"Shit, shit." I bolt upright. "Reese, wake up. Your mum—"

"Olivia, sweetie. Are you awake?"

"Fuck." His eyes find me, wild and full of panic. 'What do I do?' he mouths, and my eyes dart around my bedroom.

"The bathroom. Go hide in the bathroom." I start pushing him out of bed and he growls under his breath.

"It's not my fault you overslept," I snap back, all the ways this could play out running through my head.

None of them are good.

I'd been so happy last night when Reese climbed into bed with me, but even I can appreciate this is a clusterfuck.

Reese grabs his jeans off the floor and his t-shirt and shoots me a displeased look as he dives for the bathroom.

"Oliv—"

"Coming," I call, hurrying to the door before she comes inside. "Morning." I smile as it swings open, hoping to God that I look normal and not like a girl who spent the night tangled up in her son's arms.

"Is everything okay? I thought I heard voices."

"I was on a video call to Charli. She woke me up."

"Oh. Well, I wanted to bring you a coffee, sweetheart. You slept like the dead, it's almost ten."

Ten.

Crap.

Clearly, drunk Reese cannot be trusted to set his alarm.

"Oak is downstairs. Your father and I thought we could all have breakfast together. I'm about to go and wake Reese. Oak said he didn't stay at the Chapel, so he must be here."

"N-no," I blurt. "I'll do it."

"What?"

"I mean, I can wake him. We should probably talk anyway... after everything. Clear the air before family breakfast."

She thinks on it for a second and then smiles. "That's probably a good idea. I'd prefer it if Oakley and Reese could try not to kill each other over pancakes."

"No problem. Just give me ten minutes, then we'll be down."

She steps forward, cupping my cheek in her hand. "I'm so glad you're okay, Olivia. I know I'm not your mum, but you and your brother mean a lot to me. I hope you both know that. And maybe one day—"

The blare of my mobile phone cuts through the air and she drops her hand.

"It's probably Charli," I say. "I cut her off earlier."

"Okay, well, I'll leave you to it. Please tell that son of mine we expect him at the table whether he wants to be there or not."

"I will."

She takes off down the hall and I close my bedroom door, inhaling a shaky breath.

That was a close call.

Too close.

Marching across the room, I pluck up my phone, surprised to see Reese's name on the missed call notification.

As I approach the bathroom, my heart thumps in my chest. We almost got caught and yet, all I can think about is kissing him again.

I've barely got the door open when his arm darts out and he pulls me inside.

"What are you—"

He pins me against the wall, pressing his head to mine as he stares at me.

"I take it she bought your lies." His jaw tics as he says the words.

"What is that supposed to mean?"

"Nothing." Something flashes in his eyes, but it's gone before I can latch onto it.

"I'm sorry I slept in."

"Wait a second, is the cocky Reese Whitfield apologising?"

"Don't get too used to it." His lips slide over mine.

"Reese," I breathe, curling my fingers into his crinkled Henley. "Did you hear what your mum said? They want us to go have breakfast with them... and Oakley."

"Fuck." He steps back, running a hand down his face.

"I told her I'd come and get you."

"Smart thinking." He kisses the end of my nose. "We should probably go face the firing squad then."

"They don't know anything, Reese," I say.

He moves away from me, the temperature cooling around us as he looks back at me, and his expression tightens, sending a sinking feeling through me.

"Let's hope you're right."

6

REESE

I follow Olivia downstairs with dread and anticipation flooding my veins.

We were so close to being discovered. If Mum was a little less considerate of Olivia's privacy and more concerned with her recovery after everything that happened Friday night, she'd have stumbled in and found the two of us a little too comfortable.

The fear of her storming in was a surefire way to sink my morning wood. Just the sound of her voice on the other side of the door was the ultimate antidote to having Olivia's round arse pressed up against me.

Fuck. Just the thought of waking to her in my arms is enough to give me a semi once again.

Reaching down, I readjust myself right as Olivia looks back over her shoulder.

She stares me dead in the eyes for a beat, taking the last few steps to the ground floor blindly, before they drop to my waist.

Her brows shoot up as she registers what I'm doing. "Looking forward to this breakfast?" she asks with a smirk.

"Oh yeah, can't fucking wait," I mutter, storming past her and pulling my hand from my boxers.

All eyes turn on me the second I step through the doorway, but it's Oakley mine fall on as guilt surges through me. Only this time, it's stronger than when I looked into his eyes last night. Now, it's not because of the weight of Olivia's injuries and everything she went through pressing down on my shoulders, but also that I spent the night wrapped around her, that I finger-fucked her until she was trembling against me, my name nothing more than a plea on her lips.

My stomach knots and my steps falter as I swear he drills me with a knowing look.

"Are you going to get out of the way, or what?" Olivia snaps behind me, the venom in her voice making me snap out of my panic.

She's right. Oak doesn't know. No one does.

And they can't. Because as bad as it would be for them to find out I've been fucking her, it will be nothing compared to what happens when I follow through with my plan and leave her—and them—broken in my wake, regretting the day they ever convinced me to come back here.

Unease washes through me at the thought of walking away once more. But one quick look between Mum and Christian, and then Olivia as she takes a seat beside her brother, and I'm reminded of their lies and the betrayal they all brought into our lives. Fury surges through me. And when I meet my best friend's eyes once more, a fierce need to expose the truth and to follow through with my plan slams into me.

He deserves to know everything, to know all the lies his family was happy to tell him for months on end.

"I hope you were nice when Olivia came to wake you up," Mum says, her voice so sweet it sets my teeth on edge.

"I'm always nice," I grunt, pulling out the chair opposite Oak and falling into it.

Without missing a beat, I reach for the stack of pancakes

sitting in the middle of the table and dump more than necessary on my plate.

"Hungry, Reese?" Christian asks with a smirk.

"Something like that." *I was awake most of the night watching your daughter sleep soundly after I made her come so hard she pretty much passed out.*

"You're hanging," Oak points out helpfully, studying me harder than I'd like him to.

"And what? You don't exactly look fresh this morning," I shoot back.

"Where'd you go?"

"I came back here after you made it more than obvious I wasn't welcome at the Chapel."

Tension crackles between us as we glare at each other across the table.

He still blames me, and rightly so. I'm more than aware whose fault all this shit is. I just wish he'd ask fewer fucking questions. He already wants to hurt me. If he were to find out...

"You got wasted alone in your room?"

"What about it?" I hiss, getting really fucking bored of his insinuations that are hitting a little too close to home.

"Oakley," Christian warns, shaking his head as if he's bored of his son's antics. "Can we please just have one meal together that doesn't descend into an argument? You two used to be so close. I know things have been... strained." I scoff at that assessment but allow him to continue. "You need to remember what brought you together and put all this behind you."

"We'll see what we can do," Oakley mutters, willing to at least attempt to follow his father's orders.

"So, aside from the obvious, what's happening with you all? How has school been this week?"

We all mumble some variation of 'it's okay', while Mum rolls her eyes at our lack of enthusiasm.

"Olivia, I've already spoken to Mr. Porter and informed him that you'll be spending this week recuperating from your ordeal."

"What?" Olivia screeches, her knife and fork clattering to the table as she releases them in shock.

"It's okay, sweetheart. He more than understood and thought that it was the right thing to do, given the circumstances."

"The right thing... given the circumstances," she echoes in disbelief. "That's bullshit. I'm going to school tomorrow."

"No, sweetheart. I think your father is ri—"

"You're not going to school, Liv," Oak agrees, talking right over my mother.

"You can't stop me from continuing my life. I'm not some poor, innocent victim here."

"They're right," I parrot, unable to argue with them.

She's still covered in cuts and bruises, the evidence of that monster's touch glaringly obvious. It's going to turn all eyes on her, and I don't want that for her. For her to have to tell the story over and over, or worse, hear the bullshit lies I'm sure have already been made up after we all bolted from our own party. The rest of the team kept things moving, but our absence was noticed the second we all walked away.

"You're not serious?" she asks.

"Deadly." My deep voice perfectly conveys how seriously I'm taking this.

Olivia's eyes narrow on mine. But I refuse to back down.

Well, not until Oakley's confused stare makes my face burn red-hot.

"I mean, imagine what shit Darcie has been blabbing about you. You don't want to be dealing with that yet."

"Careful, Reese. You're meant to like her, remember," she seethes.

"Yeah," I hiss. "I think our happy couple time might just be coming to an end."

"You're seeing Darcie Porter? I didn't realise it was serious," Mum asks, clearly oblivious to the alibi I used to get away with sending Dale fucking Starling's car to kingdom come.

"No. She was a means to an end."

"And she's got plenty of detailed stories about your 'end'."

A growl rumbles deep in my throat as Olivia stares at me in an attempt to show the rest of the room that her words mean nothing.

I see it, though. The hurt that flickers through her eyes, the jealousy that tightens her muscles as she even thinks about some of the bullshit Darcie has been spewing about me.

"Reese, you shouldn't use people like that," Mum chastises.

My chin drops at her audacity. "Are you actually shitting me right now?"

Her lips part in shock, but she wisely shuts the hell up when she realises what a hypocrite she is.

Oakley remains silent opposite me, studying me, making me squirm with the intensity of it.

"You want to come out on a double date with me Thursday night?" he asks out of nowhere.

"Uh..."

"It's Misty's birthday, and I promised to make it up to her—"

"Don't wanna know, Bro," Olivia barks.

Oak rolls his eyes. "A night out. Jeez, Liv. What do you think of me?"

"There's no thinking, Oak. You're a dog, and we all know it."

"Okay, that's enough, kids," Christian says with a pained laugh. "No arguing and no discussing things that will make Fiona and I have nightmares about our babies."

"Because you were better when you were our age," Oak scoffs.

"Oh, he wasn't," Mum helpfully adds with a wide, mischievous smile.

"Overshare," Olivia mutters.

"Anyway. Me, you, Darcie, and Misty, Thursday night, yeah?"

"Why the fuck do you want to double date with Darcie?" I bark, unable to fight the shiver that rips down my spine as I think about being forced near the leech.

"It'll be like old times," Oak says with a wink.

Images of the things our past double dates with the Heir chasers at school have entailed flick through my mind, making me even less interested.

My eyes shoot to Olivia as she sits silently, waiting for my answer, and the second my skin heats with her brother's attention once more, I know there's only one I can give.

"Sure, why not."

Turning to look at Oak, I force a fake excited smile on my lips, but not before I see the way Olivia's entire body jolts in shock.

"I'm more than happy to be your wingman, if you need the help to get laid."

"Reese," Christian barks as tension thickens the air.

A plate rattling across the table hits my ears, but I don't look away from Oak. I can't. He's suspicious, I can see it in his rich brown depths that look alarmingly like his sister's.

"Excuse me, I'm going back to bed," Olivia says, standing from her chair. "I need to rest so I'm ready for school in the morning."

"No, Olivia. That's not—"

"It's happening, Dad. I'm practically an adult, and I can decide for myself if a couple of bruises are enough to keep me from school or not. And I say not."

Without hanging around to hear Christian's response, she takes off toward the stairs, leaving nothing but the sound of her footsteps in her wake.

"Well then," Christian says, stabbing an innocent piece of pancake with more aggression than necessary.

"It's your fault, you know," Oak mutters.

"Mine?" Christian asks incredulously.

"Yeah, you brought her up to be all independent and headstrong."

"She knows her own mind, exactly as every young woman should." Mum smiles proudly as if she had something to do with that.

"And I would usually agree. But the kids at school will—"

"You need to stand your ground with her," Oak barks, also pushing to stand. "She doesn't need the shit she's going to get tomorrow."

"Where are you going?" Mum asks when he scoops up Olivia's almost full plate and mug of coffee.

"Taking her breakfast, seeing as we've all managed to ruin another meal."

"Maybe next time, sweetheart," Mum says to Christian in the soft, irritating voice she seems to have dragged up from somewhere when she speaks to him. I certainly never heard her talk to Dad that way.

Stuffing what's left of my breakfast into my mouth, I lift my plate from the table, more than ready to walk away.

I get as far as the dishwasher when Mum's voice stops me in my tracks.

"Reese, can you please return your father's calls? He only wants to check in with you. He's concerned."

My spine stiffens as I think about the unread messages from him that are still sitting on my phone. He's started calling daily now, although it's not having any effect other than to piss me off.

"Then maybe he should have reconsidered sending me back here," I hiss, more than ready to blow out of this room and away from this bullshit.

"This is your home, Reese. Your destiny."

"Yeah, well, have you ever considered the fact that you might be the only one in our family who actually agrees with that?"

I'm halfway toward the stairs before she finds her voice. "You belong here, Son. With us. With Abigail."

"Fuck that," I mutter, blowing out of the house like a storm about to strike, and I don't stop running until my legs are like jelly and my lungs can't keep up with my racing heart.

I don't realise my mistake until I look up at my resting place and find the Rock up ahead.

All I see is her.

Her and everything I shouldn't fucking want but can't stop thinking about.

7

OLIVIA

Olivia

When I walk into All Hallows' Monday morning, it's like the world stops to watch. I hate it. Their stares and whispers, the way some people point like I'm an exhibit at the zoo.

Despite my father's promise that Dale Starling will never hurt me again, I guess he couldn't stop the rumour mill of Saints Cross. People know something went down—of course they do. And although I've always envied my brother and the Heirs and the way the town worships the very ground they walk on, I never wanted to end up in the spotlight.

Not like this.

I keep my head down as I cut through the early morning stream of bodies, but a saccharine voice gives me pause.

"Oh my God, Olivia. What happened?"

Turning slowly, I come face to face with Darcie and her less-than-genuine concerned smile.

"None of your business," I snap.

"No need to be a bitch, Liv. I'm only looking out for my fellow students."

"Sure you are," I murmur. Not wanting to waste another breath on her, I spin on my heel and take off. But she isn't done, calling after me.

"If you ask me, you probably deserved it."

"Darcie," somebody snaps, and I glance back to find Tally Darlington glowering at her.

"Oh look, if it isn't Miss Goody Two Shoes. Piss off, Tally. This has nothing to do with you."

"You might be the Queen Bitch of All Hallows', Darcie, but girls are supposed to stick together over things like this." Tally offers me a sympathetic smile, and my worst fears are confirmed.

Everyone knows about what happened. Or at least, some watered-down version of events.

Darcie sneers in my direction, but before she can land another blow, I take off down the hall.

"Olivia, wait," Tally calls after me, but I don't stop, bursting into the girls' bathroom. She follows me inside, barking at the girl at the basins to get out.

"Are you okay?" she asks me.

I heave a ragged breath, gawking at her. "I... God, I hate her."

"Darcie Porter is everything that's wrong with this world. But I didn't follow you in here to discuss all her shortcomings. Are you okay?"

"I'll live."

"You shouldn't be in school, Olivia. You need time to—"

"I'm not going to hide away at home. What happened wasn't even really that—"

"I swear to God, if you try to tell me what happened wasn't that bad, I will scream." Her expression turns angry.

"You're kind of scary when you're like this."

"Being Head Girl isn't easy, you know." A faint smirk traces her lips. "Especially in a school like All Hallows'."

"Well, thanks, I guess. You didn't have to stand up for me like that."

"We might not be friends, Olivia, but I think we can agree that we share a common enemy." She gives me a wry smile.

"I guess we can."

"Do you want me to stay? Get Oakley? I can—"

"No, no. I need a minute, but you don't need to stay."

Tally nods. "You might be an Heir's sister, but you're okay, Olivia Beckworth."

Before I can reply, she slips out of the bathroom and leaves me alone.

The vibration of my mobile phone startles me, and I dig it out of my pocket.

Reese: We need to talk.

Talk.

He can go to hell for all I care.

Another text comes through, and I roll my eyes at his obvious frustration.

Reese: I swear to God, Olive. Stop acting like a little brat and talk to me. You know why I had to say yes.

Of course I know why he agreed to go out with my brother on a stupid double date, but it just had to be her.

It had to be Darcie.

I start typing a reply but think better of it and delete the message.

Everything has gotten too confusing, the lines more blurred than ever.

I like Reese. I shouldn't, but I do.

I don't want him to go out with Darcie or to be promised to Abigail, but tradition—the stupid fucking rules the Heirs have to adhere to—mean I don't get a say.

I can choose Reese. I can tell everyone that he's the one I want, but ultimately, unless he decides to choose me, to fight for me, it means nothing.

I manage to avoid Reese and my brother for the next three days. Oak texts me throughout the day, checking in with me, but he doesn't push. And I'm grateful.

The truth is, some space has been good for me. Last night, I went over to Charli's house and we watched some trashy TV show and ate our body weight in ice cream. Part of me wondered if Reese would show up in the middle of the night and climb into bed with me, but he didn't.

Because he's going on a date with Darcie.

It's all she's talked about. Telling everyone and anyone who will listen that she's dating an Heir. She makes me sick, the way she uses him for her own ends. She doesn't care about Reese, she cares about his name, and his status in All Hallows'.

Still, she'll be the one on his arm tomorrow night. I heard her telling her friends that the guys are taking them to the Wilde Terrace, a highly exclusive bar and restaurant on the outskirts of Oxford.

The thought of them together makes my stomach churn.

The second class is dismissed, I shove my things in my bag and hurry out of there. I have to be quick, or else Oakley might see me as he's in the class right down the hall.

I slip into the stream of bodies and keep my head down as everyone fights their way out of the building. But I don't make it, someone grabbing my arm and yanking me into the storage closet.

"What—"

Reese cups his hand over my mouth and pushes me up against the wall, his eyes glittering with dark intent.

"What the hell are you doing?" I whisper-hiss against his palm.

"Drastic times call for drastic measures, sweet cheeks. Now, if I remove my hand, can I trust you not to scream?"

My eyes narrow to deadly slits.

Reese slowly unfurls his fingers but drops his head to mine, caging me there.

"You're a hard girl to track down."

"You know exactly where to find me if you try hard enough," I spit back.

"And risk getting caught sneaking into your room every night when your brother already suspects something..."

"I didn't take you for a coward."

The venom in my voice shocks us both. I get it, I do. But I can't accept it. At least, my heart won't. Some part of me wants Reese to fight for me. It wants him to choose me.

He lets out a heavy sigh, his mouth so close to mine I have to fight the urge to kiss him.

"I'm trying to play this the right way."

"Trying to protect yourself, you mean."

"What do you want from me, Olivia?" His eyes dance with uncertainty as he watches me. I begin to fold under his gaze, trying to press myself into the wall. Because I can't admit it—I can't tell him the truth.

Not yet.

"How's Darcie?" I snarl, hating how jealous I sound.

His lip curves. "You think I want to go on a fucking double date with your brother, Misty, and her? Trust me, I don't."

"Could have fooled me. I know, why don't I come too? I could ask Ben. He seemed like a nice guy. We could all—"

Reese's hand snaps out, collaring my throat. "Go anywhere near that prick and I'll—"

"You'll what?"

"You know, it's funny, you seem to have forgotten who this pussy belongs to." He releases me, dipping his hand between our bodies and cupping me over my skirt and underwear. "This. Is. Mine."

"Touch Darcie, and this will never be yours again."

"Bold words for a girl who doesn't hold any power."

"I think we both know what power I hold." I arch a brow, smirking at him.

A beat passes and then we collide, all teeth and tongue.

"Fuck, you drive me crazy." He kisses me hard. Punishing. Kissing me like he hates me. Like he hates himself for wanting me.

"We can't," I cry. "Not here." Not with half the student population on the other side of the door.

"I'm not letting you walk out of this door without at least one of us coming," he pants, still kissing me. Still running his lips all over my jaw, my neck, and collarbone.

Pushing him away slightly, I gaze up at him. "Then I guess that one of us is you."

"Olivia, what—"

I sink to my knees, grasping at his trousers. Reese's hands slide into my hair. "I wanted to feel you," he complains.

"Break off the date with Darcie and you can."

"I can't— fuck," he breathes as I wrap my tongue around the tip of his dick and suck.

"Fuck, that feels good."

I take him into my mouth, hollowing my cheeks so he can go deep. Reese thrusts a little, pushing my boundaries. Pushing me. But I take it. I take it all, because I need him to know I can handle this. Him.

Us.

He doesn't need to turn to girls like Darcie or her shallow, vain friends. Not when I can give him exactly what he needs.

His fingers fist my hair, guiding my head up and down his hard length. Reese might think he has all the power, that he's controlling me, but as I close my fingers around the base of his shaft and start pumping, working him in synchrony with my tongue and mouth, the power switches.

"God, yes, Liv. Take it. Take it all…" My fingernails dig into the backs of his thighs as I swallow him down again, choking on his dick and slowly pulling back up. He's close. So close, his muscles are drawn tight, his muted groans filling the storage closet.

"This mouth was made for me." He rubs his knuckles down my cheek, gazing down at me with raw emotion. It flickers right there in his eyes, and I know he feels it.

In this moment, Reese feels the connection burning between us.

"I'm almost there… fuck, don't stop. Don't—"

I rip myself away from him and climb to my feet.

"What the fuck are you doing?" He glares at me.

"You'll get the rest when you break off the date with Darcie."

"Olivia, come on. Be reasonable. Oak—"

"This isn't about Oak, it's about you and me and Darcie. Anyone, anyone but her, Reese. I mean it. I know you want to throw my brother off the scent. I get it. I do. But not her."

"I swear to God, Liv. If you don't get back on your fucking knees and—"

"Shh, you'd better keep it down in case anyone overhears." I sass while smoothing the flyaway hairs from my face.

"You're seriously going to leave me like this?"

"You're a big boy, I'm sure you'll live. Or I could send Darcie in to finish the job. I'm sure she'd be more than happy to oblige."

"You'll regret this," he seethes, tucking himself back into his trousers.

"Actually," I grin, "I don't think I will. See you around, Whitfield."

I duck out of the cupboard and close the door behind me, hurrying out of the building before my resolve shatters.

8

REESE

"You could at least look a little excited about tonight," Oak says as he joins me in the kitchen at the Chapel where I'm sitting, picking at a label on a bottle of beer.

"Oh, I'm ecstatic," I mutter to myself. "I'm sure it'll be great." I force a smile on my face when he comes to stop in front of me, his eyes narrowed and assessing. "What?" I ask when his attention doesn't waver.

"You can bail if you want," he offers.

There's a huge part of me that wants to agree. I'm fucking desperate to. But I know it's a trick. This whole night is his way of testing me, to try and figure out if his suspicions about Olivia and me are founded or not.

I hope it's enough to banish that look in his eye. But something tells me my lack of interest in Darcie won't be enough.

Why the fuck did he have to choose her for the stupid fucking double date? He could have offered for me to spend the night with almost anyone else at All Hollows'. Fuck, I'd even put up with Miss Goody Two Shoes, Tally Darlington and her bullshit opinions and rose-tinted outlook on the world over desperate Darcie.

"Nah, man. I've got your back. You need a wingman, I'm your man." I wink at him before lifting my bottle to my lips and downing the contents. "Where are Theo and Elliot?"

"Elliot's gone to see his old man. Fuck knows about Theo. You ready?"

No. "Yeah."

"Great. Let's go, then."

Fan-fucking-tastic.

Dropping my phone and my wallet into my pocket, I follow Oak out, telling myself that this night can't possibly be as bad as I've made it out in my head.

When Oak pulled up outside Misty's house and the two of them appeared wearing practically nothing, I quickly discovered that my night was going to be even worse than I expected.

Oak forcefully shoved me out of the car to allow Misty to take my place in the passenger seat, giving me little choice but to sit in the back and get molested by Darcie the second she slid right up beside me.

The only good thing about the girls' appearance was the fact that Oak's attention was finally off me and instead focused on Misty's tits. I mean, with the way she was falling out of her dress, it was hard to look elsewhere, even for me who has zero interest in her.

"You never said if you liked my dress or not," Darcie purrs, her palm sliding up my thigh beneath the table as the fingers of her other hand trace the plunging neck of her dress. It isn't as revealing as Misty's—not on the top half, anyway. The bottom is almost too obscene to be worn out in public, and I don't need to look too hard to know she's foregone underwear again. If that's meant to make me want her, then I can say without any hesitation that it's fallen far from the mark.

"It's..." A moan from the other side of the table distracts me, and when I glance up, I find Oak's got his fingers twisted in Misty's hair and his tongue so far down her throat I'm amazed she's not choking on it.

"Reese?" Darcie breathes, her hand moving dangerously high on my thigh.

Dropping my hand beneath the table, I wrap my fingers around her wrist, stopping her before she makes contact with my bored dick.

"It's nice," I say, remembering that she's waiting for something.

"Nice?" she spits as if she just watched me kick her favourite puppy.

"Yeah, it's..." I run my eyes over the scrap of fabric. "Blue."

Her eyes widen in shock as her lips twist in frustration. "B-blue?" She looks down at herself. "It's green."

"Is it though?"

She forces a smile on her lips. "I guess it doesn't really matter. What's really important is what's beneath it, right?"

Absolutely fucking not.

Hooking her finger under the hem of her skirt, she drags it up so I have no choice but to get a shot at her bare cunt.

Thankfully, my phone buzzes in my pocket, giving me something else to focus on. Ignoring Darcie's pissed-off stare, I pull my phone out, keeping it hidden from prying eyes.

A smile twitches at my lips as I find Olivia's name staring back at me.

> Olivia: What excuse did you use to get out of tonight?

> Reese: You know I couldn't do that.

> Olivia: Then I guess you're not interested in finishing what we started yesterday.

> Reese: Sweet cheeks, you know I'm more than interested in that. I'll come to you once I'm done here and prove it to you.

> Olivia: Don't bother. I'm out on a date. I'll blow Ben's mind instead.

Anger knots my stomach, fury turning my blood to lava as I imagine her sitting opposite Ben like I am Darcie right now.

> Reese: You're lying.

> Olivia: Am I?

"Fuck," I hiss, slamming my phone down on the table, making everything on top of it rattle with the force of it.

"Everything okay?" Oak asks, finally coming up for air.

"Yeah, great. Darcie isn't wearing any underwear. Was a bit of a shock. Excuse me."

Pushing my chair out behind me, I stand and storm away from the table in favour of the peace of the bathroom.

"Fuck," I bark as I swing the door so hard it crashes back against the wall with a thud. "FUCK."

Marching toward the urinal, I do my thing, thankfully in solitude as I try to figure out how the hell I'm going to get away from Darcie and her freshly waxed cunt without making Oak even more suspicious.

Fuck it. Do I even care?

Maybe I should speed up my plans and let him discover the truth and drop Olivia as quickly as I picked her up.

My chest twists uncomfortably at that thought, but I tell myself it's because I haven't gotten everything I want from her yet.

I want her trust, her truth... her heart.

Until I get that, I don't hold enough power over her to do what I need to do. And fuck, do I need it.

The need for vengeance surges through me once more as I think through my plan. Expose her, leave, and start over with the money I've been siphoning out of my trust fund.

No one even has to know where I go. I can disappear and start over somewhere far, far away from Saints Cross and All Hallows'.

I've just tucked myself back into my trousers when the door swings closed. At first, I fear that Darcie has followed me and is about to jump me in her need to finally stop lying about getting up close and personal with my dick.

I breathe a sigh of relief when I find Oak watching me as he makes his way to my side of the room. "What?" I ask, already more than fed up with his assessing gaze.

"Anyone would think you don't want to get laid."

"Maybe I don't," I mutter, heading for the row of basins to wash my hands.

His eyes follow me, and I watch as he studies me in the mirror. "Darcie is fucking gagging for it, man. And she's not wearing any knickers."

"Then you fuck her. I'm not interested in her sour cunt."

"You know, you never used to be this fussy."

"And you never used to be such a prick, but things change, huh?"

He continues to glare at me, his jaw ticking with frustration.

"What?"

"When are you going to start telling me the truth?" he asks, making my heart lurch and my stomach turn over.

"I am. I don't want Darcie's overused pussy. Can't get more honest than that. If you're so concerned about her getting off tonight, then invite her to join you and Misty. Something tells me she'd be more than up for it."

"That's not the fucking truth and you know it."

"Do I?" I hiss, shaking the water from my hands and finally turning to face him.

Tension and all the things that are currently going unspoken between us crackle, turning the air thick and unbearable.

The little boy who used to live for time with his best friend begs for me to be honest with him and take the beating that's sure to come. But the bitter, angry, and betrayed man that is standing before him has very, very different ideas.

"I need you to prove me wrong, Whitfield. I need you to get these fucking crazy ideas out of my head before I do something really fucking stupid."

His shoulders relax a little as he silently begs me to do something to prove I'm not fucking his sister.

"And how exactly is fucking that desperate whore out there going to prove anything?"

"It just fucking will."

"If I wanted her, I could have had her a million times over by now. You're not exactly dangling a tempting carrot here, Oak."

He takes a step toward me, his fists curling at his sides. "I'm fucking watching you, Whitfield. I want to believe you're not that fucking stupid, and that she's not so fucking blind. But I know you. I know how your mind works, and I know you don't stop at anything to get what you want. I might fucking love you, but I swear to fuck, if you touch Liv, if you hurt her, I will fucking end you."

Without another word, or even attempting to take a piss, he blows out of the bathroom as if I imagined that whole thing. But as his threat lingers in my ears, I know it was very, very real.

Goddamn it.

I give myself two more minutes before I convince myself to return to the table and force myself to sit beside desperate

Darcie as she flashes her pussy at me every few seconds and Oak glares at me any time he's not distracted by Misty's tits.

Fuck my life.

"You're both coming back to my room, right?" Misty asks once we've paid the bill and headed out to find Oak's car.

"Damn right we are. Right, Whitfield?"

"Actually, we've got a game tomorrow and—"

"Whitfield," Oak growls.

"What? Elliot will cut your balls off if you have a late night. You've already pissed all over his *no alcohol three days before a game* rule.

"Fuck Eaton's rules. I'm not his little bitch."

My brow lifts as I stare at him, wondering who this version of my best friend is.

Deep down, I know it's my fault. My leaving, and my fucking his sister, even if he only suspects that to be the case.

"We'll be back by midnight, and the tyrant will never know."

"You wanna fucking bet?"

"You need to lighten up, Reese," Darcie purrs, slipping her hand beneath my black shirt.

"And you need to keep your fucking paws to yourself," I warn in a tone low enough to ensure Oak can't hear as he follows Misty up the stairs toward her dorm room.

"What the hell is wrong with you?"

"Nothing," I spit. "I'm just not interested in someone who's whored themself through not only the entire student body but also the teachers at All Hallows'."

Her face turns purple with frustration.

"I haven't—"

"I don't wanna hear it, Darce. I'll follow you upstairs, but rest assured, you're not so much as getting a look at my cock."

"And what about the girl you've been messaging all night? Is she off-limits too?"

"What? I haven't been messaging a girl," I argue, but it's weak at best. I spent most of the night ignoring everyone around me in my quest to discover if Olivia really was lying about spending the evening with Ben or not.

As of yet, I don't have my answer. And I really need Oak to be distracted by something so I can slip away and find out the truth.

She might have threatened me with not finishing me off if I were to spend the night with Darcie, but it's going to be so much worse for her if I discover she's got anywhere near that motherfucker.

9

OLIVIA

I wake to numerous messages off Reese. Threats mostly.

Overbearing prick.

After I told him I was on a date with Ben, I'd ignored him. Of course, I wasn't on a date. I was at home, trying to keep myself distracted. Trying not to imagine Darcie all over him, trying her best to seduce him.

My fingers fly over the screen as I text Reese back a piece of my mind.

> Olivia: I hope she was worth it.

Ugh.

I slam my phone down on the bed, anger rippling through me.

Did they spend the night together?

Did he fuck her like a good little lap dog, all because my brother told him to?

I wouldn't put it past Oakley to do something so cruel.

If he suspects something is going on between me and Reese, it's not me he'll punish. It's him.

Because they have their stupid bro code. I'm an Heir's

sister. That makes me untouchable. Off-limits. It doesn't matter what I want.

God, sometimes I hate this place. This town and their antiquated, chauvinistic ways.

I guess part of me had hoped Reese would choose me, that he'd come clean to Oakley—or at the very least, manage to get out of their double date.

My phone vibrates and I snatch it up.

> Reese: I told you, it's not that simple.

>> Olivia: Did you fuck her? Because if you did, I hope your dick rots and falls off.

> Reese: I like you like this, jealous and angry...

>> Olivia: Jealous? Of Darcie Porter? She's slept with half of the rugby team AND the football team.

> Reese: Meet me somewhere before class...

>> Olivia: After you spent the night with her? Go fuck yourself.

> Reese: Why would I do that when it's so much more fun fucking you? Besides, sweet cheeks, you owe me.

>> Olivia: I'm sure Darcie will be more than willing to oblige.

> Reese: It's not Darcie I want...

>> Olivia: Could have fooled me.

I turn my phone off, done with his mind games.

So maybe I am acting a little immature, but I'm entitled to lick my wounds. Maybe he doesn't remember that night all those months ago when he humiliated me at the initiation party. Humiliated me and then kissed Darcie.

I hate her.

Once upon a time, I hated him. But the line between love and hate is razor thin. And although I don't think I'm in love with Reese, I am definitely falling for him.

God, when did things get so complicated?

I leave my phone off for the rest of the day. It burns a hole in my pocket, daring me to look and see if Reese has texted again. But seeing Darcie's smug smile everywhere I turn is enough to stop me from switching it back on.

"Liv," Oak's voice rises above the hallway chatter. "Don't you dare run," he barks as I double around and head in the opposite direction. "Olivia, I swear to God, will you just wait?"

He intercepts me, grabbing my elbow and steering me out of the stream of bodies.

"You're avoiding me."

"Actually, I'm avoiding all of you. Problem with that?"

"Come on, Liv. That isn't fair and you know it."

"Whatever, Oak." I refuse to look at him.

"Is this about Reese? About last night? Because I swear to—"

"Reese?" I spit his name. "What the hell would he have to do with anything?" My eyes narrow, and Oakley runs a hand through his hair.

"So it's not about Reese?"

This is it, my chance to tell him. To come clean and admit what's been going on. But what if I fess up and Reese denies it?

I'm not sure I'll survive that, so I swallow the confession.

"Did you hit your head in practice?"

"But I thought—"

"Whatever you thought, you're wrong, Oak. Me and Reese are... trying to get along, for Dad and Fiona's sake."

He studies me, searching my face for a sign I'm lying. But he won't find it. My poker face game is strong, and the second relief flits across his expression, I know I've won this round.

I just don't expect him to deliver his next blow.

"Thank fuck. Because he was all over Darcie last night. Practically fucked her right there in front of me and Misty."

His words are like daggers, plunging into my back. He watches me still, waiting for my reaction. But I shove it down, refusing to take the bait.

"How nice for him," I say coolly. But no more coolly than usual where Reese is concerned.

"Is that all you wanted to tell me, because I need to go."

"You'll be at the game later, right?"

"Actually, I won't. I have a thing."

"A thing?" His expression darkens. "What the fuck, Liv? I need you there. I need—"

"I'm sure you'll manage without me."

I had planned to go to the game, to cheer on the Saints, but I'm not feeling very sisterly where Oak is concerned right now.

"You're really not coming?"

"No, I have plans with Charli."

"But—"

"Yo, Beckworth," someone yells, and we both look up to find Elliot at the end of the corridor. "Team meeting, let's go."

Oakley glances back at me, regret swirling in his eyes. He knows what he's done, but it's too late.

"Come, please. I need you there, Liv. I... fuck." He walks off, punching the lockers as he goes.

The sound reverberates inside me, making me flinch, but I don't regret telling him no.

Maybe now he'll stay the hell out of my business.

Charli cancelled, so I'm stuck at home, by myself. Dad and Fiona are heading to the game straight from the office, which means the house is deathly silent as I make my way upstairs with a sandwich and glass of pop.

Even if I wanted to go to the game, I won't on principle. Oak was out of line earlier. And Reese... he can rot in hell, for all I care.

After devouring my sandwich, I grab my AirPods and stuff them in my ears, cranking up my relaxation soundtrack. It's probably a bad idea to exercise on a full stomach, but I need the distraction.

I need to get out of my head.

What did I really think would happen when I started fooling around with Reese? That he would fall for me? That he would denounce everything he's ever known... for me?

I should have known better.

I'm a game to him.

A toy.

Reese Whitfield doesn't have the capacity for emotions.

But I know that isn't true. I've seen another side to him. A side not many people get to see.

Irritated with myself and my inability to stop thinking about him, I roll out my yoga mat and stand tall, inhaling a deep, calming breath. Over and over, I inhale and exhale, letting the oxygen flow through me and open up my lungs, centring myself.

On the next inhale, I bend at the waist, sliding my hands down my legs into a half fold, holding the tips of my toes for a count of eight. Then, I return to a mountain pose, inhale again and this time push myself into a forward fold, the stretch of my spine almost too much. But I manage to hold it, breathing into the pose. Moving back into the mountain pose, I ready myself to move into the downward dog, widening my stance and bending at the hips. Right as my door flies open.

"What the— Reese." I whirl around on him. "What the hell are you doing?"

"You've been avoiding me."

"Yes, that's the whole point when you're ignoring somebody."

"I didn't like it."

"I didn't like you going on a date with Darcie, but shit happens."

"Jesus, woman. I already told—"

"And I don't care," I shriek. "Anyone. It could have been anyone but her."

His eyes drop down my body, full of lust and hunger. "Those fucking leggings," he murmurs.

"You need to leave."

"I will. After you give me what I need."

"What— oh my God, you're serious. You think that I'm going to what, get on my knees and—"

Reese pounces, grabbing me and pushing me up against the wall. "I told you what would happen, sweet cheeks."

"And I told you, go get what you need from Darcie. Oh wait... according to the rumours, you already did."

"I didn't fucking touch her."

"That's not what Oakley told me," I seethe. "He said you were all over her. That you practically fucked her in front of him."

Anger blazes in Reese's eyes. "Motherfucker," he hisses. "He knows, Liv. He knows, and he was testing you. I didn't touch her, I swear to God, I didn't—"

"Why?" My voice quivers. Reese frowns and I add, "Why didn't you touch her?"

"Because I don't like her."

I scoff at that.

"What?" he growls.

"That's a coward's answer and you know it."

"What do you want me to say?" He leans in, the air

shifting around us, crackling with tension. "That I couldn't go through with it because I want you? Because every time she rubbed herself on me, I imagined you?"

"I hate her."

"Join the fucking club." He smirks, lowering his face to mine, so close I can almost taste him.

"I told you if you went with—"

"I didn't have a choice. Oakley knows, and if it comes out..."

"What are we doing, Reese?" I ask, my voice an uncertain whisper.

"Honestly, I don't know." He toys with the ends of my hair, his gaze dropping to my mouth. "But I'm not sure I can stop."

His mouth crashes down on mine, hard and unrelenting, his strong body pinning me to the wall. My hands curl over his shoulders as I hold on while he devours me.

"Reese," I pant. "The game. You can't—"

"There's time. I have time." His hand shoves between us, cupping my pussy. "I need inside you. I need to feel you clamped down on my dick, screaming my name."

"This doesn't mean I forgive you."

His fingers flex around my throat as he stares down at me. "Don't worry, sweet cheeks. You can go back to hating me the second I'm done fucking you." He starts tearing at my clothes. My leggings and knickers go first, followed by my sports bra.

"You too," I say, grabbing at his t-shirt. "I want to feel you."

"You only have to ask once." Reese steps away, tearing off his clothes like he can't wait a second longer. He stalks toward me, wearing nothing but a devious smirk.

"Reese," I gasp as he picks me up and presses me into the wall, his thick cock sliding between my wetness.

"Remember what I said about this body?" He runs a hand down my waist, hitching my legs around his hips and slowly impaling me onto his dick. "It belongs to me now."

10

REESE

"Oh fuck. Yes," I groan as she drags me deeper into her body.

I've needed this since she left me in the cupboard at school, fucking aching for her.

"Fuck, your pussy is magic," I growl against her throat as her fingers curl around my shoulder, her nails cutting into my skin, the pain only adding to my pleasure. "A week has been too fucking long."

Threading my fingers into her hair, I drag her head back, positioning her exactly where I want her.

"Fucking addicted to this, sweet cheeks," I confess, completely consumed by her to even question the words that are rolling off my tongue.

"Reese," she cries when I piston my hips, forcing her to take every inch of me as her nails dig deeper into my skin.

"Fuck, yeah. Take it, babe. Let me feel you stretching around my cock."

"Arg—" I cut her scream off with my lips. The house might be empty, and I might want to hear her losing herself to me more than I want to pump her full of my cum right now, but it's still a risk.

As far as I know, Oak didn't see me slip out of the Chapel while he was sulking about Olivia fucking up his pregame ritual. Little fucking pussy. He might as well play poker alone and let himself win. It's basically what she does before every game.

My tongue licks deep into her mouth, mimicking the movements of my cock, and she meets each of my moves with a hunger that matches my own.

"Reese," she murmurs into our kiss, her body already beginning to tighten down on my dick.

"Fuck, yeah. I wanna feel you coming on me, Liv. Show me how good it feels."

Ripping my lips from hers, I kiss across her jaw before biting down on her throat as her orgasm begins to crest.

"Reese, Reese. Shit." Her nails claw at my back as her pussy clamps down on me so hard it takes all my self-restraint to hold my own release back.

The second she's done, I drag her from the wall and throw her down on her bed.

"Whoa, shit. What the—" She looks up right as I drop to my knees before her, spreading her thighs wide and diving for her cunt. "Oh fuck," she screams as I suck her clit and push two fingers inside her, curling them exactly as she likes.

Her back arches off the bed and her thighs clamp around the side of my head as I bring her to ruin, leaving her crying out my name for anyone who might care to listen.

"Reese, I need you. Please," she begs once she's come down from her high to find that my head is still between her thighs.

"Oh, so you're going to admit it now."

"I want your cock, not your arrogance, prick."

"I love it when you say such sweet things to me."

"You don't deserve it. Now get on with what you came here for, so I can get on with my day."

Crawling onto the edge of her bed, I loom over her, taking

in her heaving chest, aching nipples and the red flush that covers her skin.

Yeah, she's fucking breathtaking.

"You just want me for my cock, little liar?"

"It's certainly not your personality," she quips.

"Oh, I don't know. I think you like me more than you're willing to admit."

"No, I don— Argh," she screams when I flip her, dragging her onto her hands and knees and positioning her exactly where I want her. "I hate you," she hisses.

Crack.

"Argh. You're a fucking— REESE," she screams when I push back inside her, filling her in one quick thrust of my hips.

"Go on, sweet cheeks. Try to convince me how much you hate me while you're full of my dick."

Grabbing a handful of her hair, I twist it around my fist and hold her head up.

Her breath catches when she finds me in the reflection of the mirror at the end of her bed.

Oh, fuck yeah.

Her pussy gushes as she watches me own her.

"You like that?"

Her moan of agreement rips through the air as I slow my pace.

"You fucking love it, don't you? You make out that you're a good girl. You judge all the Heir chasers at school, when really, all along, this is what you wanted, isn't it?"

"No," she cries, although from how wet she is for me and the way her back arches to take me deeper with every thrust, I have a hard time believing her.

Wrapping my hand around her throat, I lift her from the bed.

She gasps as she stares at us, at my possessive hold of her, at the way we look connected like this.

"Jesus, Reese," she moans when I snake my other hand

around her body and cup her breast, pinching her nipple between my fingers.

"Admit it. Tell me how long you've been imagining this."

"Never."

"Was it always me? Or did you imagine snagging Elliot or Theo, or even both? All of us?"

"Fuck you, Whitfield."

"Oh babe, I'm pretty sure you're the one getting fucked right now."

I roll my hips to prove a point, and she mewls in pleasure as my cock hits all the right places.

Dropping my hand down her stomach, I find her swollen clit.

She gasps as I pinch her.

"You're going to come for me again, aren't you, sweet cheeks? And then you're going to let me fill you up before I go and kick arse on the pitch."

"Oh shit," she moans as I begin to pick up speed, the sound of our skin colliding filling the room along with our heaving breaths.

"And you're going to come to the game, aren't you? You're going to stand there and watch me while you can still feel me inside you."

"Reese." Her muscles clamp down once more, and I have to grit my teeth to stop myself from falling.

"Say yes, Olivia," I grit out, upping the pressure on her clit with my need for her to break first.

"Oh God. God, Reese."

"Say. It," I growl in her ear before biting down on it.

"Yes. Yes. YES," she screams as her body locks up tight as she flies off the cliff, dragging me right alongside her.

"Fuck, Liv. Fucking can't get enough of this," I groan, pumping her full as aftershocks rock her body.

I've barely come down from my high and am more than a little reluctant to release her when my phone starts ringing.

"Motherfucker."

"You'd better get that," Olivia says, pulling at my arm that's banded tight around her body.

"You don't mean that."

"You've got a game to get to."

The second my hold on her lessens, she slips away from me.

Grabbing my tracksuit trousers, I pull my phone free as she pads toward her bathroom.

A wicked smile pulls at my lips when I find Oak's name staring back at me.

"Hey, man. How's it going?" I ask innocently, switching the call to loudspeaker just to be a prick.

"Where the fuck are you?" Oak growls, making Olivia pause in the doorway, her bare arse and the sexy curve of her spine making my dick harden for round two.

"I'm coming, keep your fucking hair on."

"Elliot's losing his mind. If you don't get your arse here in the next..." I throw my phone onto Liv's bed and storm toward her, spinning her around and pushing her back against the cold tiled wall of the bathroom.

"What the hell are you doing?" she whispers so quietly I barely hear her.

"Stealing a good luck kiss. Something tells me that your brother needs all the wins he can get tonight."

My heart thunders in my chest as I think about his reaction to this. But fuck him.

I need this.

I really fucking need this.

Slamming my lips down on hers, I take the kiss I'm so desperate for, one that I hope will tide me through until after our win and I get to celebrate with round two in a few hours.

"WHITFIELD," Oak booms down the line.

"Five minutes, I'm on my way right now."

Releasing a pliant and more-than-ready Liv panting

against the wall, I cut the call, drag my clothes on and march toward the door.

Spinning back around, I find her in the doorway once again, still naked and still looking as panicked as she is turned on.

"I'll see you later, yeah? You don't need to wait up, I can wake you."

Lifting my fingers to my lips, I make a show of sucking her taste off them before I turn to leave.

The second I walk into the locker room and Oak's eyes turn on me, I know I'm in for a fucker of a night.

Suspicion oozes from his every pore as he watches me run over to my spot and begin stripping down to get ready.

"How nice of you to join us, Whitfield," Coach Walker barks, his eyes boring holes into my back.

"What the fuck are you playing at?" Elliot hisses in my ear, his anger palpable.

"Just a little pregame ritual. You know all about those, huh?"

"Not ones that make me almost miss kick-off, you fucking dick."

The atmosphere in the room grows heavy, and I'm sure it's not helped when I refuse to look at Oak.

He can see my betrayal written all over my face, I'm sure. And if he gets too fucking close, he'll smell her too, I have no doubt.

"Let's fucking go, ladies. You might have left the Bulldogs whimpering like puppies last year, but don't think that they're not going to come back fighting."

Elliot shoves me toward the door the second Coach demands we do so. And as if they've fucking planned it, he and

Theo stay between Oak and me until we have little choice but to get into position.

The heat of his stare burns into me, but I still refuse to give him my attention.

Despite what Coach said about the Bulldogs, the game is a piece of piss. They could have smashed them even if I decided not to show my face and spend the rest of my night between Olivia's thighs.

I successfully manage to stay the hell away from Oak as we celebrate out on the pitch while our home crowd goes wild.

I search the stands, desperate to see if Olivia followed orders and showed her face, but I don't spot her in the crowd.

Disappointment tugs at my insides, but I refuse to dwell on it.

"You were on fucking fire, man," Theo says, throwing his arm around my shoulders as we make our way to the locker room. "The girls are gonna be all over you for that performance."

"Here's fucking hoping."

The second we turn the corner, he's there waiting for me, his eyes narrowed on me.

The rest of the team is lingering behind us, waiting for us to shower so they can get cleaned up for the party.

"Not here, man," Elliot instructs, shoving Oak in the direction of his locker.

"You'd better have some fucking good evidence to prove his suspicions wrong about where you were and how you got those scratches up your back, or he's going to fucking kill you," Theo warns ominously in my ear.

"I'm not fucking scared of Oak."

"Clearly not, if you've been doing what we think you've been doing."

"Shut your fucking mouth, Ashworth," I bark, stripping out of my kit and marching toward the showers, all the while wondering how well my girl scratched up my back earlier.

Nothing is said as the four of us shower. Oak might be gunning for me, but he's still a good little Heir who will follow Elliot's orders to keep this private.

All that changes when we're halfway back toward the Chapel and Oak turns on me.

"Tell me I'm wrong," he booms, his palms slamming down on my chest. "Tell me I'm fucking wrong and the girl's perfume you turned up stinking of didn't belong to my fucking sister."

I swallow harshly but don't say anything.

"I swear to fucking God, Whitfield. If you don't start talking, then I'm going to assume she was the one who mauled your back and fucking end you for this."

11

OLIVIA

I chew my thumb as I wander toward the Chapel.

I'd gone to the game—I couldn't stay away if I tried. Not after what had happened with Reese. I could still feel his touch, hear his filthy, possessive words as he fucked me into oblivion. God, the way he handled me... I should have hated it, but I didn't.

Because I'm so gone for him. And maybe it makes me a fool, maybe I'm asking for heartache and disappointment, but he feels it too.

I know he does.

Coming to the Chapel is probably a really bad idea. But I need to see him, and I need to try and fix things with Oakley.

The second I turn the corner, though, their raised voices stop me in my tracks.

"Tell me I'm wrong," Oakley booms, his palms slamming down on Reese's chest. "Tell me I'm fucking wrong and the girl's perfume you turned up stinking of didn't belong to my fucking sister."

Crap. I duck behind the building, my heart racing in my chest.

"I swear to fucking God, Whitfield." Anger coats my

brother's every word. "If you don't start talking, then I'm going to assume she was the one who mauled your back and fucking end you for this."

I inhale a sharp breath, waiting for Reese's reply.

Part of me knows it'll be bad, really bad if he admits it, but part of me wants him to claim me. To say fuck you to the Heirs and tradition and responsibility... and choose me.

"Assume what you like, Beckworth. It's none of your fucking business."

"You smug fucker."

"Okay, knock it off," Elliot says, and I peek around the corner to find him standing between my brother and Reese. "This is not the time or place. We have a win to celebrate."

"Like I'm going to celebrate anything with this sneaky fucker. He's fucking Liv, I know he is."

Reese's expression gives nothing away. He isn't admitting it, but he isn't denying it either. And I don't know how to feel about that.

"So what if I am? She could do a hell of a lot worse."

The laugh that bubbles out of Oak isn't normal. Bitter and strangled, it's full of disgust and distrust.

"Got something to say, Beckworth?"

"Yeah, I've got something to say. You're not good enough for her, you fucking piece of shit."

"Oak," Theo warns.

"He left," my brother spits. "When things didn't go his way, he fucking left us. We can't trust him. He's a snake. And doesn't deserve someone like Olivia. He'll never deserve her. She's good, she's the best of us, and he's dead inside. He doesn't have a fucking heart."

Reese releases a maniacal laugh that sends a shudder through me. "You're so fucking full of yourself. Thinking the sun shines out of Olivia's arse when really, she's no better than the rest of us."

Blood roars in my ears as I stand here, frozen to the spot.

"What the hell does that mean?"

"It means, she's not the girl you think she is. Not when she gets on her knees and begs so—"

Crack.

The sound of Oak punching Reese reverberates through me, but it's his words that cut me to the bone.

"I'll kill you," my brother yells. "I'll fucking kill you for touching her."

"You'll have to catch me first," Reese taunts, inching backward while Elliot and Theo hold Oak firmly.

"Maybe you should walk away, Whitfield. Let him cool off."

"Cool off? I don't need to fucking cool off, I need him gone. You should have stayed gone. We were fine without you. Olivia was fine without you."

"You want me gone, Beckworth?" Reese's voice is icy cold.

"Damn right I do."

"Consider it done." Spinning on his heel, Reese takes off in the opposite direction of the Chapel.

"Fuck. *Fuck!*" Oak roars, kicking the ground.

"Relax," Elliot commands. "Everyone needs to take a fucking minute and cool off.

But I know he's wrong. I saw the defeat in Reese's eyes, the dejection. He believed every word Oakley spat at him.

And I need to know why.

I need to know what's going on in his head.

Thunder claps overhead as I catch up to Reese.

"Wait," I cry, right as the first fat drop of rain falls.

"Go home, Olivia."

Not Olive. Not sweet cheeks or Liv.

Olivia.

"Not until we talk."

"There's nothing to say." He reaches his car and wrenches the door open.

But I rush over to him and grab his arm. "You might not have anything to say, but I do."

His eyes narrow, rain hammering down on us, soaking us both through. "What the hell was that back there?"

"What?" he grits out.

"This... us... what does it mean to you?"

"Mean to me?"

"Stop playing dumb, Reese. You act like you hate me, like you hate yourself for wanting me... why? What did I do? Just tell me what I—"

"What you did?" He grabs my arm, pulling me close. "You know what you did. You destroyed me."

"W-what? I—"

"You want to know what this means to me?" He motions between us. "Nothing. You. Mean. Nothing."

"That's not—"

"What, the truth? It's a game, Olivia. It's always been a game."

My heart shatters. "You don't mean that. You feel it, I know you do. Reese—"

"You were a good fuck, babe. A means to an end. That's all it was."

"Liar." I shove down the emotion clogging my throat.

He's hurting.

Lashing out because of what Oakley said.

He doesn't mean it. He doesn't—

"I love you." The words spill out in a rush. I can hardly breathe through the rain, through the pain rattling inside me.

"What the fuck did you just say?" Reese sneers.

"I-I'm falling in love with you."

A dark glint lights up his eyes, his mouth twisting with smug arrogance. "God, you made it so easy."

"W-what?"

"Olivia?" someone calls across the car park.

"Abigail?" I blink away the raindrops clinging to my lashes.

Reese murmurs something under his breath before yanking out of my hold.

"N-no," I reach for him again, but he pushes me away, climbing inside his car. "Reese, don't do this, please."

The cold haunted look he gives me makes my chest crack, and I feel like I can't breathe.

"Reese, please." I slam my fists against the glass, but the car roars to life as he stares at me like he doesn't even know me.

The car lurches forward and takes off, leaving me in a puddle of tears and rain.

"Olivia?" Abigail reaches me, wrapping her arm around me. "What happened?"

"I-I don't know." I stare after Reese's car, but it's already gone, swallowed by the sheet of rain.

"Come on, let's get you somewhere warm." She leads me toward the imposing Chaucer Building.

"Isn't it locked?"

"Don't worry." She gives me a small smile. "I have a key."

She does?

Abigail lets go of me to dig a small key out of her pocket. She slips it into the lock and the door clicks open.

The strip lights flicker to life as we enter the long corridor. The overpowering smell of chlorine fills my lungs.

"I haven't been out here for years." When we had mandatory swimming lessons in year seven.

"My dad and Mr. Porter have an arrangement. In return, I'm allowed after-hours access to the pool."

"Huh."

Little Abigail Bancroft sure is full of surprises.

"I take it you swim."

She nods, her eyes darting away from me. "But I... I can't swim in front of people."

"Because of your scars?"

Another nod.

"You shouldn't be ashamed of them."

"Easy for you to say," she murmurs, leading to the end of the corridor and into a room I've never been in before.

"What is this place?"

"You'll see." She hits an illuminated switch on the wall, and the pool lights up beyond the glass windows lining one side of the office.

"Pretty."

"It's one of my favourite places. Here." She hands me a towel and a fluffy robe. "I'll give you a moment to get changed and go and find us some hot chocolate."

Abigail heads for a second door, but I call after her. "Wait."

"Yeah?" She glances back.

"Thanks."

With another small smile, she slips out of the room and leaves me alone.

"This is good," I say, sipping the rich hot chocolate. She even found some marshmallows to melt into it.

"I keep a little stash of supplies in the kitchen."

"Just how often do you come here?"

"Whenever I need to escape."

"Did you watch the game?" Guilt flashes in her eyes, and my lips curve. "You did, didn't you?"

"I... maybe, just a little."

"Next time, you can sit with me."

"Why?"

"Because we're friends, aren't we?"

"I don't know. I've never really had a friend before."

That makes my brows knit. But before I can ask her why not, she adds, "So you and Reese, huh?"

"I'm sorry you had to see that."

"I'm not. I don't like Reese, Olivia. It would make my life a whole lot easier if he could find someone else. Then maybe our parents would drop this stupid arranged marriage thing."

"I'm not sure I'm the girl to help with that."

The things Reese said. Cruel, hateful words.

"He cares about you."

"I'm pretty sure his words and actions earlier would suggest he doesn't."

"Love and hate are two sides of the same coin, you know. It's easy to get the two confused."

"I think I'm falling in love with him," I admit. "I don't know how it happened, but it's like he's crawled under my skin and I can't get rid of him."

"If anyone can tame him, it's you."

"Everything is a mess. I shouldn't have let things get this far."

"So why did you?" she asks, but I find no judgement in her eyes.

"Because... for once in my life, I wanted to do something for me. Not my brother or the Heirs or my father. Just me."

"It's not easy, being a girl living in this man's world."

"No, it isn't."

"What will you do about Reese?"

"I don't know."

"What do you want to do?"

I want to go after him, to make him admit what I know in my heart to be true. But he's still hiding things from me. And until I know what, I don't see how we can move forward.

"You should go after him."

"W-what?"

"If you care about him, you should go after him."

"You're right," I say, a sense of resolve washing over me. He doesn't get to run from this—to run from me.

Not after I admitted how I feel about him.

Grabbing my phone off the arm of the sofa, I pull up our text chat.

> Olivia: We need to talk.

A minute passes and he doesn't reply.

> Olivia: Reese, please…

Nothing.

A sinking feeling spreads through me, but I refuse to be deterred. Hitting call, I wait for it to connect, but it sends me straight to voicemail.

"Damn you, Reese," I murmur.

"Maybe he needs to cool off."

"Yeah, maybe."

But as I say the words, the knot in my stomach tightens.

And I can't shake the feeling that something bad is about to happen.

12

REESE

The rain pounds down on the windscreen as I press my foot harder on the accelerator, my need to get away from this town too much to deny.

A bolt of lightning illuminates the sky a second before a crack of thunder makes my car shudder.

Oak's words reverberate through me, sinking their claws into the insecurities I try my best to hide from the world.

But that's the thing about someone who's known you their whole life, who knows you better than you know yourself. They know exactly where to strike when they really want to hurt you the most.

I can't even claim that the words he spat at me were lies.

They weren't.

I'm not good enough.

Not even for a liar like Olivia Beckworth.

I'm nothing.

No one.

And this town would be better off without me. Just like Oak pointed out.

I think of her, of the words she said to me before we were interrupted. They were everything I wanted to hear. My entire fucking purpose for coming back here. I wanted her to fall, and I wanted to watch her fucking pay for the lies she'd been covering up. For the pain she caused, for the destruction.

I should be fucking delighted that all my hard work has paid off. That despite being a royal fucking cunt to her, she's still blinded enough by my cock and the few orgasms I've gifted her to fall for it.

She claims not to be anything like the rest of the girls at All Hallows'. But one taste of an Heir's cock and she's fallen into the same bullshit trap as them.

Dick blind.

I can't help but smirk as I think about it being my dick she's drunk on.

Reaching down, I tug at my trousers as the memory of being buried deep inside her only minutes before the game earlier comes back to me.

Fuck. She might have been nothing more than a game to me. But she was fun.

More fun than she probably should have been.

With her cunt squeezing me so tight I practically saw fucking stars, it was easy to forget all the reasons I hated her.

The ping of my phone startles me a beat before a message pops up on my screen.

> Dad: Great game tonight, Son. Proud of you.

I scoff at that. His messages have been coming more frequently this week.

Apparently, I should have forgotten by now that he was the one who sent me away like a stray dog that he no longer wanted sniffing around his new life.

Betrayal rips through me once again. He promised me time and time again that the second he found a way to get out, he'd take me with him. That we'd start over together. That he'd sever the ties I had to this place, to Abigail, to Mum.

But he did none of that. Just when I thought we were embarking on what was going to be a new chapter of our lives, he ripped the rug from beneath me and sent me back here like he never made any of those promises.

Like he didn't even fucking care.

Anger surges through me once more when another message comes through.

I expect to find his name there again, begging me to talk to him, to visit. But to my surprise, when my eyes drop, I find Olivia wanting to extend her torture for some fucking bizarre reason.

> Olivia: We need to talk.

"What the actual fuck is wrong with you?" I scoff, taking a turning too fast and almost putting my car into the ditch.

Ignoring her, I turn my music up in the hope it'll help ease some of the tension in my shoulders and the ache of my jaw from Oak's less-than-gentle punch.

He wanted more. I could see his need for blood shining bright in his eyes. I bet he's fucking gutted the others held him back, stopping him from taking what he really wanted.

> Olivia: Reese, please...

"I know I'm good, but fuck," I murmur to myself. "You're giving Darcie a run for her money here, Liv."

I shake my head, both loving and hating that she's playing right into my hands.

I thought she might pose at least a bit of a challenge. I guess I should have seen it coming after I got between her legs so easily on initiation night.

My grip on the wheel tightens as I remember pushing into her that night. Fuck. Her pussy blew my fucking mind. It damn near killed me to pull out and not take what I'd been craving. But pulling away, snapping those photos, they'd been exactly what I needed at the time.

I thought I was about to walk away, to never see her again.

Maybe I'd have done it a little differently if I knew what the next few months were going to hold.

Or maybe I wouldn't...

I can't help but laugh when my phone starts ringing this time. I throw my head back and really bark out my amusement at how pathetic she's being.

Surely, playing little miss clueless is going to get boring for her soon. She can't keep pulling the 'I'm innocent and have no idea why you hate me' card.

"Get the fucking clue, Liv. I don't want you."

But as those words echo around inside my car, I know they're lies.

Because I do want her.

I want her again, and again, and again.

"FUCK," I bark, slamming my hand down on the wheel as my frustration gets the better of me.

The sign thanking people for visiting Saints Cross comes and goes, and I'm soon on a road in the middle of nowhere with no other cars to be seen.

> Dad: I know you're going to be celebrating tonight, but maybe call me tomorrow?

I suck in a deep breath as I think of all the things he said to me when he sent me back here.

"Yeah, yeah. How about we have this out a little sooner than that?"

I press my foot down, speeding faster along the desolate road.

I barely remember the way to the place Dad now calls home. I was here over two months, but I didn't venture out all that often unless it was to head down to the beach.

The solitude was needed, although I can't deny that it made me miss my boys more than I should have done, seeing as I walked away without so much as a second glance.

Dad's SUV is parked up out the front of the modest beach house he found for himself, but the space beside it is empty.

I pull up, killing the engine the second I've stopped, plunging myself into silence.

I half expected Dad to spill out the second I pulled up, but despite the lights being on inside, there seems to be no sign of life as I stay sitting there.

My phone rings again, Olivia's name lighting up the screen, and the sight of it is the final push I need to get out of the car.

Pulling my keys from my pocket, I make my way toward the front door. I don't bother knocking—I figure that he's been begging me to talk to him for over a week, so there's no way he won't welcome this visit.

My lips part to call out for him once I'm in the hallway, but my voice is cut off when a loud cry rips through the air.

"Oh fuck, Richard. Yeah, just like that, Daddy."

Disbelief, shock, and maybe a little bit of pride wash through me.

I know I should back away, but a sick and twisted part of me forces me to walk toward the woman's continued cries, although I come up short of the door when my dad joins in.

"Krystal, fuck, baby. I love you. I love you so fucking much."

Krystal?

Krystal?

Slamming my hand down on the ajar door, it swings back against the wall with a loud crash, startling the loved-up couple beyond.

Rounding the corner, my eyes fall on exactly what I was expecting, what I feared. Dad's sitting on the sofa with my mother's best friend astride his lap, her traitorous cunt full of his dick.

"Reese, fuck," Dad barks, instantly flipping them in an attempt to protect Krystal's fucking virtue.

Bit late for that, if you ask me.

"You're fucking her? Krystal?" I balk, disgust rolling through me as Dad reaches for his shirt and throws it at her in a rush. "Don't worry, old man," I spit when he fumbles. "I have no interest in her fucking tits."

After tugging his boxers on, he turns to me, his face tomato red. Although I'm not sure if it's with embarrassment or anger.

"What the hell are you doing here?" Dad booms, getting up in my space while his slut scrambles to her feet.

"Me? I fucking came to see you like you've been begging me," I bark back. "How long?" I ask, throwing my arm out toward Krystal.

"Reese," he soothes, instantly calming down, but it does little to abate my anger.

"How fucking long?"

He pales, giving me all the answer I need.

"I fucking stood up for you. I stood by you when Mum was the one doing the dirty, and you lied to my fucking face. How long have you been fucking *Aunt* Krystal, Dad?"

He rubs a hand down his face, guilt etched into his expression. "There's no easy answer to that, Son."

"Yeah, there really fucking is. A month. Two. A year. Five?" I rattle off. "How fucking long?"

His lips part, but he seems to forget any words exist.

Luckily for him though, Krystal, a woman I have known since I was just a kid, the woman who is my mother's best and closest friend, speaks for him. "Twenty years," she whispers.

Silence falls after that confession, but her words continue to ring out in my ears.

"T-twenty fucking years?" I repeat, my voice eerily calm despite the red-hot fury flooding my veins.

But that means...

No.

No fucking way.

"It's complicated, Reese. It's—"

"You motherfucker," I roar, flying toward my dad, but he's ready for me and blocks my first few blows.

A red haze descends on me, one that rivals the moment I discovered this exact same thing with my mother and Christian. And all because of *her*.

Olivia.

But this isn't her fault. She didn't know I was heading here tonight. She didn't set this up. She wasn't the orchestrator in shattering even more lies and bullshit than my life is apparently drowning in.

After a couple of minutes with Krystal screaming behind me, I manage to overpower my dad and land a few solid punches to his jaw and gut.

But it doesn't make me feel better.

The betrayal from both of my parents, from people I've trusted all my goddamn life, cuts me so fucking deep I can't see anything else.

"Reese, please, stop. It's complicated, but I've always loved your father. And he's always loved me. We tried to do the right thing," she pleads, pulling at my jacket in her attempt to protect my lying cunt of a father.

"All my life. All my fucking life you've all been lying to me," I yell, my entire body shaking with anger.

"It's not like that, Son."

"Don't fucking *son* me. I'm nothing to you but an inconvenience. No wonder you wanted me gone. Go on, admit it, you wanted me gone so you could play happy fucking families with her." My voice doesn't even sound like my own as I scream at him. I sound manic, unhinged. But everything

I've been bottling up for weeks, months, is finally coming to a head, and it's being aimed right at the man who promised me the world and then sent me straight back to hell to accept my fate.

"Did you ever love her? The woman who carried your kid for nine months? The woman who gave up her fucking life for you? Does she know you've been in love with her best friend all this time?"

Dad stares at me, blood trickling down his chin as he remains mute.

But I have no intention of hanging around for those answers. I can't cope with hearing any more.

"Fuck this. Fuck all of this and your bullshit lies. I'm done. So fucking done. With all of you."

I fly out of the house, my legs moving faster than my brain can register. Before I know it, I'm at the local corner shop and I've got two bottles of vodka in a bag, the promise of oblivion closer than ever.

I stumble down onto the beach and find myself a secluded spot in the dune, hiding away from the rest of the world. I twist the lid on the first bottle and chug it until my throat can't take the burn any longer.

The nothingness doesn't come fast enough, but when it does, there's only one thing I can think about. One person. And before I know what I'm doing, my phone is pressed to my ear, its ringing cutting through the haze as I lie back on the sand, my need to hear her voice more desperate than I could ever begin to explain.

13

OLIVIA

It's late when I get back to the house. Abigail was good enough to dry my clothes for me before I drove her home.

She's not what I expected. But then, I guess I've never given her the time of day before. She's smart and empathetic, and there's a strength inside her that people don't see.

I like her, and I meant it when I said we were friends. Or at least, I'd like to be friends with her.

Abigail isn't driven by power or status or popularity. She's just a girl trying to survive each day and find her place in the world. Something I can relate to.

"Olivia." Fiona rushes out of the house the second I climb out of my car. "Thank God."

"What happened?"

"It's Reese, sweetheart. He took off and... his father called. Reese went to Lymington to see him but— oh dear." Her lip quivers as she holds back the tears clinging to her lashes.

"What happened, Fiona?"

Lymington is almost a ninety-minute drive. So whatever has happened, it must have only just happened.

"We should have told him. I knew we should have told

him, but it's complicated and he's so angry... I didn't want him to find out like this. Have you talked to him?"

"No." *He won't respond to my texts or calls.* I swallow the words.

"Can you try to call him? I'm worried he's going to do something stupid. He and Richard got into it, and Reese took off."

"I don't understand. What exactly happened?"

"Oh, sweetheart. It's a long and complicated story. But let's just say Reese found out that our marriage wasn't the happy family he always thought."

"I—"

My phone blares and I quickly dig it out of my pocket, hoping to see Reese's name.

"Is it—"

"It's Oak." Disappointment floods me. I hit decline, not ready to deal with my brother.

"I'm worried," Fiona says. "It's late, and the storm... If he's driving in this or—"

"Shh." I pull her into my arms. "I'm sure he'll be okay. He probably just needs some time."

"I never wanted to hurt him," she murmurs through her tears.

"Come on, why don't I make you a cup of tea? I'm sure he'll call or text eventually."

"Thank you, Liv. You're a good girl." She hugs me before walking off down the hall.

I check my phone, unsurprised to find no reply from Reese.

> Olivia: Please let us know you're okay. Your mum is worried. I'm worried. Even if you need space, just... reply, Reese. Please.

I follow Fiona into the kitchen, hoping he might.
But it never comes.

Something rouses me from a fitful sleep.

Not something.

The blare of my mobile phone.

"Hello?" I mumble, barely awake.

"Little liar. Such a pretty little liar. You ruined everything, Olivia." Reese slurs down the line and I sit upright, rubbing the sleep from my eyes.

"Reese? Where are you? What time is it?"

"I hate you," he goes on. "I fucking hate how much I want you. You're like poison, sweet cheeks. You're in my blood, in my fucking blood, and now I can't get you out. I can't…"

"Reese." I slip out of bed. "Just tell me where you are, and I'll come and get you."

"No, you won't. I'm not good enough, remember. Not good enough for you or the Heirs or my parents. Everyone lies to me. Lies. Lies. Lies."

"Reese, give me something. Anything…" Panic rises up inside me. It's late, the middle of the night, and he's drunk. More than that, he's hurting. And I want to be mad at him—I am mad at him—but I'm also worried.

"I'm here, Reese. Just let me help you," I plead, pulling on a hoodie over my shorts and vest top.

A crack of lightning lights up my bedroom, and I hear Reese mutter something under his breath.

"Reese…"

"I should probably go. I'm all out of vodka… and you know what they say. No vodka makes Reesey a dull boy."

"For God's sake, Reese. You need to sober up and tell me where the fuck you are."

"Or what, sweet cheeks? What are you going to do about it? Because we both know you're not going to drive ninety minutes to Ly— oops."

Gotcha.

Relief pours into me. He's still in Lymington. I just needed to pinpoint where. And there's only one person who can help me.

"Stay where you are," I snap down the line at him.

"Ooh, giving me orders, Beckworth." He chuckles darkly, but it's tinged with sadness. "Not sure I could move right now, anyway. My legs appear to not be working."

Jesus, give me strength.

"I'll be there as quickly as I can."

"Yeah, yeah. Such pretty lies from your pretty, pouty mouth."

I roll my eyes, slipping out of my bedroom and creeping down the hall to Dad and Fiona's room.

Gently opening the door, I peek my head inside. "Fiona," I whisper. "Fiona."

"Olivia?" Her voice is thick with sleep. "What is it? What's wrong?"

"I need to talk to you."

Dad murmurs something, but Fiona soothes him back to sleep. She grabs her silk dressing gown and joins me in the hall.

"What is it?"

"Reese, he called me."

Confusion bleeds into her weary expression. "He did?"

"Yes, he's drunk. I think he's still in Lymington, but I don't know where. Is there anywhere you can think he would go?"

"I... you can't be thinking of going after him? I should—"

"I'm going."

"But..." Her brows knit tighter. "Olivia. Is there something you're not telling me?"

"It's not important. But I really need to find Reese, Fiona."

"The beach. He always loved the beach."

"The beach, okay." I nod. "I'll call you when I find him."

"Let me wake your father. We'll all go. It's—"

"I don't think that's a good idea. He's angry and upset and..." I need to do this alone. I need to prove him wrong.

"Are you sure?" Uncertainty flickers in her gaze.

"I'll be fine."

"Okay." I go to leave, but she grabs my arm. "Olivia?"

"Yeah?"

"I don't know what's going on between you and Reese but it doesn't change anything, sweetheart. One day, he'll marry Abigail."

Her words hit me like a wrecking ball.

"Even if it's not what either of them wants?"

Sadness washes over her. "Even then. I didn't see it before. But you care about him, don't you?"

I school my expression, and she gives me a sympathetic smile. "One day, he's going to be your brother. Your family. You have to know it can't ever work out."

"I don't know what you want me to say."

"Save yourself the heartache, sweetheart. Reese is... he's not the right person for you."

I pull my hand away and take a step back. "I should go."

Fiona gives me a small nod. "Call me as soon as you're there."

"I will."

I walk away from her and don't look back.

All while pretending she didn't just drive a knife right into my heart.

It takes me less than ninety minutes to get to Lymington. The whole town is asleep, the roads quiet, and the houses steeped in darkness.

I follow the signs for the seafront and park in the small car park. After sending Fiona a quick text to say I'm here, I turn the flash on and take off down to the beach. The rain has cleared a little but the storm lingers, thunder rumbling in the distance.

There's no sign of Reese or his car, so I dig out my phone and call him.

It rings out.

"Answer, damn it. Answer."

But the wind is too noisy, whipping around me like an angry howl. Pulling my hoodie up, I trudge toward the row of little beach huts. They're all closed except for the last one. The door rattles against the frame and I yank it open, shining the torchlight inside.

"Thank God," I breathe, relief flooding me at the sight of Reese curled up on his side, a bottle of vodka next to him.

"Reese?" I whisper, nudging his foot with mine. "Reese."

He murmurs something nonsensical but doesn't wake. I quickly text Fiona and let her know I've found him. She texts me straight back.

> Fiona: Is he okay?

> Olivia: He's sleeping off a bottle of vodka. I'll stay with him.

> Fiona: Are you sure? Maybe we should come get you?

> Olivia: Do you really think that's a good idea?

> Fiona: No, but I don't like the idea of you there all alone with him.

> Olivia: We're safe and dry. I'll tell him to call you in the morning.

> Fiona: Okay and thank you.

Her gratitude feels empty when she pretty much told me that Reese isn't right for me.

"Okay," I murmur, glancing around the beach hut.

It's small, barely deep enough for Reese to lie down. Somehow, he's managed to do it. I can probably lie next to him, but it'll be snug, and if the small trinkets and ornaments lining the shelves are any indication, we're trespassing. But he's out cold, and I'm not sure I want to try and fight with him to go somewhere else.

So I do the only thing I can think of. I grab a towel off the rack, roll it up, and place it on the floor next to him. Then, I lie down and slip my arm around his waist.

He looks so peaceful like this, I can't resist reaching out and tracing his slightly furrowed brows with my fingers.

He inhales a deep breath as if my touch soothes him. I like to think it does. But he's drunk and passed out. He has no idea I'm here.

"Oh, Reese," I whisper, snuggling closer as the storm rages on outside, the wind howling through the hut.

He shifts beside me, murmuring something again. Then, his arm slides round me and he buries his face in my neck, sending a bolt of heat through me.

"Mmm, Liv." His words rumble through me.

"I'm here, Reese. I'm right here."

I close my eyes, holding onto the broken boy who has stolen my heart.

But when I wake up sometime later to a crack of thunder, Reese isn't asleep.

He's awake.

Staring right at me.

And he doesn't look happy to see me.

My heart tumbles.

"R-Reese," I say. "You're—"

"I'm going to ask this once and only once, Olivia. What the fuck are you doing here?"

14

REESE

My heart thunders in my chest and white noise races past my ears as my head spins with confusion. My mouth is dry, my tongue thick from way too much vodka last night.

But what the hell else was I meant to do after finding out that everything I thought I knew about my life, my family, is nothing but lies. All my life, Mum and Dad made out that they were happy, that they were in love. But the reality of that seems to be very, very different.

Why lie? Why try and cover it all up? Did they want to fuck me up beyond repair, to shatter my trust in the two people I should be able to rely on?

The question I growled at Olivia hangs in the air between us. I know what I want her to say, but at the same time, I also want to believe that this isn't real. That she's a figment of my imagination. Because why would she come here? We're ninety minutes away from Saints Cross. Why would she have driven here in the middle of the night in a howling storm?

I squeeze my eyes closed for a beat, hoping like fuck that when I open them again, the world starts making more sense.

But when that time comes, I still find her lying right in

front of me, chewing on her bottom lip as if she's trying to come up with yet another lie.

"Olivia," I growl, having less than zero patience with bullshit right now.

"I came for you," she blurts, reaching forward and resting her hand on my chest.

I swat it away the second she makes contact with me.

"Well, you shouldn't have bothered. Did you want to come and gloat that karma had kicked me in the arse?"

"What? No. I was worried, and then I got home and your mum said—"

"She said what?" I spit, pushing to sit up, although I regret it instantly when the world spins around me.

Fuck. How much did I fucking drink last night?

One glance at the empty bottle of vodka in the corner of the small beach hut gives me a serious clue.

"Your dad called her. She said something had happened and that she was worried. So I—"

"Came to rub salt into the wound. You should go home, Olivia. I'm not good enough for your concern, remember?"

"Fuck that, Reese." She pushes to stand, putting me at a serious height disadvantage as she places her hands on her hips and glares down at me. "I was worried, and scared that you were going to do something stupid. And I..."

"And you..." I prompt, needing her to continue. Needing some honesty, if that is what's falling from her lips right now.

She sighs, her eyes dropping from mine for a beat as her anger at my reaction ebbs away. "I didn't want you to be alone. What Oak said... it wasn't true. You're not—"

"Don't," I spit. "Don't fucking stand there and lie to my face. Everything Oak said was true and you know it."

Ripping my eyes from her, I storm toward the door, which doesn't take all that much effort seeing as this beach hut isn't much bigger than my sock drawer.

"No, Reese. Wait." Her fingers wrap around my upper

arm, but her weak grip is nothing, and I rip myself free with ease.

Spinning on her, I force her back against the wall, pinning her arms beside her as I glare down at her.

My breath is rank, but she doesn't so much as flinch, staring up at me with as much fire in her eyes as I feel burning through my veins.

"I don't need you, Olivia. I don't need your pity or your—"

"This isn't pity, Reese. It's concern, because I... because I care. There, you happy? I care, okay? I care about what Oak said to you, I care about what happened with your dad, about why you left this summer, about why you think it was my fault. I fucking care, and I shouldn't, I know that. You've been nothing but a fucking dick to me for years. Even when we were friends, there was something different between us, like you only put up with me because Oak wouldn't have it any other way."

"Yeah, because that was how it was."

I shake my head. "I don't believe you."

"So? Do you really think I care about your opinion about me?"

"Yes. I do."

My chest heaves and my nostrils flare as I try to keep it together. Try not to wrap my hand around her throat. I've no idea if I'd squeeze the life out of her or kiss her until we both drown in each other. I'm too confused over her coming after me when everyone else is happy enough to wash their hands of me.

"I... I can't fucking do this."

I release her in a rush and storm to the door once more, swinging it open and wincing against the morning sun.

The storm might be long gone, but evidence of it covers every inch of the beach beyond.

"Reese, please don't do this," she begs.

But it's too late. I'm gone.

I can't fucking do this.

The thought that she's telling me the truth, that she does actually care, is too fucking much.

"Reese," she cries, her voice cracking as my legs take me away from her.

The lingering wind from the night before blows my hair as the sun warms my skin.

Pulling my phone from my pocket, I check that I turned it off before continuing forward and once again leaving her behind.

"Reese, please. Come back." Her voice barely carries to me, and I'm not sure if I'm impressed or disappointed that she's not chasing after me.

It's not until I've hit the car park and am heading toward one of the seafront cafés that I realise I probably fucked up.

I look back over my shoulder, half expecting to see her watching me, and my heart sinks when I don't.

"Fuck," I mutter, my fists curling at my sides as confusion wars within me.

Did she really come all this way so that I wasn't alone after what I discovered last night?

Everything I've planned since driving back into Saints Cross after my summer here begins to crumble at my feet with all the lies and bullshit from my parents.

The blare of a horn scares the living shit out of me. I spin around in a rush, finding an old woman staring at me from behind the wheel of her car.

Jesus, is there anyone on this planet who doesn't want me out of the way?

The girl you just left behind.

Squashing that thought almost as quickly as it appeared, I move my arse out of the way and step up to the takeout window. The middle-aged woman behind the counter smiles at me sympathetically, clueing me in to how shit I look.

Reaching up, I comb my fingers through my hair to smooth it down before ordering coffee and breakfast.

"Double shot?" she asks with an amused smirk.

"Sure. That sounds like a good idea. And two bottles of water."

"You got it. And in case you wanted any advice, you'll never find the answer you're looking for at the bottom of a bottle. I'll give you that one for free." She winks before turning toward the coffee machine and kicking it into action.

"Thanks, I'll try to remember that next time." It's a big fat lie and we both know it, but thankfully, she leaves it at that.

Movement beside me catches my eye and my heart jumps into my throat and hope fills my veins. But when I look over, all the air rushes from my lungs when I find the old woman who was trying to park.

She also gives me a sympathetic smile but thankfully doesn't offer me any nuggets of advice from her years of life experience.

"Thank you," I mutter, snatching up my order the second I've paid for it and taking off.

My heart is in my throat as I climb over the short wall that leads me back to the beach. This could be a mistake. A massive fucking mistake.

But the second the order rolled off my tongue, I'd sealed my fate without even realising it.

But if Liv is gone—if she's turned her back on me, got in the car and headed back to Saints Cross—then it's going to wreck me.

My hand trembles as I hold the tray of coffees, the beach hut I spent the night in getting bigger before me. But there's no clue as to whether she's still inside or she's done the sensible thing and run.

She should.

After everything... The way I've treated her. The things I've said... She should run and never look back.

But what if... what if I'm wrong about everything?

Last night, although painful, taught me a lot of things. Mostly that everything I've ever believed in my life has been a lie.

So what if everything I've allowed to fester inside me, to poison me for months is also wrong?

What if she really is here because she wants to be?

That thought blows my fucking mind.

But it's possible. Right?

The wind has blown the door closed, so as I get closer, I have no way of telling if she's decided to wait me out.

My heart races at a million miles a second as I juggle everything in my hands and reach for the door.

I close my eyes as I pull it open, praying it's not going to be empty inside, and all the air rushes out of my lungs when I open them again and discover my answer.

"You didn't leave," I breathe.

"Yeah. Apparently, I'm a fucking idiot," she mutters before her eyes drop from mine. "Is one of those for me?"

Stepping back into the small space, I hold the tray of coffees out toward her. "I got double shots."

"Good call," she mutters.

She plucks the cup from the tray before her eyes find me again, studying me.

I lower my arse to the towel I slept on last night and throw the bag of pastries between us as something of a peace offering.

"I'm waiting," Olivia mutters.

"Waiting for what?" I ask innocently, although I know exactly what she means.

I take a sip of my coffee, my need for caffeine getting the better of me despite knowing it's going to be too hot.

"Ow, fuck. Shit," I hiss when the boiling liquid burns my tongue.

Olivia watches me with her brow quirked and a smirk on her lips. "Some might say that's karma."

"I don't care about what anyone thinks but you," I confess.

"Oh, so you actually want to hear me out now?"

"Uh... well," I rub the back of my neck awkwardly. I don't do this. I don't have heart-to-hearts with anyone. Especially not girls. And especially not my best friend's sister.

Fucking hell, Oakley is going to fucking castrate me when he finally gets his hands on me again.

"Yeah, I guess I do."

Her expression hardens, and a frown crinkles my brow.

"Well, that's tough, because I'm not the one who needs to do the talking. You're the one with the explaining to do, Whitfield."

"Oh, you're surnaming me now, huh?" I mutter, desperately needing to lighten the mood.

"Don't try to be cute. You—"

"You think I'm cute?" I ask, unable to fight my smile.

"No, I don't. Not in the slightest. Now start talking."

My mouth opens and closes a few times, but no words come.

"Start with what happened before the summer. Why did you suddenly turn on me, Reese?" Pain and confusion war in her eyes, and it makes the anger I felt back then—hell, the anger I felt last night when déjà vu smacked me upside the head—surge through me.

My blood runs red hot through my veins and I squeeze my eyes closed at the image that's been imprinted in my brain since the night I discovered the truth.

Since the night she sent me into it and began the process of my entire life crumbling before my eyes.

"Take your time. We've got all weekend."

My brows shoot up. "You want to spend the weekend with me?" I ask, shocked to my core.

She shrugs. "I guess that all depends on how the next hour goes, huh?"

My fists clench and unclench in my lap as I stare at her in disbelief.

"What do you think I did, Reese?" she urges when I don't offer anything up.

"You knew. You knew about them, and you never told me," I blurt, my voice rough with emotion and betrayal.

"W-what?" she stutters, her brows pinching tight.

"You knew about my mum and your dad, and instead of having the fucking balls to tell us, to tell me to my face, you used it against me. You made sure I found out in the worst possible way."

I stare down at my hands as bitterness floods my body. Forcing myself to stay seated instead of getting up and storming away is physically painful. But I do it. It's time we finally had this out.

It's been festering inside me for too long, rotting every single piece of good, of light I once possessed, turning me into a dark, revenge-fuelled monster.

I hate the person I've become, but I haven't been able to stop it.

The lies.

All the lies have built up, and if I don't start talking, if I don't let some of it out, I'm pretty sure I'm going to explode as nothing more than a fireball of hate and anger.

When she doesn't respond, I have no choice but to look up. My breath catches at the sight of her pale face, and some of the fire inside me dies.

"That's what's been eating you up inside? Reese... I didn't know," she whispers, pain woven into every word. "It was after you'd gone that they sat Oak and me down and told us that they'd been seeing each other. Your dad, you, had left by then. She told us that their marriage had been over for a long time and that they were finally happy."

"No, that's bullshit," I spit, even though deep down, I know she's telling the truth. But letting go of this quest for vengeance is a terrifying thing. I need something to hold on to, to focus my anger at. And if it's not her and what I truly believed she did, then what will happen?

"It's not, Reese." She sits forward and reaches for my hands.

I flinch away, but she refuses to accept that and moves closer, her hands cupping mine, her warmth seeping into me.

"Tell me. Tell me what you thought I did."

I shake my head, the memories of that night playing out in my mind as clear as if it only happened yesterday. "Like you don't know exactly what you did. You act so innocent but you wanted to hurt me. You wanted to—"

"Reese, you're not making any sense." Her brows furrow.

"You remember that night you were at Elliot's, working on that group project Miss Allenby gave us?" I ask, staring into her eyes, hoping that I'll find the truth within them.

"Uh... y-yeah. I went with Oak and Elliot and you got kept behind for being an arse in Mr. Marsh's class," Liv murmurs.

I nod. "After Mr. Marsh had finally stopped ripping me a new one for my attitude, the school was deserted, only my car was left in the car park. I dropped into the driver's seat when my phone rang."

"I called you to stop by our house to get the textbook I forgot. I'd left it in the summer room where I was writing notes for us the night before," Liv remembers.

"I didn't think anything of it other than it being weird talking to you on the phone. You never called me, you never asked me for anything."

"Because you were always such a dick. But Oak's phone died, so I—"

"I thought it was a set-up." Shame burns through me as realisation begins to sink in. "I thought you'd planned it to hurt me. To finally get back at me for all the bullshit jealousy I'd harboured toward you over the years."

"No, we just needed the book. I'd asked Oak to go for it but he was being a lazy sod and we knew you were going to be driving by. What the hell did—" She gasps as reality hits her. "You walked in on them?"

"Yeah, sweet cheeks. I did."

"And you thought that I... that I sent you to find them."

I shrug.

Fuck. It sounds so ridiculous now.

My entire body trembles as I picture them up against the hallway wall as if they couldn't even wait long enough to get upstairs.

They were so wrapped up in each other they didn't even hear me shut the front door, or sense that I stood there for long enough for the ground to rock beneath my feet.

She gawks at me, a mix of sadness and disbelief glittering in her eyes. But then something flashes there. "You came back with the book and asked me if I'd spoken to my dad, and I said he was at the house having a meeting with your mum."

Tugging my hands from hers, I scrub them down my face. "I waited for you to fess up. To tell everyone what you knew. But when you didn't, I got things twisted up inside..."

"I didn't have a truth to tell. I didn't know."

"Fuck, Olivia." I push to my feet and begin pacing, but the confines of this stupid beach hut don't give me what I need. "I can't do this. I can't fucking do this."

I blow out of the door and storm down the beach, my name nothing but a desperate plea on Olivia's lips.

But I don't stop as my feet begin sinking into the soft sand.

Unlike when I first emerged, there are now others on the beach, people running and walking their dogs. But I ignore every single one of them as I make a beeline for the shore.

"FUCK," I bellow when I come to a stop. Pain, anger, and

confusion collide within me like a firestorm that wants to drag me into its ugly clutches.

My fingers thread through my hair, and I pull until I can't take it anymore. Bending over, I rest my hands on my knees, regrets threatening to take me to the ground.

"Reese, please don't run from me. From this."

My entire body jolts at the proximity of her voice. "Don't, Liv. I don't deserve for you to still be here."

"I'd never lie to you and Oak about something like that. If I knew, if I had any fucking suspicion, I'd have told you. Both of you."

"Dad's fucking Krystal," I blurt, too many thoughts rolling around my head. "Mum's best friend. The woman I grew up calling my aunt, for fuck's sake. It's messed up. Everything is so messed up, Liv."

Her sharp breath is the only clue that I actually spoke those words out loud.

"All my life, they played the part of being the perfect family, having the perfect marriage. It was all bullshit. All lies. My entire life has been one big fucking lie, Liv. And I don't... I just... FUCK," I roar.

"It's okay, Reese," she soothes, her hand resting on my upper arm as she steps up beside me.

"No, it's not, Liv. None of it is fucking okay. I trusted them. I believed they loved each other, that they were happy. But all this time they've been fucking everyone else, making a total fucking fool of me."

"You're not a fool, Reese. You're angry. You feel betrayed, and I understand that."

"Do you? Both you and Oak seem to be perfectly okay with this new set-up. You've welcomed Mum into your home like she's the missing part of your puzzle, leaving me on the outskirts of your new family."

"In a way, she is, Reese. Our family, our dad, has been broken for a long time. He has done everything he could for us, but since our mum died, he's never truly been happy. I don't think I realised how bad it was until I saw the way his entire face lit up the night he told Oak and me about your mum.

"They're happy, Reese. So fucking happy. And that's all I've ever wanted for my dad."

"Jesus," I mutter, hanging my head. "Your family has been made whole, and mine has been shattered into a million pieces."

"It's your family too. You don't have to be the enemy here, Reese. There is space for you in our home, in our lives."

"As your stepbrother?" I ask, my voice deepening at the possibility of that being the only connection Olivia and I can claim after all of this.

"I... uh..."

"This can't work, Liv."

"Says who? Oak? Your mum? My dad? At this point, after what our parents have done, I'm not sure their opinions hold any weight."

"Abigail?" I ask, my chest twisting even mentioning her name.

The wind whips up around us, making Olivia's dark hair blow across her face and sending a shiver through her body.

"We should get out of here," I say, taking a step toward her.

Despite everything I've confessed, all my misdemeanours, the magnetic pull between us is as strong as ever.

Lifting my hand, I cup her cheek. "Why are you still here, Liv?" I whisper, my voice so quiet I'm amazed she actually hears me.

"Because you need me to be."

Her words hit exactly where she intends them to.

"Fuck." Leaning forward, I press my brow to hers, letting her warmth, her strength seep into me. "I don't know who I am anymore, Liv. My parents... if they've been fucking about all this time, how do I even know that Richard Whitfield is even my real dad?"

"Don't say that. They're not bad people, Reese. They just... made mistakes like all of us."

I blow out a long breath as she shivers.

"We should get out of here."

Her eyes widen at my words, and I swear I see disappointment wash through her.

"Uh..."

"Were you serious about spending the weekend with me, sweet cheeks?"

"Yeah. I'm not in a rush to get back. You?"

"To hear Mum's excuses and bullshit cover-up for all the lies, and to have Oak lay into me again? No, can't say that I'm all that excited about the prospect of returning anytime soon."

"Oak will come around," Liv assures me as we both turn back toward the beach hut.

"No, he won't. I broke one of the Heir cardinal rules by hooking up with you."

"Hooking up? Is that what we've been doing?" she asks lightly. I appreciate her attempt to lift the tension, but it falls flat.

"No, not really. If it was just that, there wouldn't have been so much pain."

"It doesn't have to be that way."

"I'm not sure I'm capable of anything else now, sweet cheeks. They broke something inside me with all this. I'm no longer the boy you grew up with. The man I'm turning into isn't someone I even want to know, let alone be."

"You're hurting, Reese. That's okay. Lashing out is okay too. But you've got to stop bottling everything up. All you had to do was talk to us and none of this would have happened."

"I know," I confess quietly, regrets swirling around inside me.

"Come on, let's find somewhere to go. I need a shower. I smell like the beach."

Dropping my nose to her hair, I breathe her in. "You smell perfect to me. But I would totally be up for that shower."

15

OLIVIA

"Oak again?" Reese asks as I glance at my phone.

"Yeah." I turn the damn thing off and drop it on the table.

I texted Fiona earlier. She knows that we're both safe and okay. She wasn't too happy when I said we wouldn't be back until tomorrow. But Reese needs this.

I need this.

We're not in Lymington anymore. After Reese begrudgingly told me what happened with his Mum and Dad, the lie they'd lived for his entire life, we left the beach hut and drove in our own cars to a hotel just outside of Winchester. Reese didn't want to be anywhere near his father, and it wasn't like we could stay in the beach hut and wait to be arrested for trespassing.

So here we are, in some small country hotel. We grabbed a few things on the way here. Snacks and toiletries. But despite talking all morning, the atmosphere between us is tense.

"Penny for your thoughts?" Reese asks from the bed as he flicks through the TV channels.

"I still can't believe you thought I..."

"Come here." He pats the bed and I go to him, curling up

into his side. Reese holds me close, dropping a kiss on my head, and contentment washes over me.

Even now, after everything, I still want him. I want him so freaking much.

I guess Abigail was right. Love and hate are two sides of the same coin. And sometimes, those lines blur. They become a big, tangled web that's impossible to unravel.

"You have to see it from my perspective," he says. "We were always at each other's throats. I was jealous of your bond with Oakley. You were always so judgemental of the Heirs, of me. *Especially* me."

"Reese, that's not—" He stares down at me and lifts a brow. "Okay, maybe I was a little judgemental. But you were always so full of yourself and the older we got, the more possessive of Oakley you got. Like you didn't want me around, ruining all your fun."

"Fair point. I was full of myself." He smirks, dragging me closer, until I'm half-lying on him. "But you weren't his annoying sister anymore, Liv. You were all grown up, and I didn't like it. I didn't like the way you made me feel."

"That is such a boy thing to say." I roll my eyes.

"It's the truth." I shrug. "Anyway, when I got to your house and saw them... in my head, you'd wanted me to find out. You'd wanted to hurt me."

"Reese." I sit up, palming his cheek. "That's not true. I would never be so malicious."

"I know that now. Maybe some part of me has always known that," he exhales a steady breath, "but I was blinded by anger, Liv. By betrayal. I wanted to hurt you, Oak, and your dad. I knew things would never be the same again after that I found out and I wanted to..." He stares off at the wall, but I tip his face back to mine.

"You wanted to what?"

"I wanted to hate you so fucking much," he admits, and it breaks something inside me.

Reese carries so much pain and anger around with him, but part of me gets it. His entire life has been a lie. His parents stayed together out of obligation, not love. And although I don't doubt they both love Reese more than anything, their lies have come around to bite them, and Reese got caught up in the crossfire.

I stroke his brow, leaning in to kiss him. "I'm sorry, for all of it."

"Shouldn't I be the one apologising?"

"Yes." I chuckle, sliding my hands to his polo shirt. "And I plan on making you grovel a lot. But I can't imagine what you're going through."

"It's all a lie, Liv. My childhood. Every happy memory. They weren't happy, neither of them. They were just fulfilling their obligations. I was nothing more than a burden."

"No, Reese. They love you." I touch my head to his and hold his face in my hands. "They love you."

"They lied. All this time..."

"To protect you, Reese. To give you the childhood you deserved."

"That's bullshit, and you know it." Anger ripples off him. "He's been fucking Krystal this entire time. A woman who I've grown up with. Who's sat at our dinner table. A woman I called auntie when I was a boy, for fuck's sake. That's messed up, Liv."

He's right. It is.

But I don't know what else to say. I can't know what Fiona and Richard were thinking, only that I have to assume they were doing it out of love for the life they'd created together.

"He told me he could get me out of the arranged marriage, you know."

"What?" My brows pinch, and Reese nods.

"When I found out about your dad and my mum, my dad said we could leave Saints Cross and never look back. He promised me. It was all I could think about. Leaving this life behind. The pressure and responsibility. The betrayal." His eyes flash with emotion, and I wonder if he still hates me.

Even now he knows the truth, is Reese too damaged by everything that's happened to trust me?

The thought makes my heart ache.

Because if he can't trust me, how can we ever move on?

"He could have told me then. He could have fessed up and explained... but he didn't. Instead, he took me with him and then sent me back the second Mum clicked her fingers. I can't trust either of them. I can't trust anyone."

"That's not true," I whisper. "You can trust me, Reese. Oak and Elliot and Theo. You can trust us."

"I want to believe you, Liv. I do. But—"

"I'm here. I came here for you." I kiss him, hard and bruising, refusing to let go. He needs to know I care about him. He needs to know that I would never hurt him.

"Liv—" He tries to push me away, but I refuse to budge.

"No, Reese. You need this. I need this." I press another kiss to his mouth, flicking my tongue over the seam of his lips. His body shudders beneath me, his hands curling into my hips and lifting me over him. One of his hands splays over my arse, pulling me closer.

"When I think about the things I've done to you... the things I've said..." Guilt shines in his eyes as he gazes at me.

"I'm not glass, Reese. You won't break me."

"I don't deserve you," he whispers.

"I'm here, aren't I?"

"I'm promised to Abigail. My mum isn't going to let me walk away from that. She's made that perfectly clear."

His words cool the rising heat between us, and I let out a soft sigh, dropping my gaze.

"Look at me," he commands, sliding his fingers under my jaw. "I should walk away, Liv. You should walk away."

"Is that what you want?"

"What I want has never mattered."

"Maybe it should," I challenge.

There's every chance I'm setting myself up for a world of heartache, but it's not fair. We shouldn't have to stop this because of some old-fashioned arrangement. It's the twenty-first century. Reese and Abigail shouldn't have to marry each other on their parents' say so.

They should be free to choose who they love, who they want to spend their lives with.

"What do you want, Reese?"

He stares at me blankly, as if he can't process the words. "No one has ever asked me that before."

"Well, I'm asking you now."

"I want to choose my own future. I'm not bothered about uni or working at the firm, but I want to be free to choose who I... if I ever settle down."

My heart drops.

"What?" he asks me, and I school my wounded expression, giving him a little shake of my head.

"Nothing." I force a smile.

"Olivia, I—"

"It's okay. You didn't make me any promises."

I slide off his lap, unable to meet his eyes. "I need to use the bathroom."

He lets me go.

Reese lets me go, and it feels symbolic.

I came here to fight for him, to show him that he's not alone. But maybe it wasn't enough.

Maybe I'm not enough.

After hiding in the bathroom longer than I should have, I find the courage to go back into the hotel room and face him.

"Should have grabbed a phone charger," he says, waving his phone at me. "My battery died."

"We can head back, if you want to."

I'd stupidly thought we would stay and it would be this magical romantic weekend.

God, why did I let my heart run away with herself?

Reese had the perfect opportunity to tell me how he felt, and he didn't.

And now everything feels so confused in my head. It's possible this is nothing more than a game. That he wanted to use me to get back at my father and his mum. That I became collateral in a war that pitted us as enemies.

But I was never Reese's enemy.

"Do you want to go back?" he asks, watching me with a closed-off expression.

I wish I knew what he was thinking.

"I think we both know this isn't about what I want, Reese."

"Come here." He shuffles to the end of the bed and plants his feet on the floor.

"What—"

"I said, come here." Reaching for my hand, he tugs me over to him, banding his arm around my waist. I gaze down at him. He's so infuriatingly handsome, it isn't fair. I can't think straight when we're this close. When he's touching me, looking at me like I'm all his dreams come true.

"You're upset with me."

"I'm... it doesn't matter."

"I'm not good at this, Liv. I'm not good at letting people in."

"I know."

"But you came. You came for me."

I nod, too overwhelmed to reply. He looks so lost.

"I don't deserve—"

"Shh." I press my finger to his lips. "Let's not rehash things. We've both done and said things to hurt each other."

"You're so strong, Olivia." His hand slides up my stomach,

resting over my chest. My heart. "You're one of the strongest people I know."

"I have to be when I'm surrounded by Heirs."

"Can I kiss you?"

My heart flutters at his simple request, and I nod again.

Reese pulls me down onto his lap, pushing my thighs apart so I'm straddling him. His hand curves around the back of my neck, holding me right where he wants me as he fixes his mouth over mine, firm and unyielding.

I fist his polo shirt, needing to be closer. Needing everything he'll give me.

How can I walk away now that he owns a piece of my heart?

Things are such a mess, but when he kisses me like this, I can't help but fall deeper under his spell.

Reese Whitfield is broken—and I want to be the one to piece him back together.

"I need you, Liv," he murmurs against my lips, his tongue tangling with mine in slow, lazy licks.

Sliding my palm against his cheek, I touch my head to his and smile. "Then take me, Reese."

I'm yours.

16

REESE

With my tongue still twisted with hers, I grip her arse and stand to my feet, taking her with me.

"Reese." My name is nothing but a needy plea as I move with her.

I walk across the huge room I booked for us for the night, and she panics when she realises I'm getting farther away from the bed.

"Wait, what are you—"

"You're dirty, remember?" I murmur, my lips connecting with her neck. "I promised you a shower. And I figure if I'm going to dirty you up even more, then I should do the gentlemanly thing of cleaning you up after."

She shudders as I suck on the sensitive patch of skin beneath her ear and kick the bathroom door open.

"Never had shower sex before," she moans, my fingers gripping her arse hard enough to leave bruises.

"Good. I like having firsts with you."

"Not sure you've got any left for me after being such a man whore, huh?"

A laugh falls from my lips, but there's a bitterness to it as I very briefly reminisce on all my... activities over the past couple of years.

"I'm not that bad," I argue.

"Is that right?" she chuckles.

Pulling away from her neck, I stare down into her eyes. They're dark with hunger, still edged with anger over my confessions earlier, but thankfully, there's no jealousy in them.

"Don't believe all the gossip you hear in the hallways at All Hallows', sweet cheeks. The girls like to... exaggerate."

"I know full well how much bullshit they spit, Reese. But I'm also aware that there's no smoke without fire." Her brow lifts.

"Olivia, I—"

"I don't care about them, Reese," she confesses as I lower her onto the counter, sliding my hands around her hips and pushing them under her hoodie and vest, loving the softness of her skin against my rough hands. "Just..." She shudders as I cup her breasts and pinch her hard nipples.

"Just what, Liv?"

"Just promise me that you never touched Darcie. Please, tell me it was all—"

"I never touched the bitch. I'd rather saw my own hands off."

Her head falls back as I squeeze her tits harder.

"I need you naked, babe. I need your legs wrapped around my waist and my cock buried deep inside you."

"Your mouth is filth, Reese Whitfield."

Wrapping my fingers around the bottom of her hoodie, I drag that and her vest from her body, throwing it to the floor behind me.

"You love it," I groan, staring down at her resting back on her palms and allowing me to take my fill of her body.

"Do I?" she taunts.

"Yeah, your cheeks are flushed, your chest is heaving, and

these..." I reach out, pinching her nipples again and making her squirm on the counter. "You're wet for me too, aren't you?

"Reese," she moans, arching her back, begging me to give her more.

Tucking my fingers under her waistband, I give her a second to get with the program and lift her hips, helping me out.

Dropping to my knees before her, I tug the fabric free from her ankles and press my hands on the insides of her knees, spreading her wide for me.

"Reese," she gasps, fighting against me.

"Too late to be shy now, sweet cheeks. I've already tasted it, and I'm fucking starving here."

"Jesus."

"I fully intend to spend our whole time here with your taste coating my tongue. When we drive back into Saints Cross, I don't want there to be any doubt of who owns you."

"And what about you?" she asks, finally letting her legs fall open to expose what I really want.

My mouth waters as my eyes feast on her.

"Fuck, I need you." Her cunt glistens with need, and my brain totally misfires as I'm utterly consumed by my desire for her.

"What about you, Reese? Who owns you?"

"Do we need to do this now?" I ask, ripping my attention from her pussy in favour of her eyes.

"I can't be yours if you can't be mine," she says so fiercely that I half expect her to jump off the counter and walk away.

My grip on her tightens in the hope that she can't feel my hands trembling.

With every touch, every word, every glance, my plans for breaking her, for turning my back on everyone, Saints Cross and All Hallows', crumbles around me.

I thought it was exactly what I needed to do.

Break her heart and leave her world rocked, the foundations she thought were so solid shaking around her.

But everything I believed isn't true.

Even now, hours after talking it out, the evidence of my stupidity makes my head spin.

She didn't know.

She didn't send me to the house that night to discover my mother's infidelity.

She's as much a victim of our parents' lies and betrayal as I am.

Why couldn't I have thought that to be the case when it happened?

Because you were so blinded by anger.

In a move I didn't see coming, I lean forward, pressing a chaste kiss to the inside of her knee, my eyes still locked on hers as my heart thumps to a furious beat in my chest.

"I'm yours, Olivia. We'll figure it out. We'll—"

"But Abigail..."

"I've never been an easy person to put up with, Liv. You of all people know that."

She sucks her bottom lip into her mouth, running it between her teeth as she swallows nervously.

"But I'll find a way. I fucking promise you. I'm not letting this go."

She stares at me as if she can't believe the words that are coming out of my mouth. And quite frankly, I don't blame her.

I wouldn't believe me either.

I've done some horrible things, things that she's not even aware of yet. I don't deserve for her to be here with me right now, let alone listening to her tell me that she's mine.

"But—"

"No more arguing, Liv. For the rest of the weekend, it's just us. We can pretend that the world outside these rooms doesn't exist and that everything is simple."

"You make it sound so easy."

"Because it is, isn't it? Me and you, this." I gesture between us. "Despite everything. It's been so easy, so right. And I know you feel it too. We're meant to be, Liv."

Her teeth sink into her bottom lip as she studies me. Her eyes flick over every inch of my face. I have no idea what she can see reflected back at her, but I allow her the time she needs to consider everything I've said.

My heart jumps into my throat when she finally speaks, and there's a part of me that's already preparing to have to walk away, that she's decided I'm nothing more than the liar I've accused her of being all this time, and that I'm not worthy.

But that's the opposite of what falls from her lips.

"Get on with it then. I don't intend on spending all night waiting for you to make me come."

"Oh shit. Fuck. You're perfect."

Spreading her legs as wide as they'll go, I finally get what I've craved since the moment I got her in here.

Her taste explodes on my tongue as I tease her, circling her clit and barely giving her what she needs.

"Reese," she groans, her fingers threading into my hair, attempting to drag me closer.

"Greedy girl."

"Reese," she warns, her voice holding a little more bite this time.

She tugs my hair again, sending a bolt of pain down my neck, and I take pity on her, flattening my tongue against her and pushing two fingers deep inside her.

"Oh fuck. Yes."

"Tell me how good it feels, babe," I demand, determined to make her mouth as dirty as mine is.

"So good. Your tongue... God." Her head falls back, her hips rolling.

"My tongue what?"

"It's so good. M-must be all the... fuck," she moans when I find her G-spot. "All the practice."

"Cheeky bitch," I mutter, finger-fucking her harder and focusing all my tongue's attention on her clit.

"I'll take it. I'll take it. Fuck. Reese, fuck," she screams, her voice echoing off the tiled walls surrounding us.

I don't stop as she rides out every wave of her release, my eyes locked on her face, totally enthralled as I witness her fall for me.

Once she's done, I sit back on my haunches. My cock is trying to bust out of my tracksuit bottoms, but I ignore it.

"Do you remember what you said to me in the car park at school last night?" I ask, my mouth running away with me.

I didn't have any intention of bringing it up. The whole situation is too terrifying to even think about, but it seems I lose my damn mind whenever I'm with this girl.

She nods, her cheeks only getting redder as she thinks back.

"Did you mean it?"

She can't have. It was a knee-jerk reaction to make me feel better after the shit Oak threw my way. She was trying to calm the shitstorm that was already raging within me.

"What do you think?" she asks softly.

I shrug like a fucking idiot and slip my hand into hers the second she reaches for me, and get to my feet.

Her eyes drop to the tent in my trousers and her brow quirks.

"I think you were trying to make me feel better," I blurt, refusing to take the easy way out of this for once.

"Huh, well. You always have been more of an action over words guy, so maybe we should try it this way."

She hops off the counter and pulls my shirt from my body before shoving my trousers and boxers down until they pool at my ankles.

My cock bobs as she stares at it with hunger in her eyes.

"The Heir chasers got one thing right," she mutters. "You've certainly got plenty to work with."

"I'm not so sure," I say, kicking my trousers from my ankles and wrapping her hair around my fist to take control. "I think you might need a closer inspection."

Taking myself in my hand, I drag her forward until she has no choice but to take me in her mouth.

"Never been this good, Liv. Never," I grunt, needing her to know that it doesn't matter how many girls might have gone before her, none of them ever brought me to my knees like she does. "You fucking own me, babe. Fuck. Yeah, take it all the way."

She deep throats me like a pro, like she was fucking made for me.

And the second she starts humming, sending vibrations down the length of my cock, my orgasm rips through me. But for once, I don't want to finish in her mouth.

I pull out, dragging her away by her hair as my cock jerks in my hand.

"Reese," she gasps in shock as I come all over her.

"Fuuuck, Liv. Fuck."

My cum drips down her tits, marking her as mine in the most primal way, and I swear my heart fucking shatters at the sight.

"What?" I ask when she stares up at me in disbelief. "I told you I was going to dirty you up some more. Looks like I've got plenty of cleaning to do now."

I drag her to her feet before me and lift my hand to the mess I've made.

"You look like a filthy whore, Olivia." My voice is deep, cracked with something so overwhelming, I'm not sure I could understand it if I even tried. "My filthy whore," I breathe, writing my name in my own cum across her chest. "And I never want it to be any other way."

Her chest heaves as she watches me watch her.

"Tell me what you're thinking," I demand, needing to know where her mind is at.

"I'm thinking... I'm thinking how much it's going to hurt when you slam me back against the wall of that shower and fuck me until I don't know my own name."

Her scream of shock rips through the air as I lift her into my arms and give her the answer to that musing not three seconds later.

17

OLIVIA

"Again?" I murmur, feeling Reese grow hard against my stomach.

We're lying naked in bed, tangled up together like we can't get enough. Like neither of us wants to let go in case something rips us apart.

"I'll never get enough of you." He nuzzles my neck, sucking the skin there and sending a bolt of lust straight through me.

"You already had me twice."

Once in the shower and then again the second we got dried off and climbed into bed.

"And I want you again and again and again."

"I always knew rugby lads had stamina, but I didn't know — Reese." I shriek as he begins tickling my waist, laying me back in the soft sheets and hovering above me. Reaching for his hair, I brush it out of his eyes and smile up at him. "This is nice."

"Yeah. Too bad we have to go back to reality soon." A shadow passes over him.

"Reese?"

"Are you hungry? We could order room service."

"Are you sure? This room must have cost enough." The hotel is upmarket. When we checked in, the receptionist looked at us like we were joking.

"I'm good for it," he says, a little defensively.

"Reese, I wasn't being arsey. I don't want to take advantage."

"Jesus, Liv. It's just a hotel room and some room service. It's not a big deal. Shit, I'm sorry. I didn't mean to snap."

"Are you okay? You're acting weird."

"I'm fucking starving." My brow arches and he adds, "For food, sweet cheeks. I need actual food."

"Oh."

Something feels wrong between us, but I don't understand what changed. Everything was great until I brought up the cost of the hotel room.

But before I can ask another question, Reese covers my mouth with his, kissing away every insecurity I have.

"Sorry," he whispers. "I'm a grumpy shit when I'm hungry."

"Apparently so."

"What are you in the mood for?" I lean over and pluck the room service menu off the bedside table.

"Order one of everything." He grins. "I need to take a piss."

I can't help but watch as he clambers off the bed and strolls naked into the bathroom, his Heir tattoo on his shoulder rippling as his muscles contract. He's so bloody hot, it hurts to look at him.

Heat floods my cheeks as I think about all the filthy things he's done to me since we got here—all the filthy things I still want him to do.

How can we ever go back to hiding this now we've crossed this line?

The answer is, we can't. I don't want to. But it's not that simple, either.

Our parents. Oak. Abigail. There are so many obstacles in our way, but he said it. Reese said we're meant to be, and I want so desperately to believe him.

"Get extra chips," he calls from the bathroom. "And see if they have onion rings."

"Anything else?" I chuckle.

"Whatever you want."

My lip quirks as I think about what I want, because it doesn't include anything on the menu.

After ordering Reese a ridiculous amount of food, I try to turn on my phone, only to discover the battery is dead.

Oak is probably going out of his mind, but I can't find it in myself to care. Not today. Not after everything that's happened.

"Hmm, now there's a sight for sore eyes." The heat in Reese's voice sends shivers through me. I glance over my shoulder at him and give him a sultry look.

"I ordered you one of almost everything."

He stalks toward me, leaning down and sliding his hands up my ankles, and he tugs me sharply to the end of the bed. His knees hit the floor and he lifts both of my legs over his shoulders. "Change of plans," he says. "There's only one thing I'm hungry for right now."

"Oh yeah?" I sass, swallowing the moan caught in my throat as his lips find the soft flesh along my inner thigh.

"Yeah, sweet cheeks. You."

"You sure you don't want to drive back together?" Reese asks me as we walk to our cars.

"It seems silly to leave one car here when we'll only have to come back for it."

"Yeah, I know." He buries his face in the crook of my neck. "But I'm not sure I can let you go."

"You're just sad there's no chance of a car journey blowie."

I arch a brow and he explodes with laughter.

"I've created a monster."

"And she bites too." I snap my teeth together, leaning up to kiss him. "Thank you for last night. It was..." Amazing.

"I think I should be thanking you."

"What happens now?" My stomach sinks.

"We'll go back to Saints Cross and deal with Oak, and then figure out how to deal with my mum and Abigail."

"Promise?" I hate how vulnerable I sound, but I need to know that he's in this thing with me.

"I promise." Reese grips the back of my neck and drops a kiss on my head. "I'll meet you back at the house, okay?"

I nod, climbing into my car and waiting for him to do the same.

Connecting my phone to the in-car charger, I leave it to power up and turn on the engine. My car rumbles to life, the radio blasting out a sad song about heartbreak and regrets.

Just what I don't want to hear.

Switching the station, I pull out of the car park and pass Reese. His gaze lingers on me as he follows.

I can only imagine the shitshow we're going to return to. Oakley knows something is going on, and I all but admitted to Fiona that I care about Reese.

God, I wish we could stay here, leave all the bullshit behind and just be together.

Reese is different in Saints Cross. He has to be, because society, his mum, and the Heirs expect him to be. They don't see the side of him that I do.

It isn't fair, yet I know nothing in life rarely is.

About thirty minutes outside of Saints Cross, my phone begins to vibrate.

Oak.

Dread plunks in my stomach but I ignore it, choosing to remain in ignorant bliss for as long as possible. But with every mile that passes, I can't shake the feeling that something is wrong.

By the time I pull into our driveway and cut the engine, my hands are shaking.

Twelve missed calls, numerous voicemails, and texts from Oak, Charli, and Dad.

I don't have a chance to read them before Oakley comes racing out of the house and storming toward me.

"Oak, what's wrong?" I ask as I climb out of the car.

"Liv, thank fuck." He pulls me into his arms.

"What's going on?" Rearing back, I look my brother in the eye, his expression stormy and full of concern.

"You don't know?"

"Know? Know what?"

Just as Oak opens his mouth to reply, the familiar rumble of Reese's Subaru fills the air and my brother goes rigid.

"I'll kill him, I'll fucking kill him."

"Oak, wait." I try to grab him, but he's too quick as he stalks over to Reese. "Oak, come on—"

"You motherfucker." Oak smashes his fist into Reese's face as he climbs out of his car, and I scream.

"Please, Oakley. Don't do this. I... I love him. I'm in love with him."

"What?" My brother's eyes snap to mine, pure rage shining there. I've never seen him look so angry. "You love him? After everything he's done to you? What the fuck is wrong with you?"

"It was a misunderstanding, Oak. It was all a big misunderstanding. We've talked it over and I—"

"There's a video, Liv. Photos..."

The world goes quiet around me as I stare at my brother, trying to comprehend what he's saying.

"N-no," I whisper.

It isn't possible. It isn't—

But the expression on his face tells me it's true.

"This piece of shit shared them to the school's email system. Everyone in the registry received a link to them last night. If you'd have answered your phone, I would—"

"You released them?" I'm not looking at Oak now. I'm looking at Reese, who's staring back at me, pale and bloody.

"No, Liv. No fucking way. I didn't do that. I swear to God, it wasn't me."

"It was your fucking email, Whitfield." Oak slams him against the side of the car again, spittle flying from his mouth as he bellows, "I saw what you did, you fucking scumbag. I heard every word of it."

Oh my God.

God.

An ugly sob crawls up my throat as my world tilts sideways.

Reese released the photos, and there was a video. A video of that night. Of him degrading me. Leaving me broken and half-naked in the mud.

I clap a hand over my mouth as I retch. Everyone will know what happened. Because Reese shared it to our entire school while he lay in bed with me, pretending to care.

"You bastard." My feet carry me over to him, and before I can stop myself, I slap him across the face. "I came for you. I fucking came for you, and all along you'd planned to do this."

"Liv, listen to me. I didn't fucking do this. Yes, I planned to hurt you, planned to skip town and never look back, but I didn't plan to release that footage. You have to believe me."

"W-what did you just say?"

"I didn't plan—"

"No, not that part." I inhale a shuddering breath. "You were going to leave."

Reese stares at me, regret glittering in his eyes as he realises his slip of the tongue.

"I... yeah. Once you fell in love with me, I was going to

break your heart and then leave. But I did not send that email, I swear it."

"What the fuck is going on?" Oak glances between us, still fisting Reese's t-shirt.

"I see." I stare at him, realising what an absolute fool I've been. "It was all a lie, wasn't it?" Everything you said..."

Every touch, every kiss... it was a lie.

I take a step back. And another. Slowly moving away from him. From the boy I love.

The boy who stole my heart and then shattered it.

"Liv. Olivia. We need to talk about this... we need to—"

"No," I hiss, cold and detached as my chest cracks wide open. "I never want to talk to you again."

"Olivia!" he yells as I turn and walk away, tears streaming down my face.

"You're a lying piece of shit, Whitfield, and you're done here."

I don't turn back at the sound of them fighting. Of the crack of bone and grunts of pain. I have nothing left to give.

Because I gave it all to Reese, and he broke it.

He ruined me.

Just like he always promised.

"OLIVIA!" My name echoes through the air like a battle cry.

But I ignore it.

I ignore him.

Because whatever I thought Reese and I shared was never real.

It was all a game.

And I lost.

18

REESE

Oak's fist ricochets off my cheek, and pain explodes inside my skull, making my head ring. But it's nothing compared to the agony ripping through my chest from what he accused me of doing when he first dragged me out of the car.

We knew we were walking back into a shitstorm. I knew he was still going to be angry and that the time we've been away will have done little to calm his need to hurt me. But I never could have imagined this.

Those photos. The videos. They were for me, to fuel my sick need for the girl I shouldn't have been thinking about, let alone craving and jerking off over every chance I got.

I might have taunted her by threatening to share them, but I never had any intention of doing so.

Those moments between us... They were just that. Between us. And like a fucking lovesick puppy, I treasured those stolen moments with her, especially when she was sleeping and I was able to pretend that she didn't hate me, that we had no chance of being together. In those few minutes, I was able to pretend. Just like I did this weekend.

Talk about coming back down to earth with a fucking bump.

"You're fucking done here, you lying piece of shit."

His fist meets my jaw this time, and I swear something fucking snaps.

"Boys, that's enough," a loud voice booms as heavy footsteps crunch in the gravel.

But if Oak hears his dad, then he doesn't let it stop him. If anything, he only gets a whole new wave of energy as he goes at me like a man possessed.

His final blow to my gut sends me crashing to the floor.

"Oakley, I said enough."

I spit a wad of blood out on the Beckworths' driveway and blink back the tears of pain in my eyes before looking up.

Christian is holding Oakley back as he stares down at me like a wild beast. Pure hatred fills his eyes, his teeth are bared, and his chest heaves. His fists are still clenched, covered in a mixture of both our blood. Nothing but death and the need for pain oozes from him.

In this moment, he's not my best friend. The boy I relied on for everything almost all of my life. He's nothing but a bitter, hate-filled monster.

And despite not doing the things he's claimed I've done, I know that I deserve it.

I might not have released those intimate images of Liv. But I've still done enough awful things to her to deserve this.

"Let him go, Christian. Let him have his fill. I won't fight back."

"You fucking piece of shit. I wanted you dead when I figured out you touched her. But this... you're fucking dead to me, Reese. Dead."

"Oakley," Christian barks. "Get in the house. Now!"

"You know what he did. Why are you stopping this?"

"Just do as you're told, Son. Get in the bloody house and clean yourself up."

The tension between us crackles, Oak's eyes promising me a whole world of more pain than I'm in right now the next time he sees me.

"Fine," he finally huffs, shrugging his father's hands from his upper arms.

I suck in a breath when he steps forward, but the pain never comes. Instead, he spits at me as if I'm nothing more than a piece of fucking rubbish.

"I'll never fucking forgive you for this, Whitfield."

Then, without another word, he takes off across the driveway and storms into the house, the loud slam of the door echoing behind him.

"Shit," I hiss, collapsing to the ground as the pain gets the better of me.

"Up you get, son." Christian's hand appears before me and I frown up at him.

"Shouldn't you be kicking me while I'm down too?" I mutter, refusing his help.

"I'd rather hear the whole story first. But rest assured, if you have done this, I won't be letting you off this easy."

"Great, I'll end up in some shitty juvie with Dale fucking Starling, won't I?" I scoff.

"We'll see. Juvie might be too good for the likes of Starling."

"But not me," I grunt as I get to my feet. "Good to know."

"Get in your car, we're leaving."

I watch as he drops into my driver's seat as if it's his own car, but the second he closes the door, my eyes drift up to the house.

A figure in the hallway window makes my breath catch.

I desperately want it to be Liv. But disappointment floods me when I discover it's Oak, still glaring at me as if my mere presence is ruining his life.

I knew him hating me was inevitable, but I'd planned to be long out of town before the truth was revealed. And I was going to be taking those photos and videos with me, not leaving them for the entire student body of All Hallows'.

Fury bubbles up inside me as I think about all those horny teenage boys jerking off over my girl.

My fucking girl.

The need to chase after her, to call for her, burns through me.

But I don't.

It would be pointless right now. She won't listen to me.

Hell, she might never listen to me again after this, but the least I can do is allow her to cool off and then try to have a rational conversation about it all. After I've figured out who the fuck did this to us, of course. Because I will work it out, and I will sell their soul to the devil for thinking they could cross us.

"Reese," Christian barks, leaving me little choice but to limp around to the passenger side of my car, holding my aching ribs which jolt with each step.

A loud groan rips from my lips as I fall into the seat, but Christian doesn't say anything. Instead he glances over at me with anger, and I swear pride in his eyes.

Yeah, he can play the big man all he wants, but deep down, he wants to do exactly what Oak did to me for hurting his daughter.

I get it. He should.

"Where are you taking me?" I ask as we head across town, the tension in the car too unbearable.

"The Manor," he states coolly.

"Why?" I ask, confused as to why he'd want to take me to one of the most expensive hotels in town while I look like this.

"Because," he sighs. "You need to cool off. All of you do. And this way, your mother won't hurt me for not treating you right."

"Ah, of course. It's all about my mother and what she wants," I spit.

"Reese, I—" He slams his lips shut, cutting off whatever he was about to say.

I might be curious as to what it was, but not enough to ask when he remains silent.

Only a few minutes later, we pull into the grand driveway of the fancy hotel. Christian pulls to a stop and lifts his phone from inside his jacket.

"Sharon," he barks down the line the second it connects before stepping out of the car so I'm not party to his conversation.

I sit there waiting, wallowing in self-pity while he paces for a few minutes.

Only seconds after he places his phone back into his pocket does a perfectly made up middle-aged woman come bouncing down the stairs with a key in her hand. She points around the side of the building and I sigh as I realise what this is.

They're sneaking me in so I don't bring the tone of the place down.

Why didn't he head out of town and dump me in the closest shitty B&B? Surely, he can't think I deserve this kind of luxury?

No sooner has she bounded off again is my passenger door ripped open.

"Come on, then. I don't have all day."

I glare up at Christian, but his expression gives nothing away. I guess it should be expected, seeing as he spends his entire life fighting for arseholes who don't deserve it.

With a less-than-gentle shove in the right direction, we move around the building to the side door and then step into the lift.

He takes me right to the top floor, and I silently follow him out to one of the best rooms—suites, I guess—the place has to offer.

"Wow, anyone would think you actually like me," I mutter, following him through into the lavish living room.

"Take a seat," he says coldly.

Knowing my only other choice here is to run and never look back, I do as I'm told and lower my arse to the sofa.

Christian doesn't move, though. He just studies me through assessing eyes. "Tell me the truth, Reese," he demands.

"I didn't share those photos," I state confidently.

"But you did take them?"

My stomach knots. "I... um..."

"Reese."

"Yeah. Yes. I took them. Olivia and I, we've been... uh..." How the utter fuck do I explain to her dad what it is we've been doing. "Fooling around?" I finally say, although it's not meant to come out like a question.

"Did she know you have photographic imagery of her?"

"She was aware of some of them, yeah."

"You're aware possessing them without her consent could leave you with a criminal record?"

"I'm aware," I confirm. I might be a dumb-arse where Olivia is concerned, but I'm not a fucking idiot.

"Why did you take them?"

"Do you really want to know the answer to that?" I ask, my brow lifting, the cut Oak left me with opening up as I do so.

When Christian stares back at me, I figure he really does want to know.

"I... uh... Shit," I hiss, rubbing the back of my neck awkwardly. "I like her, Christian. Like, really like her."

"So much that you've allowed her to be violated like this?"

"They were never meant to be seen by anyone but me," I shout, hating that he could ever believe I'd want to hurt her like that.

"I'm going to need you to explain all of this to me, son."

"I'm not your son," I spit. "Right now, I have no idea

whose son I actually am. You stand there judging me for this, but none of you are any better. How long were you fucking my mum, huh? How long were you going behind my 'father's' back? And what about Krystal? I spent years calling her my fucking auntie, and then I find my dad balls deep in her. How about you start spilling some home fucking truths?"

"Jesus," he mutters, scrubbing his hand down his face before moving to sit on the coffee table in front of me. "I love your mum, Reese. I have for... I have for a long time."

"Great, good for you. But that doesn't answer any of my questions."

"No, of course it doesn't." He sucks in a deep breath. "I really think your mum should be the one to tell you all this."

"Maybe, but she's not the one who's here, is she?" And honestly, if she was here, I'm not sure I could handle it.

"Fine," he relents. "Your dad was with Krystal before he was with your mum."

"I gathered that when Krystal said they'd been fucking for the best part of twenty years."

Christian's expression gutters. "Do you think you're the only one with a complicated love life, Reese? Oakley is your best friend, but that didn't stop you, did it?"

"I guess not," I mutter.

"Your dad and Krystal broke up after she went to a different university, and your mum and dad started spending more time together. She fell pregnant with you, and they embarked on life as a family. They wanted you to have everything you deserved, and they believed them being together was a part of that."

"But they didn't want to be together?"

"They were happy. For a lot of years, everything worked for them. But eventually, their friendship wasn't enough. Krystal came back into town, and your dad realised that he never really got over her."

"So he cheated?" I spit, a hint of the betrayal I felt on Friday night coming back to me.

"No. Your father never cheated. Just like your mother and I never did. Everyone was aware of the situation."

"Everyone?"

"They agreed it was best for you if your parents were to show a united front."

"While getting their kicks elsewhere?" I scoff, hardly able to believe what I'm hearing.

"Reese, you're more than aware that life in this town is complicated. Your mum had married your dad, and in your grandfather's eyes, that was how it was going to be."

"Fucking bullshit traditions."

"When Jeremy died, we all started making plans for our future."

"But I fucked that up by walking in on you fucking my mother six ways from Sunday." He gasps, telling me what I already knew. He had no idea they had company that day.

"Uh... yeah. We all just want to be happy, Reese. And we want our kids to be happy too."

"And that involves me being forced to marry a girl I barely even know?"

"That arrangement has nothing to do with me, son." He holds his hands up. "That's between your mother and Judge Bancroft."

Silence falls between us, a million and one unspoken words, accusations and threats hanging there.

"So what now?"

"Now, you all calm down. And if you're telling me the truth that you didn't release those images, then you need to find a way to prove to me, to Oak, and most importantly, to Olivia."

"And what about me and Olivia?"

"I don't know, Reese. That's something we're all going to need a little time to process."

19

OLIVIA

"Liv, come on, open the door."

"Go away, Oak," I yell, my body trembling with anger, heartache and shame.

"Please, Sis. We need to talk."

"I have nothing to say to you."

"Olivia, I swear to fucking God, if you don't let me in—"

Leaping off the bed, I storm over to the door and rip it open. "You'll what? Beat me into a bloody pulp?"

"Fuck, no." The blood drains from his face. "I would never. I just wanted to make sure you're okay."

"Well, I'm not. So if we're done here..." I go to close the door, but he sticks his foot in the way.

"We need to talk."

"No, we really don't."

"Liv, please..."

"Oakley, I... I can't." I feel sick thinking about the fact that everyone has seen those photos. And a video. God, I had no idea Reese was filming me.

Tears burst from my eyes as I bury my face in my hands. My brother's arms envelop me as he pulls me into his chest.

"Shh, Liv. I got you. I got you." He walks me back into my bedroom, kicking the door shut behind him.

"Come on, let's sit." He pulls me down on the bed and wraps his arm around my shoulder. "We can talk or just sit here, but I'm not leaving you alone."

"Everything is such a mess," I murmur through the tears.

"Want to tell me what happened? It might help to get it off your chest."

"Or give you more ammunition to go after Reese." I peek up at him, and his jaw clenches so hard it must hurt.

"Reese is a dead man, Liv."

"N-no, Oak, please... you can't."

"He took photos of you, Liv. He filmed you, for fuck's sake. That shit doesn't fly with me. You have to know I can't just stand by and—"

I grab his bloody hands and lift them up. "I think you already made your point."

"He deserved it."

I can't exactly argue with him, but I don't want Oak to go after Reese and do something he might one day regret.

"He thought I betrayed him," I whisper, resting my head on Oak's shoulder.

"What?"

"Before the summer, Reese found out about Dad and Fiona, and he thought I'd set it up that way."

"The fuck? That doesn't make any sense."

"I know that and you know that, but Reese got things all twisted up in his head. You know it's always been weird between us. He's always been jealous of our relationship."

"Which is why I'm having a real fucking hard time understanding how you two ended up... I can't even say it." Disgust coats Oakley's words.

"It wasn't like I planned for it to happen. It started off as a game..."

"A game? Fuck, Liv. I don't like this. I don't like it at all."

"I didn't mean for it to happen, Oak. I didn't mean to fall for him."

"Shit, Sis. You can't be serious. You can't mean—"

"I do." A fresh wave of tears overwhelms me and I sob into my hand, my heart aching at Reese's betrayal.

"But none of it was real, Oak. Reese played me. He made me believe we had something real…"

"Shh, come here." He wraps me tighter, holding me as I break apart.

Here I was, planning how to come clean to Oakley and Dad, while Reese was planning on breaking my heart and then leaving town.

I'm an idiot.

A lovesick fool.

I let my emotions cloud things.

Reese hasn't changed. He's still that manipulative, cruel boy from before the summer. He lured me into his game, and I fell for his ruse.

Hook, line, and sinker.

"Olivia?" Dad's voice pulls me from a fitful sleep.

"Come in," I murmur, leaning over to check the clock on my bedside table.

Ugh. It's too early. Even if it is Monday morning.

"How are you feeling?"

"Hoping yesterday was an awful nightmare."

His expression gutters.

"No? Well, there goes that hope." I sit back against my headboard and let out a weary sigh.

"I came to check on you last night, but you must have been sleeping."

I hadn't been. But I hadn't wanted visitors. Not after my conversation with Oakley.

He finally left me and I'd curled up in bed, sobbing quietly as I clutched my pillow.

Pathetic, maybe, but I needed some time alone to process everything and figure out how the hell I was going to face everyone at All Hallows' in light of the email.

"Listen, sweetheart, I talked to Reese—"

"Don't. Please, Dad. I can't..."

"Oh, Olivia." He perches on the edge of the bed and takes my hand in his. "This is a mess, sweetheart. And I'm not only talking about the photo footage, which, by the way, I've already dealt with."

"You have?"

"Of course I have. Mr. Porter is aware of the situation and assured me that anyone sharing it will be dealt with swiftly. The link has also been traced and removed. We can't stop people from sharing their own copies, but there will be an announcement this morning outlining the punishment for anyone who does."

"Oh my God." Dread fills my chest.

"Now, I need to ask you something, and it isn't... well, it isn't something any father wants to ask of their daughter. But did Reese ever hurt you?"

"No, Dad. N-no. Everything we did was... consensual."

"The photos... they didn't look very—"

"Do we have to do this?" Shame burns through every inch of me.

"If I'm going to fix this mess, sweetheart, it's important I'm armed with the facts."

"It was a misunderstanding."

"And more recently, the two of you have been... seeing each other?"

"Yes."

"I see." He strokes his jaw as if contemplating something.

"It wasn't supposed to turn into something serious, but it did. At least, for me."

"I don't think it's one-sided, sweetheart."

"What?"

"Reese cares about you, Olivia. In his own strange way, he—"

"N-no. He did this. He did all of this."

"He says he didn't."

"Did he also tell you he planned this, Dad? He wanted to make me fall in love with him and then break my heart and leave me. Leave town. All because you and Fiona..." The words stick in my throat.

"No, he didn't. But it explains some things."

"You have got to be kidding me? You're taking his side?"

"Trust me, sweetheart, I am not taking his side. But you're important to me. Both of you. And we have got to find a way to move forward. Now, is it possible that someone else leaked that footage?"

"It came from Reese's internal school email."

"He swears he didn't send it."

"I don't know what to tell you. That footage is on his phone, Dad."

"But it could be possible that someone else sent it?"

"I guess. But it doesn't change the fact that while I was falling for him, he was planning to break my heart."

"You're right, it doesn't. And that isn't something I can fix so easily. Even if I could, Reese is promised to Abigail. Something Fiona is very unwilling to compromise on."

"Why?"

"What?"

"Why is she so dead set on it? It's the twenty-first century, Dad. Stuff like this isn't supposed to happen anymore."

"You know our world is more nuanced than that, Olivia."

"Something happened, didn't it? With Judge Bancroft?" It's the only thing that makes sense.

"Olivia..."

"I hate it, Dad. I hate that even if I could forgive him"—

and I'm almost certain I can't—"it would be for nothing, because one day, he'll have to marry Abigail. A girl who wants it even less than Reese does. How is that fair?"

"It isn't, sweetheart." He lets out a steady breath. "It isn't."

"So I guess it doesn't really matter if I hear him out or not, because the end result is the same. We were doomed before we ever got started. Maybe this is karma's way of driving her point home."

"Olivia, don't—"

"I'm tired, Dad. You can go now."

No way in hell am I going to school today.

He squeezes my hand gently before standing. "I'll talk to Mr. Porter again. Of course, nobody expects you to go in today."

"Good, because I hadn't planned on it."

"You know, Olivia, it feels hopeless now, but you're young, sweetheart. You have your whole life ahead of you. There will be other boys out there. Other relationships. Ones that are less complicated."

I lie down and turn my back on him, crushing a pillow to my chest.

"Get some rest. I have to head into the office, but I'll call you later."

He hesitates for a second, but when I don't answer, he slips out of my room, closing the door behind him.

As I lie there, it occurs to me that he didn't mention where Reese is. Whether he's still in Saints Cross or gone.

Just like he planned.

I hide out at home until Wednesday. By then, I'm going stir crazy and I decide to go back to school.

The longer I wait, the harder it will be. Besides, I have nothing to hide.

At home, it's like Reese doesn't exist. No one talks about him around the house. No one talks much at all. I think Fiona is avoiding me, and Dad has been preoccupied with work.

So I'm a little taken back when I walk into All Hallows' and hear nothing but Reese's name on people's lips. Of course, my name is a hot topic too, but I tune it out as best I can.

"Olivia." Abigail catches up with me.

"Hi."

"How are you?"

"I... I'm not going to lie, it's been a rough few days."

"I heard what happened."

"You and everyone else."

"I didn't look." She gives me an apologetic smile. "I mean, I did. But as soon as I realised—"

"Don't worry about it."

"Who do you think sent the email?"

"Reese—" I start, but Abigail cuts me off.

"You don't really believe it was Reese, do you?"

"It came from his email, Abi."

"Yeah, but that doesn't mean anything." She shrugs. "Somebody could have gotten his login details or tampered with the system."

"I don't want to talk about it."

"Of course, sorry. I didn't mean to upset you."

I let out a small sigh. "You didn't. I'm just fed up of dealing with... this." I motion to the huddle of girls all staring in our direction.

"Ignore them. I do," Abigail says, pulling her hair around her face.

I wonder if she knows she's doing it. Hiding herself. Using her hair as a shield.

"You know, you don't need to do that."

"It's a bad habit," she says.

"You're a good person, Abigail."

"If only being good was enough..."

"Listen, would you like to get lunch together?" I ask, and she gives me a warm smile in return.

"I'd like that."

"Great. I'll see you later then?"

"I'll be there." She starts walking backward. "And Olivia?"

"Yeah?"

"For what it's worth, I don't think it was Reese."

Her words stay with me as I head for my first class. But even if she's right, even if it wasn't Reese, he still planned on breaking my heart.

I was still a game to him.

How can I ever forgive that?

20

REESE

"Reese, open the door," Elliot booms after this round of hammering on it ends.

I groan as I shift on the sofa.

The room spins and my stomach convulses, threatening to puke up the liquid diet I've lived on since Christian dropped me here.

He's hiding me. That much is obvious.

They're all ashamed of me and what I supposedly did.

But I didn't do it.

Yeah, I wanted to hurt Olivia, but I never would have done something so... so...

"Reese?" Elliot booms again.

I figure that the longer this goes on, the more likely they are to be removed by security.

I'm not sure that even Elliot Eaton can get away with throwing his weight around in The Manor like he owns the place.

"Fuck off," I grunt, although it's nowhere near loud enough for them to hear as I swing my legs off the sofa. My need to take a piss overrides the alcohol that's flowing through my system which is meant to be numbing everything to nothing.

Those videos, the photos I took... all of them are out there for the world to see. The entire school has seen her, seen her in a way that only I was meant to.

My stomach twists violently, and I quickly find myself running toward the bathroom before I hurl into the toilet, attempting to purge all my misdemeanours and bad intentions. But it's not enough. It'll never be enough.

"Ugh," I groan, resting my head on the basin as my body burns up, sweat coating my skin.

It hurts, but I deserve it.

I deserve all of it for being stupid enough for thinking I could have something as good, as pure as Olivia Beckworth and keep her to myself.

I should have known something like this would happen.

"Reese?" The pounding on the door starts up again, making my brain rattle in my head.

"FUCK OFF," I bellow, needing to do something to make it stop, to make it all stop.

But it doesn't. And knowing Elliot, it never will.

He's like a dog with a bone at the best of times, so I can't imagine this will be any different.

Olivia might not be an Heir, but she's one of us. Always has been. And I hurt one of our own.

But I didn't do it.

My brain races—or at least attempts to—as I try to figure out the puzzle here.

Someone else got their hands on my phone in order to get those photos.

But who?

And who would be fucking stupid enough to go up against us like this?

They have to have a death wish, I know that much.

Stumbling to my feet, I somehow manage to get my body

to comply enough to brush my teeth and attempt to freshen my mouth up.

Everything outside the room has fallen eerily silent, so I naïvely allow myself to believe that security has finally shown up and thrown Elliot's arse to the curb.

That hope comes crashing down around my feet when I step out of the bathroom in only my boxers to find both Elliot and Theo standing in the middle of the suite.

Elliot's top lip is peeled back in disgust as he looks around at the state of the room.

Theo's eyes, though, are locked firmly on me, allowing me to see the hatred and the anger that burns within them. But he doesn't get a chance to say or do anything, because as always, Elliot takes charge.

"What the fuck do you think you were playing at?"

I stare at him for a beat, my fists curling at my sides as pain and regrets rip through me.

"It's got fuck all to do with you," I scoff, not willing to go back over it all just for his pleasure.

"You hurt one of us, you hurt all of us, Whitfield. You know that."

"Yeah well, fuck it. What's done is done. Now, are you finished? I've got really important shit to be doing," I say, swiping a bottle of vodka I haven't yet finished from the table and moving toward the sofa.

But my body doesn't move quite as smoothly as I was hoping for, and in only a beat, Elliot is right in front of me and the bottle is ripped from my hand and thrown across the room, colliding with something and shattering.

The entire suite is fucked after my two-day binge and rampage. Furniture is upended, picture frames, glasses and mugs are broken. But other than opening the door to accept more alcohol, I haven't allowed any motherfucker to step inside.

Until these two pricks.

"How did you get in?" I growl when Elliot steps into my space.

He sniffs none too discreetly before that lip curls. "You're a mess."

"Newsflash, dickhead. My entire life is a fucking mess."

"Are you really still playing that card? Oh, boo fucking hoo, your parents have been fucking about. Since when did you believe life was fucking perfect, Whitfield? That any human on this fucking planet behaves in the way they should? How has being a part of this town, an Heir, not shown you that that kind of life is a lie, a fantasy?

"Our world is corrupt, full of lies, bullshit and manipulation. I have no doubt that all our parents are out there doing shit they shouldn't be just for kicks. That's what people with more money and power than fucking sense do." He leans in closer before delivering the final blow. "It's what *we* do."

"Nah," I say, lifting my hands and shoving him back out of my space. Or at least, I attempt to. The motherfucker comes straight back for more.

"We don't hurt innocent fucking people. We focus our wrath on those who deserve it, on those who torment others, who do us wrong," I shout back, trying to defend our actions. Fuck knows why. Elliot is our leader, he knows what we do and how we do it all too well.

"So that's how you rationalise all this to yourself? You thought Olivia did you wrong, so you sought justice. How very fucking noble of you, Whitfield."

Hearing her name after days of nothing but wishing I could rocks through me like a bullet to the heart.

"I didn't send that fucking email. I'd never, never do that to her."

"But you wanted to hurt her," Theo butts in, speaking for the first time.

"Yeah, I did. But not like that. Never like that."

"Why did you even have the videos if you didn't want to use them against her?"

"Because I want her," I snap, the words rolling off my tongue before my brain has caught up. "Because I want her, and the nights I was locked away in hell with you... that was the only bit of her I could have."

Elliot's lips part to say more, but no words come out.

"I didn't send that email. I never wanted a soul to see those images of her. They were mine. And mine only."

"You never should have taken them."

"Yeah, well... there are a lot of things we all never should have done. But I didn't send that email, and I need to figure out who the fuck did."

"While you're hiding, off-your-arse wasted in here? How are you getting on with that?"

I bare my teeth and snarl at him in response. "I won't hurt her more by turning up. I need help, I need—"

"You want us to help you flush out the guilty?" Theo asks without any kind of hesitation.

"You believe me?" I blurt, not expecting to have either of their support on this.

"Yeah. I believe you. I've seen the way you look at her. I don't think you'd have done that to her."

"Well, fuck." All the air rushes from my lungs, and I have the weird urge to go over and hug him.

I don't, but fuck, I want to.

Silence follows his confession until I start to wonder if either of them is going to speak again. But when Elliot's voice fills the room, I get exactly the words I was hoping for.

"Fine. We'll look into it. Ask around to see if anyone has overheard anything. But in the meantime, you need to sort yourself out. At some point, you're going to need to leave this room and deal with Oak and Olivia, and you're in no fit state to do that right now."

It's been two days since Elliot and Theo burst their way in here and promised me that they'd try to figure out the truth behind all of this.

I know I should probably man up and leave the hotel, but doing that means seeing her, and as much as I might crave that, I know my presence is only going to cause her more pain. And I've already caused enough.

I need to at least prove my innocence over that email before I can attempt to put everything else right.

I might have had intentions of ripping her heart out and leaving, but everything has changed. And I need her to know that. The thought of walking away from her now rips me apart.

I need her.

I need her like I never thought possible.

I sit back on the sofa and scan the room. It's still a mess, but as Elliot and Theo promised to help me, they wouldn't let me off with making a few of my own, starting with sorting this shit out. Knowing that they could clear my name, I didn't exactly have a choice in complying.

School finished two hours ago, and seeing as there's no game tonight, they'll have had practice and then probably headed back to the Chapel for a party.

My chest aches as I think about everything I'm missing out on. It was easy during the summer when Saints Cross was nothing but a memory in my mind. But right now, I'm still here, and my life that I'm not sure I hate quite so venomously is in touching distance. Yet, I'm on the outskirts, looking in. All my fault, of course, but I can't help the pain of that ripping through me.

I'm flicking through the music channels on the TV when a knock comes from my door, and unlike before, I get to my feet and pull it open.

"You look better," Elliot mutters, running his eyes over me.

"I showered and everything," I mutter, pulling the door wider, but my words are cut off when I find two girls standing behind him and Theo that I was not expecting to see.

"What the hell are they doing here?" I bark, my voice holding more anger than I was expecting.

"Let's go," Elliot demands, reaching back and wrapping his hand around Tally's upper arm, dragging the furious girl into my suite.

"You don't need to manhandle me, jerk."

"I'll do what the hell I want," Elliot snarls. "You were the ones who came to us," he reminds them.

"They came to…"

"Just turned up at the front door, demanding to know where you were," Theo adds, guiding Abigail into the room a little gentler than Elliot did Tally. I'm hardly surprised—there's no love lost between Miss Goody Two Shoes, Tally Darlington and the Heirs.

"Well, I'm honoured, but I'm not really in the mood for a three-way so—"

"Shut up," Abigail spits, making all our brows hit our hairlines.

"Oh?" I mutter, closing the space between us and studying her closer than I ever have before. "I think I might have underestimated you."

"Yeah, you and everyone else who can't see past my scars."

Shock rocks through me, and I look over my shoulder, finding both Elliot and Theo staring at her like she's sprouted an extra head. Tally, though, looks smug as hell.

"You've found him. Now, for the love of fuck, will you tell us what this is all about?" Elliot growls, his impatience with having to put up with the two of them more than obvious.

"You know, you could be a little nicer, seeing as we have the information you want," Tally hisses. "Maybe we should take it to Oakley in—"

"You have information?" I ask, barking over her. "You know who did this?"

A wide smug smile curls at Tally's lips.

"We do."

21

OLIVIA

I inhale deeply as I move slowly into the cow pose, pushing my hips upward and pressing my chest forward, letting the tension melt away. Lifting my head, I relax my shoulders while gazing straight ahead. And then I exhale into the cat pose, rounding my spine and pushing my tailbone forward.

The cat-cow pose is great for stress relief, something I need after the week I've had. Every day, I've had to face them. Listen to the whispers and sniggers, tolerate the stares.

Dad was right, though. Whatever he said to Mr. Porter worked, and no one has outwardly bothered me about the footage. Well, no one but Darcie. She gave me a murmured insult or two in passing.

Nothing new there.

The sound of the ocean ripples through the room, letting me sink into the pose, finding my inner calm.

Yoga might help with the stress and frustration, but it does nothing for the ache in my heart. The giant hole left by Reese and his betrayal.

I haven't heard a single word from him.

Nothing.

I heard Dad telling Fiona that he's safe and laying low while things blow over. Whatever the hell that means. But she still hasn't tried to talk to me about it.

Not that I really blame her.

I interfered with her plans for Reese.

She probably hates me.

Releasing the pose, I sit up and roll back my shoulders, inhaling another deep breath.

"Olivia?" Dad calls, shattering my peace. "You have visitors."

"I don't want to see anyone."

But voices travel upstairs, growing closer, and with a heavy sigh, I drag myself over the floor and go to my door, ripping it open.

"I said I— Tally?" I gawk at the girl standing outside my bedroom.

"Hi, Liv. Can we talk?"

Abigail peeks out from behind her and gives me a warm smile.

"Abi? What is going on?"

"Let's go inside." Tally motions to my room. "We'll explain everything."

"Who's downstairs?" I ask at the sound of male voices. "Is that—"

"Come on." Abigail takes my hand and ushers me back into my room.

"Why is Reese downstairs?" My voice betrays me, quivering.

"Oak, Elliot, and Theo are, too."

"They are?" A strange sensation goes through me. I don't like it. "I don't want him here. I can't..."

"Shh. It's okay, Liv." Abigail guides me to my bed and we sit.

"Will somebody please tell me what the hell is going on?"

"Reese didn't send that email," she blurts.

"He... he didn't?"

I think deep down, I knew it wasn't him. But after everything we've been through, I couldn't trust him fully not to do something so malicious. But I'm not sure it changes anything. Not after learning he planned to hurt me all along.

"No," Tally adds. "It was Darcie Porter."

"*What?*" I spit.

Tally nods, disapproval thinning her lips. "I overheard her bragging to her friends about it after school, outside the common room. She stole the images off Reese's phone and tricked one of the media nerds into showing her how to hack the system, probably promised to get on her knees for him. Stupid slut."

"Does she know you heard her?" Anger floods my chest.

Darcie.

Darcie did this.

All because she's a jealous, petty bitch.

"No, she has no idea. She obviously assumed no one else was around, but I stay late sometimes. I told Abigail, and she suggested we go straight to the Heirs."

"But she sent it from Reese's email. Without proof, it's her word against yours."

Tally's eyes light up with delight. "That's why I recorded their conversation."

"Shit, you didn't?"

"Oh, I did. Darcie Porter thinks she can get away with anything just because her daddy is the headteacher, and I'm sick of it."

"Did you play the recording to my brother and the Heirs?"

She nods. "They already have a copy."

"Why?"

"Excuse me?" Tally balks.

"Don't get me wrong, I appreciate it, I do. But why help me and Reese? You despise the Heirs."

"You can thank Abi for that. She seems to think that maybe I'm wrong about you."

The two of them share a look that makes me frown.

"Well, either way, I'm grateful."

"Your brother wanted to tell you, but we figured you'd probably appreciate hearing it from us first."

"You would be right."

I'm not ready to face him or Reese yet.

Especially Reese.

"What do you think they'll do to her?" Abigail asks.

"I don't know."

But whatever it is, it won't be good.

"It's about time someone knocked her down a peg or two." Tally smirks.

"Liv?" My door bursts open and Oak stands there, concern pinching his brow.

"Seriously, Beckworth," Tally sneers. "You couldn't just give us ten minutes?"

"Bite me, Prim."

"Bite me, Beckworth."

"What is going on right now?" I ask, glancing between them.

"Nothing," they both snap in unison.

I hold my hands up and murmur, "Sorry I asked."

"Where is—"

"In the kitchen." Oak grimaces. "Don't worry, I told him if he even so much as thinks about coming up here, I'll break his fucking nose."

"Oak," I sigh.

"He doesn't get a free pass just because he didn't send that email. Fuck that, Liv."

"I didn't say anything."

"No, but I can see it in your eyes. You're thinking about going down there to talk to him."

Am I?

I don't want to, but my brother is right. The urge to go to Reese burns through me.

He doesn't deserve my sympathy or empathy, though.

He doesn't deserve anything from me.

"Liv's old enough to make her own decisions," Tally says.

"Stay out of it, Prim."

"Prim?" Abigail asks.

"Yeah. Little Miss Prim and Proper. Also known as a right stuck-up bitch."

Tally scoffs. "You are such a prick."

"Fuck—"

"Oak!" I hiss. "If you only came up here to argue with Tally, you can leave."

His expression drops as he drags a hand over his face. "I came to make sure you're okay."

"I'm fine. At least, I will be. What are we going to do about Darcie?"

"We?"

"I don't remember her wronging you." I point out.

"Fuck that. She came after you and Re—" He stops himself, and my chest tightens at his slip. "She came after you, which means she came after us. You know we can't let that fly."

"I don't want you to." Darcie deserves to be taught a lesson. But I don't want them to do anything stupid or reckless.

"I want to decide her punishment," I add.

"Consider it done." Elliot nods.

"Not tonight, though. I need some time to figure things out."

"On that note, we should probably go," Tally says.

"Actually, I was wondering if you and Abi want to stay and hang out?"

"What about me?" Oak has the audacity to look offended.

"Sorry, Brother. It's girls' night."

"Girls' night? You're seriously going to send me away after—"

"You're a big boy. I'm sure you can handle it. Besides, you and Reese probably need to work out your differences... without beating the shit out of each other."

"He deserves everything he gets."

"Maybe," I whisper.

Silence crackles between us and then Oak lets out a heavy sigh. His eyes flick to Abigail and back to me. "Since you're throwing me out, walk me down?"

"I'll be back," I say to the girls. "Make yourself at home."

We walk down the hall before Oak grabs me and pulls me close. "I can't believe I'm going to say this, but he's really cut up about this, Liv. And don't get me wrong, I'm so fucking mad at him for touching you. But he's one of us."

"I know."

"You two need to talk."

"I can't, Oak."

"He's a mess. I've never seen him like this. Ever."

"I don't know what you want me to say. He's promised to Abi. I never should have—"

"I'm not talking about Abigail right now. I'm talking about you. What do *you* want, Liv?"

"I... I don't know."

I'd wanted Reese. But it wasn't real. Every secret touch and stolen kiss... it was all a lie. A game.

"I know I can be an overbearing arse sometimes, but it's only because I care about you. And I don't want you to settle for less than you deserve."

"I know."

"I love you, Liv." Oak pulls me into his arms. "Nothing you've done or do will ever change that. And although I'm not sorry I beat Whitfield's arse, I promise to try not to do it again."

"Okay, who are you and what have you done with my brother?" I laugh, but it comes out strangled.

"I'm worried about you. He broke something inside you, didn't he?"

Tears prick my eyes as I nod.

"Which means it was real." Oak lets out a steady breath. "I didn't want to believe it... but here we are."

"Here we are."

"Just a heads up," he says. "Elliot says Reese can come back to the Chapel."

"Fine by me. I just won't be coming around anytime soon."

"Liv, maybe—"

"I should get back to the girls."

"Fine. But you can't avoid him forever."

I flash my brother a bitter smile. "Watch me."

He rolls his eyes before heading downstairs.

But the second I make for my room, my resolve crumbles. Because I want to see Reese. I do. I'm just not sure I can trust anything that comes out of his mouth.

And if I can't trust him, how can I ever forgive him?

"I never thought I'd find myself in an Heir's bedroom," Tally says.

"You know I'm not actually an Heir, right?

She shrugs, rubbing her fingers over the photo on my desk of me, Oak, and the lads.

"Okay, the sister of an Heir." She casts me a knowing glance, and I shake my head with silent laughter.

"If it makes you feel any better, I never imagined you would be here either."

"How do you think I feel?" Abigail says. "I'm supposed to marry him."

That kills the mood, the three of us falling into an awkward silence.

"Sorry," Abigail adds. "I didn't mean—"

"No, it's okay. I guess all three of us have our reasons to be guarded."

"Well, here's to breaking the mould." Tally grabs her can of pop and thrusts it in the air. "Something about this year feels different. Maybe it's time for us girls to steal the Heirs' crown and run All Hallows'."

"God, can you imagine?" I stifle a laugh.

"Oh, I'm not sure I want that," Abi murmurs. "I'm not good at being in the spotlight."

"You're better than you think." I offer her a reassuring smile. "I know I've already said it, but thank you, for doing this. For coming here. I really do appreciate it."

"We might not be friends, Liv. But I think we can all agree that we share a common hatred of Darcie Porter and her special brand of bitchery."

"Here, here." I raise my own can in the air and give Tally a small nod.

"So what do you think you'll do to get revenge?" she asks, a devious glint in her eye.

"I... I don't know."

"Well, whatever it is, you need to make it good. That bitch has had it coming long enough."

"Actually, I might have an idea," Abigail chimes, and we both look at her.

"You do?" My brows furrowed.

"Yeah. It's a little bit crazy, and we'd probably need the Heirs' help, but it'll send a message for sure."

I glance at Tally and she nods.

"Okay." I meet Abigail's wary gaze. "Tell us your idea."

22

REESE

"Home sweet home," I mutter as I follow Oak and Theo through the huge doors of the Chapel.

I didn't want to come back here. But equally, I didn't really want to go back to The Manor either.

I wanted to be at... home.

Home.

Not a name I thought I'd ever give to the Beckworths' house. Or at least, not recently.

But that's what it is. And not because of the house, or the fact that my mum lives there.

It's all because of her.

The girl who's wormed her way beneath the armour I wear 24/7 and set up camp in my heart.

Oak says nothing, just marches toward the kitchen with his shoulders pulled tight and rips the fridge open, immediately reaching inside for something.

"You good?" Elliot asks as he steps around me.

"Uh... yeah. Could you two give us a few minutes?" I ask, although hesitantly.

Oak hasn't said a word to me since Elliot called him and

demanded he meet us at his dad's house so he could hear what Abigail and Tally had to say.

Hell, he hasn't even looked at me.

He's pointedly ignored and avoided me at all costs.

I'm not sure if that's better or worse than him flying at me again and taking his anger out on me with his fists.

Elliot glances over his shoulder as Oak knocks the top of his beer off and lifts it to his lips.

"Sure. Just shout if you need us."

"I won't," I confirm. "If he wants to kill me, he can have at it. I know I fucked up, that I deserve it."

"And that's exactly why he won't. Just talk to him, yeah. And be honest. No matter how hard that is."

"I'll see what I can do."

After grabbing beers for both him and Theo, the two of them disappear up the stairs, leaving me alone with my former best friend and the reason my face is still completely fucked up.

He watches them leave, still refusing to so much as glance my way.

And it's not until a door closes upstairs and silence falls around us that I finally say something.

"I'm sorry."

His entire body jolts at my words, yet it still takes a good ten seconds of unbearable tension before he finally moves his eyes to me.

"Not good enough," he spits, his voice full of venom and hatred.

"I fucked up, Oak. I saw something that didn't actually exist and latched onto it. I needed someone to hate, I needed someone to blame for the fact that my entire life had been a lie, and unfortunately it fell on her."

"Still not fucking good enough. She did nothing wrong, Reese. Not a damn thing."

"I know," I say, lifting my hand to rub the back of my neck as shame burns through me. "Fuck. I know. But I couldn't see that at the time."

"You could have thrown it my way. Any fucking way but hers."

I stare at him, not having any words for him. The air crackles between us, and my head spins with all the things I should probably be saying right now but am too chicken shit to allow out of my mouth.

"You're gonna need to start talking, Reese. I need a solid fucking reason not to break your fucking nose this time."

My chin drops, my lips opening and closing a couple of times.

"Spit it the fuck out," Oakley barks, slamming his empty bottle down and marching toward me.

I take a step back, not really in the mood to let him lay into me again. I can hardly fight back—it's not like he deserves the pain like I do.

His hands lift and he shoves me hard in the chest, forcing me to back up again. "Tell me, Reese. Tell me why I shouldn't," he begs. It's almost as if he doesn't want to hurt me despite the hunger darkening his eyes that tells me otherwise.

"Oak, I—"

"You what, arsehole?"

My back collides with the wall, my head ricocheting off, sending a bolt of pain down my neck.

Oak's breath races over my face as he stares me dead in the eyes, daring me to lie to him, begging me not to open up so he has a reason to hurt me.

"Because I've fallen for her," I whisper, barely able to believe I'm saying the words out loud.

"You motherfucker," he barks, and I wince when he pulls his arm back and throws his fist forward. Only, it never collides with my face. Instead, he plants it firmly into the wall beside me. "You motherfucking, cock-sucking..." He continues spitting insults at me that I can't decipher as he drops his head into his hands and backs up.

"Oak?" I question when he stops in the middle of the room and does... nothing.

His knuckles are split wide open again from that hit, drops of blood falling to the stone floor beneath his feet.

"You were never meant to touch her. She's meant to be off-limits."

I'm the one who falls silent this time.

Oak and I have been tight for as long as I can remember, but we've never really dived into anything as deep as this, as serious as this. In the past, any disagreement has been resolved by a fight or a battle on the Xbox. Never has it been like this.

The cavern that opened up when I left this summer is stretching wider as we stand here staring at each other.

"Do you love her?" he finally asks, his voice cracked with emotion.

"I... uh..."

"This isn't the time to fucking hesitate, Reese," he warns.

"I-I know. I just... I don't even know if I'm capable of feeling that way about anyone and I'm..." His eyes narrow in anger. "I'm fucking terrified, okay? I've hurt her. I've hurt her in a way I'm not sure she's ever going to be able to forgive me for, and I don't know what to do about it. How am I meant to come back from this?"

His brows jump to his hairline at my question.

"Are you really standing there asking for my advice for how to get my sister to forgive you for this?"

I shrug. "You know her better than anyone. Who else do you suggest I ask?"

His jaw pops and his teeth grind. "I think right now, you know her better than I do. I had no idea she was capable of lying to me quite as successfully as she has for the past few weeks."

"I'm sorry I caused that. I'm... I'm just fucking sorry, Oak. But Liv, she's... fuck." I scrub my hand down my face, feeling all kinds of awkward. "She's fucking everything."

"Fucking right she is. She deserves the world, not to be treated like she's nothing but a piece of shit on your shoe to sate your need for revenge."

"I know. I fucked up. But I don't know how to fix it."

"Well, you're gonna need to figure it out or you're going to lose her."

His words are like a bat to my chest.

"How is she?" I ask.

Being in their house was a special brand of torture. Knowing she was right above my head, that all it would have taken was for me to climb the stairs and crash my way into her room to see her was almost too much to bear. But I had to do it. I had to do it for her.

She's asked for space, and all I can do right now is follow orders.

I hoped that time might be enough for her to calm down and want to talk about it, but as each day passes, I know I'm kidding myself.

I'm going to need to do something, and it's going to need to be something epic. And even then, it might not be enough.

"She's a mess, Reese. You might as well have shoved your hand into her chest and ripped her heart out."

"Really?" I ask, an embarrassing amount of hope in my tone.

"You don't need to look so happy about it," Oak scoffs.

"I'm sorry," I say, rubbing my jaw and trying to tamp down my joy at his statement. "It just means she cares."

"Jesus. You two are as fucking bad as each other," he mutters, spinning on his heels and making a beeline for the fridge again.

"I need her, man," I confess as he pulls another beer free. Only one though, I notice.

"I don't wanna give you my blessing here, you know that, right?"

"Your fists on Sunday clued me into that, yeah."

"I want the best for her. For her to be treated like a queen, not fucked around for kicks."

"That's not—"

"I'm not finished," he growls, downing half his beer. "I want her to be happy, Reese. More than anything, I want to see her smile. And right now, she's fucking miserable, and I don't even think it's because of what you did. It's because she fucking misses you.

"So no, I'm not fucking happy about it. But if you can swear to me that from here on out you'll never do anything to intentionally hurt her, then I might—and I emphasise that might as strongly as possible—be able to get on board with it."

"Why do I sense a huge *but* coming?"

"Because there is." He glares at me, showing me how serious he is about this. "You will make this right, you will prove to her—and me—that you are serious, that she's it for you. You will not look at any other girl, and you will not breathe a word against her, because the only one of us that deserves shit talking about them is you."

I nod, unable to do anything but agree.

"If you can attempt to be the kind of man she deserves, then I might get behind you both, because I want to see her fucking smile again, and something tells me that you're the answer to making that happen."

"If I can figure out a way to make her talk to me, let alone how to forgive me, I'll do everything I can to make it happen. I fucking swear."

"Good. Now get the others down here because I might just change my mind if I have to spend too much time being reminded of what you did."

"S-sure, yeah. Okay."

"And you can get your own fucking beer. I'm not your slave."

"There's still one huge fucking problem," I confess, making him pause halfway toward the sofa. "Okay, so I've got a lot of problems right now. But this one is an issue."

"Shoot."

"I need to get out of this marriage bullshit with Abigail because..." I swallow nervously. "The only girl I want to be tied to is Olivia. And not because we have to be."

"Fuck my life." He balks. "You telling me you want to be my brother-in-law one day, Whitfield?"

"Hey, it could be worse."

"How?"

"It could be Theo."

"Fuck you, man. I heard that," Theo scoffs from upstairs, cluing us in to the fact that they're listening to this whole conversation.

"You're a whore and you know it."

"Meh, boys have gotta have fun, right?" he asks, jogging down the stairs to join us. "Besides, there's too much pussy in the ocean to settle down anytime soon."

"Just you wait, Ashworth." I snort. "One day, a girl will come along and knock you clean off your arse."

"Nah, never going to happen. You think I want to go to uni tied down to some chick who only puts out twice a week."

"Thank fuck I only have one sister," Oak mutters, grabbing the Xbox controller and falling down on the sofa.

"We good, yeah?" Elliot asks, looking between the two of us.

"For now," Oak agrees. "Reese still has a massive fucking hole to dig himself out of, though."

It might be Friday night, but none of the guys make any attempt to attend any parties or even bring one to us.

We spend the night like we used to, shooting the shit, drinking, battling on the Xbox, and ignoring the elephant in the room which is what the fuck we're going to do about Darcie fucking Porter.

That shit can wait until the morning. None of us need our night ruined with thoughts of that bitch.

It's just a shame that it's the first thing we're faced with when we're all woken up by the pounding on the front door by three determined-looking girls.

23

OLIVIA

Elliot greets us, his brow arching up in that arrogant way of his.

"This is a surprise," he drawls, his eyes running over each of us but lingering a little longer on Abigail.

I half-expect her to shrink under his icy cold gaze, but she stands firm, staring right back.

Interesting.

"We need to talk," I say.

He yanks the door open and steps aside, and I gently nudge the girls forward.

"I guess it's true what they say."

"And what is it they say, Tally Darlington?" Elliot asks.

"You really are a bunch of little rich boys playing at being kings." Her eyes drink in the Chapel.

"Watch it, Miss Perfect."

"Tally." I shake my head. The last thing we need right now is them going at it.

"Sorry, it's just... a lot."

"Jealous, Prim?" Oak appears, leaning against the door frame.

She scoffs, otherwise ignoring him.

"Where's Re—"

"Hi."

My heart tumbles at the sight of him. The bruises along his cheekbone and jaw are fading, but he's still a mess. I want to go to him, to make sure he's okay. But I don't.

I can't.

Because he hurt me in ways I'm not sure I'll ever recover from.

And his defeated expression tells me he knows that.

"How are you?" he asks, taking a step forward. His presence, the havoc he wreaks on my insides, sucks the air from the room.

"I'm fine." I glance away and walk over to the sofa. Abigail sits beside me, shoulder to shoulder, an offer of support. I give her an appreciative smile.

"I... we wanted to talk to you about Darcie."

"What's this?" Theo strolls into the room, drawing up short when he spots the three of us.

"The girls want to talk to us about Darcie," Elliot parrots as the three of them take a chair each. Reese stays standing, his eyes fixed on my face.

"I want you to let us handle it."

"It?" Elliot's eyes narrow.

"Retribution," I clarify.

"And what do you have in mind?"

"Elliot, man, come on. We should—" Theo starts, but Elliot cuts him with a hard look.

"Let's hear it, Liv."

"Abigail found out some interesting things about Darcie. Something we can use to knock her off her pedestal at All Hallows'."

"Care to tell us what it is you have?" Elliot asks Abigail, and she glances at me.

"You have to trust us," I say. "But rest assured it'll ruin her reputation and land her in a whole heap of trouble with her father."

"Interesting."

"Eaton, come on. We have the—"

"Darcie went after Olivia." Elliot gives me a small nod, cutting Theo off. "Vengeance should be hers." He relaxes back against the sofa, oozing arrogance and malice. "You're sure it'll have the desired effect?"

"It'll ruin her," Tally says with a smug smile.

"And you want that, Liv? Because once you walk this road, there's no going back."

"I know," I say. "But I've made my decision."

Maybe it makes me as bad as her, but Darcie Porter deserves everything coming to her.

"Olivia, wait," Reese calls after me as I follow the girls back to Tally's car.

"What do you want?"

"Can we talk?"

"I have nothing to say to you." My heart clinches.

"I deserve that. But it doesn't change the fact that I have plenty to say to you."

"I-I can't do this, Reese. I'm sorry."

"Liv, wait." He grabs my arm and a bolt of electricity goes through at his touch. "Please, hear me out and then we can—"

"Olivia, are you coming?" Tally calls.

Reese mutters something about, 'interfering bitch' under his breath but releases my arm.

"You should go," he says.

Without so much as a word, I force myself to walk away from him. I want to scream at him, to hurt him the way he's hurt me, but I'm too emotionally drained to even reply.

I've almost reached Tally's car when his voice stops me. "Liv?"

I glance back, immediately regretting it. Because his expression is guttered, shame and guilt shining in his eyes.

"It was real," he chokes out. "I know I fucked up, but I need you to know that it was real."

A sad smile tugs at my lips. "I wish I could believe you."

I slip into Tally's back seat and belt up.

"Are you okay?" Abigail asks me.

"No."

I can't help but look back at Reese, standing there, watching me watch him. He talks a good talk, almost had me believing him. But how can I trust anything he says now?

"I know what you need," Tally adds. "Some of Dessert Island's red velvet cake. It always makes me feel better."

"You don't have to do that."

"Do what?" she asks, finding my gaze in the rear-view mirror.

"Try to make me feel better."

"It's not like I have anything better to do. Abigail?"

"I don't know. I don't tend to go there."

"Why not? Dessert Island is the best cake shop in town."

"I..."

Noticing her obvious discomfort, I say, "Tally is right. The cake is to die for. And who doesn't love cake?"

"Okay, I'll come."

"You don't have to hide, Abi," I add. "Not with us."

She gives me an uncertain smile. "Thank you. Is it wrong I'm looking forward to seeing Darcie's face Monday morning at school?"

"Hell no." Tally chuckles. "Desperate times call for desperate measures. The only way to win against a person like Darcie Porter is to fight fire with fire. And thanks to your snooping," she grins at Abigail, "we have the match we need to light the fuse on her reign at All Hallows'. If that doesn't deserve cake, I don't know what does."

By the time Monday rolls around, I'm a ball of nerves.

Declaring war on someone like Darcie is a dangerous thing, but you can't negotiate with the likes of her. She demands total annihilation of her enemies. But she's about to find out that no one messes with a Beckworth and gets away with it.

Abigail picks me up and the two of us ride to school together.

"Are you nervous?" she asks me.

"A little. There could be fallout."

"But your brother and the Heirs will protect you, right? And your dad?"

"Yeah but she's still—"

"The headteacher's daughter."

I nod.

"Well, I hope he realises what a conniving, vile bitch his daughter is after this."

"Abigail Bancroft, I didn't know you had it in you."

"She makes me so stabby. She's always made my life a misery. Ever since the accident."

All Hallows' looms in the distance, rising out of the trees like a castle.

"I'm sorry," I say. "If I've ever made you feel—"

"You didn't. But I appreciate the sentiment."

"Yeah, but I didn't exactly give you a chance either."

"Nobody is perfect, Liv." Abigail pulls into the school car park. "Have you talked to you know who yet?"

"I have nothing to say to him." She gives me a pointed look, and I balk. "What?"

"You have plenty to say. You care about him."

"And he hurt me."

"If it's any consolation, he looked just as miserable Saturday."

"He did look pretty miserable, didn't he?" A faint smile traces my mouth.

"Maybe you should hear him out."

"You're not going to let this go, are you?" I glower at her.

"No."

"Well, you're wasting your time."

"Or you're not being honest with yourself."

"You know, I liked you when I got into your car this morning. But now, now I'm not so sure."

"It's not me you hate, Liv. It's that you still care. Even when you think you shouldn't."

Shouldering the door, I climb out and inhale a sharp breath.

She's right.

Abigail is right, and I don't know what the hell to do with that.

Reese doesn't deserve my forgiveness. He doesn't deserve anything from me. But the thought of us being done, just like that, hurts so damn much.

"I can't think about Reese right now," I admit as she rounds the car to meet me.

"You're right, let's deal with our little problem, and then we can talk some more about him." Abigail gives me a knowing smirk, and I find myself smiling back at her.

She's not the girl everyone thinks she is. And something tells me this is the year she'll truly find herself and her place in the world.

I'm glad I get to be here to see it.

"You have to meet my friend Charli soon. She will love you," I say as we head toward the building.

"Charli. Why does that name sound familiar?"

"She used to go here, but she got expelled in year eleven."

"I remember. There was a scandal with her mum."

"That's the one."

"You really want me to meet her?"

"Of course. She's my friend, you're my friend..."

"Okay. I'd like that, I think."

"Fair warning though, she'll probably try to corrupt you the second she gets her hands on you."

Abigail blushes.

"Don't—"

A commotion inside the corridor catches my attention and Abigail smirks up at me. "Ready?"

I take a deep breath and nod. "Ready as I'll ever be."

We step into the building and cut through the morning crush down the corridor to the emergency stairwell. Checking the coast is clear, Abigail beckons me inside and we take the stairs up to the second floor. It's quiet up here, like we knew it would be. Abigail moves ahead of me toward the mezzanine, pulling off her backpack. She digs out a stack of flyers.

"No going back," she says, handing me half the pile.

"No going back."

Together, we move to the balcony. It overlooks the entire main corridor, the students below oblivious to the two of us above them.

"Ready." Abigail lifts her hands over the balcony and I do the same. "Three, two, one."

We both throw the flyers into the air, watching as they drift down to the ground floor.

"Quick, come on." She grabs my arm and pulls me back toward the stairwell. We slip inside and race down.

"Oh my God. I can't believe we did that."

"Now the real fun starts." We burst through the door in a fit of giggles, joining the stream of bodies.

It starts as a rumble. People grabbing the flyers and gasping, whispering to their friends, laughing and muttering their disgust.

"Holy shit, did you see this?" Someone shoves a flyer at us and I take it, feigning shock as I study the collage of black and white stills of Darcie and a man twice her age in various states of undress.

"Darcie Porter likes daddy dick," someone bellows, and the corridor explodes with laughter.

But it all dies down the second she and her friends step into the building.

"What's going on?" Her voice rings out over the chaos as she snatches one of the flyers out of someone's hand. "What is — No. No," she cries, her expression wide with dismay.

"Oh my God, Darcie, is that Mr. Nelson?"

"N-no. It's not what it looks like. Someone must have photoshopped them. It's not... I'm..."

"Ew, gross. Isn't he like, forty something?"

Darcie rushes past us, storming straight into the girls' toilets.

"Oh, how the mighty have fallen." Tally steps up to us and smirks. "Tell me that didn't feel good," she says.

"Maybe. Just a little."

"Admit it, Liv. You liked it."

"I..."

A trickle of awareness goes through me and I glance down the hall to find my brother, Elliot, Theo, and Reese watching. Oak grins with pride while Elliot gives me a sharp nod. But I can't place the emotion in Reese's eyes.

Or maybe I don't want to.

"Yeah," I finish, holding his gaze. "I liked it."

Far more than I probably should.

24

REESE

"Oakley Beckworth and Reese Whitfield, Mr. Porter would like to see you in his office immediately," Mrs. Pearce says, reading from the note one of the lower school runners just delivered.

Poor little shit looked like he was going to piss his pants being forced to walk into an upper sixth class when he first stepped through the door.

All eyes turn on the two of us sitting at the back of our psychology class, curiosity burning through each of them. Although I'm not sure why.

Since the stunt the girls pulled yesterday morning, our names have been whispered through the entire sixth form as the culprits who finally brought down Queen Bitch, Darcie Porter.

Unsurprisingly, she hightailed it straight off the All Hallows' campus the second she discovered what had happened, and no one has heard a peep out of her since.

We knew this was coming, though.

Even if our names weren't on the tips of everyone's tongues, we knew that the blame would land at our feet. After all, Elliot has already told her that he has evidence. Lucky for us though, that's in the form of a video, and after watching it last night—for research purposes only, obviously—it was immediately clear that it was of another rendezvous entirely.

So as far as we're concerned, we'd never seen those photos that were distributed yesterday, and we have no idea that Darcie was fucking her father's friend, colleague, behind his back.

"Well, go on then," Mrs. Pearce encourages. "I don't need my lesson disrupted more than necessary."

With a frustrated huff, she turns her back on us to write on the whiteboard.

"I wonder what this could be about," Oak mutters as we shove our books into our bags and get to our feet.

Things are still tense between us. He might be putting up with me moving back into the Chapel and hanging around, but he's far from happy with it. I don't miss the angry glances he shoots my way when he thinks I'm not looking, or the judgemental way he looks me up and down as if he's sizing me up as a potential brother-in-law.

My stomach knots as I think about the reality of that situation.

Not only have I somehow got to achieve the impossible by getting Olivia to even talk to me, but some-fucking-how I've got to get Mum and Judge Bancroft to rip up that stupid contract they concocted all those years ago binding me to Abigail.

I'm sure she's nice enough. Hell, she's sure shown us in the past few days that she's got more about her than we ever gave her credit for. But she doesn't do it for me. She doesn't light a fire inside me like Olivia does. She doesn't make my heart race and my cock swell with one look.

Jesus. I'm so fucking screwed.

I follow Oak out of the classroom and we head for the main exit of the sixth form building. Mr. Porter's office is in the main school building, a place we've hardly visited since we finished year eleven. But I guess incidents like proving his daughter has been fucking his staff ensure we skip the arse ripping by our head of sixth form and go straight to the top.

It comes as no surprise when we walk through the main reception and past the admin offices that we find Theo and Elliot sitting on the seats in the waiting area outside the head's office.

"Well, well, well, isn't this a coincidence," Theo mutters with a smirk.

"Anyone would think that the rest of the school doesn't hate her as much as we do," Oak scoffs, dropping into the seat beside Elliot.

No one gets a chance to respond, because footsteps click down the hallway behind us, and when I turn around, my eyes widen at the sight of Christian marching toward us with Olivia right at his side.

"Good morning, boys. Always a pleasure," Christian greets with a smug-as-fuck smirk playing on his lips.

He knows what we did. It's written all over his face. And something tells me that he'd be encouraging us to do it again. Hell, I'm pretty sure if he could dig up anything worse than we already found that he'd be handing it over willingly after what that bitch did to his daughter.

"Dad," Oak breathes. "You okay, Liv?" His eyes narrow as he studies her, but despite the dark circles lingering under her eyes and the way her lips pulled down at the corners when I first looked at her, she plasters a smile on her face and whispers, "Of course."

I keep my eyes locked on her, unable to look anywhere else, even as both Oak and Christian watch me do it.

I can't help myself. I need my fill.

It's been too fucking long since she's been this close to me. And it might make me a pussy, but I fully intend to make the most of her proximity.

The door opening on the other side of the space we're all

congregating in startles me, before a deep voice bounces off the wall. "Ah good, you're all here. Please, come in."

We allow Christian to go first, and the second he reaches his hand out to shake Mr. Porter's, I step up beside Olivia, dipping my head so that I can breathe in her scent.

She tenses, probably waiting for me to say something. But I bite back the words. The time for us to talk is coming, but right now isn't it. Not when we're about to have to fight for our innocence.

"As nice as it is to be invited into your office, Mr. Porter, do you mind explaining to me why me and my kids are here right now? Seems to me that you might have bigger issues on your hands," Christian says, talking about us as if we're his.

It's the way of the Heirs. Any of our parents—well, maybe not mine so much right now—protect us as if we're their own. It's why Mr. Porter hasn't called them all in. Although why he chose Christian is beyond me. He can get a murderer who was caught red-handed a non-guilty verdict in the courtroom. Something tells me Mr. Porter is going into this knowing that we'll be walking straight out of this office and heading back to class with our slates still clean in less than thirty minutes.

He's doing what he needs to do. Ticking those boxes to ensure the school board is happy.

It really says something considering the 'victim' here is his daughter. It also makes me curious as fuck as to what Mr. Porter might be involved in if he's going to allow this shit to slide.

"Rumour has it that your boys, and daughter, had a hand in the photographs that were distributed around the sixth form yesterday."

"I'm sorry, sir," Christian says, as slick as you like. "I have no idea what you're talking about."

Mr. Porter's face turns purple in frustration. He clearly doesn't want to have to spell it out, but Christian isn't the kind of opponent that makes any of this easy.

FILTHY JEALOUS HEIR: PART TWO

With a sigh, Mr. Porter is forced to—vaguely—explain what a filthy slut his daughter is to a very shocked-looking Christian. I swear to God, if he ever failed at being a defence lawyer then he'd make a killer actor.

The two of them go back and forth for a few minutes while the five of us sit mute, aware that our input isn't needed while Christian has our backs. And thank fuck for that, because with Olivia standing next to me, her body heat warming my side and her scent still filling my nose, Darcie fucking Porter couldn't be further from my mind.

Exactly as I predicted, and without any evidence to back up Mr. Porter's claims that we were involved in any way, the five of us are allowed to leave.

Liv and I are shoulder to shoulder as we walk toward the door, neither of us slowing down when we get to it. I know I should be a gentleman and let her go first, but the thought of her closing those final few inches when we have to squeeze through is too much to ignore.

She doesn't back down either, and when she twists to the side to exit, her hand brushes mine, sending a spine-tingling bolt of electricity shooting up my arm.

Sucking in a sharp breath, I fight my need to grab her and back her into any wall I can get to to kiss her like my life depends on it.

Instead, I do the total opposite, and after thanking Christian for his support, I hightail it away from the main building like someone set my arse on fire.

"Abigail, wait up," I call down the hallway when I spot her trying to disappear into the crowd at the end of the day. I have to give her credit, she's got the art of blending in down to a tee.

She hesitates, probably not used to anyone calling after

her, and when she turns around, her eyes widen when she discovers the voice belongs to me.

Her husband to be.

Ugh. Why did I even think that?

"Hey, how are you doing?" I ask when I finally reach her.

For the first time since she left her classroom, people actually look her way, and I quickly notice her trying to hide behind her hair. "You shouldn't do that, you know? You shouldn't let anyone here have so much power over you that you feel the need to hide." A weird kind of protectiveness washes through me.

"People stare. It's easier to take away what interests them so much."

"Fuck them, Abigail. You should be proud of those scars."

"And what would you know about it, Mr. Perfect?" she asks, finding a little of the spunk she showed us at the weekend.

A sad laugh falls from my lips. "I think we both know that I'm hardly perfect."

"Personality, maybe not. But you're pretty to look at." Her cheeks blaze red at her confession.

"Pretty? I'm a rugby player, Abi. I'm far from pretty."

"Yeah, well. You know what I mean. People stare at you because you're hot, not because you're disfigured. It's different."

"And how would you know they're not staring because they think you're pretty?" I ask, hating listening to her talk about herself this way.

Yeah, sure, the scars are... a little distracting. Shocking at first, but only because you don't expect them. But they're her, they show her strength. She's pretty, hot even. All she needs is a confidence boost, and I'm sure everyone will start looking at her differently.

"Trust me, I know. Anyway," she says, trying to steer the conversation away from her, "is there something you wanted?"

"Uh, yeah," I say, rubbing at the back of my neck a little awkwardly. "I... uh... I need your help with something."

She comes to a stop beside her car and turns to me, her eyes narrowing in suspicion.

"You need my help with— ohh... Right, well. Get in, I'm all ears."

She shoots me a knowing look and I march around her car to get into the passenger seat so we can have this little chat in private.

25

OLIVIA

"Well, that was an hour of my life I'll never get back." Tally sits beside Abi and unwraps her sandwich. When neither of us replies, she glances between us.

"What's the matter with you two?"

"Liv won't come to the match later."

"I already told you, I'm—"

"Busy, yeah. You're also a terrible liar."

"I'll come," Tally says. "I've never really been to a rugby match. It could be fun."

Hell.

It will be hell watching Reese get all sweaty and muddy.

All week, he's given me space. Feels a lot like he's avoiding me, if I'm honest. We shared a moment when we left Mr. Porter's office the other day, but that was it.

Even Oakley has been quiet on the whole me and Reese scandal.

It's weird.

I expected... well, I don't know what I expected, but complete avoidance wasn't it.

I guess it makes things easier, though. We can't be

together. Not unless Fiona and Judge Bancroft decide to free Abigail and Reese from their obligations.

Even if we can be together, can I ever forgive him?

All I know is that it hurts. It hurts that he betrayed me, and it hurts that we've barely spoken.

I didn't plan on falling for him, but I did. Even though my head knows it's probably for the best that things worked out this way, my heart won't accept it.

Going to the game, being around him any more than I have to right now feels like the worst kind of torture.

"We should all go," Tally announces. "We can watch the match and then go to my house and binge ourselves on fruit cider and pizza."

"You want us to come to your house?" Abigail turns a pale shade of green.

"Yeah, well." Tally shrugs like it's no big deal. "Unless you don't want to—"

"I'm in." Abigail smiles. "Liv?" They both turn their attention on me. "Please, you have to come. It won't be the same without you."

"She's right, you know. Besides, you won't only be there to cheer on Reese."

"Tally," I warn.

"What?" She holds up her hands. "I'm not saying a word."

"Hmm." I stuff a stick of pepper into my mouth.

"So you'll come?" Abigail glances at Tally.

"Why are you pushing this?"

"Because you can't let him win."

"Win?" I scoff. "I didn't realise it was a game." But the second the words leave my lips, I regret them.

Because that's exactly what it is—what it's always been.

"You know what I mean," Abigail adds with a small smile.

"Fine. I'll go to the game. But I'm not setting foot near the Chapel, so no after-party."

"Like I'd ever be caught dead at one of those things." Tally scoffs. "Now, what does one wear to a rugby match?"

Abigail chuckles and I roll my eyes.

Jesus, what am I getting myself into?

The roar of the crowd is deafening as Elliot tackles a player to the ground, snatching the ball right out from under him.

"He's... good," Abigail breathes.

"Something you want to tell me?" I ask over the noise. She blanches, shaking her head.

"N-no. I'm just saying, he's good."

"They're all good, Abs."

"Abs?" Her eyes grow wide.

"Sorry, that just came out."

"It's okay. I've never had a nickname before."

I smile. She's cute in an endearing, sad kind of way. But I'm grateful for her friendship. Especially since Charli hasn't been around much since everything happened with Dale.

"Go, go Saints. Run... Yes!" Tally shouts and we both look at her. When she notices us, she drops her hands and frowns.

"What?"

"Nothing." I smirk. "Nothing at all."

"It's invigorating."

"Invigorating, sure."

"Oh, piss off."

"I think we've created a monster," Abigail whispers.

"Who'd have thought it? Tally Darlington, a closet rugby fan."

The Saints score and the crowd goes wild, Tally shouting and clapping right along with them. The lads descend on my brother, celebrating his try.

But I'm not looking at Oakley, drawn instead to Reese as he jogs over to them. His long, muscular legs eat up the field, his brows drawn tight in concentration. He always looks so serious and brooding, but then a smile breaks over his face as Oak hugs him, and my heart stutters in my chest.

"Liv?"

"Y-yeah?"

I don't look at Abi.

I can't.

I can't pull my eyes off Reese and my brother, the two of them wrapped in an embrace. They need this. They need to repair the damage between them. But as I watch them, I can't help but think that I'll never have that again. Reese and his arms wrapped tightly around me. Emotion surges inside me and I check my watch for the time. Thankfully, the match is almost over and we can leave.

"Are you okay?"

"I'm fine."

She takes my hand in hers and squeezes gently. "Everything will work out, you know."

I wish I could believe her. But I can't. Because some girls don't get the boy or the happy ending. All they get is memories and heartache.

Damn you, Reese Whitfield.

As if he hears me across the field, his head lifts and he finds me in the crowd.

"Wow," Abi murmurs. "I hope someone looks at me like that one day."

"I..."

Words fail me, because Reese is still standing there, staring at me.

"I can't do this." I snatch my hand away from Abi's and push through the crowd. I shouldn't have come. It hurts too much.

All week, I waited for him to barge his way into my room or drag me into a store room at school and make me listen.

God, I half-expected him to get down on his knees and beg for forgiveness. But he didn't.

And I know why.

I know, I just don't want to admit it.

But as I get out of there and suck in a ragged breath, I can finally acknowledge the truth.

He's letting me go.

"Olivia, wait," Abigail calls after me, but I keep moving toward the car park. I can't be here, I can't—

"Will you wait a second?" She grabs my arm and tugs me backward.

"I can't, Abi. I can't do it. I can't pretend everything is fine. I am not fine." Tears burn the backs of my eyes as I fight to keep them inside.

"You can. I know it hurts, but—"

"No, Abi. You don't get it. I expected him to fight for me. I expected him to make me listen and he didn't. And I know it sounds crazy because I should hate him, but that hurts more than anything. Knowing that he just let me go."

"Liv, he didn't—"

"I want to go."

"But I thought we were going to Tally's?"

"We can. I just... I need to get out of here."

Something passes over her expression as she glances back toward the stadium.

"Tally, is—"

"Right here." She appears out of nowhere. "Sorry, I wanted to watch the end of the match."

"You should go watch it, I'll be fine."

"No way. I promised you a girls' night, and that's what you're getting. Come on." She digs her car keys out of her shoulder bag.

"So, I was thinking we should stop at Dessert Island on the way home and get some cake to take with us."

"Sure, whatever," I murmur, climbing in her car.

An almighty cheer fills the air and Tally says, "They must have won."

"Probably."

Abigail and Tally share another look.

"I'm fine," I mutter.

"You sound fine." Tally snorts. "But I'm sure tonight will remedy all that."

"Tally," Abigail hisses.

"Abi is right. It might take a little bit more than red velvet cake and fruit cider to pull me out of this mood."

Tally catches my eye and smirks. "We'll see."

"What do you think she's doing in there?" I ask Abigail as we wait for Tally to collect our order from Dessert Island.

"Maybe there's a queue."

"A queue?" I scoff. "We've been waiting half an hour."

"Knowing Tally, she's getting them to make us something from scratch."

That makes my lips twitch. I can totally see Tally doing something like that.

"Have you heard from Oakley?" Abigail asks and I shake my head.

"He'll be in a shower full of naked guys right about now."

"W-what do you mean?"

"How do you think they all get clean after a match?"

"I guess I've never really thought about it. So you're saying the changing room will be full of naked boys?"

"Do they look like boys to you?" My brow arches and her cheeks flush. "Didn't think so."

"What was it like..." She hesitates. "Being with one of them. An Heir, I mean."

My stomach sinks. It's the last thing I want to think about, but I humour her. Because something tells me it took a lot of guts for her to ask that.

"Why do you ask?"

"No reason. I've never..."

"You're a virgin."

"What do you think?" Her hand goes to her hair.

"You'll meet the right guy one day. A guy who will see past your scars."

"Yeah, I'm not sure that will ever happen."

"Of course it will."

"I can't imagine..." Her mobile phone vibrates and she checks the message.

"Is it Tally?" I ask, growing impatient. "Is she almost done?"

"Uh... she needs us to go in there."

"What, why?"

"I don't know. Come on, before she makes a scene." Abigail climbs out of the car and reluctantly, I follow. I want to get the damn cake and go to Tally's house.

"There isn't even a queue," I say as I glance through the windows, spying Tally at the counter talking to one of the cute shop assistants.

"I'm sure she has her reasons," Abigail says, checking her phone again.

My brows knit, a strange feeling trickling down my spine.

"Abi, what's going on?"

"What? Nothing. We're getting—"

"Olivia."

His voice makes my breath catch and I turn around to find Reese standing there, freshly showered and more gorgeous than ever.

"What are you doing—" My gaze slides to Abigail and guilt washes over her.

"Don't be mad. He knew you wouldn't agree otherwise."

"Agree to what? What the hell is going on?"

"You're not coming with me and Tally," she says.

"I'm not?"

"No, you're going with Reese."

"Like hell I am." Anger floods me.

"You need to hear him out, Liv."

"Why?"

"Because I did, and I believe him."

"You two talked... about me?" Betrayal fists my heart.

"It wasn't like that. Reese came to me and asked for my help. He—"

"You gave me no choice, sweet cheeks." He takes a step closer.

"But you ignored me. All week you—"

"Fuck, Liv. I wasn't ignoring you. I was giving you space. I was trying to figure out a way to fix things."

"And did you?" I challenge.

"The jury's still out on that." His eyes flash to Abigail.

"I'm going to go find Tally. Just... promise me you'll hear him out." She leans in and whispers, "Everyone deserves a second chance."

Abigail disappears into the shop, leaving me alone with Reese.

"How are you?" he asks, rubbing the back of his neck.

"Annoyed. Confused. Did I say annoyed?"

"You did. Come with me?"

"Why?"

"Because, Olivia Marie Beckworth," he steps forward and tucks a strand of my hair behind my ear, "I need to fix this." His head drops to mine, my heart squeezing at his proximity.

"I need you to let me fix this."

26

REESE

I thought she was going to say no.

The way her face dropped when I showed myself, the way her eyes darkened with anger and her lips twisted in irritation. I was convinced she was going to turn me down and ruin everything Abigail and I had been planning.

Asking for her help had been a risk. She could have immediately gone running to Olivia to spill my ideas, but I was confident. I'd seen the way she looked between the two of us when we'd been close. She wanted us to talk. She wanted her new friend to be happy again. And I had to hope it was enough to get her on side.

Thankfully, it was, because Abigail jumped at the chance to help. And it turns out, it was a killer decision, because that girl is a true romantic who is going to help me steal back Olivia's heart.

I think...

She might have agreed to come with me, but since the moment her arse hit my passenger seat, she hasn't said a word. I'm not sure if that's a good thing or not. I figure that she could have immediately started shouting and attempting to rip me a new one, so there is that.

It's not until we've left Saints Cross far behind in the distance and I begin to slow to take the turning we need that she finally twists to look at me.

"If you're about to take me into the middle of nowhere in the hope that no one will find my body after you're finished with me, can I suggest you let me out here?"

"I'd never hurt you, Liv," I say, although I wince as the words leave my lips.

She scoffs in response, folds her arms over her chest and turns back toward the window, acting as if I'm not even here.

I get it. I deserve it. But fuck. It hurts.

I turn off the quiet road and onto a dirt track. It's so dark now that the sign to the place we're heading toward isn't visible, giving Olivia no clue what to expect.

The tree cover overhead makes it even darker as we bump down the seemingly endless track.

"This had better be good," Olivia mutters.

"I think it's your idea of heaven," I confess.

"You're here, so I highly doubt it."

"Fair," I mutter, pulling the car to a stop in the same place I did when I was here last night, setting everything up. "Ready?"

She looks back over at me and my breath catches at the pain in her eyes, although I swear to God there's a little hope in there too.

"Is that a serious question?"

"Come on, sweet cheeks. I've got a surprise that I think you're going to love." I jump out of the car, slam the door, and rush around the bonnet so I can open hers for her.

She's too fast for me, but I do manage to take over and offer her my hand to help her out.

"Wow, did you dive headfirst into a bucket of chivalry or something?" she deadpans.

"Just learning from my mistakes and stupidity."

Ignoring my hand, she climbs from the car without my

help, and I fight like hell to keep the wounded puppy look that threatens from spreading across my face.

"That's a start," she mutters, stepping around me and scanning the tree line to try and spot something. "Show me what you've got, then." Liv picks a direction and takes off.

"Wait," I say, reaching for her arm and pulling her back. My palm burns where I touch her, my heart rate picking up as I drag her close enough that the heat of her body burns into mine.

I stare down at her as her eyes slowly roll up my chest and lock on mine.

"Hey," I breathe, my pulse racing. "Can I take you out on a date?" I ask like a moron. It works, though, because her face softens for the briefest moment and I see behind the mask she's pulled on.

"I don't date knobheads."

"Good. You shouldn't. You should date someone who knows how to show you a good time and treat you right."

Sliding my hand down her arm, I twist my fingers with hers and take off toward the trees.

"Reese, what are you— oh shit," she breathes when we break through the undergrowth and my surprise is revealed.

There, in the middle of the vast field, is one single tipi covered in twinkling fairy lights. The perfect relaxation yoga retreat in the middle of the Oxfordshire countryside. Or at least, that was what I was going for.

"Reese, this is..."

"Heaven, right?"

Silence falls between us as she stares at the view ahead of us.

"You did this?" she asks, in total awe.

"Well, I had a little help, but yeah."

"Why?"

"Liv," I sigh.

"You've avoided me all week—"

"No, I was—"

"Giving me space, you said. But that's not how it felt."

"I knew dragging you into an empty classroom and making you listen wasn't going to be enough. I needed to go big or go home." My lips twitch into a smile. "So this is me... going big."

Her chest heaves as she stares at me, a million and one things happening behind her eyes.

"Talk to me, Liv. Tell me what's going on in that pretty little head of yours."

"I don't know if I can trust you," she confesses.

"I understand that. I do. But I know that I can't live without you. These past two weeks... Fuck, Liv." My chest tightens. "They've been the hardest of my life. Not having you there, knowing I couldn't come to you, that you truly hated me... It's been hell."

"Yeah, well things haven't exactly been all sunshine and roses for me either."

"I know, and I'm sorry. I'm so fucking sorry. If I thought for a second that anyone would find those photos then I—"

"Wouldn't have taken them?" she offers.

"Uh..." I rub the back of my neck with my free hand. "I would have hid them better," I confess.

"Reese, that's not—"

"It's the truth, Liv. Do you have any idea how many times I've wanked off over those photos, how many times I've had your moans playing in my ear while I come all over myself?"

"Stop, please," she begs.

"I promised you the truth, babe. This is it. Me, unfiltered. Real."

She stares up at me with wide eyes, eating up all of my confessions.

"Then I'm going to need more," she says hesitantly.

"Good, because I have it. You can have every truth, every secret, everything. Anything." I take a step closer to her, leaving our bodies less than an inch apart. "As long as you're here with me. Because I need you, Liv. I'm fucking drowning without you."

She fights it, I know she does. I see it in her eyes. Her need to stay strong as her head screams at the rest of her to do the right thing, to remember all the hurt I caused. But her heart, her desire, is louder, more insistent, so when I dip my head and brush the lightest of kisses over her lips, she doesn't pull back. Instead, she freezes in position, letting me have that briefest taste of her. But it doesn't sate my need. If anything, it only fuels it.

I pull away before I'm unable to resist anymore and pull her back to my side.

"Come on, I want you to see inside, and we need to start the fire."

"Fire?"

"Yeah. You want to toast marshmallows, right?"

"Uh... who are you and what have you done with that arrogant piece of shit, Reese Baron Whitfield?"

I throw my head back on a laugh, so fucking relieved that she's agreed to be here with me, that she hasn't lost her spark through all this bullshit.

We walk around the little bonfire I built last night and head toward the tipi. It's not much more than a glamorous tent, but I did manage to organise a huge blow-up bed for us—assuming she lets me in it—for us to sleep on, so at least it'll be comfortable.

We've got a little makeshift kitchen, and there's even a portaloo outside. But it's ours for the weekend if she's willing to put up with it.

The one thing I ensured was here waiting for her is the first thing she latches onto when we step inside.

"Reese, why are there two yoga mats?"

"I thought it was about time you taught me some of those moves."

"For real? The big bad rugby player wants to do yoga?"

"Sure, why not? You look hot as fuck when you curl up like a pretzel. I'm sure I can make good use of myself."

"Sounds like you have something else in mind other than yoga."

"As long as it helps you relax, I'll be whatever you need, babe. Plus, I was doing some research, and there are a few positions that are great for—"

She slaps her hand down over my mouth, stopping my words. "Let's not run before we can walk, huh?"

I shrug, wrapping my arm around her waist and dragging her into my body. "As slow as you want, sweet cheeks. I just need one thing."

"Oh yeah, what's—"

I make the most of her parted lips and fuse mine to them, licking into her mouth in deep strokes.

"Dickhead," she mumbles, but the second I lower my hands and grab her arse, crushing her tighter against me and allowing her to feel my cock growing between us, she caves to my kiss, stroking her tongue against mine and letting me believe for those brief moments that everything is going to be okay with us.

I reluctantly break the kiss long before I'm ready for it to end and rest my forehead against hers, holding her heated stares.

"It's going to take more than one sweet gesture and a knee-weakening kiss," she warns.

I nod, fully aware of that situation. "Your knees are weak, huh?"

"Oh shush," she mutters, playfully slapping me on the shoulder. "Your ego doesn't need any kind of stroking."

"Maybe not, but I know something that does." I roll my hips, letting her feel how much she affects me.

"Reese, I'm not interested in any of this if it's nothing more than a hookup. I'm done with all the sneaking around. If, and I mean a really big if, we can get past all this, then I want it to be real. I want the world to know."

"Same, babe. I want exactly the same." Releasing her arse, I slide my hand up her side, loving the way she shudders at my touch before wrapping my fingers around the side of her neck and cupping her jaw. "I want it all. With you, and I want every motherfucker and their wife to know it."

"But Abi—"

"Shh," I breathe, grazing my thumb over her full bottom lip. "Abi and I are going to sort it. Tonight wasn't the only thing we discussed."

"But—"

"There's time for all that. But right now, I want to go outside, light the bonfire, and lay out under the stars with my girl. I want to tell her how much she means to me, and how fucking sorry I am until she has no choice but to start believing me."

"Reese," she breathes, uncertainty glittering in her eyes.

"It's true. I was wrong, Liv. So fucking wrong. I needed a target to focus my blame on, but it never should have been you. Ever. But I want this, I want you, us, so fucking bad it hurts, and not just because I let your brother beat the shit out of me for it."

27

OLIVIA

The flames lick the sky, the stars winking above us as we lie on the blanket. Reese is feeding me toasted marshmallows, getting the sticky sugar everywhere. Probably so he can clean me up with his hungry, wet kisses.

"You taste so fucking good, Liv," he rasps, running his tongue over the seam of my lips.

"This is nice."

"It is. I like being alone with you. Away from everybody else."

"Away from Saints Cross?" I ask, and he nods.

"Have you talked to your mum yet?"

"No. She keeps hounding me, turned up at The Manor and tried to see me, but I wouldn't open the door. She and my dad want to sit down and explain everything, but fuck that, I don't want to hear it."

I stroke the hair from his face. "You know you'll have to talk to them eventually."

"I know, but everything is messed up."

"I know." Leaning up, I kiss him, letting my tongue tangle with his. Reese tightens his arm around my waist, dragging my body closer. Desire shoots through me but I hesitate, and it's enough for him to stop. He touches his head to mine and lets out a heavy sigh.

"Sorry, I—"

"No, Liv. Don't do that. We go at your pace, okay? I fucked up, but I want to fix things. I want to—"

"Shh." I press a finger to his lips.

"No," he pulls my hand away, "I need to get this off my chest, please."

"Okay."

"You're fucking under my skin, Liv. In here." Reese grabs my hand and presses it to his chest. "I need you. I need you to forgive me—"

"Reese—"

"I know, I know. It'll take time. And it's more than I deserve. But I swear to you, I'm done with the secrets and games and lies. I was wrong, so fucking wrong about everything. But I let my anger blind me and there's always been this, this rivalry between us. You were a scapegoat. A pawn in my game. And it nearly cost me everything."

The haunted look in his eyes makes my stomach twist. He reaches out and brushes his thumb along my jaw. "It almost cost me you."

"Reese." My voice is cracked with emotion, just like my heart.

"It's you and me, sweet cheeks. You and me against the world. Just give me a chance, Liv. Say yes."

"Yes." The word spills from my lips. "But I swear to God, Reese, if you screw me over again—"

"I won't." He ghosts a kiss over my jaw. "You're mine now, Olivia. I'm not ever letting you go."

His words fist my heart, filling the cracks inside me. Maybe I should fight him more, make him grovel, but Abigail was right. Everyone deserves a second chance. And this is his.

"What are you thinking?" he asks, rolling me underneath him.

"That maybe you should get on your knees and grovel."

"On my knees, huh?" A wicked glint flashes in his eyes. "I think I can do that." He leans down, kissing me. Slow, lazy licks, exploring my mouth with his tongue. Reese pours every ounce of his apology, his shame, and regret into every slide of his lips against mine. I feel it in every caress.

"I'll never get enough of this," he murmurs, his hand wrapping around my throat and holding me right where he wants me. "You want me to get on my knees and beg? I'll do a damn sight more than that." He presses one final kiss on my mouth before dropping down my body.

"Wait," I cry, grabbing his shoulder.

He lifts his face and frowns. "You don't want—"

"I do, but not out here."

"Nobody is out here but us, Liv." He cups my pussy, rubbing me through my leggings. "I'm going to peel these from your legs, bury my face in your pretty little pussy and make you scream so loud even the stars hear you."

"Is that a promise?" I smile, my blood heating at his dirty words.

"No, it's a fact."

Reese wastes no time in pulling off my Converse and leggings, sliding his arms under my thighs and spreading me wide. "I'm going to fucking devour you."

He leans in and runs his nose along the lace of my underwear, breathing me in.

"Reese," I gasp at his hot breath right there, teasing me. My hand slides into his hair, gripping as he licks me over the delicate material.

"Did you wear these for me, Liv? Secretly hoping I'd fuck your sweet little pussy with my tongue?"

"God," I choke over the breath caught in my throat.

"Tell me what you want, Olivia."

"I..." I press my lips together, trying to suppress the moan building in my throat.

Reese licks me again, kissing me there. Pressing his tongue inside me even through the thin scrap of lace that separates us.

"Liv..."

"More," I breathe. "Please..."

"Like this?" He hooks my knickers aside and takes a long, sweeping lick, groaning as my taste hits his tongue. "So fucking good." He dives back in, flattening his tongue over my clit.

"Reese, ah..." My body bows off the blanket, demanding more as sensation riots inside of me.

"This pussy is mine," he murmurs, pushing two fingers deep as he continues tonguing my clit. "Now, tomorrow, and every day after that."

The sheer possession in his voice sends my heart careening in my chest. I want that—I want to be his. Always.

But I keep the words trapped behind my lips, only allowing myself to moan and cry out his name as he pushes me toward that invisible ledge.

"More... more..." I try to writhe against his mouth.

"I'm in control here," he hisses, nipping the soft flesh of my inner thigh with his teeth, sending a delicious sting through me.

My fingers tighten in his hair as he plunges his tongue inside me, circling my clit with his thumb, working me into a boneless, breathless mess.

"Reese, God... I'm coming... I'm... ahhh." My cries fill the night sky as Reese licks me through the waves of pleasure rippling through me.

When he's done, he crawls up my body and kisses me hard and bruising, forcing me to taste myself on his tongue.

"Was that enough grovelling for you?" he asks with a cocky smirk.

I lift a brow and smile sweetly as I say, "We'll see."

"God, Olivia, I can't get enough of you." Reese's hand slips down my body, drawing lazy circles on my hip.

We came into the tent a while ago, after he fed me more s'mores and then pulled me onto his lap and let me ride him.

It was intense, being above him, in control of every touch, every slide of our bodies. He didn't try to overpower me or flip the tables, he simply handed me the reins and let me use him.

"I want you again." I twist to look at him over my shoulder, meeting his hooded gaze. My hand dips between us as I reach for him, both of us naked under the blankets.

"Liv—"

"What are you scared of?" I ask, rolling over to face him. He's been different since we came inside the tent, like a wall has gone up between us

Cupping his cheek, I lean in to brush my lips over his.

"I keep thinking this can't be real. You can't actually be here with me, you can't want this. Want me."

"I'm here, Reese. And I want this. I want you."

Uncertainty flickers in his eyes and I hate that he doesn't trust my words or the connection between us.

His gaze dips and I whisper, "Reese..." Gripping his jaw, I force him to look at me. "I meant what I said before. I'm falling in love with you."

"Fuck, Liv. I don't—"

"Shh."

I replace my fingers with my lips, kissing away his doubts. I guess we both have a way to go to heal after everything that's happened. Reese was betrayed by his parents, the people he should have been able to rely on no matter what. Those kinds of scars need time to fade.

"I'm here," I whisper again, breathing the words onto his lips until I begin to feel the tension leave him.

But Reese still holds back, and I let out an exasperated sigh.

"What can I do?" I ask.

"Just you being here is enough." He gives me a weak smile.

Frustrated that things had taken a sombre turn, I decide to take matters into my own hands.

"What are you doing?" he asks as I slip out of the blanket and retrieve one of the yoga mats.

His heavy gaze follows me, making my stomach tighten as his eyes burn into my skin.

"You wanted me to teach you some yoga, so here goes nothing."

"But you're naked." He pushes up on one elbow, interest flaring in his gaze.

"Consider it motivation." I smirk, rolling out the mat and sitting down with my legs folded, my back straight, and my hands resting on my knees. "We call this the easy seat pose."

I take a couple of deep breaths, closing my eyes. There's something sensual about knowing he's watching me, his hungry gaze drinking in the sight of my naked body.

He clears his throat, sounding a little pained. "Just how flexible are you?"

I open my eyes and grin. "Want to find out?"

He nods, and I get to work, moving through pose after pose, making sure to add some extra sass to each one. A brush of my hand over my breast, a little sigh of relief as my muscles stretch and relax.

"Fuck, that's hot." Reese shifts closer, watching as I move my body through the cat pose into the cow pose.

Rising on his knees, he begins to come toward me but I pin him with a hard look. "This is the observation portion of the lesson. No touching."

"You're joking, right?" He gawks at me.

"Do I look like I'm joking? In a minute, you can have a go at some of the poses."

"What about together? Can we practise them together?"

My heart flutters wildly in my chest. Who knew yoga could be so sexy.

"If you're a good student, maybe you'll get rewarded."

I stand, moving into the downward facing dog pose, making sure to give him a full view of my arse.

"I think I died and went to heaven," he murmurs, and I glance back at him, smirking. "Are you teasing me, sweet cheeks?"

"Teaching you," I remind him, focusing on my breathing.

"How about now?" His body is suddenly behind me, his knuckles running up the backs of my thighs.

"Reese." I breathe, shivers zipping through every point of my body.

His hand keeps going, moving higher and higher until his fingers slide between my slick folds.

"Hmm, you really like yoga, don't you, Olivia?"

"I..." Reese bites my arse cheek, and I almost topple over but his hands grip my thighs, holding me steady.

"Do you think you can hold this pose while I make you come?"

God.

Wildfire licks my insides at the dark promise in his words.

"Answer me, Liv. Use your words."

"I— Mmm," I moan as his fingers make another pass over my core.

"Yeah, I want to eat you like this. And then I want you to show me all the ways you can bend and stretch."

"Oh God," I pant, my body trembling with anticipation.

"Not God, Liv. Your Heir. And it's time for this Heir to worship his Queen."

28

REESE

I sit back on my haunches, at eye level with her slick pussy. My mouth waters as I grip onto her arse hard enough to leave bruises tomorrow. The thought of finding my mark on her in the morning makes my cock jerk with need.

"Reese," she moans, holding herself in position but rocking her hips temptingly.

"Fuck, I can't resist you, Liv."

I lean forward, dragging one long sweep of my tongue from her clit right to her arse.

"Oh," she gasps, leaning forward a little as I take her by surprise.

"Don't move. You need to hold this pose until you've come all over my face. And then, I'll let you switch."

I dive forward again, sucking her clit into my mouth and grazing it with my teeth until her cries for more echo off the walls around us.

Her entire body trembles as she fights to keep herself up as her orgasm builds.

"Come for me, sweet cheeks," I growl against her, pressing

my thumb against her puckered hole. Her entire body stills at the sensation.

"R-Reese, I've never—"

"Shh... trust me, babe."

Her body rocks as she nods her agreement, and I push a little deeper. Her muscles clamp down on me and her pussy floods my mouth as I up the pressure on her clit and work her until she's screaming.

Unable to hold her position any longer, she crashes to her mat in a panting heap.

"That good?" I ask, watching as she fights to catch her breath.

"Th-that was... filthy."

"I thought you'd figure out by now that I am filthy, babe." The blush on her cheeks deepens as I watch her.

"So what's next?" I ask, wrapping my hand around my length and stroking slowly, wishing I was pushing into her body instead.

After a second, she rolls onto her back, plants her feet on the mat and lays her arms down by her sides.

"Not very original, but I'm not exactly fussy rig—" My word cut off as she tenses her glutes muscles and lifts her hips from the mat, basically offering herself up to me.

She stares at me as I remain kneeling. My heart beats so fast, I can feel it in every inch of my body, and there's so much fucking blood in my dick that my head spins.

"Fuck, Liv. I need you so bad."

Her brow quirks in amusement. "So what are you waiting for?"

"Fuck knows."

I shuffle over to her, my eyes locked on her in the hope that she can see the truth of everything I've said to her since we got here.

I come to a stop with her knees on either side of my hips and skim my hands down her thighs.

She shudders at my touch, her nipples puckering.

"You want me, babe?"

"You know I do."

"And you're confident that you can hold this?" I ask, moving forward and rubbing the head of my cock through her wetness.

"Y-yes," she breathes as I dip myself inside her ever so slightly, her muscles trying to suck me deeper.

"Fuck, I love how desperate you are for me."

"Please," she whimpers, her stomach muscles pulsating as she keeps herself in position.

I hold myself right at her entrance, teasing her with everything I can give her as I stare into her eyes.

"I missed you so much," I tell her honestly, my fingers squeezing her hips to help drive the point home.

"I-I need you."

"Only want me for one thing, huh?" I quip.

"I should after everything you've done. You were going to leave me."

I hang my head, although I don't rip my eyes from hers, needing her to see all my regrets, my shame.

"When I first got back here, yes, that was my plan. But as time went on, as we got closer, there was no way I'd have been able to go through with it."

"Where were you going to go?"

I sigh, hating that she wants to have this conversation right now, right as we're on the cusp of something so mind-blowing.

"I was moving money out of my trust fund so that I could rent a place far away from Saints Cross."

Pain flickers through her features as I say the words.

"I wouldn't have done it, Liv. I couldn't have left you."

"Why?"

"Because I—" Panic floods me and I swallow the rest of the words. "Because I need you. Because I need this, what we've found."

"I shouldn't forgive you."

"I know. You shouldn't, but I'm going to do everything I can to prove to you why you should."

Without warning, I thrust forward. I might have been the one to instigate this conversation, but I'm done now. I need actions, not words.

"Reese," she screams as the force of my movement sends her shooting up the yoga mat.

"Hold your position, babe. You can't release it until my cum is dripping out of your cunt."

"Filthy."

"You love it."

"Yeah," she confesses. "I think I do."

My grip on her hips tightens as I fuck her with abandon until sweat is trickling down my spine and my chest is heaving as I try to drag in the air I need.

Releasing one of my hands, I press my thumb against her clit. She almost instantly falls. Her back arches as her release rolls through her. Her pussy clamps down tightly on me, my name nothing but a plea on her lips.

Only seconds later, my balls draw up and my cock jerks, filling her up.

Leaning over her, I claim her lips in a wet and dirty kiss as my cock softens inside her. As I press my weight down on top of her, she finally crashes to the mat with a grunt.

"I'm impressed with your stamina, sweet cheeks," I confess against her lips.

"I'm still waiting to see yours."

"Oh yeah?" Reaching down, I hitch her leg up around my waist and roll my hips, my semi sending aftershocks through her.

"Show me what you've got, bad boy."

My phone buzzes, dragging me from sleep, and I groan as I reluctantly release Liv and blindly reach over to find it.

"Turn it off," Liv groans, wiggling against me, making my morning wood even harder.

This weekend has been perfect. Everyone knows where we are and they promised not to reach out unless it's an emergency, and there's only one person I'm expecting to hear from.

My heart drops as I think about what we need to do. But it has to happen. I need to prove to Liv how serious I am about our future together.

Lifting it in front of me, I blink a few times to clear my vision before the name I'm expecting appears before me.

> Abigail: Dad's back in town. Ready when you are.

Another text comes straight through.

> Abigail: I hope you've both had a good weekend.

Stuffing it back under my pillow, I curl myself around Liv again, burying my face in the crook of her neck and breathing her in.

"We're going to have to go back soon," I confess.

"Is your other woman calling?" she mutters lightly.

"There is no other woman on the face of the Earth, as far as I'm concerned."

"Such a smooth talker," she mutters as I shift us so that I can take her from behind.

She gasps as I push inside her.

"Sore?" I ask. It's entirely possible with how much time I've spent inside her this weekend.

Fuck, it feels good to be together. No lies or secrets or games. Just us and the truth. Well, almost. There are still a couple of words that seem to get stuck on my tongue every time I go to confess them.

"A little, but I'm sure I'll manage."

By the time we've packed up and left our little slice of heaven, I've made sure that Liv won't be able to forget me while I head off to do what I need to do the moment we get back into town.

"You're nervous." It's not a question, just a statement, proving how well she can read me.

"Yeah, I'm going to meet Abigail and her dad," I confess as we pull into the Beckworths' driveway.

"Oh?" she asks, turning toward me with wide eyes.

"It's time to get everything straight and set us both free."

A smile twitches at the corner of her lips, but she doesn't look as hopeful as I would like.

"Do you think it's possible?"

"We're about to find out."

Silence falls between us as we come to a stop and the engine cuts out.

"So I guess this is where we part, then."

"Nah, babe. I'm never leaving you, not ever. Let me deal with this, then I'm going to come back and take you out for dinner." She stares at me in disbelief. "What? I can take you out for a date, can't I?"

"I think I like this version of Reese Whitfield."

"Good, because I fucking love this version of Olivia Beckworth."

It's not until her eyes go all glassy that I even realise those words fell from my lips.

"Reese," she breathes as my heart picks up speed.

"I mean it. I fucking love you, Liv. I think a part of me always has. I was too dumb to see it."

"You mean you're no longer dumb?"

I can't help but laugh.

"I'll always make mistakes, Liv. But I promise to always talk to you about them so you can help steer me in the right direction."

"I think I like the sound of that," she says, reaching for my hand before leaning over to claim a kiss.

Leaving her is the last thing I want to do, but the second Liv pushes the door open and climbs out, I spot Oakley loitering in the window, not so discreetly watching us. With a heavy sigh, I let her go, knowing they need to talk.

With the two of them inside, I head back across town to meet Abigail. The second I pull up out the front of her house, she's stepping out of the front door.

"Hey," she says as I climb out, unable to miss the fact that she's not wearing any make-up. There's a part of me that likes that she doesn't feel like she needs to cover up, but equally, I hate that she feels the need to try and hide who she really is when she's at school. "How was it?"

"Amazing," I breathe, unable to keep the smile off my face.

"She heard you out?" she asks, sounding hopeful.

"Yeah, and then some."

Heat colours her cheeks and she looks away from me, embarrassed.

I might be becoming a lovesick fool, but I can't help hoping that she'll find someone who will make her feel like Liv makes me feel. She lights me up inside by being close. Her touch makes me burn from the inside out. Abigail deserves that too. It was never meant to be me.

"Ready for this? I ask when she fails to respond to my comment.

"Not really, no. My dad is... he's a formidable man."

"Yeah," I mutter. I've never actually spent any time with him, but I'm more than aware that Judge Bancroft is an enigma around town.

"He's in his office, come on."

Abigail leads me through her lavish house. The sheer size of it puts the Eatons' estate to shame. My eyes shoot everywhere as I follow her down the wide hallway.

She stops in front of a closed door, very briefly looks back at me, and lifts her hand to knock.

"Daddy?" she calls.

"Yes, sweetheart."

She sucks in a steeling breath before pushing the door open and stepping inside. "Hi, Daddy. We wondered if we could have a chat?"

"We?" Placing his pen down, Judge Bancroft slowly looks up. His eyes find his daughter first and his eyes light up with fondness, before they roll over to me.

Surprise flickers through his features before a smile settles on his lips, clearly getting the wrong idea about me and his daughter being in the same room.

"Yes, of course. What would you both like to discuss?"

Taking a step forward and holding herself tall, Abigail takes control of the situation as if she's been trained to do so. "We want you to forget about the deal you made with Mrs. Whitfield-Brown in regard to the two of us."

Judge Bancroft's brows shoot up in surprise, but he refrains from saying anything, instead allowing his daughter to continue with what she's come to say.

"We appreciate that you had an agreement, that you're only doing what you think is best… for me. But both Reese and I agree that we are completely incompatible, and he's in love with someone else. Someone," she quickly adds when his lips part, I guess to argue, "who is quickly becoming a good friend of mine. They belong together, Daddy. They love each other. And I'm so happy for them. I want it for them. I want it for myself too one day, but I know that Reese isn't the man who's going to give it to me. So please, we'd like you to reconsider allowing us to choose our own paths in life."

She falls silent and I swear you could hear a pin drop as

the atmosphere in the room turns so thick, I struggle to suck in my next breath.

By the time Judge Bancroft's lips part again, I'm sure I'm about to pass out with anticipation. "Well then," he leans back in his wingback chair, steepling his fingers, "it seems like you know exactly what you want out of your life, sweetheart. But..."

His expression drops. "I'm not sure it's going to be that easy."

29

OLIVIA

"Of all the guys in the world, it had to be Whitfield?" Oakley asks me as we sit in the den. I'm curled up on the soft leather sofa while he's sat rigid in one of the wingback chairs.

"We didn't plan it, Oak."

"Yeah, I know," he murmurs. "Doesn't make it any easier to hear."

"I love him. I'm in love with him."

"Fuck, Liv. That shit is going to take some getting used to. After what he did—"

"I'm not asking you to forgive him, Oakley. Not yet, at least. I know it'll take time, and I know there'll be an adjustment period. But it's him."

He's the one I want.

The one my heart and soul want.

"I hope you made him get on his fucking knees and grovel. Actually," the blood drains from his face, "don't answer that. I don't ever want to think about— shit, I need a drink."

"It's barely lunchtime," I chuckle.

"Yeah, well learning your sister and best friend are getting nasty between the sheets will do that to a guy."

"I need you to be okay with this, Oak," I whisper, my heart squeezing at the thought that he might not be able to get past it.

Reese has always been a thorn in mine and Oakley's relationship, but never like this. But I have to stay true to myself and what I want. Even if it causes a rift between us.

"I... fuck, Sis. I don't know what you want me to say."

Getting up, I go to him and perch on the roll arm of the chair. "I'm sorry." I reach for his hand.

"Yeah. I know. It's just... going to take some time."

"Promise me you won't go too hard on Reese."

"Fuck, Liv. You can't ask that of me. It's my prerogative as your brother to give your boyfriend shit."

"Fine. Just promise not to hurt his face again. I kind of like it." My lips twist with amusement, but Oakley looks less than impressed.

"Liv? Oak?" Dad calls. "Lunch is ready."

"I can't believe they're staging an intervention," I grumble.

When I'd gotten home earlier, Dad and Fiona requested that we all sit down and talk about things... together. Reese should be here soon, but I still haven't heard from him.

"Dad is on your side," Oak says as we stand.

"How do you know?"

"Because it's Dad and you're his favourite."

"I am not his—"

Oakley pins me with a knowing smile. "You're his daughter, Liv. All he wants is for you to be happy. Fiona, on the other hand... you might have a way to go persuading her that you and Reese are a good idea."

"Gee, thanks for the vote of confidence."

"Anytime, Sis. Any fucking time." His laughter follows me out of the room. We make our way down the hall to the kitchen, where we find Dad and Fiona talking in hushed conversation.

"Is Reese here yet?" Fiona asks, her voice edged with disapproval.

"No, I haven't—" Her mobile phone starts ringing and she frowns at the incoming call. "I need to take this."

She slips out of the kitchen and Dad ushers us to sit down. "Did you both have a good talk?"

"I think so." I glance at Oak and he smirks.

"I promised not to break Reese's face again. It's a start." He shrugs, helping himself to a piece of bread.

I check my phone again, wondering what could possibly be taking Reese so long.

He said he would sort it.

He said he and Abigail had a plan to set them free.

God, what if Judge Bancroft refused? What if—

"Hello?" Reese calls out, and relief floods me.

I practically scramble out of my chair to go and meet him. Oakley mutters something under his breath and I give him the bird before slipping into the hall.

"What happened?" I ask, studying Reese's expression for a clue. "Did he—"

"Reese, Olivia, come in here please."

He visibly flinches and my brows pinch. "Reese, what's going on?" My stomach sinks. "Why didn't you call—"

"Reese Baron Whitfield-Brown, get in this kitchen, now," his mum shouts, and Reese lets out a heavy sigh.

"Come on, let's get this over with." He takes my hand and tugs me toward the kitchen as dread snakes through me.

"Mum, Christian," he says as we enter the room. Oak flashes him a shit-eating grin as if the whole thing amuses him.

Arsehole.

"Sit. Down." Fiona notices our joined hands and narrows her eyes with disapproval.

"Fi," Dad says. "Let them—"

"Why don't you tell everyone what you did, Reese?"

We all sit, the air thick with tension.

"How do you know?" Reese asks her.

"Samuel Bancroft called me, thought I might like a heads up. Damn it Reese, you had no right. Not without talking to me first."

"Why does it matter?" he says. "I don't want to marry Abigail, and she sure as hell doesn't want to marry me."

"That wasn't your call to make."

"Why?"

"Excuse me?" Fiona blanches.

"Why did you broker that deal in the first place, Mum? What are you hiding?"

"Reese Baron—"

"Okay, okay. Why don't we all just take a breather?" Dad pats Fiona's hand, giving her a reassuring smile.

"He agreed?" I whisper to Reese, squeezing his hand under the table to command his attention. His dark gaze snaps to mine and he nods.

"He did. We're free."

"For God's sake, Reese. You can't—"

"Already did, Mum. We spoke to Judge Bancroft. He agreed. It's done."

"What did you promise him?" she asks quietly.

"What do you mean?"

"What did you offer him to make him renege on the deal?"

"N-nothing. We explained that we didn't want to go through with it. Abigail—"

She lets out a heavy sigh. "This was all to protect her..."

"Fi." Dad shakes his head. "It's not our place."

"Not your place to what?" Oakley pipes up.

"It doesn't matter, Son. What's important is that Judge Bancroft has cut Reese free so he and Olivia can—"

"Christian, be reasonable. They're family. One day they might be stepsiblings. It's—"

"Unconventional, yes. But you saw how miserable they both were. You know what it's like to..."

"Go on, say it." Reese stiffens beside me, anger and pain rolling off him.

"Reese, son, I didn't mean—"

"I know exactly what you meant, Christian."

"Christian, is right." Fiona lets out a weary sigh. "This isn't helping anything. But I have to ask, are you both absolutely sure this is what you want? You're so young and—"

"We know," I say, clutching Reese's hand in mine. "At least, I know." My eyes find his again and his expression softens a fraction.

"She's it for me," he confesses.

"And let me guess, you're going to pursue this thing between you with or without my blessing?" Fiona fixes her attention on her son.

He doesn't look at her as he nods and says, "I won't walk away from Liv. Not again."

"Very well, then. You're eighteen now, I suppose I have to accept your decision. But don't think we're done talking about the fact that you've been siphoning money out of your trust, young man."

"Good. When we talk about that, we can also talk about Dad and Krystal."

Fiona's whole demeanour changes, hurt flashing in her eyes.

"You two clearly have a lot to talk about," Dad, ever the peacekeeper, says. "But right now, I would like to sit and eat a nice lunch with my family. And yes, Reese, that includes you. We all make mistakes, son. I trust you won't be making any more anytime soon."

"Uh, no, I don't plan on it." He almost chokes over the words and Oakley explodes with laughter.

"You should see your face."

"Fuck off, Beckworth."

"Make me, Whitfield."

I let out an exasperated groan, and they both look at me. "Is this how it's going to be now?"

"Probably," Oak shrugs as Reese mutters, "Yeah, until he stops being a dickhead."

"Language," Fiona scolds. "Maybe we should reschedule lunch," she suggests.

"Better get used to it, darling." Dad smiles at her. "This is only a snippet of things to come. Wait until Oakley meets the girl of his dreams."

"Yeah, never going to happen," he murmurs, stuffing a stick of pepper into his mouth.

"What about Tally?"

"Tally?" He balks. "As in Tallulah fucking Darlington?"

"Language," Dad and Fiona both snap.

"Yeah, why not? Something tells me she'd give you a run for your money."

Reese sniggers.

"Nah, she's not my type. Besides, I'm not ready to settle down."

Dad chuckles. "That's the thing about love, Son. It strikes when you least expect it." His warm gaze falls on me, and it's then that I know everything is going to be okay.

Things might be messy and strained and weird for a while, but ultimately, we're family.

And we'll ride out this storm as a family should.

Together.

"Jesus, Liv. Do you have any idea how fucking good your pussy feels clenched around me?" Reese thrusts into me slowly, punching his hips in the most perfect way.

"Quiet," I chide. "We need to be quiet." His hand slides around my jaw and covers my mouth as he fucks me from behind over the sink vanity.

He drops his mouth to my neck, his eyes fixed right on mine in the mirror.

"Look at you," he murmurs, biting down and making me gush around him.

"Reese." My muffled cry is drowned out by his palm.

"I love your body... your pussy, the way you grip me like a fucking vice." He slides out and pushes back in, teasing me, his fingers curling around my hip.

I'll have bruises but I don't care. I need him. I want him like this. Raw and real and unfiltered.

"It's a shame Oak didn't stick around. We could have had some fun taunting him."

"Reese!" I nip his hand and he collars my throat, bringing his mouth to my ear.

"I'm thinking he doesn't believe I'm serious about you. About us, Liv. Maybe he needs proof. Maybe he needs to hear you screaming my name over and over to really drive the point home."

"Oh God." An intense wave crashes over me as my legs tremble.

"That's it, babe. Give it to me."

Reese lets me have it—hard, brutal thrusts that drag out my orgasm until I'm whimpering uncontrollably, murmuring his name like a whispered prayer.

"You're mine, Olivia." He kisses my collarbone, still watching me in the mirror.

Watching us.

"I want it all."

"Yours," I breathe. "Yours."

"Fuck." He drives into me and stills, holding me as close as possible while he fills me up.

Fisting my hair, he drags my face up to his and kisses me with so much intensity, my heart swells in my chest. "I love you, sweet cheeks. So fucking much."

"I love you too, Reese."

"No regrets?" he asks, his body shuddering against mine.

"I..." The words get stuck in my throat as I consider his question.

Our relationship isn't born out of truth and honesty, it's forged from pain and heartache, lies and games...

But sometimes, you have to walk through the flames to get to the other side.

Pulling his face down to mine, I kiss him. Once. Twice.

And then, I whisper against his lips, "No regrets."

30

REESE

"Be quick," Liv says as I kiss her shoulder and roll out of bed.

We haven't ventured out of this room since we managed to get out of the family lunch Mum and Christian insisted on. We had no need to when all we wanted was each other. But as the hours have gone on, hunger has started to get the better of both of us. We decided against that date I'd promised Olivia—for now, at least—in favour of hanging out in bed together.

It's late. Too late really to be sneaking down to the kitchen like a naughty child for midnight snacks, but fuck it.

My girl has officially exhausted me, and I need some fuel.

The lights in the hallway went out an hour or so ago, letting us know that Mum and Christian had gone to bed, and unsurprisingly Oak never reappeared to hang out with us.

Pulling on a pair of sweats, I slip into the bathroom to take a piss before heading downstairs on my mission.

I promised my girl something decent to snack on, and I fully intend to deliver.

The house is in darkness as I make my way to the kitchen. If I were in our old house, I'd be able to do this in the dark. I knew that place like the back of my hand. Knew where to find everything, which floorboards creaked and which windows were the easiest to break out of.

I might have spent almost as much time here as I did at home, but I never learned it quite the same. Instead, I relied on Oak to worry about escape plans, food and alcohol runs.

The second I step over the threshold, I slide my hand up the wall to find the light switch. My eyes burn with the brightness, but that's soon forgotten when a figure nursing a glass of whisky at the breakfast bar makes my stomach jump into my throat.

"What the fuck are you doing?" I bark, glaring at Mum while my heart thrashes wildly in my chest.

"Can't sleep."

"So you thought you'd sit there in the dark, waiting to scare the shit out of someone?"

"Language, Son," she chastises. Honestly, I don't know why she bothers. She's been trying since I was about thirteen so far and it's made very little difference to the words that come out of my mouth.

Ignoring her, I march forward, more than happy to grab what I need and leave her to it.

"Would you like a drink?" she offers, making me pause halfway across the room.

"Do I want a drink, or do I want to sit and drink with you?"

Hurt flicks across her face, but she locks it down fast. "With me. I think it's time we talked, don't you?"

Flashbacks of finding her with Christian all those months ago and then Dad with Krystal recently fill my mind and anger swirls in my belly.

Talking about it is the last thing I want, especially while my girl is upstairs in her bed, naked and waiting for me.

My lips part to say no, but then she gives me a look that

makes me feel like a little boy and I find myself moving toward her and taking a seat.

She grabs another tumbler off the tray beside her and pours me a generous helping of whisky as if she knows I'm going to need it to hear what she wants to say to me.

I'm not sure if I'm relieved or downright terrified of what I'm about to be forced to listen to.

"I'm sorry, Reese," she says, pushing the glass over. "You were never meant to find out everything you did... the way you did."

"You mean, I was never meant to walk in on both my parents fucking other people? Right, I'll remember that."

"Reese, please," she sighs.

"No, don't try to placate me. You both fucked up here, Mum."

"I know. And I'll take full responsibility for the fact that we should have sat you down and talked to you sooner."

"Christian said—"

"I love your father, Reese. I always have. But it's been a long time since I tried to convince myself that I was in love with him."

"Why didn't you do the right thing when you figured it out?"

"Because I couldn't. I'm Jeremy Brown's daughter. I'd made my wedding vows, and in his eyes, that was how it had to stay. You know your grandfather was traditional to his very core."

"So screwing around on your marriage was better than a divorce so that you could both be happy?"

"We weren't screwing around. We both knew the deal."

"I'm not sure if that makes it any better or worse. How long was Dad sleeping with Krystal, Mum?" I ask, wondering if she'll give me the same answer that Krystal did.

She swallows nervously.

"All those times she came for dinner, to my birthday

parties, for Christmas. All the times I called her aunt. She was banging Dad, wasn't she?"

"Yes, but we were happy, Reese. We made it work. And that's all we ever wanted for you, a happy family."

"But it was all a lie."

"No," she argues. "The love we have for each other was real, and the love we have for you is real. Maybe it wasn't conventional, but it worked for us."

"You should have been honest. I get that maybe you couldn't do it while Grandad was alive. I understand the high expectations he had of you. But after he was gone, I was old enough to understand. All you had to do was tell me, I—"

"We were going to," she assures me.

"Well, you weren't fast enough. Watching you get fucked against a wall, and then Krystal grinding down on Dad were both things I never, ever needed to see."

Her cheeks turn such a bright shade of red, I'm surprised her head doesn't go up in flames.

"We're sorry, Reese. For all of it. We handled it badly, just like you did."

"Oh no, don't turn this on me. I fucked up, I know that." I really fucking know it, and I'll spend a lot of time trying to make up for it. For ever hurting Olivia the way I have. "But it all could have been prevented if you trusted me with the truth. I might not show it, but all I want for the both of you is to be happy, and if you'd explained the situation, then yeah, it might have been hard to swallow, but I'd have understood. People change, I fucking get that."

She hangs her head in shame while I throw back the measure she poured for me.

Silence falls between us, and I push the stool back ready to put an end to this, but Mum's next words stop me.

"You shouldn't have gone to Judge Bancroft like that today."

"Why not, Mum? It wasn't like you were doing anything to

get me out of it. You can't actually believe that it would have worked, that Abigail was the girl for me. You just described what happens in a marriage where love isn't enough to conquer all. What did you expect us to do? Put up with each other until he died and then go our separate ways?"

I don't need her answers to confirm that that was exactly her plan.

"He's sick, Reese. He's..." She winces. "Not going to be around forever. I hoped that... maybe... you wouldn't have to fulfil your obligation."

"You hoped he would die before we got married, is that what you're saying? That's messed up."

She shrugs, guilt covering her face.

"But why, Mum? Why sign me away like a prize fucking cow when you knew I wouldn't want it?"

"Because I didn't have a choice," she finally confesses.

My eyes narrow as I study her. "What really happened between you and Judge Bancroft, Mum?" A trickle of unease rolls down my spine.

Reaching for the bottle, she refills her glass. "It's complicated, but I didn't have a choice. I needed something..."

"It was bribery, wasn't it?" I ask when she trails off, clearly not willing to talk about it.

"He wanted to make sure Abigail is looked after when he's gone and I... well, I needed him to make something go away."

It all starts to click into place. "A case," I spit, anger flooding my veins. "You signed my life away for a fucking case? Unbelievable."

"In the world we live in, Reese, people don't always play by the rules. Sometimes you have to fight fire with fire."

"That's not an excuse," I mutter, disbelief coursing through me.

"One day, Reese, you'll have kids of your own, and you'll understand the lengths you'd go to protect them. To give them the life they deserve."

Pushing the stool out behind me, I take a step back. "You know, I really, really hope I don't." I can't imagine I would ever understand why any parent would want to force their child into something they didn't want.

"I'm going back to bed," I say quietly, half hoping she doesn't hear me.

"Your bed, I assume."

"We'll see," I mutter under my breath before taking the stairs two at a time to get back to my girl.

The TV is still illuminating the room when I slip back inside, but when I turn the corner, I find Liv is no longer watching it and is instead slumped down, fast asleep.

Finding the remote in the sheets, I turn it off, plunging us into darkness, drop my sweats and slip in beside her.

She moans as the heat of my body presses up against hers, aligning myself with her and wrapping my arm around her waist, holding her tight.

Dropping my lips to her shoulder, I whisper, "I love you, Olivia."

"Love you too, Reese," she says sleepily, snuggling back into me. "Everything okay with your mum?" she asks, telling me that she snuck out to see what was keeping me.

"Yeah, everything is good, sweet cheeks."

Walking into All Hallows' the next morning with my fingers intertwined with Liv's and Oak, Theo, and Elliot following us is surreal.

I thought Elliot was going to shit a cactus when I turned up with her in tow for breakfast at the Chapel this morning. But if he thinks I'm going to be hanging out there without my girl, then he should really reconsider giving me my key, because we come as a package deal now.

With every step we take, more and more eyes land on us.

Students whisper to their friends, pointing us out. And by the time we get into the building, I've heard the words stepbrother, wrong, and off-limits more than I ever thought I would.

But fuck their judgement. The only person's opinion I care about now is the girl at my side, and Liv continues to walk through the crowd with her head held high, letting all their opinions roll off her. Pride for my girl swells within me, just like it did the day I watched her and Abigail soak up the praise for their stunt that got Darcie Porter suspended.

Her absence is only temporary, unlike that fucker Starling, who has been shipped off to some private school up north for troubled kids, which apparently has a reputation for its military-style treatment of its more-than-deserving students. That motherfucker is in for a world of pain. Couldn't happen to a more deserving person, if you ask me.

"Liv," a female voice calls before Abigail's red hair flashes in the crowd before she and Tally bounce toward us.

"It's too early for fucking Barbie and her playmate," Oak complains behind us.

"Shut up," Liv snaps before greeting her friends with a wide smile.

"So the rumours are true then?" Tally asks sceptically.

She's happy for Liv, that much is obvious. But their new friendship means that she's going to be hanging around us more. And I'm not sure there's anything on Earth that Tally Darlington hates more than the Heirs, or more specifically, Oakley Beckworth.

The Darlington and Beckworth rivalry isn't anything new. They've been battling in the courtrooms for years, and since we all started school, Oak and Tally seem to have followed in the footsteps of their fathers by rubbing each other up the wrong way at every possible opportunity.

She's done everything she can to strip us of power over the years, but seeing as she doesn't have all that much sway, even now she's been elected Head Girl, she's never really succeeded at anything.

But even though we've got a connection to her through Liv, I can still see that need for her to ruin us burning bright in her eyes.

"What's up, Darlington?" Theo asks, wrapping his arm around her shoulder, much to her disgust. "You look a little uptight. Those goody two shoes boys not quite hitting the spot? You know what you need— Ow," he grunts when she elbows him impressively hard in the ribs, forcing him to back up.

"If you so much as suggest anything that involves you touching me again, then you're going to regret it."

"Leave Prim alone. She's too stuck up and frigid to be any fun," Oak grunts.

"Oh, bro. You know as well as I do that breaking the innocent ones can be the wildest."

"Don't you three have somewhere to be?" Liv hisses, glaring at her brother.

"You know what will get rid of him?" I whisper in Liv's ear. But before she has a chance to answer, I back her up against the closest wall, hitch her leg up around my hip and slam my lips down on hers.

"Oh, for the love of fucking God. I can't watch this shit. Let's go," Oak growls while Liv chuckles against me.

Long before I'm ready to break the kiss, the sound of their retreating footsteps disappears and Liv presses her hands to my chest, forcing me to back up.

"You can't do that every time he's being a numpty," Tally says with a smirk.

"A numpty?" I ask, fighting a laugh.

"You know, using foul language doesn't actually make you cool, or hard," she sneers.

"Nah, the only thing that makes me hard is my girl."

"Oh my God." Tally throws her arms up in disgust, but

surprisingly Abigail stands there, silently laughing at her friend. She really is coming out of herself, and I can't help but think there's a pretty awesome person hiding behind her mask.

"I can't do this. I've got a student council meeting to prepare for." Tally scurries off without a backward glance.

"Everything went okay with your mum then, I take it?" Abigail asks once the three of us are alone.

"She was pretty pissed, but yeah, all good. What about you?"

"Yeah, yeah. Everything's great. Not being shackled to you sure is a weight off my shoulders."

"Harsh, Abs. Harsh," I chuckle as the bell rings, and we all move toward where we're meant to be.

Which sadly means I need to part ways with my girl—but not until we've made use of another wall, and I send her into her first class gasping for air, my name a plea on her lips and a promise of what's going to come later.

31

OLIVIA

"Abi, Tally, this is Charli. Charli, these are my new friends."

"I love your hair," Charli says to Abigail, who shrinks under the attention.

"Uh, thanks."

I smile at Abi. I know what she's thinking. Why isn't Charli staring at her scars?

"And you. Tallulah Darlington. I remember you."

A ripple goes through the air as the two girls lock eyes. I half-expected Tally not to show. Things were a little weird today at school. She still hung around with me and Abigail at break, but I could tell being around the Heirs makes her uncomfortable. Especially my brother.

"Never expected to see you fraternising with the enemy." Charli's eyes slide to mine and then back to Tally.

"Olivia isn't an Heir," she points out.

"True. But she's with one now and related to one. How's that going to work out?"

"Charli!" I hiss.

"Relax, Liv. I'm only looking out for you. For all we know, she's using you to plot her revenge on them."

"I'm not."

"I hope for your sake that's true." Charli flashes her a feral grin, and for a second, I think Tally might bolt.

But she sits back in her chair and smirks. "I like you."

"Yeah, well the jury is still out on you." Charli picks up her menu like she didn't just issue Tally a veiled warning. What's good?" she asks.

"Everything," Abigail answers.

"Sorry about her," I whisper to Tally.

"It's fine. I get it. I've always been a bitch to you."

"I wasn't exactly friendly in return."

"I don't agree with a lot of what the Heirs get away with, that will never change. But I am glad we got to know each other, Liv. I need you to know that."

"I do. Just promise me you won't go after them. It'll make things hella awkward between us if you go to war with them."

"I'm Head Girl, people expect me to—"

"Tally, if you go after them, it won't end well."

"Fine." She huffs, giving her menu her full attention.

"I've never seen so many types of cake," Charli says. "How the hell am I supposed to choose?"

"The red velvet is amazing. The carrot cake, and raspberry and coconut are up there too. Then you've got the coffee and walnut, funfetti, and lemon cake. All solid options."

Charli gawks at Tally like she's grown a second head.

"What?" Tally shrugs. "I like cake."

My phone vibrates and I dig it out of my pocket, smiling at the sight of Reese's name.

"Oh God," Charli groans. "She has that look."

"No, I don't."

"Hate to break it to you, Liv," Tally sniggers. "But you do."

"You so do," Abigail adds.

> Reese: Just got done with practise. Heading back to the Chapel for some boys' time. See you later?

> Olivia: Yeah, okay. I'm at Dessert Island with the girls.

> Reese: Have some cake for me. Better yet, get a slice to go and we can have some fun with it later.

> Olivia: Reese!

My cheeks heat as I shield my screen from prying eyes.

> Reese: What? I'm craving cake… and pussy. Your pussy. I'm sure we can make it work.

> Olivia: Filthy boy.

> Reese: You haven't seen nothing yet, sweet cheeks. I have this fantasy of you wearing my rugby shirt and nothing else and me fucking you all over the Chapel.

> Olivia: I think Elliot, Theo, and my brother would have something to say about that.

> Reese: You're probably right. We could always go for a little trip into the woods and finish what we started all those weeks ago.

I ponder his words. Maybe I've lost it or maybe I'm blinded by love. But my fingers fly across the screen as I fight a smile.

> Olivia: The throne. I want you to fuck me on that stupid, ridiculous throne.

> Reese: Fuck. Yeah okay. Although now I'm going to have a serious fucking hard-on while we're playing Xbox, thinking about you riding me.

"Liv?" Charli barks, and my head snaps up.

"Yeah?"

"Three times. I asked you three times what you want to order."

"Sorry. I was—"

"Sexting Reese, if the colour of your cheeks is any indicator."

"I wasn't—" Her brow lifts and the words die on the tip of my tongue. "Sorry."

"At least one of us is getting some."

"What's it like?" Abigail asks, surprising the crap out of us. "Sex, I mean."

Tally and I both look at Charli and she rolls her eyes. "Don't look at me. I'm not the one fucking an Heir."

"You have such a way with words," I groan.

"Yeah, but you love me." She smirks. "Sex can be really, really good or really fucking awful. It all depends on who you're doing it with. Take him, for example." Charli points to a guy seated across from us. "He looks like he'd be a wham bam thank you man kinda time. But hottie behind the counter?" she swings her gaze to the guy that Tally talked to on the way in. "He looks like he'd give you the ride of your life."

"Callum?" Tally says. "He has a serious girlfriend."

"Shame," Charli snorts, and we all burst out laughing. Even Abigail.

This is nice.

Being here with my friends. Talking about boys and sex and all the things eighteen-year-old girls should be talking about.

"What are the guys up to?" Charli asks, mischief sparking in her eyes.

"Why?"

"Because I was thinking after we get done here... we should go say hi to them."

"Charli, I'm not sure that's a good idea."

"Sounds like a great idea to me," Tally says, making my eyes widen in shock.

"I should probably ask Reese."

"Nah, we can surprise them." Charli grins. "We can take them cake."

Oh God.

I fight another smile.

If only she knew.

"I'm not sure about this," I say as we reach the Chapel. My heart is a wild thing in my chest, beating erratically as Charli nudges me toward the door.

"What's the worst that can happen?" she asks.

"We could find them all balls deep in Heir chasers?" Tally scoffs.

My stomach plummets. He wouldn't.

Reese would never—

"Relax." Tally touches my arm. "I didn't mean Reese."

"They said they were playing Xbox."

"Boring." Charli grabs the ornate knocker and raps it on the door.

A minute later, the door swings open and Oakley appears. "What the fuck?"

"Surprise." Charli thrusts a takeout bag at him. "We brought you cake."

"Cake? What? Liv, what the hell are you doing here?"

"Bad time?" Tally says coolly.

"Yeah," he drawls. "I was just about to fuck..."

I suck in a breath, hoping he's not about to say what I think he is. "The guys over on COD."

"Cod?" Abigail frowns. "You're playing fishing games?"

He gawks at her, shaking his head, and Charli and Tally

use his momentary disbelief to slip past him and enter the Chapel.

Oakley lets out a frustrated groan, pinning me with a hard look. "You thought this would be a good idea, why exactly?"

"I don't know. The girls thought we could all bond."

"Bond? With Tally Darlington? Have you forgotten she's had it out for us since... forever?"

"I think we were wrong about her," I say.

He makes a derisive sound in his throat. "Well, you can deal with her. And Elliot, when he realises you're gatecrashing gaming night." He storms off into the house but pauses at the last second, glancing back. "And Liv?"

"Yeah?"

"No fucking Reese in the Chapel. I love you both, but I swear to God, if I ever catch the two of you—"

"Beckworth."

Reese's voice rolls through me like thunder, sending a shiver down my spine. Our eyes collide and the faintest of smiles traces his mouth.

"Hi."

"Hi."

"Fuck's sake," Oakley mutters, grabbing Abigail's hand. "Come on, Abs. Let's leave the lovebirds to it."

Reese takes a step closer, the air growing thin around us. "You're here."

"I'm here." His brows pinch, and I add, "We brought cake."

"You did, huh?" Desire and hunger swirl in his eyes as he reaches for me, cupping my face. "I missed you this afternoon."

"It was only a few hours."

"A few too many." Reese dips his head, fixing his mouth over mine and kissing me. Tiny sparks of electricity shoot off round my body, my skin vibrating with need.

"Hi," he breathes.

"Hi."

"Fuck, Liv. The things I want to do to you." He touches his head to mine.

"We can't," I sigh. "Not here. Oakley will kill you."

"It'd be worth it though." A wicked glint lights up Reese's eyes.

"Yo, lovebirds," Elliot bellows from the living room. "Get in here before Tally and Oak kill each other."

"Oh, shit," Reese chuckles, pressing a kiss to my forehead. "Later," he promises.

I smile, emotion clogging my throat. "I'll hold you to that."

"Oh my God, we did it. We beat you." Tally holds up her hand to high-five Charli, the lads looking dumbfounded at the girls' domination of their silly video game.

"That's not... how is that even possible?" Oak asks. "Are you sure you two haven't played this before?"

"Seriously?" Charli frowns. "We're not that lame."

"I'm hungry," Reese whispers, pulling me closer into his side. "For cake and—"

"Stop." Heat flows through me, making my stomach curl.

It's been nice, being here at the Chapel with them. Charli and Tally give as good as they get where the lads are concerned, which is probably a good thing considering the simmering animosity between my brother and Tally.

I smile to myself. I know how easily hatred can turn to something else, and I can't help but wonder if maybe another Heir will lose his head and heart over a girl soon.

"What's that look for?" Reese asks, his lips brushing the shell of my ear.

"Nothing. Just thinking..."

"Am I going to have to tickle it out of you?" His fingers dig into my waist and I smother a yelp.

Everyone glances in our direction.

"What?" I feign innocence.

"I can't believe I've got to spend the rest of the year watching my sister and my best friend get off with each other." Oak rubs his jaw.

"Fuck off, Beckworth. You're only jealous."

"Dude, that's my sister. My sister..."

"Yeah, and later I'm going to balls deep inside her and—"

Theo snorts. "You're asking to get your arse beat, Whitfield."

"Nah, Oak's all talk. Now we've got Mum and Dad's blessing, he can't touch me." Reese kisses the side of my neck, his arms tightening around me.

"Fucking wanker," Oakley mutters, getting up and padding out of the room.

"Don't be a dickhead, Reese," Elliott warns.

"What? He started it."

"He kind of has a point."

"What do you want us to do? Pretend we're not a thing? Because fuck that."

"Just... tone it down a bit, yeah? Let him come to terms with it before you ram it down his throat. We still have the rest of the season to get through. I'd like my two favourite players not to be at each other's throats every time we get on the pitch."

"What do you mean, your two favourite players?" Theo pipes up.

"Relax, Ashworth. You're my third favourite."

"Prick. That's not what you were saying when we played golf last weekend."

"Hold up, you played without us?" Oak pokes his head around the door. "What the fuck?"

"You don't even like golf, Beckworth." Theo shrugs. "Besides, we don't all have to be kissing each other's arses all the time, you know."

The girls all laugh.

I cuddle closer to Reese, still hardly able to believe we've made it to this point.

A second later, Oakley approaches us.

"What the hell is that?" Theo asks, and my brother drops some boxes into my lap.

"Oak!" I blush, staring at the boxes of condoms.

"You two want to go at it like rabbits, then be my guest. But I swear to God, Whitfield, if you knock her up anytime soon, I will fucking kill you."

"Oh shit," Theo chuckles.

"I can't believe you did that," I say, my cheeks on fire.

Elliot meets my eyes and gives me a wolfish smile. "You really are one of us now, Liv. Better get used to it."

32

REESE

"Reese, you need to go," Olivia breathes between kisses.

I found her—okay, stalked her—after her last class of the day and dragged her into an empty classroom so that I could have some much-needed alone time with my girl.

"I know, I know," I confess, kissing down her neck and sucking on the soft skin beneath her ear.

I'm still inside her after taking her against the wall, but despite only filling her up seconds ago, my cock is already hardening for a second round.

"Elliot is going to kill you for being late," she moans as I squeeze her tits through her school shirt.

"Fuck, Eaton. He'd understand if he had access to your pussy."

I pull my head back in time to see her brow quirk at my words.

"Okay, not your pussy. This is mine, and only mine," I say circling my hips, making her muscles tighten around me. "Some other girl's pussy."

"You really think he's going to let someone past that cold mask he wears?" she scoffs as her pupils continue to dilate.

"Yeah, I have no doubt someone will wiggle their way in. Now, are you done thinking about one of my best friends while my dick is inside you?"

"Umm..." she teases. "I'm not sure. Maybe you should remind me why I should only be thinking about you."

"I thought you were worried about me being late."

"Well, you already are now. What's a few more minutes?"

"My filthy, filthy girl. You just want to make sure someone catches us fucking in here, don't you?"

She shakes her head, but her body betrays her as her pussy gushes around me.

I take her chin in my grasp and hold her eyes captive as my hips piston. "You love it, don't you?"

She nods—well, as much as she's able to with my tight hold on her face.

"Good. Because I fucking love you."

"Reese," she moans as I drop my hands to her arse and drag her lower half from the wall, leaving her at the angle I want. "Oh shit."

"Fuck, yeah. Look at you taking my cock at school like a good girl."

She gushes again.

"I want to see you playing with your clit, babe. Then I'm going to fill you so full of my cum that you'll be walking around feeling me inside you for the rest of the day."

"Fuck, your mouth."

"Maybe later, filthy girl."

Whoops and hollers go up around the locker room when I eventually stumble my sated arse and spent cock inside.

"What fucking time do you call this, bellend?" Oak calls the second he looks over.

"Sorry, man. You know how it is." I wink, shamelessly

lifting my hand and sucking the two fingers I had inside his sister not so long ago into my mouth.

"You're a fucking cunt, Whitfield," he scoffs.

"You're also fucking late," Elliot fumes.

"Oh, keep your frilly fucking knickers on, Eaton. I'm here now, aren't I? And not all of you are ready, so I don't know why you're having a bitch fit."

He rolls his eyes at me but steps aside so that I can make my way to my locker.

Sniggers and excitement bubble up behind me, making my hackles rise, and I soon find out why they're acting like a group of pre-teens looking at their first pair of tits.

"You motherfuckers," I grunt the second my locker comes into view.

Pinned across the front of it is a banner with 'pussy-whipped' written across it, and the entire thing is covered in bows and streamers.

Laughter erupts behind me as I step toward it and rip it all off.

"What? So you're okay with the disgusting PDA all over school, but this pisses you off?" Oak asks, the amusement in his tone telling me that this is his handiwork.

"I couldn't give a fuck who knows that I've handed your sister my balls, Oak."

His jaw pops at my words. He's going to get used to it one day, but fuck, I really hope he doesn't, because winding him up about it is too much fun.

With everything littering the floor, I reach for the locker and pull it open. I regret it instantly when glitter and streamers float down around me.

"Wait, wait," Theo says, coming up behind me. "There's one more thing."

Something scratches the top of my head, and when I glance over my shoulder, I find that he's pinned a fucking veil into my hair. Before I can stop him, he thrusts a fake bouquet at me too.

"I'm going to fucking kill the lot of you," I hiss, clutching the bouquet like a fucking idiot.

But despite my irritation, I can't fight the smile that spreads across my lips as my eyes move between my boys.

Coming back here for the beginning of the school year was the last thing I wanted. Being pulled back into this world seemed akin to Hell. But the reality is that it's where I belong —surrounded by my best friends, with my girl by my side.

Saints Cross might be one fucked-up town, but there's nowhere else I'd rather be.

"Hey, Oak," I call, and he glances back at me.

"Yeah?"

"Catch." The bouquet flies through the air and he catches it, brows pinched in confusion.

"What the fu—"

"Congratulations, dickhead." I wink. "It's your turn next."

EPILOGUE

Olivia

"I can't believe I let you talk me into this," Tally frowns, downing yet another shot.

"I'm glad you came," I say. "But maybe you should go easy on those."

"Pfft," she snatches up another off the tray. "If I'm going to survive a party at the Chapel, I need alcohol, Liv. Lots and lots of alcohol. Just don't let me do anything stupid, okay?" She gives me a serious but slightly glazed look. "I'm trusting you. I do not want to end up giving my virgin—"

Tally's eyes widen in horror. "Oh my god. Forget I said that. Please god, forget."

I chuckle. "There's nothing wrong with being a virgin, Tally."

"Ssh. Keep your voice down." She glances around the room. "The last thing I need is your brother and the Heirs learning that I'm... that. They'll never let me live it down."

"I'm sure none of them care about your sexual history."

"Come on, I want to dance." Tally grabs my hand and tugs me toward where the other girls are dancing. A couple of Darcie's friends shoot me a look of disdain but I let it roll off my back. They don't like that I'm here, with Reese, but they can suck it. I've always been close to the Heirs but now I get to call one mine.

Victory never tasted sweeter. Although I have to put up with my fair share of Heir chasers since I'm around the lads more. It's a small price to pay for loving Reese though.

"Hmm," a pair of hands slide around waist, "you look far too sexy to dancing alone."

"Reese," I breathe, leaning back into his strong body. A body I know almost as well as my own.

"Seriously, you two. Can't you keep your hands off each other for more than—" Tally goes rigid, clapping a hand over her mouth.

"You okay there, Darlington?" Reese asks.

"Fine." She swallows. "I think I need some air."

"I'll come with by you," I say.

"No, no. I'll be fine." Waving me off she starts weaving through the sea of bodies.

"I should probably go after—"

"Relax". Reese kisses the curve of my shoulder. "No one here would dare touch her."

I crane my neck, gazing up at him. "How can you be so sure?"

"She's your friend. And you're my girl. Anyone would have to have a death wish to touch something that belongs to me, even by proxy."

"Hmm, I like it when you talk dirty to me."

"That's because you're filthy, sweet cheeks." Reese kisses me, turning me in his arms so he can run his hands all over my ass.

"Get a fucking room," Oakley yells from somewhere behind us, and I chuckle.

"You think he'd be used to us by now."

"Don't give a shit, Liv. I love you and not even your brother can take that away from me."

After a while of dancing and kissing with Reese, I go in search of Tally. He's right, anyone would have to be stupid to try something on with Tally, but it doesn't mean she hasn't fallen over in a bush or passed out somewhere.

God, I should have switched her to water sooner. But we all need a blow out occasionally and it can't be easy being Tally Darlington, head girl, daughter of the straight and narrow Mr. Darlington.

"Have you seen Tally?" I ask Elliot in passing.

"No. Why?"

"She went to get some fresh air but it's been a while."

"You need me to come look for her with you?"

"No, I'm sure she's okay. Probably making friends with some of the first years."

"Shout if you need me."

I smile. Elliot is... well, he's still he usual cold, guarded self. But he treats me with respect and has accepted Abigail and Tally's presence in our lives thanks to my blossoming friendship with them both.

I slip out of the Chapel, ignoring the debauchery going on around me. You get used to it after a while.

"Tally?" I call, scanning the tree line. It's dark and eerie out here, always has been.

Rustling catches my attention over by the trees and I take off in that direction. "Tal—"

She staggers out of the trees, covered in mud.

"What the hell happened to you?"

"Funny story," she cackles, barely holding herself together.

Jesus, she's drunker than I realised.

"I wandered down here and Oak—"

"Hey, Liv." My brother appears out of the darkness and I gawk at them both.

"What the hell is going on?"

Because this looks bad... it looks just like the time Reese and I had a moment in the woods before the summer.

"Did the two of you-"

"What? Fuck, no," Oakley hisses. "She's wasted. I saw her wander out here and tried to talk to her into coming inside." He runs a hand through his hair. "She tripped and fell. This was the result."

"It's true." Tally hiccoughs. "I fell."

I study them a little closer. Tally is drunk. Too drunk. And Oak seems a little skittish. But then he's probably drunk and high.

"I'll leave you to deal with her," he says, stalking off toward the house muttering something about' 'girls who can't handle their alcohol'.

"Are you sure you're okay?" I ask Tally, hooking my arm around her waist.

"Me?" Another hiccough. "I'm fine. But my outfit is ruined."

"Come let's get you cleaned up. We can use Reese's room. I keep some spare clothes in there."

I lead her back toward the chapel, but I can't help but think there's more to the story than she's telling me.

"I know you always shout at Abi when she asks you this," Tally hesitates. "But what's it like... sex with an Heir?"

I glance over at her and frown. "Why are you thinking about sex with an Heir?"

"I'm not. I mean sex in general, I guess. With a lad who knows what he's doing."

"Tally, is there something you want to tell me?"

"N-no. No. I guess I'm just curious. I've waited and waited to do it and now it seems like this big magical thing." She drops her gaze. "It's not like I have a ton of friends to talk to about this."

"Sex can be intense. Especially with the right person. But it should also be fun and comfortable and feel good. And consensual. Definitely consensual when you're sober and in the right frame of mind."

Tally snorts. "Thanks for that, mum. I'm not going to do anything stupid, you know. I have more self respect than that. I'm just curious is all. And drunk. Definitely drunk. I think it's time I head home."

She stands, swaying a little. I rush over to her side and lace my arm through hers. "Come on, I'll ask Reese to call you a cab and walk you to the front gates."

"Thanks."

We head downstairs but I draw up short when we hit the bottom step. "Jesus, he's a dog."

"Who—oh." Tally goes rigid beside me at the sight of Oakley practically fucking a girl against the wall.

Dread snakes through me as I watch the usual sparkle in her eyes gutter.

"Tally?"

"W-what?" She jerks her head to mine.

"Are you okay?"

"Yeah, I'm fine. Just didn't expect to see... that."

"He's a dog."

"Yeah." There's a tightness in her words as we head for Reese.

"You know, Tally, I love my brother dearly, but he isn't the kind of boy you want to get tangled up with."

"You think... god, Liv. No. No way. I hate Oakley. He's like the bane of my existence."

"Okay." I nod. "If you say so."

"I do."

She's sounds convincing enough but I know all about the fine line between love and hate.

I just hope Tally knows better than to try and walk it...

Especially with someone like my brother.

Want more of Reese and Olivia?
Get your FREE Filthy Jealous Heir Bonus Scene now!
DOWNLOAD HERE
https://dl.bookfunnel.com/bgdikh7fz5

Oakley & Tally's story is up next!
BUY CRUEL DEVIOUS HEIR NOW

CRUEL DEVIOUS HEIR DUET SNEAK PEEK
HEIRS OF ALL HALLOWS' DUET TWO

Chapter One
Tally

Nervous energy thrums through as I wait backstage in the hall.

"Hey, you good?" Sebastian Howard asks me.

I nod, gnawing the end of my thumb.

"You don't look—"

"I'm fine," I snap, instantly feeling guilty. "Look, I'm sorry. This is a big deal. It's—"

"Yeah, I know." He gives me a strange look.

"Tallulah, Sebastian." Mr. Porter approaches, smoothing down his All Hallows' silver and green tie. "Are you both ready?"

"We are, sir," I answer.

"And you're absolutely sure you want to do this?"

"We are."

"Good, well, let's get this show on the road." He doesn't look very pleased about it, but as Head Girl and Boy, it's mine and Sebastian's job to launch a campaign that will elevate student voices and improve well-being. Even if the headteacher doesn't like it.

Even if this year's campaign is set to make waves.

I've always had a strong moral compass. It hasn't made life at All Hallows' particularly easy for me, but when your father is Thomas Darlington, a beacon for integrity and social justice, people tend to be wary of you.

It's never really bothered me before. I like flying the flag of fairness and equality. It's why I became Head Girl, after all. But it's the final year of sixth form, and suddenly, I'm doubting myself. Doubting all the sacrifices I've made in the name of doing the right thing.

This is the right thing, though; I silently reassure myself. I've always believed in using your platform to fight injustice and speak on issues that are important. And now's my chance.

Mr. Porter ushers us onto the stage while the student body files into the grand hall. It's one of my favourite buildings on campus with its vaulted ceilings and original stained-glass windows.

I stand awkwardly next to Sebastian, clutching my presentation notes in my hand. Of course, he volunteered me to do most of the talking, since it was my idea. Public speaking has never really bothered me before, but today is different.

Forcing myself to take a deep breath, I scan the crowd, instantly regretting it when Olivia spots me and gives me a little thumbs up.

A strange sensation snakes down my spine. My friendship with Olivia Beckworth is... complicated. She's Oakley Beckworth's twin sister. And he's an Heir. He and his three best friends—Reese Whitfield-Brown, Elliot Eaton, and Theo Ashworth—rule the halls of All Hallows' with an iron fist and their special brand of debauchery. It's how it's always been in Saints Cross. The elite families and their evil spawn take what they want, when they want, with little consequence.

It makes me sick. It's always made me sick.

Which is why I've always done my utmost to avoid them.

But then, at the start of second year, I struck up an

unlikely friendship with Olivia. Like me, she seemed to despise the patriarchal system ingrained in our town's history. Until she went and fell for an Heir, that is. Now, she's deeply in love with Reese, and I'm trying really hard to not let it come between our new friendship. But it's not easy.

Not when being around Olivia ultimately means being around them.

Around *him*.

I hear them before I see them. The All Hallows' Saints, led by none other than the Heirs.

Elliot leads them into the hall, barely acknowledging anyone as a low rumble of murmurs and even a couple of cheers goes around the room. The teachers start demanding order, but it does little to dampen the excitement their arrival stirs.

Please.

I fight the urge to groan.

They're rugby players, not royalty. Yet, because of the names they bear, the legacies bestowed on them, they're placed on pedestals and worshipped like gods.

"Darlington," Seb grits out, and my eyes nap to his.

"What?"

"I said your name like three times."

"Oh, sorry. What's up?"

"We're almost ready." He motions to the lectern and a wave of nausea rolls through me.

Breathe, Tally, just breathe.

I've been over this presentation so many times, I could probably recite it in my sleep. But when Mr. Porter approaches the lectern, my heart begins to crash violently in my chest.

"Okay, okay, settle down." He waits until silence falls over the room. "This morning, I want to welcome our Head Boy and Girl onto the stage to present to you this year's student campaign. As you're all aware, every year, we encourage our student voice team to come up with an idea for improving student life here at All Hallows'. Tallulah Darlington and Sebastian Howard are going to introduce you all to this year's campaigns. Let's give them a warm round of applause."

Mr. Porter leads the room in a half-hearted applause. I'm used to my fellow students' apathy, though.

"Hello," I say into the mic, letting Seb adjust it a little. He gives me a reassuring nod, despite his initial reservations about this campaign.

"This year, Seb, myself, and the rest of the student council have chosen something tangible. Something that will make a real difference to the students of All Hallows'. Therefore, we're proposing a new home for the student welfare committee and the excellent work they do for the students of All Hallows' around supporting and improving mental health and well-being.

"We're all aware of the difficulties facing the committee in recent years. Mental health and well-being has never been more important for young people. They need safe spaces to meet and talk and get advice. Safe spaces to be themselves. And right now, they do not have the space, resources, or budget to provide this."

I take a little sip of water from the table beside the lectern, letting my eyes run over the sea of faces all watching, listening, daydreaming about wherever they would rather be than here, listening to me and my pie-in-the-sky ideas.

But I don't let it deter me.

"We all know that the school prides itself on the success of the rugby and hockey teams." A raucous cheer goes up around the room and I silently fume.

This is exactly the problem. People don't care about facilities for student welfare; they care about new equipment for the athletic department. Because a successful athletic department means more investment. Better facilities. More publicity.

"The education board pumps money into athletic teams. But what about the students who need extra support with other things? Counselling? Access to extra tutoring? Help with access issues?"

Mr. Porter shifts uncomfortably in the wings, no doubt unappreciative of my assessment of the school's priorities. But everyone knows the truth. Certain things matter more at All Hallows'.

"Now, we could petition the board for extra funding for a new student welfare facility. Or we could redistribute the resources the school already has to ensure a better commitment to supporting the welfare and well-being of students at All Hallows'."

I glance up at Seb and notice his stalwart expression. His eyes seem to say, 'You don't have to do this.' But the thing is, I do.

I have to do it—for more reasons than one.

Which is why I take a deep breath and stare out at my classmates. I find the Heirs in the crowd, letting my eyes run over each of them. Elliot. Reese. Theo... and Oakley. He shoots me a cheeky smile. One that might have made my stomach flutter a couple of weeks ago.

Not anymore.

Before I lose face, I clear my throat.

"Therefore, for this year's student voice campaign, we are proposing that The Chapel be decommissioned as the Heirs' private on-site residence and be reimagined into a brand new student welfare facility that the entire student population at All Hallows' can access."

As my words land, and their implication with them, Oakley's smile falls, replaced with confusion and anger. His brows pull tight as he levels me with a look that makes me wither. But I stand tall, letting Mr. Porter take over to usher the room into silence once more.

Because Oakley isn't the only one reacting.

A ripple of surprise, shock, and disbelief goes around the room, and Seb mutters under his breath, "Here we fucking go."

"Shut up," I hiss, and he slides his eyes to mine, giving a little shake of his head.

"What did you really expect, Tally? You just declared open war on the Heirs."

"I..."

"I hope you have a good insurance policy," a shiver goes down my spine at his warning as he continues, "because you're going to be public enemy number one now."

"Tally, wait up." Olivia jogs after me as I hurry down the hall before the rest of the student body empties out.

I don't know what I was expecting after I delivered my presentation, but it wasn't for the room to fall into complete chaos. Mr. Porter struggled to regain control, but, at that point, I slipped out, needing to catch my breath—and lie low until the dust settled.

"Tally." She grabs my arm and I whirl around, pasting on a weak smile.

"Oh, hi," I say to Olivia.

"What the fuck was that?"

I wince at her harsh words. "I..."

"So that's why you've been avoiding me all week? Because you knew you were going to pull that bullshit." Her brow lifts, accusation glittering in her eyes. "I thought we were friends. I thought—"

"We are. I mean, we were..."

"Were?" She pales. "Jesus, what the hell is wrong with you? I know you've never liked the Heirs, what they stand for. But do you have any idea how awkward you just made things for me? I stood up for you. I vouched for you." Disbelief coats her words, and I feel a stab of regret.

But I can't tell her the truth. She won't understand.

"What's really going on?" Her eyes narrow. "You've always been a thorn in their side, but you've never openly declared war on them before. And you promised me—"

"It's time," I say, lifting my chin in defiance. "They're out of control, and the student welfare—"

"So befriending me? Befriending Abigail? What was that? A way to get close? To infiltrate the enemy? Because I don't buy it."

"It doesn't matter. I'm committed to this campaign. I already have permission to take the petition live. If I collect enough signatures, Mr. Porter will present it to the school board and they'll have to consider the request."

"Unbelievable."

"We can still be friends," I blurt, my conviction wavering. Because I like Olivia. I like having a friend.

"Seriously? And how do you propose that's going to work? I mean, Jesus, Tally. You didn't even give me a heads-up. I'm with Reese. I *love* Reese. Not to mention Oakley is my brother."

"So you're choosing them, then?" My heart sinks, but I shouldn't be surprised.

Of course she's choosing them.

"It's not like you chose me, either."

"It's only the Chapel, Liv. I'm sure they can live without it."

Bitter laughter spills off her lips as she pins me with a look of sheer disappointment. "You're more stupid than I thought if you truly believe that."

Download the CRUEL DEVIOUS HEIR DUET to continue reading.

ABOUT THE AUTHOR

CAITLYN DARE
DELICIOUSLY DARK ROMANCE

Two angsty romance lovers writing dark heroes and the feisty girls who bring them to their knees.

SIGN UP NOW
To receive news of our releases straight to your inbox.

Want to hang out with us?
Come and join CAITLYN'S DAREDEVILS group on Facebook.

ALSO BY CAITLYN DARE

Rebels at Sterling Prep

Taunt Her

Tame Him

Taint Her

Trust Him

Torment Her

Temper Him

Gravestone Elite

Shattered Legacy

Tarnished Crown

Fractured Reign

Savage Falls Sinners MC

Savage

Sacrifice

Sacred

Sever

Red Ridge Sinners MC

Crank

Ruin

Reap

Rule

Defy

Heirs of All Hallows'

Wicked Heinous Heirs

Filthy Jealous Heir: Part One

Filthy Jealous Heir: Part Two

Cruel Devious Heir : Part One

Cruel Devious Heir : Part Two

Brutal Callous Heir : Part One

Brutal Callous Heir : Part Two

Savage Vicious Heir : Part One

Savage Vicious Heir : Part Two

Boxsets

Ace

Cole

Conner

Savage Falls Sinners MC